The Mon

M.R.C. Kasasian was raised in Lancashire. He has had careers as varied as factory hand, wine waiter, veterinary assistant, fairground worker and dentist. He lives with his wife in Suffolk in the summer and in a village in Malta in the winter. He is the author of two previous historical mystery series, published by Head of Zeus, including the bestselling Gower Street Detective series.

Also by M.R.C. Kasasian

The Violet Thorn Mysteries

The Horror of Haglin House
The Montford Maniac

M.R.C. KASASIAN

THE MONTFORD MANIAC

CANELO

First published in the United Kingdom in 2024 by

Canelo
Unit 9, 5th Floor
Cargo Works, 1–2 Hatfields
London SE1 9PG
United Kingdom

A CIP catalogue record for this book is available from the British Library.

Print ISBN 978 1 80436 610 3
Ebook ISBN 978 1 80436 617 2

Cover design by Sarah Whittaker

Look for more great books at www.canelo.co

Printed and bound in Great Britain by Clays Ltd, Elcograf S.p.A.

1

For Tiggy with all my heart.

1: OYSTERS, CROCODILES AND SECRET MESSAGES

I PASSED INSPECTOR Alfred Stanbury the letter. The paper was curled, brown and opaque. A message had been written in invisible ink beneath the words that Jack had penned when he had jilted me.

E-L-P, and then an *M*, had appeared briefly. I was almost certain that I had spotted another *E* at the end before the letters had vanished.

Stanbury sniffed. 'Just smells like charred paper to me.'

'It smelt of onion juice before I heated it.' I passed him the sugar. 'That was what alerted me.'

He held the page up to the light. 'It's well and truly invisible now. I can hardly make out Jack's words, let alone any secret inscriptions.'

'I read it,' I insisted.

'I'm sure you did.' Alfred stirred his coffee and glanced at the envelope. There was a small hole from when it had been pinned on the chapel door with only my name, *LADY VIOLET THORN*, written on it in block capitals.

We were seated in my William Morris box-shaped chairs in the front sitting room, half-watching the oyster man go by, pushing his barrel on a trolley.

'Orford Bay fwesh today,' he was chanting.

'More likely fwesh two days ago,' Stanbury quipped as the unwelcome odours seeped under my slightly raised window. 'Do you mind?' He brought out his battered crocodile cigar case.

'Please do,' I wafted my hand uselessly and rose to push the sash down. The days were still abnormally warm for late September.

'It's not much to go on,' my friend said as he slipped out a half-smoked Havana. At nineteen shillings a hundred he would not waste even part of one.

'It tells us Jack is in trouble,' I protested. 'Perhaps he was forced to write that letter.'

'It's possible.' He struck a red safety match. 'And I have to say I was very surprised when Jack did that. I was always under the impression that he adored you.'

When I had written in one of my Ruby Gibson short stories that words stabbed her to the heart, a critic – male of course – had said that the phrase was cloying claptrap, but I felt a pain as real as any in my breast at Alfred's statement. On what was supposed to have been the happiest day of my life, I had been greeted at the chapel by a grim Reverend Methews bearing a note from my fiancé. Jack could or would not go through with the wedding. By the time I read that, he had disappeared.

'Do you want me to kill him?' Agnust had asked and I knew that she would if she found him.

'Do not worry,' I had replied. 'I shall do it myself.' But I never really meant those words.

Agnust was a maid in Thetbury Hall, my family's seat in Norfolk, but had taken it upon herself to help raise me. Throughout my childhood she had comforted me sometimes, and scolded me often.

After the betrayal, I had fled Thetbury for the Suffolk market town of Montford but my parents had insisted that Agnust went with me. This was an act of kindness, my mother had claimed, though I suspected that they were glad to be rid of her.

I escaped to Break House, a property I had come into on my twenty-first birthday. It was an oddly arranged, wedge-shaped property, being built into a corner of Seraphim Square. I did not become the hermit that some believed me to be, but I preferred to spend more of my time with my fictional characters, especially Ruby Gibson, my lady adventuress, and Inspector Havelock

Hefty of Scotland Yard. They featured in most of my novels and short stories and rather too many of my thoughts but they could never play me false – at least not without my permission.

'But why would anyone have made Jack write it?' Stanbury wondered.

'I do not know… To explain his disappearance?'

Alfred breathed smoke though his nose.

'Why have you waited until now to show it to me?'

'I suppose I supposed that there was nothing you could do about it,' I admitted, 'and I do not suppose there is.'

Alfred dipped his head. 'I am sorry to say all your suppositions are probably correct.' He rested his right ankle on his left knee. 'Is Lady Anglethorpe still staying with you?'

'She is. But she has gone out.'

'Pity.' I did not ask to which of my statements he was referring.

Aunt Igitha, as she was known to me, had turned up uninvited, claiming that Uncle Tiberius had thrown her onto the street, though that did not sound like his style. He had always been a generous and placid man. She was penniless and only needed to stay for a few nights, she had pleaded, but that was over a month ago and she was already talking about us getting a wolfhound and what we should do for Christmas. Before she came, I had hardly known the woman.

Cane Braise rode in from Market Street, a huge, jolly man. We watched through the window as he tipped his tilted slouch hat to the ladies and tossed pennies to street children. It was difficult to believe that this amiable gentleman was fond of roasting anyone who refused to pay for the *protection* he offered. His wife gave garden parties to raise money for orphans. No doubt some of them had been made parentless by her husband.

'I would give my eye teeth to see him behind bars.' Alfred bit his cigar. 'He wouldn't have so much to laugh about with a noose around his neck.'

'It would be a brave jury that convicted him, even if you found any willing witnesses.' I watched him pass by. The hands that held those reigns were reputed to have strangled his own father in a bid for control of the Braise Shotten gang. He moved out of sight.

Ruby appeared from the back of my mind with a coupe of champagne. It was a little early for that or perhaps a little late because she was still in the same ivory gown that she had been wearing the previous evening.

'Can't stay long,' Alfred was saying, oblivious to her presence. 'I have a rather important burglary to attend to.'

'Why important?' I offered him a Nice biscuit, but he declined it with a gesture of his cigar.

'It was at Thropton Hall.'

'Paddy Padmore's house?' I checked in surprise for most robbers would stay well clear of a superintendent's property.

'Apparently only a canteen of cutlery was stolen but he has taken it very personally and all leave is cancelled until the culprit is found.'

'A powerful incentive for some unscrupulous officer to pin it on the first vagrant to venture out of the Lowers,' I commented. Lower Montford was notorious for its criminal class but there were a great many impoverished inhabitants no less honest than their more prosperous counterparts in the Uppers.

Alfred leaned forwards. 'I would not say that.'

But he cannot deny it, Ruby drained her glass, unheard and unseen by my visitor.

A pigeon fluttered noisily onto the windowsill and Alfred clapped his hands but, rather like housebreakers, winged vermin have little respect for officers of the law.

'I must go. Crime waits for no man.' He got to his feet and handed the letter back. 'I'll mull it over,' he promised, and I was sure that he would, but I knew in my heart that I had given him very little to contemplate. I did not need Ruby to remind me that we had no information as to where Jack Raven might be, nor to add, as she did, *Or even if he is still alive.*

2: CHAPTER TWENTY-NINE IN WHICH THE MURDERER IS EXPOSED

INSPECTOR HAVELOCK HEFTY surveyed the assembled household.

'Perhaps you could explain why you went to the library in the middle of the night, Carruthers,' he suggested, and the butler gaped.

'How on earth did you know that Inspector?' he asked in astonishment. 'I made sure that nobody was watching.'

Good morning, Thorn, Ruby greeted me as she rose sleepily through my grey matter. Once it had been crawling with my fictional characters, but I had cast all of them except her and Hefty into the dark recesses of my cerebellum where they slumbered until they were required.

Good morning and goodbye, I replied. *You are not in this story.*

Ruby yawned. *Can't be any good then.* She had on a rather lovely tulip pattern silk dress.

At least I always catch my man, Hefty retorted, for Ruby's arch enemy, Count Vorolski Zugravescu, had slipped her clutches five times to date.

Be quiet, I told them both and Ruby swished off to enjoy a cigarette, though she knew that I hated anybody smoking in my brain.

I went back to work and had just written – *A light smile played upon the policeman's rugged face* – when the door flew open, and Aunt Igitha came into my study. Unfortunately, I could not dismiss her so easily. My aunt was made of flesh and blood – or flesh at any rate, for her whey complexion made me wonder if dishwater flowed through her veins. Her wiry pewter-hued hair was piled so high that it seemed in imminent danger of toppling forwards. She was draped, I noticed, in a cardinal red shawl not dissimilar to one that I had mislaid.

'Good morning Veety.' I did not recall having given her permission to craft a name for me from my initials.

'Good morning, Aunt,' I replied without looking up. 'Excuse me but I must…'

I indicated to my manuscript with my Aitken, Lambert and Co Magic Pencil.

'But of course,' she acquiesced, and I returned to describing events in the lofty library of the sinister Jupiter House.

> 'Nobody needed to watch you,' Inspector Hefty informed the ancient retainer. 'I smeared the underside of the soles of your shoes with a special dye that is only visible in the light of my tinted spectacles.'
>
> 'I was b-borrowing a b-book,' Carruthers stammered.

'If I might make a minor observation,' interjected Aunt Igitha, still at my shoulder, and I was brought up too well – or too timidly – to tell her that she might not.

Kindly be quiet, Lady Anglethorpe, Hefty commanded, though there were serious doubts as to whether my aunt was entitled to be thus entitled. *This is an official investigation*. Needless to say, only I could hear him.

'Should that not be stuttered?' my aunt suggested.

'What is the difference?' I sniffed suspiciously. Was that Fleurs de Bulgarie by the House of Creed that she was wearing? It was my favourite perfume, in fact, I realised, it probably was my perfume. To judge by the vapours flooding my nostrils, she had drenched herself in an exceedingly expensive half-ounce of it.

'I do not suppose it matters,' she replied, 'for the sort of thing that you turn out.'

I warned you. Hefty scribbled in his notebook furiously while I returned to mine in much the same frame of mind.

'And which tome did you select?' The Scotland Yard's premier detective interrogated him, touching his own left shoulder with his forefinger. The scar of his bullet wound always tingled when he was close to a guilty man, and it had never let him down yet.

'The Reverend Charles Brown's sermons,' the decrepit butler replied cagily.

'Which would be on that shelf,' Inspector Hefty nodded his massive cranium to the left. 'Whereas the footprints clearly show that you went to this shelf.' The detective pointed to his right. 'Where titles beginning with the letter P are kept. Could that be P for Poison, Carruthers?'

The old servant blanched.

'You are too c-clever for me Inspector,' he stuttered. 'I am discovered for it was I who killed the archbishop.'

'Stammered,' Aunt Igitha corrected me.

The entire assembly gasped.

'That is commendably loyal of you, Carruthers,' the inspector strode to the fireplace, positioning himself with his back to it. 'But you did not take the book. You returned it because you were trying to protect your mistress from suspicion.'

'This is an outrage,' Countess Veronica Di Napoli cried.

'It would be if I were accusing you, your ladyship,' Hefty agreed readily, 'but your superannuated, though staunch, flunky was mistaken in his action. It was not you who borrowed the volume, for I painted the soles of everybody's shoes with their initials to distinguish between them. Professor Green's Compendium of Poisons was taken by somebody with the initials L.O.'

'Lancelot Overstrand!' Percival Overstrand cried in horror. 'My deranged identical twin!'

The great detective smiled sardonically.

'That is what I was supposed to believe,' he declared. 'But only this morning I received a telegrammic reply from Dr Emery Emmerson who attended your family at Overstrand Towers. He confirmed that Percival died in mysterious circumstances on the feast of St Julian, the patron saint of boatmen, carnival workers and...' Hefty's voice sank to an accusatory whisper. 'Murderers.'

'Murderers!' The countess fanned herself in shock.

'Indeed, and you...' Inspector Hefty pointed accusingly at the handsome but louche young bachelor, 'are not Percival but Lancelot Overstrand, recently escaped from the Outer Hebridean Asylum of St Ambrose for the Criminally Insane.'

'Is there such a place?' Aunt Igitha enquired.

'There is in my story.'

Excuse me, Hefty called, *but I am I trying to arrest two people.*

Two? Ruby Gibson puzzled. She liked to keep an eye on the man who rivalled her for my attention.

Lancelot Overstrand and that botheration of an aunt, he explained. *Obstructing a novelist in the course of her denouement.*

Strictly speaking Hefty had no jurisdiction outside the pages of my books but, if he wanted to try, I was not going to stand in his way.

'Anyway...' Aunt Igitha seemed unaware that she was being handcuffed. 'It is time to break our fast.' She made our morning meal sound like a religious obligation whereas I had come to think of it as a daily ordeal.

'Start yours by all means,' I suggested.

'You know I dislike eating alone.'

'I am sure that Agnust will keep you company,' I said with more confidence than I felt, for my maid had a strong antipathy to our self-invited guest.

My aunt waved a hand.

Many-ringed hand, Hefty observed for he was suspicious about how she had acquired such a quantity of jewels.

Many-ringed and scrawny hand, Ruby contributed, never having forgiven my aunt for having described her as *vacuous* and advising me to push my heroine into an active volcano.

'Servants are not company,' Aunt Igitha declared. 'They are servants.'

I decided not to argue that they were the only company I kept some days.

'They are the only company I keep some days,' I decided to argue after all.

'Why not invite the crossing sweeper to join you for dinner?'

He might be more convivial, I thought before writing,

> Lancelot Overstrand's countenance changed in a moment.

'Quite enough of that.' Aunt Igitha reached over and shut my notebook. Even by her standards this was going too far.

Run her through with a rusty rapier, Ruby urged which seemed to be a little too far as well.

'Oh, for goodness' sake, Aunt.' I opened it again. 'I planned to finish this chapter this morning and I have not even reached the part where Inspector Hefty gets stabbed.'

Don't let me interfere with that. Ruby smiled cruelly and wandered off to try on my new pair of crimson suede shoes.

Hefty's face drained. *S-stabbed,* he stammered or stuttered or gasped. *Only a glancing blow I trust.*

Probably, I reassured him though, if truth be told, my Havelock Hefty stories were hardly selling enough copies to keep him alive.

And not a poisoned blade, he bargained as I pushed the lead back into my pencil.

I never thought of that, I admitted. *It is a good idea though and might even make a title – The Scratch That Killed.*

My Aunt closed the book again. Perhaps the idea of a rapier was not too drastic after all.

Poisoned? Surely not? came desperately, but muffled, through the olive-green hand-marbled leather cover.

'Come along, Veety.'

Meekly I followed her from the room.

Have mercy, Milady, Havelock Hefty called piteously, and I was teering on wavering until he added, *I'll never call you Thumbelina again.*

I was not aware, until then, that he had mocked my diminutive size. The knowledge partly assuaged my guilt, but it is a heavy responsibility, having the power of life…

And death, Ruby said as she came by on her way to rifle my wardrobe.

–

'I cannot throw her onto the street,' I protested that evening.

'I can,' Gerrund, my man, muttered, incensed by Aunt Igitha's repeated interferences in what he saw as his kitchen. The final straw had been his finding her using one of his pans to boil what she described as her *delicates* and he described as something considerably less delicate.

Gerrund had entered my employment shortly after I had moved into Break House. He had a past, he had informed me, but something in his manner had made me trust him. I had told him that I was only interested in his future and never regretted my decision.

'Either she goo or either I goo,' Agnust, my maid, threatened, infuriated by Aunt Igitha's repeated complaints about how her bed was made – admittedly badly – or deficiencies in the dusting – another task in which Agnust took little interest.

There had been occasions when I would have instructed Gerrund to fetch my maid's trunk from the attic before she had a chance to retract but Agnust brought me food and coffee, albeit grudgingly, whilst my aunt's only contribution was to live up effortlessly to her middle name of Eris, the ancient East Anglian goddess of chaos and destruction.

I used to enjoy a hot bath but now I had trouble getting into the room for a cold one. She had rearranged some of the furniture, removed many of my ornaments and placed a glass case with a grisly orchestra of stuffed mice on top of my sideboard. She commandeered and crumpled-up my newspapers before I got a look at them. My house was not my home anymore.

Lock her in the attic, Ruby suggested.

Attractive though her proposition was, I dissented but, for once, Agnust, Gerrund, Hefty, Ruby and I were in complete accord. One way or another Aunt Igitha would have to go.

3: CROCKERY AND CARNAGE AT THE CAFE CORDOBA

I CALLED ON my childhood friend, Hettie Granger. She usually had advice for me. It was not always good and sometimes not welcome, but it was advice, nonetheless.

Hettie was titivating a life-sized portrait of Mr Verisloe, a giant Galapagos tortoise. The painting was to be a present from a member of the local gentry to his wife.

'Believe it or not, the greatest difficulty I had was getting the beast to keep still,' she told me. There was orange paint spattered over Mr Verisloe's carapace. 'It kept trying to crawl off the table or hiding and I had to lure its head out with slices of Yorkshire pudding. My patron insists it's the closest thing to what they live upon in the wild.'

Despite my concerns I laughed. Those with titles have long been permitted to behave in ways that would see their purported inferiors sent to Dewbury Hall Asylum for the Insane.

'Take your aunt out for coffee and explain that you are enjoying her company so much that it is distracting you from your work,' Hettie suggested. 'Send her on a long, inexpensive holiday abroad. Take her to the Cafe Cordoba. She will not make a scene in public. Do it first thing tomorrow.' She licked a dot of chocolate brown off the back of her hand. 'Paints never taste like they look,' she ruminated, though I would have thought that she would have discovered that before now.

–

Our table rocked as Aunt Igitha shot to her feet.

'Flesh and blood!' she howled so loudly that a new, button-nosed waitress tipped her tray, shrieking as she scalded her wrist.

This was all too much for a pretty, young lady in the corner with armfuls of artificial ferns sprouting from her head. She swooned decorously into the arms of a dapper young man in a grey ten-guinea suit.

Unfortunately, the young man, hissing, 'Flesh!' dropped her so that she hit the table spilling a pot of milk over herself and, finding her face wet, shrieked, 'Blood!' so loudly that a nervous young fop all in powder blue whimpered, 'The Montford Maniac hath returned!'

He dashed for the exit, leading a stampede of panic-stricken customers battling, bills unpaid, out of the front door.

I collect maniacs – though only in my scrapbooks. One did not, however, have to be a maniacologist – a word that I would send the Oxford English Dictionary – to know of that man and his horrible deeds. The whole town and the Hams – its surrounding villages – had been gripped by terror during his gory rampage a decade ago.

'You are throwing your own flesh and blood out onto the street,' Aunt Igitha castigated me, the enormous feather arrangement on her hat rearing up like the unhappy ostrich from which it had been plucked.

I did not like to point out that we had no common ancestors nor that her marriage to my Uncle Tiberius was of dubious validity since two other women also laid claim to the Marchionessy to which his wife would be entitled.

Mrs Chavetta, the manageress, clip-clopped over, picking her way through the overturned chairs and shattered crockery.

'I am sorry.' I gazed up into her nostrils which had flared like those of my first pony, and I hoped that she was not going to follow Pineapple's example by biting me on the shoulder.

'It is I who am sorry, Lady Violet,' she said, and probably was, for I had frequented the Cafe Cordoba two or three times a week recently, if only to get out of my own house. 'But I must ask you to leave.'

'I quite understand,' I assured her, leaving enough for our beverages, a tip and to replace the broken coffee pot. Then, seeing that her equine jaw had not unclenched, what I estimated would compensate for the unpaid bills.

Give her a sugar lump, Ruby suggested.

'The scones were stale anyway,' my aunt complained, though she had devoured three of them plastered with strawberry jam and piled high with clotted cream. There was still a blob of that on the tip of her hawk nose.

'The food was excellent,' I demurred, though my chocolate cake had been dry.

One lady in a Dunstable bonnet had not let the prospect of being slaughtered separate her from her Battenburg. 'You are mad.' She brandished a pastry fork as we passed her table.

'No I am not,' Aunt Igitha retorted, gun-metal eyes boring into her critic. 'One of my doctors said I was almost cured.' Having thus vindicated herself, she strode out onto the street, with me, her humiliated and alleged niece, reluctantly at her heels. 'After all I have done for you.' Her voice was hacksaw sharp.

Not to mention all the things she has done to you, Ruby reminded me.

I could let her stay a little longer, I vacillated.

Stiffen your resolve. Hefty dug his thumbs into his waistcoat pockets so forcibly that a seam ripped.

It would be a long time before I could return to the Cafe, I reflected gloomily. Aunt Igitha had already caused us to be banned from Thompson's Snuff Emporium. That was no great hardship for I had only gone there to keep her company, but bad reputations are more contagious than measles and much more difficult to cure.

Inspector Hefty put on his new extra-powerful-magnifying spectacles and crouched to examine a smouldering cigar butt on the pavement.

'Unfortunately,' I began, remembering Hettie's advice.

Too late, Ruby said but I ploughed on.

'I have been enjoying your company so much that...' Even before I finished my sentence, I knew how insincere it would sound. 'It is distracting me from my work.'

Aunt Igitha ground the toe of her shoe on the butt.

Hefty yelped. *She trod on my hand.*

'But I help you with your work,' she argued.

What was my friend's other suggestion?

'I fear that I have been selfish and exhausted your energies,' I began. Any sane woman would have looked at me as if I were mad and I was about to discover that an insane woman would view me in the same light. 'And...' I battled on, 'I would love to buy you a long, inexpensive holiday abroad.'

I think you were supposed to omit any reference to the cost. Hefty blew on his fingertips whilst my aunt's lips battled between an upper gnarl and a lower smile.

'Did you say *long and expensive*?'

'Well...' I faltered whilst her lips regrouped and renewed hostilities between a lower gnarl and an upper smile.

'And you would be coming with me?'

'What a lovely idea.' I forced the corners of my mouth upwards. 'But unfortunately, I have a deadline to meet.'

In truth, my agent had told me to take my time which was one way of telling me not to trouble myself or him.

Aunt Igitha crossed her eyes, a trick of which I had long been envious though I was not sure why it might be useful.

'Then I shall wait until you are finished.'

I nearly crumbled but I had promised Agnust, Gerrund and myself that I would do it.

'I am sorry...' I steeled myself against her glare. 'But you must go, Aunt Igitha though...'

Don't weaken! Ruby and Hefty cried.

'I shall, of course, give you time to find somewhere else to live,' I said, and they groaned.

'Very well,' my aunt conceded with worrying placidity, 'But that could take months.'

Years, you nincompoop, Ruby berated me, gambling that there was nothing I would do to her whilst I was not working on one of her stories.

'A week,' I said, shocked at my own callousness but, whilst that basilisk stare had not metamorphosed me to stone, it had certainly helped to harden my heart.

At most, Hefty urged, aware of the carnage that she was wreaking on his investigations. He rubbed his crushed fingers.

'At most,' I concluded, straightening to my full lack of height to look her in the Adam's apple, for she was the best part of a foot taller than me.

'A week!' Aunt Igitha's snarl matched that of the ravening hyena that had pursued Ruby along a rotting rope bridge over a bottomless ravine.

'One week,' I confirmed.

My aunt's response was drowned by the approach of a clarence, one of the four wheeled carriages known, because of the racket they made on the cobbles, as *growlers*. It passed and I was relieved to find that my throat had not been ripped out in her slavering wrath. Remembering that the honour of the Thorns, and the worth of my word, were at stake, I stood my ground.

Froze in terror. Ruby glanced desultorily in the window of a bicycle shop. It was far too inelegant a means of transport to be of interest to her.

'One week at most,' I restated firmly, wishing that I had attended when Grey Wolf had taught Ruby a secret blow for warding off grizzly bear attacks.

'Don't trouble yourself.' In an instant, Aunt Igitha cast away her frenzy. 'Send my things on,' she commanded, her great dignity only marred by snagging her dress on a rusting pram parked on the pavement and dragging it with her when she tried to rip herself free.

'To where?' I watched her struggles, wondering if I should help and knowing that I should but deciding that I would not.

'Where you goo with my treasures?' an elderly woman in a threadbare shawl croaked.

The pram was full of her day's finds – assorted rags, torn and grubby. She might be able to get a meal and a bed for the night with that haul. Most of the gatherers had no permanent homes.

'Get off me.' Aunt Igitha wrenched at her dress in renewed fury, almost toppling the woman's pram over and its contents into the gutter, but I managed to catch it and pull my relative free.

'She break the wheel.' The woman prodded it with her toe though I would bet a pound to an ounce that it was broken long ago. Some of the spokes were missing.

'Let me help.' I opened my small-change purse. 'There you are.'

The rag collector peered at the sixpence in her leathery palm and, since it was something I rarely scrutinised, I took the opportunity to do so now. There were seven lions and a voluptuous lady welded to a harp in a shield rimmed by some nonsense about *mal y pense*-ing. She bit it, something I had only known people to do in story books, though not in mine. Apparently satisfied that it was not counterfeit, she enclosed it in her scabrous fist.

'Int goh no change.'

'I do not require any.'

The woman gawked.

'You're as buffle-headed as her,' she said with a contempt that failed to ignite the warm glow one usually gets from donating trifles to those who need them to survive.

'To my home of course,' Aunt Igitha answered my question as if there had been no interlude since I had posed it.

'And where is that?' I did not think that Uncle Tiberius would welcome her back. By her own admission she had insulted most of his friends and lost him his under gardener.

'Why the lighthouse of course,' she answered airily, for where else would an averred aristocrat reside? 'But mark my words Lady Violet Elizabeth Antoinette Cordelia Thorn…' She smiled sugarishly and all the more menacingly for that. 'You will rue this day grievously for the rest of your wretched life.'

A line worthy of Lancelot Overstrand. I made a mental memo and my aunt swept away, leaving a good half-yard of petticoat tangled around the rear axle. This was beginning to look like the rag woman's lucky day.

'And you needn't presume you can keep my mouse orchestra,' she shouted over her shoulder as she stormed off. One of the troubles with shouting over shoulders is that the people in front of you think you are shouting at them. Aunt Igitha could not have had greater success at clearing a path through the approaching pedestrians had she been wielding a flail.

'Oh botheration,' I said under my breath. In the midst of all the turmoil, I had left my handbag and umbrella behind. I had plenty of umbrellas, but I rarely changed my bag, it being too much trouble to transfer all the essential contents that I seldom used. I would send Gerrund to fetch them rather than face Mrs Chavetta again.

Just as I thought. Hefty whipped off his spectacles. *This cigar is from…*

Be quiet, I said. *I am not in the mood.* With that, Inspector Havelock Hefty, Scotland Yard's premier detective and fearless fighter of fiendish crimes, slunk meekly away.

4: *THE KISS OF JUDAS*

GERRUND FILLED MY fountain with cold water. We were down to our last bucket of ice in the cellar, he informed me, and I resolved to ask my parents if they had any left. They had a deep icehouse in the grounds of Thetbury Hall that could store frozen blocks for many months. Transporting one could be a problem though, in this unseasonably warm weather. Even in canvas bags insulated with wool, a great deal would melt before it arrived.

This was the first time I had been left alone since Aunt Igitha had come to Break House and yet I felt that I was in a truce with myself rather than truly at peace.

I measured out my absinthe into a torsade lead crystal glass – one sixth of a present from Jack – placed a slotted silver spoon over the rim and rested a lump of sugar on top. A fractional turn of one of the taps at the base of the fountain and the water dripped through the sugar, clouding the spirit to create what its devotees referred to as *the Green Fairy* in part because of her alleged magical properties. Her powers were diminished, it was said, if the water were not chilled.

It used to be my habit to read Jack's letter while I drank. Now I only had the charred remains and my memory of its contents.

My Darling, he had written before going on to prove that I was not his darling at all. *We cannot marry.*

'Why?' I demanded aloud as I had countless times before. 'Did you have a wife salted away?'

You make her sound like a pickled pig. Hefty looked distinctly green though he had seen far worse than that.

I had employed a man to go through all the parish registers within a twenty-mile radius, but he had come up with nothing. The idea was absurd anyway, I decided, and I gave up the search.

I am not worthy of you, Jack had written, but everybody had told me how lucky I was when we became engaged. I did not need them to tell me that he was quite a catch. He was handsome and charming and had saved my life.

-

Jack and I had been to a performance of *Utopia, Limited*, a satire on business malpractices. Though we enjoyed it, we both agreed that it could not hold a candle to *The Yeoman of the Guard,* the only other Gilbert and Sullivan performance that we had seen together.

We had supper afterwards and experienced great difficulty in finding a cab. My parents had not been keen on us going to the Savoy Theatre unchaperoned, but Jack had not been able to purchase a third ticket, we had told them. I dreaded to think of the furore that would have resulted if we had missed our last train and were obliged to stay the night, especially as we were not yet engaged to be married. Luckily, we made it to King's Cross station with a little time to spare.

The platform ran between two lines with our train to the right. It was packed with others equally determined to make their ways home and to get seats.

'Let's try the front,' Jack suggested, and we hurried along the less-crowded left-hand side where another train was drawing in, smoke billowing and steam hissing.

A group of young men were bustling past us down the middle. They looked and sounded as if they had been celebrating something. They were on their way to watch the rugby match tomorrow, Jack told me though I had no idea nor any interest in who would be playing against whom.

It was then that I felt a blow in my back and stumbled to the edge of the platform, almost overbalancing into the path of the incoming engine. A hand grabbed my arm, hauled me clear and released me. I turned to see Jack grappling with another man. Jack was tall and athletic, but his opponent was sturdily built and fought ferociously.

'Let me go, you swine,' the man yelled. He took Jack by the throat and started to throttle him with both hands.

I flew at the stranger, but he knocked me back with such a blow to my brow that I reeled into a red-headed gentleman. He caught me as I stumbled and hauled me to my feet.

'Having a brawl?' He peered at me through his thick-lensed spectacles. 'You look too respectable for that.'

'That man tried to push me onto the line,' I explained breathlessly.

'Which one?'

'The one in brown with walrus moustaches.' I pointed. 'And now he is trying to throw my companion under the train.'

'Well, we'll see about that,' the man promised and made his way towards them. At that moment Jack's fist swung up and the moustachioed man buckled at the knees. Jack pulled the hands from his throat and the man staggered backwards, just as the train arrived. It was travelling slowly and the engine driver was leaning out of his cab. He must have seen what was happening for there was the squeal of brakes, but the man was too close, and I heard him scream as the locked wheels slid over, cutting into and crushing him.

'Don't look.' Jack twisted me away and wrapped his arms around me. He had not needed to do that for I had no desire to see the mutilation.

The police came. Jack protested that we must get home, but they insisted that we, and all those in the area, made statements. Only Jack and I and the red-headed man had any clear idea of what had happened. I had assumed that it was an accident in the first moment, but the man had lunged at me again.

My attacker was not dead, a young sergeant told me, but had fallen between the tracks and had lost his right hand and had a leg amputated above the knee. He was still conscious and, absurdly, was claiming that he had been trying to save me. His name was Arthur Beech, an architect with a promising career.

The sergeant contacted Thetbury police station who sent an officer to explain to my parents what had happened. We spent the night in the police waiting room and returned home the next morning.

A few weeks' later we heard that the injured man's story had changed. He and his friends testified that, being the worse for drink, he had stumbled into me and that he had only fought Jack and pushed me away to defend himself. He did not want to press charges and the sergeant advised us that it would be better if we did not too. Arthur Beech had a spotless record, and it was possible that he was telling the truth. I thought it unlikely, though, because of the way he had changed his account of events. Also, he had gone for me twice, an allegation that he vehemently denied. Neither Jack nor I wanted to go through a trial. Who knew if his lawyer might try to blacken our names? All sorts of aspersions could be cast on our reasons for being in London at night unaccompanied. No real harm had been done to us. I was slightly bruised, and Jack had hurt his knuckles, but we would both heal. Arthur Beech, though, would suffer for the rest of his life. We took the policeman's advice and let the matter drop.

His name was Sergeant Hefty, and I was rather taken by his calm air of authority. Shamelessly, I stole his surname and christened him *Havelock*. I also moved him from the Railway Police to Scotland Yard. I have often wondered if he ever found out how he had been used and hoped that, if he did, he would appreciate my promoting him to the rank of Inspector.

Some years later I was flattered to be interviewed by *The Daily Telegraph*. Asked about an incident in which Ruby had nearly been pushed under a train, I revealed that this had been inspired by real events and was aggrieved to find that the published article concentrated far more on that than on my writing. Most vexatiously of all I was quoted as saying something that neither I nor any of my characters would ever have uttered, *My whole life flashed before my eyes.*

–

Jack and I had been devoted to each other, or so I thought, until he breached his promise.

With all my heart, your ever-loving Jack, he had written. It was signed with an *X* which I had come to think of as the kiss of Judas.

Only after I had almost come to accept that the man I loved was a callous deceiver had I discovered his message written in invisible ink. It was a trick that I had told him about when I was trying to create a new heroine. *Base her on yourself,* Jack had recommended. It was good advice and so, of course, I ignored it.

ELP ME, I was almost sure it read before, in my anxiety to reveal the rest of the words, I scorched the paper.

I drained the sweet bitterness of my absinthe and was about to have another when Ruby – who drank almost continuously when she was not on an adventure – put her hand over my glass. *You cannot drown sorrows,* she told me. *They always float to the top.*

I was sure that she was right, but still I reached for the bottle. It was the best analgesic of which I knew.

If you can't beat them. Ruby put her glass under the other tap, and we settled together, elbows resting on the high wooden arms of my chairs. The rose and trellis upholstery matched the wallpaper and the curtains. The latter were open a crack so that we could look out across the nearly deserted square.

'What is to become of us, Ruby?' I asked aloud and she put her glass on the low table between us.

All our lives are in your hands, Thorn, she replied. *Take care they do not slip between your fingers.*

5: *PERMANENT PERMANGANATE AND THE NUMBERING OF DAYS*

AGNUST PACKED AUNT Igitha's trunk but only after she had unpacked it to remove a great many things of mine. Since we were opposite extremes of the height scale, my aunt could not wear my dresses. Also, her hands and feet were several sizes larger, so my shoes and gloves were safe. However, we discovered, she had *borrowed* a number of my shawls, scarfs and mufflers. Also, a string of pearls and three of my parasols had found their way into her luggage as had some of my silverware and a bottle of Very Old Ben Nevis Malt. The bone-handled boar bristle toothbrush was one of mine, I believed, but, since it had been used and not even rinsed, I did not want it back.

I parcelled up the mouse orchestra's cabinet, the first violinist's whiskers drooping tragically as if he were begging me to let him stay. But, rather like Agnust when she was sulking, dead mice do not talk.

I closed and strapped the lid. Gerrund was all too eager to drag the trunk into the hall and summon a cab. He helped the driver to load the luggage, *accidentally* dropping his end once, and the three of us stood on the doorstep, watching what we hoped would be the last of my aunt depart.

Goodbye. Hefty nursed his fingers, still bruised from Aunt Igitha trampling on them. He was convinced that he would lose a nail.

Good riddance, Ruby called, her pride still bruised from Aunt Igitha trampling on it. *And don't come back.* For once she spoke on everybody's behalf.

There were pork sausages, calves' liver and bacon with fried potatoes and eggs for breakfast. Gerrund had a self-given mission to make my every meal a banquet. Agnust had a self-given mission to feed me up though it was probably a decade since I had gained in height, and I had no desire to increase in girth.

'Enough to feed a regiment,' I commented as she plonked the plate in front of me.

'Well dint you go invitin' one round,' she warned as if I were in the habit of doing so.

'I shall invite whomsoever I wish.' I tossed my head haughtily, cricking my neck as she trudged off. I doubted, though, that we had space for a thousand lusty troopers, especially if they were on horseback.

I could billet a Grenadier Captain, Ruby offered but I gave my attention to my post.

There was a letter from a man who knew my dark secret but would preserve my reputation if I left ten shillings under the lid of a sundial in the Monastery Gardens. Sadly, I was unable to think of anything in my life that was disreputable enough to need suppressing. Also, it was rather insulting that he did not think me capable of creating a scandal worth more than half a sovereign.

What about the theft of the Romanov tiara? Ruby challenged. *No, actually, I took that.*

I never understood how my characters could perform acts without my knowledge, though, according to Ruby, I was very often unaware even of my own actions.

A bill had arrived from Pierre Auberge, the dressmaker, and I resolved to be furious with myself about my extravagance when I wrote the cheque. There was another bill, but I have a rule never to consume more than one at a single sitting and slipped it into my handbag. Luckily Gerrund had managed to retrieve my bag from the Cafe Cordoba with all its precious bits and bobs but, annoyingly, a dirty tea towel had been rammed inside it.

Smells like a farmyard. Ruby sprayed two squirts of Fleurs de Bulgarie into the air.

Next was a small buff envelope with my name and address scrawled upon it in red ink. Applying my analytical skills, I deduced that it was a small buff envelope with my name and address scrawled upon it in red ink. Surely, I could do better than that?

Probably not. Hefty eyed my Coleman's mustard suspiciously. Its strong taste could mask that of any poison, he warned, but still deposited a spoonful on the side of his plate.

Judging by the postmark, the letter had been sorted at the Silver Lane Post Office late the previous afternoon.

Watch out, Havelock, Ruby warned. *She is after your job.*

Few things could be further from the truth. Having been embroiled in a series of ghastly events that summer, I had no wish to be involved in any crimes ever again – except in the safety of my own manuscripts.

A female policeman? Scotland Yard's premier detective shuddered in revulsion. *It was revolting enough when we allowed women to answer our telephonic apparatuses.*

I snatched up my silver paperknife and he flinched.

Do not forget that your life hangs on the thread of my whim, I warned.

I was not sure that whims had any threads, but it was enough to make Hefty slink back behind my ascending parietal gyrus where I could no longer see him.

Inside the envelope was a letter – *Well blow me down the Old Kent Road and up Great Dover Street,* Ruby mocked – on unheaded, lined paper, rough along the left-hand margin.

Hefty reappeared, leaning in front of me but, somehow, not blocking my view.

Torn out of a Griffiths and Grout exercise book. He donned his special extra-powerful-magnifying spectacles. *And written in Peterson's Permanent Permanganate Ink.*

YOUR DAYS ARE NUMBERED, I read with him, annoyingly, reciting the words almost simultaneously.

This was not especially alarming news. I was already aware that we would all be obliged to depart this earth one day. One could not go to church without being reminded of it.

AND, I read on, while Scotland Yard's premier detective scrutinised the envelope. *THAT NUMBER IS VERY SMALL.*

This was a little more worrying as I had yet to complete my first one score years and five.

PREPARE TO MEET YOUR MAKER. It ended with no signature and not so much as a kiss.

When you do encounter your creator, ask him why he built you in miniature, Ruby suggested.

I sniffed despondently at her jibe while Hefty sniffed assiduously at the envelope. He never missed an opportunity to remind me how he had detected the onion-juice on Jack's letter.

Suspiciously scentless, he observed, *therefore, the lady who wrote it must have taken care to rinse away her Rosa Damascena perfume with an unscented soap from Southern Arabia.*

I could not be troubled to list all the groundless assumptions that he had made, especially as my life expectancy was purportedly so low.

Very likely, I agreed, in hope of getting some peace.

If that note is to be believed, you will have eternal peace soon enough, Ruby – ever one for dark pronouncements – pronounced darkly.

I briefly considered taking the letter to Alfred Stanbury, but he had probably had enough of my mysterious notes lately. Also, as before, there was little for him to go on.

We know where it was delivered from, Hefty reminded me, but there must have been at least half a dozen post boxes in the Silver Lane area.

Is that the best that Scotland Yard's premier detective can come up with? Ruby slipped the letter back into its envelope and pivoted on her heel to me. *Remember the man who wrote to tell you that a poisonous water snake would slither out of your bath tap?*

No, I replied because I had never received such a communication.

You cannot worry over every crackle-headed crackle-head, she continued regardless. *Peruse your newspaper and forget about it.*

This was better advice. I unfolded the *Montford Chronical,* familiarly known as the *Chronic.* It was a special edition – hence the added penny to its usual price of tuppence. Ten pages had been devoted to the tenth anniversary of the first undisputed murder by the so-called Montford Maniac. I had kept copies of all the original reports and so this added nothing except some lurid depictions of the event by a man posing as an artist.

I knew that would cheer you up, Ruby said.

–

Harry Salter was a clerk at Jones and Dalton, manufacturers of agricultural machinery, famed for the invention of a modified plough for dredging ditches. He had a wife and six children and lived an uneventful life in what some called *The Middles.* This was an area on the outskirts of Upper Montford extending towards the Lowers, but separated from it by the River Angle.

After attending weekly mass in the Roman Catholic church of St Etheldreda, it was the practice of the family, weather permitting, to walk home through the monastery gardens.

On Sunday 27th they had paused to look at the broken shrine of St Aegbald when Salter let out a cry and staggered back clutching his throat. He had been shot by an arrow. Foolishly, but understandably, his wife tried to pull it out, causing unknown damage during which he expired.

Inspector Shomrack was put in charge of the case but, failing to find any reliable witnesses or any sign of the weapon, made little progress.

Unable to resist the dramatic possibilities of the case, the *Suffolk Whisperer* blared inaccurately, *HAROLD KILLED BY ARROW IN THE EYE.* The idea caught the public imagination. A scurrilous tuppeny broadside was printed and sold on street corners with the events depicted in a mock recreation of the Bayeux Tapestry.

The *Montford Chronical* had the real scoop, though, when, to Shomrack's fury, they published a letter that they had received.

> I KILLED HIM WITH MY CROSSBOW, HA HA! HE WAS NOT MY FIRST AND HE WILL NOT BE THE LAST. BEWARE MONTFORD! THERE IS A BLOODTHIRSTY MURDERER IN YOUR MIDST.

Shomrack had kept one detail as quiet as he could. Only he and a few officers and the murderer could have known that the arrow was, in fact, a crossbow bolt. The letter was confiscated and formed an important piece of evidence in the fruitless hunt for the man who the press and the police had already dubbed *The Montford Maniac.*

6: LITTLE TERRORS AND PETUNIA BOTTLE

I HAD NOT actually been banned from The Café Cordoba, but I did not believe that Mrs Chavetta would greet me with anything more welcoming than a scowl.

Agnust and Gerrund had argued vigorously against my going out unaccompanied after I had received the letter, but I was determined not to spend my life in hiding. Neither would I let myself be frightened into going about with bodyguards.

I had arranged to meet Hettie Granger in The Empire Café just off Market Square. Unusually, for she was almost invariably late, she had already taken a table in the bay window when I arrived early.

'Violet.' She sprang up to kiss me.

She had changed out of her painter's smock, I was pleased to note, because it was not unknown for Hettie to forget that she was wearing it and turn up, even on formal occasions, smeared in oils. Concerningly, though, her right cheek had a small cut surrounded by an angry red swelling not far off the size of half a plum.

'What happened to you?' I asked and she touched her face with her fingertips.

'It was nothing really.'

I peered more closely. 'It looks like something really to me.'

'Sit down,' she urged. 'I've made a start on the coffee.' To judge by the granular dregs that came out of the spout, she had almost made a finish of it. I summoned the waitress for more and a clean cup. 'It was just children.'

Hettie rolled herself a cigarette with extra-large papers. She preferred to do that because she could get much more tobacco into it. The little shop-bought things – or *cigarette-ettes*, as she had dubbed them – were not strong enough to clear ones lungs, she would insist.

'Honestly those youngsters are getting worse.' She struck a match and sucked the sulphurous flame into her prodigious fabrication.

'Excuse me,' the woman in tartan called out, 'but my mother taught me ladies do not smoke in public.'

'And yet here I am to prove her wrong,' Hettie responded with the coruscating smile that she usually reserved for clients she detested but whose money she rather liked. My friend readdressed me. 'A group of urchins followed me through Bishop's Square singing *Where Did You Get That Hat?* Cheeky monkeys.'

She was not a wealthy woman, but she had a large collection of headgear, treating herself to a new one with every portrait that she completed. They were usually inexpensive and plain, but she adorned them herself with whatever came to hand. She had on an enormous floral arrangement this morning, the petals being made of brightly coloured crepe paper, and I would have been surprised had that escaped their attentions.

'There is no real harm in them – usually.'

I tried to look sympathetic. *And failed*. Ruby helped herself to a Garibaldi biscuit as the waitress brought a fresh pot.

'That's what I thought.' Hettie puffed on her cigarette. 'I don't mind that sort of thing really but then they started to throw stones at me. I think they were just trying to knock it off, but one hit me hard in my back and, when I spun round to remonstrate, I took another straight in the face.' She fingered it again.

'The little terrors,' I said. 'Did nobody try to stop them?'

'It was too quick.' She popped a cube of sugar in her mouth. 'I think I know which one it was. He still had his hand raised and it was empty. To be fair, he looked as taken-aback as I was. Then they scarpered.'

'At least there's nothing broken,' I tried to console her, 'and it should heal without a scar.'

Hettie crunched on the sugar. 'And now, as if I hadn't had enough troubles for one day…' Her face grew almost tragic. 'You have taken the last biscuit.'

She waved smoke in the direction of her new friend in tartan.

'No that was Ru…' I began, but she would never have believed me, especially with incriminating crumbs down my dress. I waved to a waitress and requested more.

'So did you manage to flush out your evil Aunt?'

'I would not describe her as evil.'

I would, Ruby and Hefty dueted.

'But,' I continued, 'I did as you suggested and took her to the Café Cordoba. Unfortunately, we overestimated her sense of decorum. In fact, we were foolish to fancy that she had one'.

Hettie frowned. 'Did she make a scene?'

'A whole one act melodrama.' I wriggled uncomfortably. How on earth had I managed to get crumbs down the back of my neck?

That might have been me. Hefty flicked his waistcoat with a large white handkerchief.

'She caused such a panic that most of the customers ran away.'

Hettie blew a chain of smoke rings. 'I am so sorry.' She adopted a tragic expression. 'That I missed it.'

Another plate of biscuits was delivered.

'It was not funny,' I said.

'I don't suppose it was.' She took the only one that was coated in chocolate.

'Then I got this.' I reached into my handbag and passed Hettie the first note.

'Your days are numbered,' she read. 'Is it some kind of a joke?'

'Probably.' I whisked a Garibaldi out of Ruby's reach. 'I hope.'

'Have you shown it to Alfred?'

I dipped my confection in my coffee. 'I think he has had enough of my mysterious letters recently.'

'All the same…'

'I will think about it.' I lifted the biscuit out, but the end drooped and splashed back into my coffee.

'I'm most awfully sorry,' a woman's voice said from behind me. 'But I could not help overhearing some of your conversation.'

The speaker came round to stand between us. She was aged about forty and smartly attired in a moss green dress with a matching narrow-brimmed hat, a ribbon tied around the crown. Her hair was copper red and her complexion marble white.

'Forgive me, but did you receive an anonymous letter?'

'Yes,' I agreed warily.

'Might I see it?'

'Might I ask why?' I proved that I might.

The lady dipped her head sideways for a moment.

'It is just that I was the recipient of such a letter ten years ago last May.' She exhaled heavily. 'It said that your days were numbered?'

'It did.'

'And so did mine. If I could...' she held out her hand hesitantly. 'Please.'

There was such an earnestness in her expression that I passed the note up to her and she raised a gold-framed lorgnette hanging on a golden thread around her neck.

'Oh, my goodness.' She dropped the lorgnette, and her hand went to her mouth. 'It is exactly the same as mine. And this is the only one you have received?'

'It is.'

'And it shall be the last, I hope.' Her hand trembled as she refolded the letter. 'I had three and, after that, he came for me.'

'Who?' Hettie and I asked.

'We cannot talk here,' the lady said. 'And my home is out of town. Is there somewhere private we can meet?'

'You could come to my house.' I found my silver case and gave her a card.

'Lady Violet Thorn,' she read aloud. 'Aren't you the authoress of the Ruby Gibson stories?'

'I fear so.'

Fear? Ruby echoed indignantly.

'Fear?' The lady returned the letter. She had a long scar on the palm on her right hand. 'I love her escapades and that detective…' She rubbed her fingers as if sprinkling salt. 'Inspector Hettie.'

Hettie and Ruby laughed. Hefty did not.

'I quite like him,' the lady said to hoots of amusement from my adventuress. 'But forgive me, I have not introduced myself.' She got out a mother of pearl case and hinged open the lid to hand me an ivory-coloured card.

Mrs Petunia Bottle, I read to myself, Hefty peering over my shoulder.

Ridiculous name, he bristled. *The woman is clearly a charlatan.*

'I am pleased to meet you,' I said, unsure that I was, and rose to take her hand.

'Would tomorrow morning be convenient? Shall we say eleven?' She slipped her hand away. 'I must go, or I shall be late for an engagement. Goodbye Lady Thorn. A pleasure to meet you.'

I sat again.

'Did I say yes?' I wondered.

'Not unless I nodded off.' Hettie blew three separate smoke rings.

Mrs Frow-Fulford, the manageress, came over.

'I am sorry, Miss Granger, but we have had a complaint about your… *cigarette?*' She used the word questioningly for it looked more like something that one might use to light a canon from a safe distance.

Gather your things Thorn, Ruby advised. *You are about to be evicted – again.*

'Oh, I am so sorry.' Hettie treated her to a hundred-carat smile. 'I shall extinguish it immediately.' She nipped and stubbed it out carefully to save the rest for later. 'If we might have the bill, please, we will pay at the desk.' *We*, I knew, meant me. 'We were about to leave anyway.'

We, that time, was both of us. I had been about to have another cup but thought it wise to follow before Hettie changed her mind and made a fuss. It would not do to be unwelcome at my second cafe in a week.

My friend surveyed the woman in tartan who was looking as smug as... *Havelock Hefty,* Ruby suggested.

'I am so sorry.' Hettie was saying as insincerely as... *Havelock again*, Ruby said again. 'If you have been inconvenienced by... your bigotry,' Hettie reclipped the silver broach that closed her collar as Ruby helped herself to a finger of the woman's shortbread. 'I note that you have not taken an exception to that gentleman's foul meerschaum nor that...' she indicated with a flap of her hand, 'Man's cigarillo.' She dropped the L's from the last word with a flourish as if she were pretending to be Mexican. Perhaps she was.

For some reason, the lady was scowling in my direction.

You stole her biscuit, Hefty reprimanded me.

Surely that was Ruby. I thought about my statement. 'Oh dear,' I said aloud and went to settle the bill.

7: HAM-FISTED HOD-LUGGERS AND DEMENTED OPERATORS

THE SKY WAS encouragingly cloudy as we stepped onto the street. The headline *NO RAIN* might sound like no news, but the situation had become desperate. After a blazing summer of *straw days* – as the dry season was termed by locals – there was still no relief from the drought in the autumn. Crops had failed and the River Angle was so low that it was difficult for cattle and even sheep to scramble down its banks to drink. Reports of farmers committing suicide were becoming tragically common.

I stepped back to let a couple pass, arm-in-arm, trying not to remember how Jack and I had walked along the same street in the same way, not much more than a year ago.

'Are you going back to your studio now?' I asked as Hettie stooped to pick up the wing feather of a pigeon and stuff it into her handbag.

'I am,' she confirmed, 'and you must come with me. Your portrait is taking so long I shall have to start putting Payne's Grey in your hair and adding wrinkles around your eyes before it's finished.'

The picture had been intended as a gift for Jack who – even if he ever surfaced – no longer deserved it. Now it was destined for Thetbury Hall so that I could gaze primly, if unseeingly, at my parents every time they took the main staircase.

'Give me an hour.' We set off, both heading towards the end of the street.

I had been tipped the wink by Gerrund that Metcalfe and Garlick were stocking a new range of scarfs in preparation for the winter, when, eventually, it arrived. Lord knew how Gerrund knew but both of them often moved in mysterious ways. If word got out, the store could be stripped of its best wares in an afternoon.

I already have half a dozen, Ruby twirled one of them over her shoulder. *To your account, of course.*

Hettie slid her cigarette stub into a cigar tube. 'If you're shopping, I shall give you two hours but no longer.'

Our way was blocked by scaffolding erected in front of the Fynce and Drove Bank. It was having a grandiose pillared face built though there did not seem to be much construction work underway.

'Oy,' a man shouted from above. 'Oy you.'

Hettie ignored him. She was more used than I to attracting catcalls from builders. I glanced up and stumbled over the edge of the kerb, a bay horse lunging towards me.

'Violet!' Hettie snatched at my arm and yanked me away. The flanks of the stallion pounded against my shoulder and sent me flying sideways into my friend's arms, knocking her back against the wall.

'Goff!' Hettie gasped, winded. She looked almost as shocked as I was.

'Stupid girl,' the rider yelled because it was eminently sensible of him to career down a busy high street. He did not even glance back to check if I were injured.

'Are you all right?' I asked my friend.

'I was about to ask you the same.'

'Just a little shaken.'

'Ditto.' Hettie patted herself to check that she was still intact and appeared to be satisfied that she was. 'Nothing that two or three stiff drinks wouldn't put right.' She nodded towards the Waggoner's Rest.

'I don't think they would serve us there,' I forecast. Entering a public house unchaperoned by a respectable man and consuming alcoholic beverages in public are just two of the innumerable things gentlemen believe that ladies should never do.

'They will if we insist,' Hettie linked her arm though mine. 'Wish I'd brought an umbrella. Looks like it might rain.' She stopped. 'I meant with rain, not rubble.' Hettie brushed her shoulders, coated with the debris that had showered on us both. 'Oh, for goodness sake. This was clean – well cleanish – on this morning.'

'And my dress,' I brushed it, leaving the back of my hand in a state not dissimilar to its condition after, as a child, I had climbed a chimney at Thetbury Hall to clear a pigeon's nest.

Never mind your clothes what about mine? Ruby fulminated for they were absolutely filthy and absolutely familiar too.

Those ARE my clothes. I fumed and she shrugged.

'Bother.' I shook the lower part of my dress, the one I was wearing. It was nothing special, but I had not been planning to throw it away. My friend's face was generously powdered with cement dust, and it was a pound to a farthing that mine was too.

'And I'll wager my effulgent hat is ravaged.' Hettie pulled the rim down to tip more dust onto her shoulder.

'I think it has been dented.' My eyes were watering from the grit in them, their lids flickering up and down like signal lamps operated by demented semaphorists.

'You ham-fisted hod-luggers!' Hettie raised her fist pugnaciously and I cringed to imagine what her parents would make of such behaviour. They had despaired long ago, of finding a good husband for her, or even a half-tolerable one. 'Clod-hopping clot-headed fat ouch.'

'What is it?' I had rather been enjoying her tirade.

'I had a pain, but I don't know where.' She patted herself again. 'Oh, it's gone. How sneaky.'

Something caught my eye, other than the grit. Was that a man silhouetted against the sun, leaning over from the scaffolding near the rooftop of the bank. If so, he pulled back the moment that I saw him.

'Are you all right?' There was something odd about her.

'It feels like there's half a brick up there.' Hettie put a hand into the foliage of her bonnet and tried to flick something off. 'How on earth has it got stuck so solidly?'

She tried to lift it by the brim and it bent but the hat stayed firmly in place.

'Let me see.'

She bent over for me to rummage through the flowers.

'There is a piece of metal sticking into it.' I took hold of the flat end of the short iron cone that projected through the material. 'That is funny.'

'What is?'

Hettie stumbled two steps into the road and almost under the wheel of a passing hansom. In a reversal of our roles, I grabbed her arm and pulled her back.

'Bit early to get swizzled,' the driver shouted as he passed.

'But not too late for you to learn how to drive,' I riposted.

He should not have been travelling so close to the pavement and certainly not so fast on such a busy street. I turned to my friend.

'Let me just...' Extracting the pins, I gripped her hat under the rim and pulled. Off it came with a ripping sound leaving a clean band across the top of her forehead.

'What?' Hettie took it off me, her hair in utter disarray. 'I don't understand.' She poked a thumb through the hole.

'Let me see,' I said.

'But...' Hettie fiddled with that which was dangling over one eye and held it out for me to see. 'It's damp.'

'Bend down,' I commanded, and she bowed. 'Dear Lord.' I put a hand to my mouth.

'What?' She put a hand to her head.

'Do not touch it,' I said urgently, and her arm fell away.

'What is it?' Hettie looked almost as alarmed as I felt. I did not want to frighten her, but I could not think of a way not to do so.

'There is a piece of metal sticking out of your head,' I told her, and I was not sure which of us was the more shocked by my declaration. It was happening to Hettie, of course, but I was the one who could see it and the blood beginning to trickle down her paper-white brow. 'A spike, I think.'

Hettie Granger stared at me aghast.

'Do not touch it,' I repeated as her hand went up again.

'A spike?' she echoed in bewilderment and stepped backwards into a gentleman in rather a nice butterscotch Inverness cape. His face was down to avoid the debris.

'Have a care madam,' he said, more in concern than reproof. He raised his head and I saw that it was my friend, Anthony Appleton. 'Oh hello, Lady Violet.' He tipped his butterscotch fedora. 'Is this lady with you?' He looked at her more closely. 'Great heavens above!'

'I am not intitoxicated,' Hettie asserted. 'Am I?' she checked with me.

'You are not,' I assured her, despite her extra syllable.

'I am not,' she assured him and crumpled, saved from tumbling into the gutter and under the wheels of a fly only by Anthony grasping her shoulders.

'Take your hands off me, you ruffian.' She pulled at his wrists but he kept a firm hold of her.

'Forgive me if I do not,' he replied with commendable calmness.

'We need to get you to hospital,' I said, instantly recruiting him to assist me.

'I know that a Doctor Feeble has a practice just up the road,' he told me. 'If he cannot help, he may well have a telephone with which we can call for an ambulance.'

My friend straightened her back, her eyes almost as wobbly as her legs.

'What a fuss over nothing.' She patted my arm, leaving a fine set of sanguinary fingerprints on my sleeve. 'All I need to set me aright is a good pint of porter.' With that and a toss of her head, Hettie collapsed into Anthony's arms.

'I have her.' Anthony scooped my friend up to cradle her like a bride about to cross the threshold.

A few people had gathered around, some out of sympathy but others getting close enough for me to tighten my grip on my handbag. As public hangings demonstrated in the bad old days, no incident is so horrible that a cutpurse will not take advantage of it.

Move along now, Hefty commanded, slapping away a stray boy's stray hand.

Hettie groaned distantly.

'Are you all right?' I asked stupidly but Hettie only moaned.

'Follow me.' Anthony set off.

'He meant me not you,' I told a ragged girl, but she tagged along regardless. 'If I give you a penny, will you go away?'

Anthony was weaving his way across the road, hopping out of the way of a donkey cart and dodging behind a butcher's van with me in as close pursuit as I could manage.

'Give me thruppence and I think on it,' the girl bargained, and I found three coppers in my purse.

We reached the opposite pavement yet still she trotted by me.

'I'm thinkin',' she responded to my glare.

'Do it elsewhere,' I instructed and, seeing that I was no good for further pickings, the girl set off in search of fresh prey. She had the rolling gait that sailors adopt when on land and the poor adopt to cope with their weak, bowed legs.

Anthony was striding at such a pace that I had to break into a trot to keep up with him. Hettie's head bobbed up and down on one side of him and her lower limbs, indecently exposed almost to the knees, on the other.

It was only when I caught up that the thought struck me, and I do not know why it had not before. From the way that Hettie Granger sagged in Anthony Appleton's embrace, her eyes glazed and unseeing, was it possible that she was dead?

8: STAG BEETLES AND PALE FRENCH BRANDY

THE BRASS PLATE on the wall read *DR UPPING FEEBLE, GENERAL MEDICAL PHYSICIAN* and was followed by a series of letters, presumably his qualifications but possibly an anagram to occupy those who were waiting, as we were, for a response to my tugging of the bell pull.

I parted the curtain of hair strewn over Hettie's face. Her eyes were closed now, and it was difficult to judge her complexion beneath the grime.

'Is she…' I could not bring myself to speak my fears.

'She's alive,' Anthony reassured me and, having his hands full, kicked the door vigorously. 'And a great deal heavier than she looks.'

I knew that was true because I had given her a piggyback ride after she had broken a foot once and my spine had castigated me for days afterwards.

'Excuse me.' I reached past and pulled the handle again. 'He probably thinks that you are trying to break in.'

I wiped some of the dirt from around my friend's eyes and they screwed up.

'I am sorry,' I said, unsure if I had hurt her, and yanked the bell pull again with a vigour that any campanologist might have envied. *Come on!* I willed the occupants of the house, but people never know when they have been willed or, if they do, they ignore it.

Hettie's arm flopped down, and I took her hand. It was clammy.

'He must be out,' Anthony said as I poked around Hettie's wrist. Her pulse, when I found it, was fast and thready.

'Surely he has a maid,' I said, and, in proof of my statement, the door swung open to reveal a small girl in a uniform intended for a large one.

'Is the doctor in?' I asked.

'Do you have an appointment?'

'No but this woman is seriously injured.'

'I shall enquire,' she replied and made to shut us out.

'If you have to ask, he is,' Anthony reasoned. 'Please be kind and let us in.'

That would never have worked for me, but I have oft observed that maids who balk at performing any task requested by a woman will eagerly obey a man who gives them exactly the same instruction.

He is better looking than you, Ruby explained though I would have described Anthony as pleasant in appearance rather than handsome. He was clean-shaven with dark brown eyes and hair but most winning, on happier occasions, was his smile.

We found ourselves in a good-sized hallway but there was little time to appraise the décor for a man, still in the process of buttoning-up his grey chalk-striped morning coat, came hurrying from a room to our immediate left. He was what the locals would, unkindly, have called *jelly-boy,* for his face and neck wobbled as he spoke.

'Deary-deary me,' he tutted. 'This is the third traffic victim I have seen this year. You ladies never look where you're going – too busy gossiping and ogling us men. Bring her through.' We went into an office, ill-lit for, of the two gas lamps, one had a broken mantle. 'Put her there.'

Anthony gently lowered Hettie into a high-backed leather armchair and stepped aside. Even in the gloom she looked awful, her eyelids quivering and her mouth agape.

'I shall wait in the hallway in case you need me,' he said, and I thanked him.

'My friend and I were walking near the scaffolding outside the bank,' I told the doctor who clicked his tongue.

'Most unwise,' he said. 'They are always dropping things. Why only last week a Mrs Brown from nine, Cushion St consulted me after a falling roofing tile had startled her so badly that she has been suffering swooning fits ever since.' Two things occurred to me, the first that this was a highly pampered woman and the second that I did not think he should be discussing another patient with a stranger. 'She may have to take nerve tablets for the rest of her life,' he concluded.

And you may have to take her money for the rest of your career, I concluded, almost as cynical as many of his profession.

'A metal spike went through her bonnet.'

'So I see,' he eyed the hat, still miraculously clutched in my friend's left hand, and inhaled sharply. 'But I doubt it can be repaired.'

'Into her head,' I continued.

'Oh yes,' he glanced over. 'Is that from Edgar's Exclusive Millinery Shop? My wife frequents that establishment… all too frequently,' he sort-of punned in that we-all-know-what-the-ladies-are-like way popular with men who have absolutely no idea about us at all.

'Does she need to go to hospital?' I asked pointlessly because, of course, she did. I looked about for a telephone.

'Hospital?' the doctor quivered in amusement. 'Goodness me no. You would not get me in one of those establishments, particularly for such a trifling matter.'

'But she has had a serious accident,' I pointed out what should have been unnecessarily, and the doctor slid a pince-nez into the grooves on the bridge of his bulbous nose, not to examine her injury but to peer over at a framed certificate on the wall.

'Just checking whose name is on that diploma,' he explained, 'and I am gratified to discover that it is not yours but mine.'

Give me strength, I prayed before asking, 'Is there anything that you can do for her?'

'But of course,' he sniffed and, turning his attention to Hettie, took told of the end of the spike and pulled.

'Should you be doing that?' I fretted.

'You want your friend to spend the rest of her life with metal shard in her skull?'

'No of course not.'

'Then I shall remove it.'

'Does she not need an anaesthetic?'

The doctor snorted. 'You think she is not unconscious already?'

'Well no… but surely it could damage her brain.'

'These things are much shorter than you fancy,' he breezed. 'It will not have penetrated all the way through. If this were a man, I should be concerned but anatomists have determined that the feminine brain is much smaller than that of the male. Why it does not even fill a half of her little cranium.'

Blimmid cheek! My tiny brain fumed, having plenty of space in which to do so.

'Then why is she unconscious?'

'Shock,' he told me, 'pure and simple. The female nervous system is much more delicate than that of the average robust male.'

Robust was not a word that I would have applied to Dr Feeble nor *delicate* to Hettie Granger. She was not a big woman, but she had pavemented a pickpocket once when we were shopping in Bury St Edmunds.

'If you are sure…' I was far from convinced for, if this was what I thought it was – though I did not know for what they were used – the ones I had seen were a good eight or ten inches long. Even taking into account my friend's thick marmalade hair, there cannot have been more than half of it jutting out.

Dr Feeble opened a glass-fronted cabinet to root through an assortment of devices, coming back up with what I hoped was a medical instrument but looked more like a pair of coal tongs to me. Holding it in both hands he grasped the spike between the pincer heads and tugged.

Hettie sat up but the spike stayed where it was.

'Do not hurt her.'

'Just needs a bit of twist' He adjusted his grip. Hettie turned towards me then to the certificate and back again. 'And a bit more,' he added, already breathing hard from his exertions. 'Well,' he rounded on me, 'if you are not going to assist…'

'What would you like me to do?'

I will wake up in a minute, I told myself without conviction. It was all too horrible to be a nightmare.

'Why hold her still of course. She keeps trying to get out of the chair.'

Hettie was not in any state to try to do anything, but I went behind her and put my hands on her shoulders.

'You will be all right,' I told her though I was not sure she could hear me or that I believed it.

'Of course I will.' The doctor grunted and heaved, and I found myself having to press down as hard as I could to stop my friend rising out of the chair but the spike was stuck fast.

'Just needs a bit of a twiggle,' he muttered. 'That's a special medical term for a twist and a wiggle.'

'I think you should leave it,' I said.

'What? To rust into rust inside her head?'

'For a specialist.'

'Who? A scaffoldingisectimologist?' he scoffed. 'There is no such word because there are no specialists in this procedure.' His watery eyes shone with messianic zeal. 'I am making medical history here today – Feeble's Spikectomy.'

Throwing his tongs onto the oilcloth floor, the doctor grasped the spike in both hands and wrenched it forwards, yanking Hettie's head down. A small cry escaped her.

'You are hurting her!' I cried.

'She is trying to thank me.'

'Stop it! Stop it this instant.'

Dr Feeble rammed the spike back, smacking the back of Hettie's head into the chair. Her eyes and her hands rose to clutch his.

'Let go, blim you,' he cursed, twisting the bar in a figure of eight and, shouldering me aside, put his knee on my friend's chest and hauled with all his might.

'Stop it!' I clawed at his fingers.

The door opened and Anthony appeared.

'Is everything…'

There was a loud crack and the doctor toppled backwards, falling heavily – but not heavily enough – onto the floor, limbs flailing like a capsized stag beetle.

'Got it!' he cried triumphantly, waving his trophy in his fist like a miniature javelin, and Hettie slumped forwards, blood pouring from the crater in her head.

I gaped down at this monster posing as a physician.

'You stupid, ugly man.' I looked about. 'Where are your dressings?'

The monster gaped up at me.

'I am not ugly.' He rolled onto his stomach and got up on all fours. At that moment he was the most grotesque life form I had ever seen – and I had visited the House of Commons – but this was no time to debate his aesthetic deficiencies. He hauled himself into a kneeling position on the arm of his chair.

'Dressings.' I barged past him to open a drawer. It was full of old newspapers. 'Where are they?'

'You can't come in here looking through my private things.'

'And yet I can.' Only by a supreme effort of will did I resist the urge to push him over as he ramshackled to his feet.

'Here they are,' Anthony announced for he had been more usefully employed in looking through a cabinet than I was in arguing with that pseudo-physician.

'Thank you.' I grabbed a fistful.

'Hold on.' Feeble tried to snatch his bandages back but I whisked them away. 'You can't just help yourself.' He grabbed my sleeve. 'Vexatious child.'

'You would do well to release her and keep quiet,' Anthony advised sternly, and the doctor, loosening his grip, snapped his mandibles shut.

The wad was saturated immediately, and I had a suspicion that no amount of them would stanch the haemorrhage. A ridiculous idea occurred to me but it had worked for Hefty when he had been shot in the shoulder.

'Find me your largest cork.'

'My largest…' he raised his hands like a costermonger, astonished that I did not want to pay extra for a maggoty apple.

'Cork,' Anthony said firmly. 'Fetch one now.' He lowered his voice. 'Why?' he asked me.

'It is a medical trick that Romulus taught me,' I lied, a remote part of me hoping that I had made a mistake and would find that I had not been lying after all. Romulus was my second cousin and a qualified doctor who had what might be a unique belief amongst his profession, that skill and ethics mattered.

Feeble flapped his arms but, finding himself unable to levitate, hurried to a tall pine cupboard.

'That is probably my largest.' He pulled the stopper from a bottle labelled *Pale French Brandy*. 'I keep it for medical purposes,' he claimed though nobody had suggested otherwise.

I took it from him. It looked approximately the right size.

'Give me the bottle.' I snatched it and poured some over the cork.

'Oh, I thought you meant to drink it,' Feeble giggled, this being an occasion for much merriment.

I poured some more over the cork, took a good swig just to annoy him – especially as I did not care for the stuff – and thrust the bottle into his arms, not even glancing back as I heard a crash.

'You didn't give me a chance to take hold of it,' Feeble whined, more concerned about the brandy than his patient. 'And I am not ugly.'

Sorry Hettie. I dipped the cork into the bubbling pool of blood. *But I don't know what else to do.* Obviously, she could not hear my thoughts, but I did not want Feeble to hear them either. Locating the hole, I pressed and, to my satisfaction, found that the cork was quite a tight fit. 'Give me a hammer.'

All doctors had them, I knew. They used them to strike unsuspecting patients' kneecaps but the tool with which Feeble presented me would have been better suited to the construction of a potting shed. It even had one of those split ends which I believed were used for pulling nails out of floorboards. This was no time to carp though. I gave the head of the cork a gentle tap then three more and it slid neatly into place.

'Jolly good trick that,' Anthony murmured before turning to Feeble. 'Do you have a telephone?'

Even standing back, as he had been for most of the time, he was splattered with blood.

'I might,' Feeble replied cagily.

'Where would you like her sent?' Anthony asked me.

'Not the infirmary,' I said. Everybody knew that, if patients exited that establishment alive, they usually did so with more diseases than they had when they entered. 'The Tennison has a good reputation.'

'Go and call them,' Anthony instructed and Feeble stiffened or, at least I thought that he did. It was difficult to tell in somebody so slackly slapped together. 'I am not at your beck and call.'

'I think you will find that you are.'

I rather liked this new, masterful Anthony though, clearly, the doctor did not.

'Nobody speaks to me like that.'

'I do.' Anthony, doubtless observing the way that I was brandishing the hammer, took it from me. 'Look lively.'

Feeble trotted off.

'You have become very assertive,' I asserted.

'If truth be told I am terrified of medical men.' Anthony smiled modestly. 'But I asked myself how Inspector Hefty would have coped and tried to follow his example.'

Before Ruby could surface and formulate a cutting remark, Hettie opened her eyes and stretched as if awakening from a delicious sleep.

'That glass of porter is a long time coming.' She licked her lips and closed her eyes again.

Please God, I prayed, *do not let those be her last words.*

A part of me knew, though, that – if she lived another fifty years, Hettie would never think of a more fitting epilogue.

Feeble returned.

'The Tennyson is not admitting anyone,' he told me. 'There has been an outbreak of gastric gout.'

'There is no such thing,' I argued.

'I know,' he admitted, 'but whatever it was called it was too big a word for me to remember. Anyway, she will be much better off at the Garfield.'

From what little I had heard of *Garry's* I doubted that very much.

'I am the chief physician there,' Feeble proclaimed which settled the matter. My friend would be nursed at home – mine, on reflection since hers was cramped and would need a great deal of tidying before it could be described as chaotic.

I rang Break House.

'I'll arrange for an ambulance, Milady,' Gerrund assured me and, twenty minutes later, he arrived, driving a delivery van. 'It was the best I could do.' He opened the doors to reveal a camp bed in the back. Anthony deposited Hettie gently upon it and went to sit up at the front with my man. Having nothing upon which to sit, I knelt on the floor, holding Hettie's hand. It was uncomfortable but before long we had stopped and Anthony was clambering in to pick Hettie up again. She looked a worse colour in my unexpressed opinion as I stumbled after them in my dusty, gore-encrusted clothes.

'Cat give birth to puppies,' the newspaper vendor yelled in my ear so loudly that I almost had kittens.

9: PUTREFIED MATTER AND THE LETTING OF BLOOD

AGNUST WAS WAITING in the doorway.

'The scrapes you get up to,' she berated me, 'not countin' the ones you get down to. She's a nice girl before she meet you.' That was probably true for Hettie was four months old when we were introduced. 'Give her here.' She took Hettie from Anthony. 'S'prised at you,' she scolded, 'canoodling in public.'

'I was...'

'Daint make it worse by telling me a whole string of truth,' she warned and bore Hettie like a child in her arms, not even puffing as she tramped up the stairs.

'Just as well we keep the bed in the main guest room made up,' I commented in her wake.

''Tis,' she agreed. 'And just as well I change your sheet this marnin'.' I was not sure why that was pertinent until Agnust turned right instead of left. 'Much more comfortable in your luxurious bed.' She waited.

'Yes, I suppose she will be.' I went ahead to pull the bedding down.

Agnust deposited my friend with a gentleness that she had never exhibited to me, not even when I had been crushed by a hay waggon and she had told me to get up and stop making a fuss. In hindsight this may have been so that I could not see how concerned she was. There again, she might just have been cross with me for bleeding on her apron.

'Dint tuck her in so tight. She wint be able to draw her last breath.' She watched dubiously as I tried to make Hettie comfortable. 'Now it's so loose she fall out and burst her chitterlin's.' On my fourth attempt I performed the task to an enthusiastic, 'S'pose tha' have to do.'

Hettie opened her eyes and stretched lazily.

'What a lovely bed.' She snuggled down into my pillows. 'This is so comfortable.'

'Yes, it is,' I agreed.

'I could stay here for ever,' she smiled, and fell promptly asleep.

-

Junkins, the valet, answered when I rang Suthy Hall. His master was not at home and his mistress was resting, he told me, but he would see if she were available. Normally I would not have dreamed of disturbing Jane. Her health had not been good for the better part of two years now and, as Romulus had gloomily admitted, after all his efforts it was showing no improvement.

'If she is asleep do not disturb her,' I said wondering what on earth I could do if she were.

His footsteps faded.

I flicked through a small pile of post on my escritoire. The first two looked suspiciously like they contained bills and could, therefore, wait. There was a letter from Bailey Waters, solicitors bearing some excellent news. I was the true heir to a fortune. They could not divulge the details until I had paid the thirty pounds that it would take for them to establish my entitlement. Strangely they only had a post office address which did not arouse my suspicions in the least. This was the second time that they had written to me so, giving them full marks for persistence, I filed it meticulously in my wastepaper bin.

Jane came to the telephone.

'I'm afraid Rommy is out on a couple of house calls,' she told me, having brushed aside my enquiries about her health, 'and you know what he's like. If somebody offers him a cup of tea, he could be gone for the rest of the day.'

Despite her assurances, she sounded a little out of breath to me.

'Do you know where he is?' I asked anxiously. 'It is just that Hettie Granger has had a bad accident – a head wound – and she is unconscious.'

I gave her a quick summary of events.

'Leave it with me, Violet,' Jane said. 'I will send Junkins out on Major.' Major was their best horse. 'The woman who called round was in a badged cloak, so Rommy is probably at King Edward's.'

This was an alms house, and those it took in were given cloaks with crests on, not as a uniform but from charity to wear if they chose. Most did for they were proud to be residents. Those who could afford to, made small contributions towards their own keep. Unlike the cruel workhouse regime, married couples were allowed to stay together in their own quarters.

'I am going to have a bath and get changed,' I told her. 'Gerrund will be here if you have any news before I come down.'

'And where will Gerrund be if I have no news?' she asked in an excellent imitation of her husband's voice.

'For goodness sake, Janey, you know exactly what I mean,' I tried with less success but at least, for all our problems, we were both laughing.

–

Hettie was snoring when I relieved Agnust from her vigil that evening.

'Another bad habit you get her into,' my maid admonished me as she left the room.

I sat on an upright chair beside the bed and took my friend's hand.

Why did you take her to that horrible man? Ruby appeared, dipping a silver spoon into a jar of caviar.

I assumed that, being a doctor, he might know something about being a doctor.

What on earth led you to that conclusion? she challenged. *Scotland Yard's premier detective knows next to nothing about being a detective.*

Are you going to let her speak to me like that?

It is too late to prevent her.

I am surprised you have the time to worry about it, she taunted him, *with a knife in your left ventricle.*

Who said it was in my heart? He patted his chest anxiously. *Have you been writing more behind my back, Lády Violet?*

'Perhaps,' I said aloud.

'Perhaps what?' Hettie opened one eye.

'How are you feeling?'

Hettie closed her eye and opened the other while she considered the question. She rolled it around her mouth, analysing *les flavours* like a Frenchman with a fine wine.

Les flavours? Ruby threw up her arms in despair for she had been engaged to be married to Le Comte de l'Hardifort. He had left her at the altar and, if I had known at the time how much being jilted hurt, I would never have put her through the experience.

Hettie smacked her lips.

'Not too bad,' she decided, 'apart from feeling giddy.'

'That is...' I was about to say *good* when she added, 'And nauseous – very nauseous.'

'Are you in any pain?'

She did not trouble to chew that one before she swallowed it.

'None whatsoever.' And I was about to have another go at *good* when she added, 'apart from this throbbing-throb-throbbing headache.'

She raised her hand.

'Try not to touch...' I reached for her right arm. 'It,' I managed too late for she had prodded a finger into the clot that lurked malevolently over her wound.

'There is still something sticking out of it.'

'A Pale French Brandy cork.'

Her eyes rolled worryingly. 'Are you mad?... Or am I?... Or are we both?'

She grasped the cork and twisted.

'Ow!' she yelled. 'It hurts!'

I pulled at her hand, but she was struggling with all the strength of one woman.

'Hettie, try not to...'

'It's painful.' Her eyes brimmed.

'I know, dear, but you must not touch it.'

Her left arm went up and I grabbed that too.

'You touch it then,' she challenged.

'We have to leave it alone.'

'Oh Violet, it hurts so much.'

It was also bleeding afresh but I thought it better not to share that information.

'What is that wet feeling?' she demanded. 'Is it...' Hettie wrenched her right arm free and touched her cheek, holding the fingers out to inspect them. 'Dudgeon gouts of blood!' she cried. 'Don't let me die.'

'Of course, I will not, darling,' I promised though I was not sure that I had much say in the matter.

Don't let her die, I prayed trying to forget that this was the same God who had taken so many of my siblings. I had made all sorts of promises to him when my little brother Marcus had diphtheria, even offering myself in exchange, but to no avail.

'You are going to be all right,' I vowed though I had no grounds for doing so.

Hettie looked at me, but her gaze was drifting and, I noticed in alarm, that her struggling was weakening.

'Are you sure?' Her eyelids were drooping like Rodrigo, my kitten's, when he was trying to beguile mice.

'As sure as eggs is carrots.' I let go of her right arm and it flopped onto the eiderdown. 'Have I ever lied to you?'

There was that time... Ruby began but even she appreciated that this was not the moment.

'There was that time...' Hettie said dreamily. She perked up. 'I say, Violet, do you remember Violet Thorn?'

In my stories that was the sort of confusion that people would exhibit when they were preparing to give up their souls. More terrifyingly, I had known real people to do the same.

'Rommy will be here soon,' I said but Hettie's eyes had closed.

She was still breathing, I was relieved to note as I locked my fingers in supplication.

I know I have not always been a good person, I prayed because I had been told he likes people to admit that. *And I should have gone to church more and said my prayers at night and I am sorry but please do not take Hettie. I do not know what I can offer you in exchange.*

Take me, Ruby said.

And me, Hefty added, and I was shocked to see tears in his eyes.

And me, a hundred voices rose in a mighty chorus.

Surely, God would listen to at least one of us?

Hettie's pulse was weakening.

What more do you want? I begged.

Her breathing was getting faint too.

This has gone far enough. I shouted in my mind so as not to startle her. *Where the hell is Rommy?* But the silence was deafening. *Now you listen to me, God,* I raged. *If you do not produce Romulus here with a cure for Hettie immediately, I will box your ears so hard that you will never hear another prayer again because they will never ever stop ringing. And I mean it. Then where will you be?*

I waited for the thunderbolt but, obviously, God could not even be bothered to strike me down. As it transpired, he had a far greater punishment than that in store though, for Hettie had stopped breathing.

I checked with my little hand-mirror, and it remained unfogged. No matter how hard I prodded, I could not detect any pulse. I ripped open the top of her nightdress and put my ear to her breast but heard nothing above the sweeping of my own blood.

'No!' I cried, but there was no point in pretending otherwise. Hettie Granger, my childhood friend who had grown into the woman that I loved more than any other, was dead.

10: FRIAR TUCK AND A BRAIN OF TWO HALVES

IN DESPERATION I lifted Hettie's eyelid, but her eye was rolled back.

'Hettie! Darling!' I cried.

'What's happening?' Romulus came into the room.

'Oh, Rommy.' I could hardly bring myself to say the words. 'Hettie is dead.'

My cousin put his gladstone bag on my recently vacated chair. His expression, already concerned, became grim.

'Let me see.' He pushed me aside to put his fingers to Hettie's throat.

'I beg to differ with your diagnosis,' he said. 'Her pulse is weak, I grant you, but nonetheless, her heart is beating.'

'Thank God.' I would apologise to him later and do some kind of penance – give up drinking coffee for a week or, maybe a morning.

'Has she regained consciousness at all?'

'For a minute or two. She was quite confused and then she touched the wound and hurt herself badly – I tried to stop her – and then she fainted.'

'How long ago was that?' If ever there were an epitome of a Thorn, it was Romulus, tall and lean, with his long, hooked nose, sapphire eyes, and thick head of straight black hair.

'I do not know. A few minutes.'

'Not a straightforward faint then.' My cousin took off his coat and threw it over the back of the chair.

'Do you think she will be all right?' I asked stupidly.

'She's a tough old bird.' He raised his voice. 'Aren't you, Hettie?'

'Do you think she can hear us?'

'Probably.'

'Then you had better look out for her right hook when she recovers,' I warned. 'Old bird indeed.'

Rommy chuckled and went to a sink in the corner of the room and opened the taps. If there was once thing for which Great Aunt Herbena could take full credit, it was her installation of an excellent plumbing system. 'This is luxury indeed,' he commented. 'Running water – hot and cold.' He rolled up his sleeves and washed his hands.

Many older doctors still ignored or even ridiculed the need for antiseptics. Diseases were caused by foul miasmas arising from putrefied matter. Their prevention and cure, therefore, were based upon fresh air as prescribed by the sainted Florence Nightingale. Some still relied on bloodletting until, or even after, the patient swooned.

'A coma is often a blessing.' He closed the taps and dried his hands on a white towel. 'It relieves the patient's suffering and gives the body time to heal itself. Also…' He went back to the bed. 'It grants me the opportunity to clean up the wound. It's going to be messy so I will need plenty of old towels.'

'I do not have any old ones,' I admitted, feeling I was rather letting him and my friend down.

'I don't suppose you do.' He rolled his eyes. 'In that case I will have as many of whatever vintage you can provide.'

The cupboard was on the landing next to the bathroom. I lifted a stack of towels and returned laden to my room.

'Wrap a big one round her neck.'

So masterful, Ruby – who hated being bossed around – purred.

How dare he speak to my wonderful and merciful ladyship like that? Hefty grovelled.

'Open my bag and wash your hands.' I did as Rommy bade. 'Scissors, the large ones.'

I handed them over. 'What are you going to do?'

'Clear the area.' He set to work, snipping off long clumps of Hettie's hair and letting it fall on the towel and bedding.

'An unusual dressing,' he commented as the cork appeared.

'I did not know what else to do. It was bleeding so heavily.' I watched him lift Hettie's hair away. 'I only hope that I have not forced it to build up inside and put pressure on her brain.'

Rommy tipped his head a fraction to the right.

'Actually, you did the right thing. The bleeding was probably coming from the bone margins, and you sealed them quite nicely.' Rommy tipped his head to the left and raised his right eyebrow. 'I am half-tempted to leave it in place but then the bone would never heal over.' He twisted the cork gingerly and extracted it. The wound was oozing but there was nothing like the torrent that I had seen before.

'Do you think it will? Heal, I mean?'

He shrugged his left shoulder. 'I have seen worse injuries repair themselves.' He wiped a clot away. 'Bone has great powers of regeneration. Cutthroat razor.'

Hettie shifted.

'I think she heard that.' I handed it to him, and he flicked the blade open.

'I'm just going to clean around the wound,' he said more loudly, shaving her with all the deftness of a member of the Worshipful Company of Barbers. 'It will all grow back again.'

In a few years, I thought.

'There's a sponge in there. Run it under the hot tap… Don't squeeze it out. Bring it here.'

I held it at arms' length but still managed to saturate the front of my dress and a stream of water followed me over my floorboards and Armenian rug back to the bed. Rommy took it from me and plonked it on Hettie's head, bloodied water cascading down her face and soaking my pillow and her nightdress.

'Rinse it, wring it out and bring it back… Hurry, girl.'

You will suffer for those words, I vowed silently.

'I am sure I shall,' he agreed.

I have a useful tip for you. Ruby had changed into a nurse's uniform. *When you wish to vow silently it is a good idea not to speak.*

Rommy was mopping the top of our friend's head.

'Same again.' He passed it back to me.

'Wrung out?' I checked, unsure whether he meant for me to start from scratch.

'Of course.'

Silly me.

He wiped Hettie cleanish and handed me the sponge.

'Finished with that for now.'

I put the sponge in the sink and returned to the bedside.

'Gauze.'

There was a wad of it cut already into squares and he dabbed the remaining clot away.

Hettie had a bristly Friar Tuck tonsure about four inches in diameter but what caught my eye with a horrible fascination was the hole in the middle. It was about an inch in diameter.

Five eights. Hefty retracted his Roe Electric Reel Tape Measure, the increments marked with perforations and rivets. He had ordered it to be delivered with my latest shipment of Beeman's chewing gum, a product to which I was addicted.

'It's a relatively clean wound.' Rommy threw the soiled gauze into the steel kidney dish that I was holding out. This was not the first time that I had assisted my cousin. 'Teaspoon.'

'Did you say…'

'There's a small silver one in one of the side pockets.' Jane had sewn those in for him. 'Watch her face. If she shows any sign of discomfort let me know.' I stepped back a little and bent sideways. 'You're in my light.'

I think you will find it is her ladyship's light, Hefty informed my cousin but I took another step back.

'Better?' I asked and Rommy grunted which I took as an affirmative. 'Well,' I observed. 'She is sleeping like a baby at the moment.'

Rommy was carefully scooping out the remnants of the clot from just inside the hole. I changed the towel and laid some more around her.

'Only a woman who is childless could imagine that babies sleep soundly,' he commented, and I grimaced involuntarily. 'I am sorry. That was thoughtless,' he added without looking up for he knew that I had expected to be starting a family by now. 'There's a large steel syringe in the bottom of my bag and a bottle of distilled water just labelled *water.* Fill the syringe for me.'

They were easy enough to find, being the largest things there. The syringe was almost as big as a bicycle pump and had a rubber tube attached to the nozzle. I dipped it into the water and pulled back the plunger. Another time I might have sprayed him playfully but another time I might not have been terrified.

Rommy wiped the spoon and dropped it into the kidney dish that I had left resting on Hettie's stomach. 'Lay some fresh towels round her neck.' He placed the tube just into the wound. 'I need more hands for this. Take it and push in the plunger but slowly. We don't want to damage her brain any further.'

Tentatively I pressed on the T-shaped handle.

'Bit harder.'

Please do not suddenly whoosh out. For once an inanimate object listened to me and I managed to get a steady trickle, fresh blood and bits of clot flowing down Hettie's face and neck into the towel.

'Same again.'

'There is only a third of a bottle left.'

'That will have to do.' We repeated the procedure. 'That's good. It looks quite clean now and we got some bone splinters out.'

I glowed with childish pride at the *we.*

'Do you think there might be more?'

'I hope not. There weren't any in the second flush.'

'What about the wound? I don't suppose you can sew it up.'

He shook his head. 'The scalp is too tight to pull any skin over the cavity.'

He placed a pack on top of Hettie's head, looped a bandage over it, under her chin and back up to tie a knot at the top.

'She is still bleeding a bit,' I commented.

'Good. We need a clot if the tissues are to grow back.'

Rommy packed his used instruments into a canvas bag, put it into his gladstone, washed his hands and rolled his sleeves down.

'Well,' he said. 'She's lucky.'

'To be spiked through the brain?'

'Not to be spiked through the brain,' he corrected me. 'As you know, the organ is in two halves.'

Everything is in two halves, Ruby stated.

I did not think that he heard her, but he continued, 'I should say two separate halves and they are joined by a bridge known as the...' Romulus pointed at me rather as his professors must have challenged him when he was a medical student.

'The cor-cally-something,' I struggled. There is an unbridgeable gulf between the knowledge acquired studying medicine and that picked up whilst helping the crammer to revise for his examinations.

'*Corpus callosum*,' he completed for me but had the grace not to mock.

I knew that, Ruby claimed. *It is how I pass from one of your cerebral hemispheres to the other.*

I was not sure that I liked the idea of my character roaming quite so freely through my head, cigarette in diamond-encrusted gold holder. It made me feel itchy but, even if I could have scratched my brain, it would probably be unwise to do so.

Concentrate, I snapped at myself while my cousin explained how the spike had passed between the two halves but not deeply enough to damage the corpus cal-something-I-had-forgotten-again-already.

'Then why is she like this?' I asked.

Hettie's eyes were still closed, though the lids flickered occasionally, and she was drooling from one corner of her mouth, something I had not known her to do since I had introduced her to absinthe, and it had not agreed with her.

'Probably shock,' Romulus diagnosed. 'You will need to change the dressing regularly to keep it clean.'

'Me?'

'Well, I wasn't talking to Ruby Gibson.'

Why not? She pouted.

'Do you think we should get a nurse in?'

'I think we can leave her in the care of Lady Violet Thorn.' He clipped his bag shut and put his coat back on. 'And on no account let that oaf, Feeble anywhere near her again.' I had never known my cousin be so disparaging about a colleague. 'Anyway, I must go, Vi, if I am to catch my train.'

'Give my love to Jane. I shall visit soon, if she feels well enough to receive me.'

'She would be delighted to see you.' He picked up his bag. 'Then you can both have more fun mocking me.'

'I cannot imagine what you are talking about.' I put a hand to my heart to emphasis my sincerity.

'For goodness sake, Janey, you know exactly what I mean,' he said in a falsetto voice, and we burst out laughing. Obviously Jane had told him how she and I had imitated his voice.

'Thank you, Rommy.' I gave him a hug.

'She's my friend too.' My cousin kissed my cheek and I saw him downstairs.

Agnust came along the hallway.

'I'm afraid I got the sheets and pillow rather wet.' Rommy gamely shouldered the blame and I waited for her outburst.

'Dint you worry your head about tha', Romulus, Viscount Thorn of Thetbury,' she smiled indulgently for she was very proud of having a visitor with a real title in the house. Mine, being a courtesy one, was dust in the wind, as far as she was concerned. 'Lady Violet will change the beddin'.'

–

It may have been the fault of the nervous young fop in powder blue whimpering, 'The Montford Maniac hath returned!'. It may just have been the horrible events of the day. Whatever the cause I had a dream about Lucy Hallam, one of the later victims. She was a lady's maid who had been contacted late at night with a message that her mother was ill and set off to visit her sometime after midnight. The Maniac had struck as she took a short cut through Freeman's Alley that ran behind her mother's terraced house. She had been stabbed in the back and neck some five times but somehow managed to stagger through the gate to hammer on the back door. Her mother had looked out and seen what she described as *a fearsome fiend* renewing his attack on her daughter in the yard and been too terrified to open the door. As a result, Lucy was hacked to death while her mother looked on. Needless to say her *cowardice,* as most saw it, was widely condemned afterwards, including by the coroner.

In my dream I was Lucy, but I was also her mother, paralysed by fear and, as the maniac stepped back into the gaslight, I saw that he had my face too. I jumped out of bed shaking in terror. It was two sticks of Beeman's before I managed to calm myself enough to fall back into a fitful sleep with a candle flickering nervously on my bedside table.

11: *SNAKE OIL AND LEECH LOVERS*

ROMULUS RETURNED THE next morning. 'How's the patient?'

'She had a good night,' I replied, 'which is more than I did. I tried to sleep in the armchair in case she needed anything.' I rubbed my gravelly eyes. 'The only thing she lacked was a cure for snoring.'

He surveyed me with a critical eye.

'You should try to get some rest. You look haggard.'

'Thank you.'

'You're welcome. I don't usually offer my opinion for free.'

There was many a family in Norfolk who could dismiss that claim. It was just as well my cousin had private means, for he could never have made a living from the number of patients whom he charged little or nothing for his services.

'She has woken up a few times. Sometimes she seems to understand what is happening,' I told him as we ascended. 'Other times she talks nonsense.'

'That's Hettie for you.' We went right at the top of the stairs. 'So, she is still in your room?'

'I thought she would be more comfortable in my bed,' I lied.

'Can't be worse than the one in the spare room,' he remarked for he had stayed the night a few times since I first occupied the house. 'I have laid on more comfortable heaps of rubble.'

I did not challenge him on that claim for he had been in the army and the Burma campaign had not been a pleasant experience, I knew.

I tapped on the panel, not something I did as a rule, before entering my own room.

'Good morning, Rommy,' Hettie beamed.

'How are you feeling?'

'Much better,' she assured him. 'My head is only pounding like a sledgehammer instead of the steam hammer that was attacking it yesterday.'

'Good.' Rommy put his bag down and took her pulse. 'Much stronger and steadier.'

'Are you?' she tried to wink but it got stuck halfway.

Rommy took off his jacket, rolled up his sleeves and went to wash his hands.

'Perhaps you could have some breakfast in bed,' I suggested, and she nodded, the colour draining from her face instantly. 'Yuck. That makes me giddy.' She massaged her brow, and her semi-wink came undone. 'Scrambled eggs would be nice.'

'I shall get Gerrund to prepare some with toast,' I promised as Rommy returned with a bowl of hot water.

'The dressing looks clean,' he commented as he unravelled it.

'I changed it three times.'

'And a very neat job too.' He sponged the top of her head, careful to avoid the wound. 'That looks clean as well with a good solid clot,' he approved. 'You would make a good nurse.'

'I'd make a good doctor too.' I waited to be disparaged.

'A tarned sight better than many a man I've come across.' He dabbed Hettie dry.

'Tarned?' I laughed and he grinned.

'I picked that up in one of your Wild West stories.'

You picked it up; you put it straight back Two-eyed Jake's hands hovered over his holsters. Tarned snake-oil leech lover. I had banned him, along with countless other characters, from intruding into my thoughts but, being from Texas, he had little respect for my authority.

'He doesn't use leeches,' I said.

'Are you sure you didn't get a head injury yourself?' Rommy asked, busily rewrapping Hettie.

'Sorry I was...'

'Wool-gathering.' He produced a brown medicine bottle. 'Two teaspoons four times a day. No more, no less,' he instructed me as he cut the bandage. 'It should relieve your headaches,' he told his patient, 'but it will make you sleepy.'

'I don't mind that,' she assured him. 'It's rather nice lying in bed all day and being waited on and Violet has told me that I can stay here for absolutely ever.'

'I am not sure I remember saying that,' I murmured before the idea became too fixed in her mind.

'Of course you don't.' Hettie patted my hand. 'You are very confused.'

'Better think about getting a new mattress,' Romulus counselled in amusement.

'Oh no, Rommy.' Hettie nestled down. 'I assure you; this is very comfortable indeed.'

-

Rommy and I went down to the front sitting room. 'Take a…' I tripped on the edge of my carpet, grabbing his sleeve to steady myself. 'Seat.' I unwrinkled his jacket.

'You seem almost as accident prone as Hettie.' Rommy unwrinkled his sleeve properly and flattened the rug with his foot. 'I think you need to sit down.'

I lowered myself into my chair by the window with exaggerated caution and he sat beside me. 'I am not sure that it was an accident.'

He brought out his silver cigarette case looking questioningly at me, and I nodded my permission for him to smoke. He knew I did not care for the habit, but I knew that he had earned his relaxation.

'You think somebody put the rug there to injure you?' Rommy tapped a cigarette on his case.

'Of course not,' I said, unfairly irritated at this man who was going to such great trouble to help our friend.

And you, like when… Ruby began.

I know, I snapped before she could start to number the numberless occasions when he had rallied to my aid.

'I mean what happened to Hettie.'

'Go on.' He lit his cigarette, shook out the match and snapped it.

'It is just that I glanced up and saw a man peering down from the roof of the bank, but he pulled away the moment he saw me looking at him.'

Rommy blew a smoke ring.

'If you dropped something off a building you would look down to see what was happening and you would pull back to avoid being seen and getting into trouble.'

'That is what I tried to tell myself.' I got up and went to my escritoire. 'But this came in the early morning post.'

Rommy scrutinised it and exhaled heavily.

'Very unpleasant.' He handed it back. 'Probably somebody's peculiar idea of a joke but I can see it has disconcerted you.'

'I feel foolish...' I hesitated and Rommy leaned towards me.

'I know I make fun of you.' He touched my hand. 'Almost as much as you do of me, but I have never thought of you as foolish.'

'I was looking through my old newspaper cuttings last night.'

The ones about me? Ruby preened herself in the looking glass, never having forgotten how the *Suffolk Whisperer* had described her as *handsome brave and resourceful,* but failing to recollect *that the Anglian Free Press* had depicted her as *muddle-headed.* I had never even shown her the *Suffolk Trumpet* review which condemned Ruby as 'a disgrace to British womanhood'.

I did. Hefty puffed on his pipe with great satisfaction.

At least I was never reviewed as dull, Ruby countered.

You wrote that, he counter-countered furiously.

'And?' Romulus was viewing me as if I were a medical demonstration.

'Sorry.' I shooed Ruby and Hefty away, but they continued to bicker in the background. 'I was...'

'Miles away.' My cousin was one of the few men I knew who could talk about my daydreams without giving the impression that he regarded me as a gossamer-brained butterfly. Jack used to laugh when I drifted away but always with rather than at me. 'Having a chat with Ruby?' Rommy guessed, and I was about to deny it, but my neck had already decided to nod my head. 'What were you reading?' He retrieved our conversation.

I toyed with the miniature tweezers on my charm bracelet. 'About the Montford Maniac.'

Rommy crossed his legs and I had an urge to follow suit but it was yet another action routine to men but forbidden to ladies. 'What about him… or her.'

We had both heard speculation that the murderer could have been a woman, but neither of us truly believed it. Women could be cruel but were rarely – Boadicea being a fortunately remote exception to the rule – savage.

Don't forget the lady novelist who tortures Scotland Yard's premier detective with the threat of imminent death. Hefty examined his thorax anxiously but Lancelot Overstand had yet to launch his attack.

'I was interested in his first murder.' Wispy clouds were gathering but I doubted they would help the farmers. 'And it occurred to me that there were certain similarities between it and recent events.'

The postcard boy ambled by. Until recently he used to pretend to be a cripple but had to give up because his grotesque contortions were turning him into one.

'The spike and the crossbow bolt.' Rommy puffed his cheeks and I waited for him to make a quip, but I should have known that I could trust him. 'It's a bit of a tenuous connection.'

He flicked his ash into my nasty Limoges ashtray. It had been a gift and I rather hoped that Agnust would break it as she had my cherished Louis XVI Sevres porcelain vase, but she treasured this receptacle as if it were a family heirloom.

'So you think that I am jumping to…' I struggled to grasp another word but it had already wriggled away. 'Conclusions,' I ended weakly.

Rommy drummed the wooden arm of his chair. 'You probably are.' He tapped his cigarette again though it was glowing cleanly now.

'Do you think that I should tell Alfred?'

He glanced away then back at me. 'I suppose it wouldn't do any harm,' he replied smokily, 'but you may find he is rather preoccupied at the moment.'

'With the stolen canteen?' I rubbed myself.

'There's a bit more to it than that.' He drew out his half-hunter by its silver chain. 'But, if Alfred wants you to know, he will tell you himself.' He smoothed down his moustaches. 'Only don't let on that I said anything.'

'But you have said nothing.'

'I have said too much.'

This reminded me of one of those annoying riddle-games parents play when they do not want their children to know what they're talking about.

'Ow.' I flapped my hand, but you cannot shake pain away.

'What happened?'

'I nipped myself with my tweezers.' The skin was red but unbroken.

Rommy tossed his head in mock despair which might, in hindsight, not have been mock at all. 'Sorry. I must go.'

We went into the hall. 'Try to get some rest.' Rommy picked up his gladstone bag. 'And, for once in your life, be careful.'

I straightened indignantly. 'When have you known me to be careless?'

'Well...' Rommy put a fingertip to his thumb, presumably to count off the occasions.

'Just one example will suffice.'

'How about the time you fell off summerhouse roof and broke your wrist?'

'That is quite sufficient,' I informed him frostily and leaned forward to kiss his cheek. 'Bless you Rommy. You are a good man.'

Romulus dipped his head modestly. 'If you have any worries...' He glanced up the stairs. 'Let me know.'

Actually, Hefty tried to buttonhole my cousin. *Do you keep a stock of antidotes?*

I stood in the doorway and watched Romulus stride away. If only I had such a man in my life, I pondered. Little over a year ago I thought that I had.

-

The boys had been playing with a rugby ball, eight of them throwing it to and tackling each other. I had neither the physique nor any interest in joining in. It was a hot day and I sat at the edge of the meadow, bored and sleepy. Idly I plucked some daisies and began to make a chain. Before I knew it, one of the boys, a pug-nosed brute, was standing over me.

'What's baby up to now?' he mocked, and I felt my face burning with embarrassment, but Jack was there and, instead of joining in the mockery as the other boys were starting to do, he sat cross-legged beside me and said, 'that's clever. Will you show me how to do it?'

'Really?'

'Yes please.'

'It's very easy. You just pinch a slit into the stem near the end and feed the stem of another one through it.'

'Like this?'

I watched but his stem split. 'You were a bit too close to the end.'

The other boys wandered off.

'Don't let them bother you,' Jack said quietly. 'They mean no real harm.'

'I felt silly.'

'You looked so intent and... sweet when you were making them.'

I felt myself blush again – a habit I grew out of later in life – and looked up at Jack. His blond hair was tumbling golden in the sunlight, and I had not known until then that a boy could look rugged and beautiful at the same time.

'How's that?' he put a crown of daisies on my head.

'Lovely,' I said. His chain fell apart quickly but I saved just one flower for my journal. Stupidly, I have it still.

12: *A FATE NO WORSE THAN DEATH*

GERRUND WAS TAKING his turn to watch Hettie. Much as I loved my friend, I was glad of the break. Rather like military campaigns, as my father had described them, there were long periods of unutterable tedium broken by episodes of barely suppressed panic. In his case this was battles. In my case, rather less dramatically, it was the moments where Hettie appeared to choke or stop breathing. Most memorably, she had sat up, cried, 'Mother they have killed me' and fallen back, mouth agape, her eyes open and rolled back into her head before slapping my hand away when I went to close the lids.

I was trying to forget my fears by working in my study upstairs but every time that Lancelot Overstrand lunged, Havelock Hefty cried out piteously. He even brought his silver-haired mother – a character I had not even created – to plead for her son's life.

Agnust came puffing up the stairs.

'Right then young lady,' Agnust held out the card on a tray as if confronting a puppy with its mess. 'Remember what happenings occur last time you let a female woman visitor in the house? You near goo get us all killed dead.'

I took the card. *Mrs Petunia Bottle.* With everything that had happened I had quite forgotten about her visit.

'This visitor is different,' I assured her. 'She is here by invitation.'

'And how do you know her?' Agnust quizzed me.

I should have told my maid that she was impertinent. *Go on,* Ruby urged for she loved a good fight. Unlike my heroine, though, I preferred a quiet life.

'I met her in The Empire Café.'

'The Empire Café?' Agnust mouthed with as much disgust as she might have expressed had I mentioned a house of ill repute. 'When?'

'Yesterday – just before Miss Granger's mishap.'

'So.' She unfolded her arms with great deliberation. 'You meet a full stranger in a public place and invite her into your home? Wha' kind of behavin' way is tha' for a young lady of old breedin'?'

On reflection, it does seem rather reckless. Hefty rolled a twist of Balkan Flake pipe tobacco.

'She may have some information about that letter,' I explained.

Agnust blinked, somehow converting the action into a laborious process that I would find too enervating to attempt.

'If you want my opinion – and you do...' She slapped a paw on my desktop, making me jump in my captain's chair and my rubber eraser leap off the edge and onto the seaweed teal rug. 'You forget the whole disrepicable business.' Though I would never admit it to my maid, I was rather taken by the adjective she had coined and made a mental note to make a pencilled note of it.

I bent to retrieve my eraser but could not quite reach it. 'She is a perfectly respectable lady.'

There is no such species, Ruby said for she had yet to meet one in her world.

'Tha's what you think.' A sentence by which Agnust was accustomed to dismissing any of my opinions. 'I'll goo tell her you int at home and you can have a nice mug of hot milk and a nap.'

Had I travelled back twenty years in one of Mr H.G. Wells' time machines? I had not read the book yet, but Anthony had devoured it enthusiastically and discoursed on the possibilities of temporal travel for so long that I *accidently* knocked his coffee into his lap.

'I do not want a nap,' I whinged so, apparently, I was in 1875 after all.

The other hand crashed down so heavily that I half-expected my desk to split in two like the table I had seen chopped by a Japanese exponent of karate.

They are called Hiawathas, Ruby stated and I almost believed her until I thought about it.

''Member what happen last time you say you dint want your nap?' Somehow I knew that she would answer the question which was just as well because I had no memory of that auspicious occasion. 'You get all grumpish and goo murderin' the wrong people.'

That last claim was not so outlandish as it might have seemed, for once, after a long night trying to meet a deadline, I had nodded off, waking to kill two men, one of whom was already dead. The other had not even appeared in the same story.

'Show her to my sitting room,' I commanded haughtily.

There was a glint in those eyes that could have frozen my blood were it not fortified with coffee and traces of last night's absinthe.

'Please,' I appended, my haughtiness evaporating like the cognac in my decanter whenever Uncle Postilius visited, and I left the room.

'Dint say I dint warn you 'cause I did...' Agnust kicked the eraser under my desk. 'Warn you.'

She plodded off and I picked up my pencil.

The knife glinted in Lancelot Overstrand's hand, I jotted.

'Put it down you fool,' Inspector Hefty said coolly. 'You cannot hope to escape justice now.'

'I will see you in hell first!' Lancelot Overstrand cursed and lunged forwards.

I put the pencil down.

Surely I will overpower him, Hefty beseeched.

He is my only child, his mother sobbed.

'Wait and see,' I said aloud and made my way downstairs.

'And those knickknacks might be nasty but they are all counted,' Agnust was muttering as she came out of the room and I hoped that my visitor had not heard. Apart from that I did not care for my *objets d'art* to be so described.

'We shall take coffee please, Agnust,' I said as she bumped past me in a one-maid slow stampede.

My parents had taught me that one never says *please* to a servant and only to thank them occasionally lest they start to think that you ought to be grateful for their services, whereas they should be grateful for their positions. Even they accepted that the rule did not apply to Agnust – one reason they had foisted her onto me.

Mrs Bottle – all in green again – stood by my mantelpiece peering at a framed photograph through a gold wire-framed lorgnette on a yellow cord around her neck.

'I am so sorry.' She put it back. 'It is a vice of mine, being nosey.'

'And mine,' I smiled. 'If the picture were private, I would not have put it on display.'

She has already rifled through your bureau and read all your correspondence, Hefty warned, though I doubted that she would have had the time.

She was even taller than I remembered, and I wondered if she had answered a newspaper advertisement for a machine to stretch her spine.

'Is it of your parents? They look very like you.'

Neither of them bore anything other than a fleeting similarity to me. Whilst I was petite, they were both tall and sturdy. I was often mistaken for a child with my soft features but theirs were strong with well-defined jaws.

'It was taken last year on their wedding anniversary.'

'They make a striking couple.' She still had my hand in a firm grip as if trying to detain me. 'Your father – is he Lord Thorn of Thetbury?'

'He is.'

'A remarkable man,' she said but did not specify what had led her to that conclusion for it was obvious, from her question, that she did not know him.

'Take a seat.' I showed her to the left hand of the two chairs overlooking the square. 'My maid will bring coffee.' I lacked the confidence to add *soon* but, for once, I could have for in she burst bearing a tray held high as if to present us with a roasted pig's head, an apple in its mouth.

I hope the ears are crispy. Hefty tucked an enormous napkin around his collar.

I rather thought you were more in need of the brains, Ruby quipped.

Prosaically and unastonishingly, the tray bore a coffee pot and all its accoutrements.

'Thank you, Agnust. I shall pour.'

'In the cups and not on the carpet,' she instructed and trod off mumbling something about how I should be working instead of consorting with… Fortunately the door closed on her final words for, in Agnust's world nobody, other than her, consorted with anybody desirable.

'Is she always that forthright, Lady Violet?' Mrs Bottle asked.

Obviously by *forthright* she meant rude.

'Most of the time.' I felt the pot and burnt my fingertips. 'And please just call me Violet, Mrs Bottle.'

'Petunia,' she said, and I would have been somewhat aggrieved if she had not. 'Why do you keep her?'

'I inherited her.' I turned the pot handle towards myself. 'And, for all her eccentricities, she has many sterling qualities.'

'I will take your word for it.'

I could have explained that Agnust had lifted a waggon off me when I was a child, consoled me when I was jilted and saved my life recently, but I failed to see why I should. It always made me feel aggrieved when people criticised her for that was my prerogative and mine alone. I had witnessed other people's maids licking spoons clean when setting tables, and butlers syphoning off good wine for themselves to pour cheap wine for the guests. I had had hot and cold drinks spilt over my dresses and a bowl of soup in my hair and rarely had I said anything derogatory to anyone about their servants. Agnust, however, seemed to be unfair game to everyone, and I was starting to feel protective towards her.

I poured our coffees. 'Help yourself to milk and sugar.'

Petunia drew her hand over them. 'I take neither.'

Enough chitter chatter. Hefty struck a commanding pose. *You have yet to write how I escape a fate no worse than death.*

'You said you had some letters,' I reminded my guest.

'Before I show them to you, might I see yours again? I did not get a proper look in The Empire.'

I fetched the note from my escritoire and she studied it, mouthing the words twice, as if it were a poem that she had been told to memorise.

'Just as I feared,' she returned it unfolded. 'It is much the same. Might I ask when you received this?'

'A few hours before I met you.' I put it back in the envelope.

'Morning,' she whispered to herself then said to me, 'And are the police investigating it?'

'I fear there is little they can do.'

'I believe you are a friend of Inspector Stanbury's.'

'How do you know that?' I asked in response to Hefty's prompting.

'There was mention of it after your unpleasant experience in the summer.'

That was true enough though unpleasant seemed rather an inadequate term for the horrors that I had faced.

'I have known the inspector since we were children,' I confirmed and wished that I had not. 'Not that there was anything between us.'

I did not need Ruby to tell me that, in attempting to make matters better, I had made them worse, but she told me nonetheless.

My visitor twirled the handle of her lorgnette between her thumb and first two fingers.

'Have you had many dealings with him? In his official capacity, I mean.'

'A few,' I replied more cagily.

She is supposed to be giving you information not vice versa, Hefty reminded me.

'Might I see your letters?'

'Of course.' She leafed through her handbag to produce them.

Like mine they were on cheap paper torn from a book. *YOUR DAYS ARE NUMBERED,* I read. I looked at the second. *YOU WILL DIE HORRIBLY AND SOON.* The third read *I AM COMING FOR YOU.*

'You said he came.' I stared at the letters.

'He did,' she whispered, and I saw her grip tighten on her saucer.

'Do you mind telling me what happened?'

Petunia chewed her upper lip. 'I really don't want to frighten you, but I think it only fair to give you warning.'

'Please continue.'

'He came for me one afternoon. It was foolish of me, but I did not take his threats seriously. I thought I would be safe in the broad daylight, and I went for a walk in the road that ran behind my house – Orchard Lane. Perhaps you know it.'

'I used to scrump apples there,' I admitted, and she smiled faintly.

'Local children still do.' Her face fell again. 'I was just over the brow of the small hill past Splitbury's Farm when a man jumped out. He had been hiding behind the beech hedge.' She clutched her handbag as if it could protect her from any danger now. 'He...' she swallowed. 'He put his hand over my mouth and stabbed... stabbed me in the stomach. Luckily, I had a corset on – they were much more heavily constructed in those days – and it deflected most of the blow. Three times he stabbed and then he put the knife to my throat. I slid my hand under it –' she held it up for me to inspect the scar that ran livid across the palm, '– and managed to hold it back, but he pulled the knife from my grasp and was about to try again when...' She waved that hand in a winding motion and touched her brow. 'Thank God in his mercy, a farmer's boy appeared from the field carrying a pitchfork. He had heard the scuffle and my muffled cries. My attacker let go of me and ran.'

'Did you see him?'

'Only from behind. The boy said it was a tall man with a muffler, but I know who it was.'

Hefty watched at her intently but said nothing. Ruby was practicing triple-flipping, a technique she had developed for shuffling cards.

'How?' I prompted.

'He struck again, the next day in the Monastery Gardens and then another six times.' She ran her fingers under her collar as if it were choking her. 'He was the Montford Maniac.'

-

The next victim was Miss Jenny Bloor. *The Suffolk Trumpet* described her as a *lady of the night*, but she was a respectable barmaid as unable to defend herself from that filthy libel as she was from the vile attack. The Maniac stabbed her, probably from behind, rather as Petunia had described, but Jenny was less fortunate and succumbed to his frenzied blows. She was wounded fifteen times in the chest and stomach. On the last blow the blade snapped on her ribs and the killer threw the knife aside and made his escape.

The next morning the *Montford Chronical* received another letter before there had been any public announcement of the crime.

> DEAR JENNIE. SHE COULDN'T EVEN SQUEAL WITH MY HAND OVER HER MOUTH BUT SHE WAS A GAME GAL AND BIT ME GOOD AND PROPER. GAVE ME SOME GOOD KICKS TOO ON THE SHINS. PITY SHE DIED SO QUICKLY. I COULD HAVE STABBED HER ALL NIGHT LONG, HA HA! YOU KNOW WHO I AM. YOU HAVE ALREADY NAMED ME, YOUR OLD PAL MM.

Like any good citizen, Frank Greaves, the editor, sent the letter straight to the police but only after he had had it photographed. It was on the front page of a special afternoon edition and sold as quickly as they could print it.

Inspector Shomrack was enraged. When a rival editor suggested facetiously and enviously that Greaves had the most to gain by the murders, Shomrack took him in for questioning. The *Chronic* had never had it so good. *MY TERRIBLE EXPERIENCES AS A MURDER SUSPECT,* complete with an engraving of the inspector, went into three editions.

Astonishingly it was two days before Shomrack calmed down enough to realise that the murderer knew poor Jennie's name and must have either known her or at least of her. Every available officer was sent into The Lowers to examine the male inhabitants' hands and legs. Unsurprisingly, given the menial manual jobs in which those who worked were employed, a great many had scars and bruises.

Yet again Greaves was to prove a thorn in the inspector's side by pointing out that the writer of that letter, with his grasp of punctuation and spelling, must have been an educated man and was, therefore, unlikely to have been a slum dweller. Reportedly Shomrack frothed at the mouth after the editor penned a provocative article offering his services to lead the investigation. In hindsight, Greaves would probably have better fist of it.

-

Hettie improved more quickly than Romulus and I had anticipated. Her confusion had dissipated, and she was in much less pain than she had been. I was still concerned, though, when I took her tray up that evening, and she announced that she was ready to get up.

'But you are still suffering from vertigo,' I argued.

'Not anymore.' Hettie flung an arm out over the side table, knocking over a water glass. 'Oh bother.' Fortunately, it was empty but, unfortunately, it cracked as it struck the floor.

'Perhaps you should wait for Romulus.' I picked up the glass. It had not been as empty as I had thought. Water had trickled between the floorboards but not enough, I hoped, to stain the ceiling below.

'We can't keep troubling him over trifles.' She gazed at the glass and then accusingly at me. Perhaps she was less de-confused than I had believed. 'Besides...' She tossed her covers towards the far side of my bed. 'You know what men are like. They are such old women.' She kicked one leg up so that the bedding slid onto the floor. 'Always fussing.' The pitch of her voice lowered. '*Don't drink any more of that bleach, Hetsi-pie.*' That was her father's pet name for her. *'Be careful with that dynamite, Muffin.'* That was her mother's pet name for her. 'Nag-nag-nag-nag-nag. Well nobody...' Hettie poked her right leg half over the side nearest to me. 'Is going to tell me what I must or must not do in your own home.' Swinging both legs over the side, she sat up as if she were on springs. 'Oh, double bother.' She put a hand to her temple and toppled forwards.

'I have got you.' I grasped her shoulders and lowered my friend slowly back onto her pillows, lifting her legs and going around the bed to cover them again.

'Perhaps I am not quite mended,' Hettie admitted. 'What's for supper?'

13: BAD BLOOD AND THE JOCULARITY OF BROCKS

ANTHONY APPLETON CALLED. I saw him crossing the square. Even in the fading light, it would have been difficult to miss him in his bright blue Inverness cape with its matching fedora. After the driest summer in living memory, it was starting to rain. This was not the downpour for which farmers would be praying but a thin drizzle, not even enough for Anthony to unfurl his umbrella, also coloured blue. His shoes, disappointingly, were plain brown.

Oh good, he's coming here, Ruby checked her golden hair in the mirror. She found him rather attractive, feelings that I – needless to say – did not share.

I took my Beeman's out of my mouth and, having mislaid the wrapper, stuck the gum under the edge of the sideboard to dispose of later.

The doorbell jangled.

My mother would have been appalled. Not only had Anthony and I never been introduced but it was well after the hours when one would normally be *at home* to visitors. Also he did not present a card to my maid nor did he wait in the hall to be announced but followed Agnust, calling cheerily, as he ambled into my sitting room, 'Good evening, Lady V.'

'Anthony.' I greeted him.

His cape hung open to reveal a darker blue jacket but a lighter blue waistcoat and a polka-dotted cravat – blue, of course.

'I hope this is inconvenient.' He clasped my hand firmly between both of his.

'Why?' I suppressed a smile.

Grinned like a badger, Ruby corrected me though I was unaware that brocks were famed for their jocularity.

'I should not like to think that you are only seeing me because you have nothing better to do.'

'I am only seeing you because you barged in,' I told him in mock severity and he availed himself of his turn to grin, revealing the upper incisor, slightly chipped from when he had fought to save my life. His nose was a little twisted despite his surgeon's confidence that it could be straightened. I put a hand to my jaw which had felt bruised in front of my left ear and was inclined to click since I had fought to save his life.

'I have not forgotten how you barged into my…' Anthony stopped, remembering that Agnust was still with us.

Bedroom. Ruby hated unfinished sentences.

Surely not. Hefty sat in two things – an armchair and shock, though the encounter had been perfectly innocent.

'Bash into you, do she?' Agnust sympathised. 'She alway is a clunchy girl.' *Clunchy* was Suffolkese for small and clumsy and, for once, she had chosen an apposite adjective. 'I goo fetch 'nother cup and…' She paused as if promising a special treat. 'Saucer.'

I listened in disbelief. Whenever I had the temerity to ask for a coffee she reacted as if the task were the thirteenth labour of Hercules.

'Thank you Agnust.' Anthony took off his cloak.

I was always expected to put away my own clothes, but Agnust held out an arm for him to drape it over and lumbered off to hang it in the hall along with his hat.

'How is Hettie?' he asked – before he had even enquired about me, I sulked, before telling myself that her health was of greater concern.

'She is improving slowly,' I unsulked.

Anthony did not really need to be told that because he had visited Hettie every day and they had engaged in ever lengthening conversations. They appeared to have become good friends.

Too good, Ruby warned for we had come across them laughing together but the slight discomfort that I felt was just a spot of indigestion and certainly not the faintest twinge of jealousy.

'Good. Is she…'

'She is asleep,' I broke in more abruptly than I had intended.

That bulge in his breast pocket is a boxed wedding ring, Hefty told me. *He intends to propose marriage.*

It is his cherrywood pipe. Anthony always carried one but rarely smoked it in my presence.

'Then I shall not disturb her.' He straightened his cuffs to show the fashionable half-inch.

'I doubt that you could.' I lifted my foot but the gum, so loosely stuck to my sideboard had dropped off and glued my shoe to the floor. 'She has taken her laudanum.'

Anthony looked at me as most men look at me – oddly.

'Give her my regards.'

'I shall.' I wrenched myself free while Anthony watched in puzzlement.

'Just when you had got rid of one houseguest,' he mused. 'No sign of the old crone then?' Anthony glanced uneasily over his shoulder though, if Aunt Igitha had any skills, the ability to materialise unexpectedly was not to be counted amongst them.

With some vague idea that the family honour was at stake, I pulled myself up to my full fifty-seven and five eighths' inches. 'I do not think you should be talking about the Marchioness of Anglethorpe in such terms.' And waited for an apology.

'I most certainly should not,' he agreed but my wait was in vain.

'It is not an inaccurate description though,' I conceded, walking stickily to the window.

'Sprained your ankle?'

'No. Why?'

'You're limping.'

'Oh that,' I waved a dismissive hand. 'I sprained my ankle.'

That was nicely done. Ruby waited in vain for him to light her cigarette.

'But...'

'To what do I owe this...' I almost said *pleasure,* but changed it to, 'visit.'

'I was just passing.' He lowered himself into one of my chairs overlooking the square, raising his trouser legs a fraction to prevent them bagging at the knee.

On your way where? Hefty unclipped his peccary skin tobacco pouch.

'A good enough reason.' I settled adjacent to him and nearly added, *Not that you need one,* but there is a line – not always fine or distinct – between sociableness and being the sort of woman who ends up in the gutter in melodramas while the man she loves walks past not recognising her with his new bride on his arm.

Or ends up a spinster darning stockings, Hefty packed the bowl of his favourite briar. It had been a present from the love of his life whose name, he was confident, began with a P – or an L.

'One cup.' Agnust burst into the room. 'And saucer.' She could not have placed them more triumphantly on my tray had they been prizes at the All England Croquet and Lawn Tennis Club.

'Bless you.' Anthony said. He had a soft spot for Agnust for she had saved his life and I had told him how she had cradled his unconscious form in her arms.

'Glad someone 'preciate my effort.' She smiled at him fondly.

'I appreciate what you do,' I said, and she tilted her head sideways.

'Oh Lady Violet.' She opened the door with a flourish. 'When you ever learn to speak the truth?' At which she quit the room.

I filled Anthony's cup and topped up my own. 'Any luck with your audition?'

I hoped so for I was mortified that he, and everyone else involved in the production, had been put out of work when my *The Devil Stalks the Strand* closed.

After its first night, Ruby emphasised, for the play in which she had featured had nearly gone into a second week.

Anthony's face fell. 'They will let me know.'

'I hope so.' I added milk to both of our coffees for I had yet to meet a man who could pour it or gravy or custard or anything in a jug without making a mess. 'I wish I could help.'

'I don't want money,' he hastened to assure me and helped himself to more milk without spilling a drop. 'Well I do, of course, but not from you.'

And what is wrong with my money? I wondered indignantly and irrationally. 'I know that you were not fishing for a loan,' I reassured him.

'I expect...' Anthony took two sugars. 'Something will turn up.'

'I hope so.' Fully aware that I was offering nothing more than platitudes, I sipped my drink. It was a few degrees below tepid.

'Montford man eats breakfast standin' on head,' the newspaper vendor bellowed. He was working later than usual, probably because he was selling few copies despite such a captivating headline.

'Perhaps he is Australian.' Anthony looked at me askance. 'You seem a little preoccupied.'

To give him credit, few men ever notice a woman's mood until she starts throwing ornaments at them.

'I have had an anonymous letter,' I got up to show it to him.

Ask to see a sample of his handwriting. Hefty peered closely at Anthony's fingers with his special extra-powerful-magnifying spectacles. *He has a permanganate stain on his thumb.*

'Lord I'd love to get my hands on the scoundrel,' Anthony fumed. 'I'd soon number his days.'

It was probably just as well that he was unlikely to come across my anonymous correspondent. The only time I had witnessed Anthony fighting, he had come off very much the worse for it.

'I expect it is just somebody's idea of a joke,' I reassured him, but not myself.

'I'm absolutely sure it is.' He gripped the arms of his chair. 'A cowardly and tasteless one.'

'Perhaps I should throw it away,' I said and he wriggled his nose.

'Might be better to keep it for now,' he said, demonstrating that he was not quite so absolutely sure after all.

A pantechnicon appeared from Angel Street pulled by a pair of Suffolk Punches. I watched them approach, impressed, as ever, by their enormous, muscular build. They were well tended and groomed, representing, as they did, Pallent's Furniture Store whose name was painted neatly on the side.

The vehicle stopped outside Unbreak House, my neighbour's to the left.

'A little late for deliveries,' I commented – especially as Mrs Hatchpenny was a widow and unlikely to want strangers turning up at dusk.

Two men got out and pulled the double back doors open and the tailgate down to create a ramp. They disappeared up it, emerging a moment later, one hauling and the other pushing a long wooden crate out, dragging it onto the pavement and a little way along to deposit it half in front of my house and half in front of my neighbour's.

'Whoops,' one faint voice said. 'Wrong way up.' And with some difficulty they tipped it on its side.

'Hope it int fragile,' the other commented, giving it a kick as if his action somehow ensured that it could not be.

Together they raised the ramp, clipped it up and closed and bolted the doors. For a moment they surveyed their delivery.

'That's that.' The first one dusted his hands together and went back to the front. 'Right then.' The second one tipped his flat cap back and, before I realised what was happening, they were off, gliding over the tarred surface of the perimeter road and back from whence they had come.

'They cannot just leave it there,' I said. 'Apart from anything else, it will get wet.'

Even if it were empty, such an item would soon be taken or broken up for the wood but, from the way the men had heaved, there was certainly something heavy inside it.

'We need to let your neighbour know,' Anthony said. 'No point in us both getting damp. I'll go.'

He went into the hall and, a moment later, I heard the front door close and saw him examine the crate before he continued on his way. Anthony moved out of sight though I heard him knocking. Two or three minutes later he returned to stand outside my window. I raised the lower sash.

'Mrs Hatchpenny is away.'

When is she not? I wondered for I had had little more than the occasional glimpse of her since I came to Break House.

'The maid insists it's not for them anyway.' He glanced back.

I had heard some hammering next door but not paid much attention. The square was rarely quiet during the day.

'Well, I have not ordered anything. There must be some mistake,' I told him. 'I shall come straight out.'

Balancing on my heel to avoid getting any Beeman's on my rugs, I went into the hall to change my shoes. Taking my cloak off its hook, I draped it over my shoulders and grabbed an umbrella out of the rack. This last item proved to be superfluous as the drizzle had converted itself into a light mist.

Anthony stood by the crate. 'You have lost your limp,' he observed.

'I put on a more supportive pair of shoes.'

Oh, what a tangled web we weave, Ruby quoted piously though she was not always welded to the truth.

'What on earth is it?' I wondered.

'Copies of your latest novel?' my friend suggested.

'I only wish that they printed so many.'

The corpse of Percival Overstrand, Inspector Hefty asserted, but it was long and tall enough to contain one coffin on top of another. *And his hitherto unknown non-twin brother,* he added less confidently.

I looked for a label but there was nothing other than a wavy arrow with *THIS WAY UP* chalked underneath.

A trio of young ladies swished past us singing *My Mother Never Told Me* in a way that suggested that they could probably have told her a thing or two. They sauntered off up Market Street and the square was quiet again. The market stalls were long gone, and it was not a pleasant enough evening to encourage people to walk in the gardens.

'Your shoelace is undone,' I told Anthony and he half-sat on the crate, resting his right ankle on his left knee. What a scandal it would cause if I were to do that.

'Strange,' he said. 'I thought I felt something bump inside.'

He finished his bow-tying and slid back onto his feet.

'There it goes again.' Anthony had his hand on the box in a pose reminiscent of Abraham Lincoln taking the presidential oath. 'And again.' He put his ear to the box and his face registered concern. 'There is something in there.'

I followed suit and heard a gasp. 'I believe you are right.' I stood up but he was still bent over.

'Or someone.' Anthony listened intently. 'I think I heard a cry for help.' He raised his head a fraction and called, 'Hello.' He pulled back in alarm. 'There it is again.'

We looked at the crate and then each other.

The top had an overhang of about a quarter of an inch. Anthony gripped the rim with his fingers and heaved to no avail.

'We could do with a jemmy,' I said. 'But I do not possess one.' I ran my fingers under one long side but could feel no hinges. 'There are some screwdrivers in the house we could probably use, but Gerrund is out, and I have no idea where he keeps them.'

Anthony tried again lifting the box a little off the ground and dropping it back heavily. The whole box shook and there was a muffled cry.

'A hammer?' Anthony suggested anxiously.

'I do not know where any of the tools are kept,' I told him in agitation. 'They are probably in the cellar, but we do not have time to ransack the house.'

Anthony tried one end of the crate, straining until the blood vessels stood out in his bulging neck muscles but his efforts were of no avail.

Whoever was in there was scrabbling urgently now.

'Hold on,' I said, as if the occupant had any choice. 'We will get you out of there very soon.'

I was not sure about the *Very soon* part.

'I can't do it,' Anthony let go of the crate.

'We could try a meat cleaver,' I suggested. Gerrund would never forgive me if I damaged it, but I would never forgive myself if I left a man, or woman, to die for the sake of a kitchen utensil.

'Just a minute,' Anthony said. 'I think I can feel a catch.' He went down on his haunches. 'Yes, two small bolts going into the woodwork.' I stood a few feet away, dreading to think in what state the person we were releasing would be.

'Are you sure it is a person?' I checked.

'I'm positive – almost,' he concluded less certainly.

'I only heard noises. It could be an animal.'

'Could be,' he conceded. 'I'd better have a look.'

'Be careful.'

'I'll just take a peek.' Anthony slid the bolts back one at a time and raised his voice, 'I am opening the side now.' But he had no need to do so for it crashed open, smashing down onto the pavement and a dark mass flew out, flinging Anthony over onto his back.

'Look out,' I shouted pointlessly, but I had to shout something.

A creature was standing on Anthony's chest – an enormous black cat – a panther – snarling to reveal a lethal array of dagger-like teeth. Ignoring my friend's efforts to push it away and shaking off a desperate punch to the side of its head, the great cat lowered its head towards Anthony's throat.

'Get off him.' I charged over, flinging my umbrella like a javelin, the ferule striking the panther's side and bouncing away, doing no damage but at least causing the animal to look at its flank in surprise. I picked up my feeble weapon to jab it in the neck. It shook its head angrily and batted at the umbrella, claws extended to wrench it from my grip.

A fly came clattering round the square. 'You want to keep that beast in a pound,' the driver shouted as he passed.

Whether it was my actions or those of the horse and carriage, I could not tell, but something distracted the panther. It stepped off

Anthony's recumbent form, but any relief died in an instant for Anthony was lying supine and the beast had turned its attention to me. We viewed each other from our very different perspectives. To him I could be dinner; to me he could be death.

Every muscle fibre strained to make me flee but I knew that it would be useless. I could never outrun a panther. I had read somewhere that you can stare wild animals down, but there was no time to put that theory to the test for it was crouching as if to bound and it would only take one leap for the beast to be upon me.

My hat, I thought in desperation, ripping it from my head and tossing it, discus-style at its feet. I had hoped that, with its feathers, it might look like a tasty morsel but, apparently, I looked like a tastier one for it paused briefly to sniff my bonnet, only to flick it contemptuously aside with one enormous paw.

Seeing that it did not need to bound and, as lazy as all cats are in my experience, the panther padded casually towards me, licking his lips like a glutton at a feast, though I doubted that it could pick much more than a morsel from my bones.

'Whistle,' I told myself aloud and, putting my charm bracelet to my lips, blew as hard as I could, expelling air, but that was all.

You are blowing on your pencil, you idiot, I scolded myself and blew on the whistle with all my might. For a small device it produced a surprisingly loud, piercing sound that even made me wince. I could not take my eyes off my would-be attacker to see how Anthony reacted or even if he were conscious, but the panther did not like it. It shrank back and I blew again but it was less disturbed by the noise the second time and my third blow merely served to annoy it. It flicked its head to shake the sound away, pawed at the ground in a way I thought only bulls were supposed to, and crouched – apparently not too lazy to pounce after all.

An upstairs window flew open. 'Quit that racket immediately you hooligans.' It was an elderly man in a floppy Ebeneezer Scrooge nightcap. The window slammed but the panther paid no attention.

In a last desperate effort, I flung my handbag and hit it squarely on the nose. It snarled again but angrily this time. Clearly, I was a highly irritating first course. I saw its back legs tense for the jump and patted feverishly in my hair, but I had thrown all the pins away with my hat. There were some nail scissors in my handbag, but I could not retrieve it. I had no weapon but a tiny charm penknife. I unfolded it and fumbled with the catch to take my bracelet off. The blade was all of about a third of an inch long but, if I got a chance to use it, it might at least hurt the panther. My shoes were too flimsy to inflict much, if any, damage. Workmen's boots would have been more serviceable but, to those who can afford it, style always wins over practicality. Other than that, I only had my bare hands and, for what it was worth, I would use them. Perhaps I could poke it in the eye.

Why was the cat taking so long to attack? Was it toying with me as Rodrigo used to taunt an unfortunate mouse? It seemed to be taking a great interest in my bag, sniffing and pawing it this way and that and licking the leatherwork.

'Get away from her, you filthy brute,' Anthony shouted and I saw him make a limping run straight towards the panther.

'No, my darling!' I cried but, like all men, Anthony did not listen. He did not even pause to discuss the matter but hurtled onwards, his right foot going back and kicking the animal a great thwack in the stomach. It grunted and twisted round towards him.

'Come on then,' Anthony challenged, backing away but beckoning it. 'Come on, you pusillanimous swine.' Another time I might have corrected the taxonomical accuracy of his challenge but, there might very well not be another time.

The panther strolled towards him. Having nothing else to hand I dived forwards, snatched up my handbag and hurled it with all my might, but my throw was wild this time and the bag skimmed off its back into the air. A young man in a light brown suit was coming round the corner.

'Howsh-jat?' he called though he had picked it off the ground. 'Bit of a tiff?' he laughed. 'Throwing bagsh at him.'

'Are you blind?' Anthony called as the man weaved towards us.

'Blind drunk,' I muttered and the stranger stopped, wobbling backwards and forwards and lifting his hand to peer under it as if being dazzled.

'Thash a big pushy-cat,' he marvelled.

'Get away,' I shouted and he frowned.

'Thash not very friendly.'

The panther twisted around, sprinted towards the newcomer, and pounced.

'Wha…?' the young man gasped in confusion as he fell onto his back, the animal on top of him. He screamed as it clawed at his hands which were trying to cover his face. His legs kicked uselessly in the air.

Anthony pushed in front of me, shielding me with his body, rooting through his pockets to get out his pipe-knife and fumbling the spike out for the blade, which would be blunt. It wasn't much but it was all he had. He stepped forwards but I grabbed his jacket.

'No! It will kill you.'

'It might but it will certainly kill him if I do nothing.' He wrenched free and glanced briefly into my eyes. 'I'm sorry,' he said, 'but I can't just stand here.'

The man had stopped screaming now and I saw the panther's jaws opening wide.

Anthony set off. It was then that the hours I had thought wasted, watching boys playing rugby, proved to be useful at last. I flung myself at my friend, wrapping my arms around his legs and sending us both sprawling into the road.

'Let go,' Anthony yelled.

I do not think that he meant to kick me in the stomach as he struggled to release himself, but the result was the same as if he had done so maliciously. I gasped, winded, and released him. We struggled to our feet. He had blood trickling from his nose.

The panther had the man by the throat now and was shaking him like a terrier with a rat. I got up.

A shout came from behind. 'Get down, milady!' It was Gerrund and he was holding his Enfield revolver. I dropped to my knees. He took his stance and pulled the trigger. Nothing happened. 'Damn it!' he pulled twice more. It clicked and nothing else.

He flung the gun at the panther and hit it on the face. It yowled furiously but returned to its prey, sinking its teeth with a horrible cracking sound into the young man's head.

Gerrund raced across the square, paused to pull up his trouser leg and carried on, this time with a short-bladed knife in his fist.

The panther raised its head, its mouth matted with gore and ran towards him.

'Oh, dear God!' I cried but the animal stopped at my handbag, picked it up in its mouth as gently as a mother with a cub and trotted away.

A woman screamed and four men were running – heroically away from her. I had not even seen them, but the panther ignored them all and trotted off through the Great Gate into the Monastery Gardens.

'Are you all right?' Anthony and I asked each other and assured each other that we were though he was gingerly touching his nose and I my stomach.

Gerrund was standing in a spreading black puddle. The body was quivering but it was not possible that the young man was still alive. His throat had been torn out and his head poured blood from two craters. I never believed that expressions remain after death for then, surely, the muscles relax. This deeply gouged face, though, was still contorted in terror.

'God rest your soul,' I said, and Anthony added, 'Amen.'

We turned away. 'Sweet Jesus,' my friend whispered.

None of this could be real. I had been working too hard and let myself confuse truth with fantasy.

You are not going to be sick, I lectured myself, for I was hot and dizzy.

'There's nothing we can do for him.' Gerrund tucked his knife back into the scabbard strapped to his left calf.

A few minutes ago, the stranger had been happily intoxicated. He was harming no-one. Did he have a wife? a sweetheart? children? parents? There would be people appalled and broken-hearted by what had happened.

'We must call the police,' I said.

'And the army,' Gerrund suggested, 'for the cat. If you ask, the police will contact them. They might not for me.' He shot a glance at Anthony who was half-turned away, his hand over his mouth. 'Looks like he's going to swoon. Can't leave him to guard the body while I get screens.'

'Of course you can,' I insisted and Anthony nodded weakly.

'I won't let anyone near him.'

'Ever held a gun?' Gerrund asked Anthony, fiddling with his revolver.

'Only on the stage.'

'Take this in case it comes back.'

'But...'

'The safety catch was sticking but it should be all right now.' Gerrund handed it over by the barrel. 'Don't kill anyone. If you wound it, you might only infuriate it then God knows what it will do. Probably best if you just fire in the air. That should frighten it off. I'll be back as soon as I've got the screens... Just had it serviced too,' he muttered.

Apart from a stray dog, Seraphim Square was deserted, but it did not take long for people to gather, curious as to what was causing the disturbance. The drizzle had stopped.

'Will you be all right?' I asked and Anthony nodded.

'Of course.'

'We'll be back in a minute.'

As my man and I headed towards Break House, I retrieved my umbrella, though I was not sure that it merited rescuing. It was badly scuffed and shredded from its service as a weapon.

Two men laughed from somewhere in the direction of the Splendid Hotel. It was unlikely that they had witnessed what had occurred.

'Where the bloody hell did that thing come from?' Gerrund wondered. It was probably very like him to use expletives but not like him to use them in my presence.

'Out of that crate,' I said. 'We thought there might be a person in there.'

'What on earth did it want with your bag?'

'It is a very good handbag,' I asserted ridiculously, and he snorted. 'What is that smell?' I wondered as we neared the crate.

Gerrund wrinkled his nose. 'Same as what cats do in your back garden.'

'There is something else though.' I inhaled. 'I know what it is.' I looked into the opening and saw a few large, crumpled rags. Reversing my grip on my umbrella, I hooked a wad out with the handle.

'Chloroform,' Gerrund said. 'I used to enjoy a sniff of that until I found it was all I got out of bed for.'

'That would explain why it did not make any noise sooner,' I realised. 'And why, at first, it made no serious attempt to attack us.'

'Strong stuff,' he confirmed. 'Maybe somebody was supposed to deliver the animal and took it to the wrong place.'

'Perhaps,' I agreed. 'Do you always go out so well-armed?'

'Not usually.' He straightened his coral cravat, his expression betraying nothing.

'Are you in any danger?' We reached the front door.

'Not now,' Gerrund said simply. 'And you have never been – not from the people I was dealing with.' He drew out a key on a chain and unlocked the door. 'If my presence put you in the slightest peril, milady, I would go immediately.' He stepped back to admit me.

'And leave me to Agnust?' I went into the hall.

'And wha's wrong with tha'?' She folded her muscular arms under her substantial bust, usually a sign that I was in trouble.

'Did you not hear the commotion in the square?' I wiped my feet on the mat before she told me to do so.

'Dint hear nothin',' she said. 'Had a thirst and knew you wint 'grudge me a glass of your cordial.' She wrinkled her nose. 'Dint taste much like pep'mint.'

It would not, being absinthe. I looked at her innocently.

'Goo off, it do.' She pulled a sour face. 'And the rest. Try 'em all and they make me ill. So I pour the lot away – save you gettin' poisonous. Pass out a while, I do.'

Another time I would have been aghast at the waste, but it was such a trivial matter compared to what we had just witnessed.

'There is a dead man in the square,' I told her.

'Oh Lady Violet!' she exclaimed. 'What do you do to him?'

'I tried to save him,' I replied, 'and so did Gerrund and Anthony.'

'Might have know you be jumbled up in it all,' she told Gerrund.

'Help him to carry some screens into the square,' I ordered her and, unaccustomed to my peremptory tone, she said, 'Yes, milady,' and seemed about to bob in a curtsy before she grabbed a doorframe to stop herself falling over.

-

Sergeant Webb answered the telephone immediately. It was still a noteworthy occasion for them to receive any calls. I described the events as briefly and as matter-of-factly as I could – for every man knows that, if a woman is upset, she is hysterical.

'Better I do let 'Spector Stanbury know,' he said. 'The super'tendent away and the army wint come out for me – not 'less I lead a rebellion 'gainst her majesty and I int abou' to do tha'. If tha's all… Who turn their telephone off first?' He seemed unsure of the etiquette of this machinery.

'I do.'

'Fare thee well and Godspeed,' he called as if I were embarking on a dangerous journey.

'Goodbye,' I said and replaced my candlestick in its cradle feeling instantly contrite. After his valediction had I been a little abrupt?

I wouldn't say 'a little'. Ruby admired herself in my looking glass and I nearly asked what I had ever done to her, but it was too large a catalogue to be recited in a single session.

–

I went up to check on Hettie. She was snoring like a walrus and the level of laudanum in the bottle by Hettie's bed was lower than I remembered. She had been taking rather a lot of it lately and I hoped that she was not going to end up like Rossetti's muse, Lizzy Siddal, fatally addicted. I removed the bottle to a drawer in my dressing table. If she ransacked the room in the night, I would know that my fears had been realised.

14: THE RIOT ACT AND THE SOUL OF THE BEAST

ALFRED STANBURY HAD been at home, reminding his children who he was, he semi-joked wearily.

'What happened?' he asked with no preamble.

'That crate was left on the pavement,' I explained. 'There was a panther in it.'

'What on earth are you taking about?'

'A big cat.'

'I know what a panther is. What was it doing in there and how did it get out?'

'Somebody delivered it and we let it out,' Anthony admitted.

'You…' Stanbury began incredulously.

'We heard a noise and thought that somebody might be trapped inside,' I explained.

Alfred groaned. 'Get a lot of people shut in boxes here, do you?'

'About as often as we get wild cats,' I retorted, and he bobbed his head.

'Point taken.'

'I was only trying to have a look.' Anthony tucked the revolver under his crocodile-skin belt, and I hoped that he had put the safety catch back on. 'But it burst out the moment I opened the side a crack.'

'What next?'

'It jumped on Mr Appleton, but he managed to fight it off.' Not quite what happened, I was aware, but people who did not know Anthony often assumed, from his thespian ways, that he was effete, though he was far from it. 'It turned on me, but he fought it off again.'

'Lady Violet fought it too,' Anthony chipped in.

'And hardly a scratch on either of you,' Alfred observed drily.

'I think it was still quite groggy,' I said. 'There were wads soaked in chloroform in the crate. I threw my handbag to try to ward it off but a young man came along. He was obviously intoxicated and thought it some kind of game.' His screams still reverberated in my head. 'When he picked up the bag, the panther attacked him.'

'And he is the dead man?'

'Yes.'

'I came out of the house with my revolver.' Gerrund – who had been standing back – was clearly unwilling to have his true motive for being armed investigated. 'But it jammed.'

'And then?' Stanbury scratched his cheek.

'It killed the man and ran off with my handbag.'

'Your…'

'Handbag,' I confirmed.

Stanbury scratched his neck. 'What on earth would it want that for?'

'I have no idea,' I replied. 'I don't keep pork chops in it.' If that sounded facetious it was not my intention. 'But I did have some pear drops,' I remembered.

Stanbury looked at me as if I were what I often thought that I might be – mad.

'You think that is what they live on?'

'Of course not but they might like the smell, just as dogs love aniseed,' I speculated. 'Anyway, it ran into the gardens.'

'Better and better,' Stanbury said. 'It could hide anywhere in the bushes.' He looked at my screens – four of them in a protective square. 'I will talk to you all again and take some statements.'

About twenty people had gathered near the monastery gates, some of them farmers with scythes and pitchforks. Two men carried shotguns. A middle-aged man in a faded Suffolk Regiment captain's uniform stood at their head.

'Follow me, my brave lads.' He drew his sword.

'For pity's sake,' Alfred groaned. 'They'll kill somebody.' He marched over. 'Nobody is to enter the gardens,' he barked, and the military man glared at him.

'This is a free country,' he said, 'and you cannot stop us.'

Alfred gazed back. 'I am empowered under the Riot Act of 1614, to order any congregation of twelve or more people to disperse or face punitive action.' He scanned the gathering. 'Jethro Woodgate, you did three months hard labour, the last time I arrested you. How does six months appeal to you?'

'I just come help,' the farmer protested. 'If there's a dangerous beast in there...'

'There are few more dangerous beasts than an armed mob,' Alfred retorted. 'It is getting dark and innocent people could be injured or killed. The army is coming soon. Let them deal with it.'

'Best do as inspector say,' Jethro told his fellows. 'Hard labour int hard, it's blimmid hard on a good day and there int none o' them.'

Somewhat deflated, the men trudged away grumbling to each other and themselves.

'Give up my pint o' strum to come here,' one complained. *Strum* was a noxious rum-like concoction made from beets. I had tried it once and that was once too often.

Gerrund was at my side.

'I know that man in uniform,' he told me. 'Runs a gambling club.' He caught Alfred's eye. 'Or so rumour has it. Anyway, he's no more entitled to wear those medals than I am.'

'You men,' the inspector called to a huddle of constables whose purpose so far had been to lounge about chatting to each other and any passing woman under the age of thirty. 'Clear the square and man the entrances to stop anyone else getting in without my authority.'

Disgruntled at having their social intercourse disrupted, they set about their task.

'How long will the army take to get here?' I asked, for they were barracked in Bury St Edmunds and Ely, neither of which were on our doorstep.

'Luckily they are camped on an exercise near Lower Downhill Up.' He kicked a pebble. 'So we can expect them fairly soon. Meanwhile…' Alfred clapped his hands together. 'I had better have a look at the body. The doctor should have been here by now. Speak of the devil.' A plump man balanced on a piebald mare appeared to be remonstrating with the policeman guarding the top of Market Street. Stanbury raised his voice. 'Let him through, Smith.'

The constable scratched his helmet. 'But you say let no-one…'

'Let him through,' his senior repeated in exasperation.

'Dint let no-one through,' Smith held out both hands. 'Let someone through. It's all too confoosin'.'

A close relation of despair drifted across Stanbury's face.

'If…'

'It's back!' a young constable stepped into the gateway, his truncheon drawn ready to strike.

'Don't be a fool man!' Alfred bellowed. 'Step aside.'

His officer jumped back and not a moment too soon for a dark shape hurtled out of the gathering gloom. I am confident that every soul in that square believed that the creature was charging at them. Only one of those people was correct and, for a change, it was me. I looked into the soul of the beast and saw its evil intent. It looked at me and, doubtless, saw the fear as it began to run in my direction.

Alfred placed himself in front of me while, simultaneously, Anthony stepped in front of us both. The great cat hurtled towards him, but he did not flinch. He raised his right arm, pointing straight at the animal. It was almost upon him when he pulled the trigger, his hand jumping up with the recoil, the explosion reverberating around the square and inside my head. The panther leapt and Anthony fired again while it was in mid-air. It crashed into him, sending him sprawling and falling on top of him.

Alfred had his revolver drawn too as he raced the few steps to them both. He pushed the muzzle to the cat's ear but there was no need to fire. It was dead.

'Good shooting, sir.' Gerrund stood over them both.

'Thank you,' Anthony gasped. 'But I wonder if I could trouble you both to lift it off me.'

'I think we can manage that.' Alfred bent over to take hold of a massive front paw.

'But could you put my gun down first, Mr Appleton.' Gerrund hesitated to approach. 'You have it pointed straight at the inspector's head.'

'Do I?' Anthony twisted his neck to look at the revolver in surprise. 'So I do.' And lowered it carefully to the ground.

Alfred and Gerrund heaved and dragged the panther off.

'Thank you.' Anthony felt his torso gingerly. 'Not sure it didn't break my ribs.' He prodded his stomach. 'Or rupture my liver.' He tapped himself. 'I'm quite certain it has fractured my spleen.'

'A stiff drink will soon put you to rights.' I reached out. 'Give me your hand.'

'Best if I do it, milady.' Gerrund hauled him up and, seeing Anthony looking all crumbled and broken but not really broken at all, I lowered my head. It would not do for any of the men to see my face. They would all have known that my brimming eyes were the result of weak feminine emotions.

It appears to have afflicted me too, Inspector Hefty snuffled. I had not been aware that he especially cared for my friend. *It's not that,* he sniffed. *But when I wrestled with the panther in the park, the stem of my briar pipe was broken.*

A likely story. Ruby flicked her Egyptian cigarette, scattering ash onto his Ulster coat, but her cynical smile evaporated when she saw that the hand, with which her rival brushed his lapel, was gouged by claw marks.

Agnust approached with the rolling gait of a sailor on land after months at sea.

'Find anozzer bottle of your cordial,' she announced. 'Taste better this time, it do.'

-

Anthony and I made a tattered pair by the time we returned to my sitting room. Our clothes were grubby and torn and my hair hung in disarray.

'When I was running towards that cat, did you call me *darling*?' he asked over a large whisky.

'Of course not,' I laughed lightly over mine.

Cackled like one of the weird sisters, Ruby corrected me, and in truth, I knew that I had overacted. The last man I had addressed so affectionately had left me hurt, confused and humiliated outside the family chapel at Thetbury Hall.

Anthony puffed out his cheeks. 'I must have misheard you.'

Don't try to squirm out of this one, Thorn, Ruby urged. *Tell him the truth.*

'I did say *darling*.' I conceded as I took up her gauntlet but dropped it immediately. 'It was from sonnet eighteen. *Rough winds do shake the darling buds of May…*'

'*And summer's lease hath all too short a date*,' Anthony continued because you can never out-bard a thespian. 'But why?'

'I find that quoting poetry helps me to remain calm in a crisis.'

'I find it helps me earn my keep during one,' he smiled. 'Or rather it used to do so before the East Suffolk Shakespeare Society closed its doors.'

Oh, for pity's sake, Thorn, Ruby scolded me. *Why are you pushing him from you?*

Do you really think I can go through all that again? I demanded, and Anthony touched my hand.

'Dear Violet,' he said. 'You look so sad.'

'I think it is just shock,' I told him and should have fallen sobbing into his arms and let him hold me, but I disengaged my hand from his and turned away.

'I had better check if Hettie is all right,' I told him. 'And I do not want her troubled with any of this.'

I trudged up the stairs to find my friend blissfully unaware of the drama that had unfolded beneath her window.

'No, I cannot make you look like Adonis, Mr Foxley,' Hettie said, though she was fast asleep.

–

Alfred Stanbury called the next morning.

Will somebody introduce the man to a competent barber? Ruby exhorted for his hair, pleasantly tousled when he was a youth, was just tousled in his maturity. I had bought him a jar of macassar oil once, but he had never applied it.

'I've been to Pallent's Furniture Store,' he told me, declining my offer of a coffee. 'It's all rather odd. According to Mr Pallent the crate was left outside their yard as they were closing yesterday, with a letter instructing them to deliver it to this corner of the square immediately. There was a five-pound note enclosed with a promise of more jobs to come if they performed the task satisfactorily.'

'For one crate?' I checked in surprise. A working man would be happy to earn that in a month.

'It ensured they did the job.' Alfred went to look out across the square. The stewed eel seller was setting her cauldron atop a charcoal burner, fortunately downwind and far enough away for the aromas not to reach us. 'And they had no idea of the contents.'

'Did anybody see who left it at Pallent's?'

Alfred cracked his knuckles. I wished that he would not. 'Apparently a small fire started at the back of the store and, understandably, they were occupied in dealing with that.'

I backtracked.

'And the instructions did not mention my house specifically?'

'Not according to Pallent.' He turned back to me. 'But I haven't seen the letter. They were told to leave it outside under a brick and it was gone in the morning.' He toyed with his watchchain. 'So we cannot say with any certainty that it was intended for you.'

'I cannot think why it would be.'

Tell him about the letter, Hefty urged.

'Though I did get a letter telling me that my days are numbered.'

'You're always getting odd notes,' Alfred piffed. 'But I've a few myself lately – the end of the world and all that nonsense.'

Thank goodness she took your advice. Ruby mixed herself a Plymouth gin and Indian tonic but did not offer me one. *You're bad enough sober.* She searched in vain for a slice of lemon.

I went to stand by Alfred, my head about level with his shoulder. 'But where would the panther have come from?'

'I have sent a man to Anglethorpe.' Alfred glanced down at his feet. 'To ask at the zoo, and there are a few private menageries in East Anglia. We'll check if they have had a panther stolen though I would have thought it would have been reported if that were the case.' He polished the toe of his right shoe on the back of his trouser leg. 'Apart from any danger to the public, an exotic animal like that must cost the earth.'

Rather like the bill for your ridiculous clothes, Ruby said, though I noted that she was wearing my new Wilber-Lowe shoes. Ruby shook the icebox. It was empty.

'It is possible the delivery of one went astray.' I watched a ladybird crawl down the upper pane. 'They might not regard it as a police matter at first.'

Alfred shot me a sideways glance. 'We're asking about that as well.'

Hefty, ever ready to defend a fellow officer, admonished me, *He does not tell you how to plot your books.*

More's the pity. Ruby blew the ladybird away.

'I am sorry,' I told Alfred. 'I did not mean to question your competence.'

'I know you did not.' He pulled out his watch and flicked open the lid. 'Perhaps I have time for a coffee after all.'

Alfred peered out while I rang the bell for Agnust.

'Looks like we will have a musical accompaniment.' He pointed into the square.

'If only that were true,' I groaned for the hurdy-gurdy man was wending his way through the stalls towards his patch in front of my house.

–

Alfred came back that evening.

'Have you found out who the dead man was?' I poured us both a whisky.

'A Mr John Black,' he replied, 'a wine merchant's assistant aged twenty-three – on his way home from a friend's birthday celebration in The Waggoner's Rest.' He pinched the bridge of his nose wearily. 'Looked after his invalid mother. Lord knows how she will cope now. He was her only surviving child.'

'How unfair life and death are,' I sighed. 'If he had stayed to have another drink or left five minutes earlier, he would have been home and safe.'

Alfred brought out his cigar case.

'We have had a report of a stolen panther,' he told me. 'From the Marquess of Anglethorpe.'

'My Uncle Tiberius,' I exclaimed.

'The very same,' he confirmed. 'The cage was found empty yesterday afternoon and they thought it had escaped. The Marquess tethered several sheep and goats in his grounds in hope of luring it back. He offered all his estate workers a reward if they spotted it but there was no trace. Then he noticed faint waggon tracks heading from the cage towards the main road.'

'Aunt Igitha.' I squirted a dash of soda into his whisky. 'Who else would be mad enough to take it? And she made threats against me when I asked her to leave.'

'What kind of threats?' He put the cigar case unopened back in his inside breast pocket.

'Just that I would regret my actions.' It sounded feeble, I knew.

Only because it is. Ruby fitted a cigarette into the mouth of the silver snake that served as a holder. She had taken that idea from a lady who had asked for my help.

'Your uncle suggested that she might be responsible,' Alfred informed me.

I knew you were right to suspect her, Hefty said, though he had not supported my misgivings before now.

'And so I called on her,' Alfred was saying. 'She vehemently denied it.'

'Of course.' I handed him his scotch.

He rubbed the back of his neck. 'She can be quite a forceful woman.'

I noted that he had not called her a *lady*.

'Adamant that she had been in all day,' Alfred continued. 'And her butler backed her up.'

'Well, he would.' I swirled my drink.

'I realise that.' Alfred seemed uncharacteristically irritable. 'But also, several people saw her in her lantern room. She had the lamp on, but it was not rotating so the lowers benefited from street lighting for a change.' He flicked back his head. 'A few ladies of the night were not very happy about their ages and imperfections being exposed.' He rolled his eyes.

Across the floor? Ruby enquired guilelessly.

If I am such a bad writer, how did I manage to create you?

I was always here. She clipped on her – i.e. my – garnet earrings. *You only discovered me.*

'I think I should pay my uncle a visit.' I struggled to quell all my mental chatter. 'And then...'

A pity you did not undiscover her, Havelock Hefty reproached me.

'And then?' Alfred prompted.

'I shall confront my aunt myself.'

'I am not sure that is wise.'

Agnust had an adage, *Wise is as wise do* and it always made sense when she said it, but it made none at all when I quoted it to the inspector.

-

There was a sad article in *The Suffolk Times* the next morning. Samuel Flowerdew was dead. He had shot himself with a twelve-bore shotgun. I had first met him when I was nine and had been invited to his tenth birthday party at the nearby village of Blockborough. His father went shooting with mine and, since they were friends, it was natural to assume that their children would be too. Happily, the assumption was to prove to be correct.

Sammy, as he quickly became, was a chubby boy with freckles and sandy hair. He shook my hand gravely when I gave him his present. I had wanted to give him a set of throwing knives – having seen an act at the circus – but my mother sent me with Agnust to Botley's Toy Shop in Thetbury town to buy him a ship in a bottle.

'I expect, being a lady, you shall marry a prince,' he predicted after thanking me, 'but I shall answer God's calling, enter the church and become a Bishop.' He giggled. 'And so we will both end up in palaces.'

I felt I should tell him that I had no such plans – for I was going to be a doctor – and congratulate him on his worthy ambition but settled for, 'I am sorry your ship cannot float.'

'It is all the better for that,' he assured me, 'because it will not get washed out to sea and wrecked upon a reef. I shall be able to keep it always.'

Off Sammy went to play cricket with his friends, marooning me with his twelve-year-old sister, Eunice. She ordained that we play school with her dolls, lining them up in chairs on the lawn and taking turns to give them lessons. I taught them about Jonah and the Whale, which I had just learned about from Miss Kidd. Eunice's lessons consisted of her shouting at her dolls to stop fidgeting – even slapping some of them. In later years I wondered how this reflected on Mademoiselle Dubois, Eunice's guillotine-faced governess.

Next Eunice declared that I should be her maid and dress her hair. Having brushed it eighty-four times and been scolded for being stupid, I had had enough. The horrid girl tried to insist that I continued and grabbed hold of my arm. I did the only thing a well-bred young lady should and punched her on the jaw. She could probably have killed me in the scuffle that followed and that may well have been her intention for she took me by the throat, brushing off my repeated blows until another boy dragged us apart.

He was tall for his age – eleven, as I discovered later – and blonde-haired with intense green eyes flecked with gold.

'A word to the wise,' he told me as Eunice ran shrieking away, kicking all her dolls out of the way in the process. 'When you make a fist, don't make it around your thumb. You could break it. Also, the chin is harder than your hand and will hurt you more than your opponent.'

Rubbing my bruised neck with my bruised knuckles, I discovered that he was right.

Sammy came hurrying over, doubtless to scold me but his serious expression broke into a broad grin.

'Good for you, Violet.' He did a little jig. 'I've been wanting to do that for years.' He indicated to the other boy. 'This, by the by, is Jack.'

Jack did not shake my hand but nodded his head and said, 'Next time go for her snout.'

From that moment the three of us were firm friends but, in the next instant, Agnust marched over to drag me away in disgrace.

'I'm shamed on you, Lady Violet Elizabeth Antoinette Cordelia Thorn.' She only used my full name when I was in trouble. 'Brawlin' in public like a street slug. Wha' kind of behavin' way is tha' for a young lady of old breedin'?' She was dragging me along by the hand towards our carriage. 'Next time goo out of sight and remember, the Good Lord give you lovely teeth for a reason. One good bite soon settle any argument.'

'But I did not even get any cake,' I wailed.

'Dint deserve none.' Agnust took me to the clarence in which we had arrived. 'But I get you a piece anyways.' She tapped her handbag and called grandly to the footman sitting sullenly aloft. 'Home, my man.'

I looked back at the Flowerdew's regency pile.

Sammy and Jack were waving.

'Nasty boys,' Agnust said but I waved back, and I noticed that she did too.

And now Sammy was dead. He had been less happy in later years, but I still found the news difficult to believe. What could have driven my friend to such despair? Could such a devout clergyman really have lost his faith to such a degree that he had gone to face God by suicide, an act Sammy regarded as a grave sin? The note he left did not really explain his motives. He could not face a life of misery, he wrote. Had he been unhappy in love? He had never had much success with members of the female sex but, equally, he had shown little interest in them. He had been an enthusiastic attender of the race meetings at Newmarket. Perhaps he had accrued unpayable gambling debts there. Whatever the truth might have been, his family maintained a silence on the matter.

15: *THE KINDNESS OF CROCODILES*

I HARDLY KNEW Aunt Igitha before she inflicted herself upon my household. I remembered a tall, sharp-nosed woman with piercing eyes coming to a garden party at Thetbury Hall some seven or eight years previously. Her thick, gun-metal hair was piled so high that Hettie and I decided it must be a horsehair wig and we hoped that it would get entangled with a low branch. I do not believe that she spoke more than a dozen words to me. She was far more taken with Jack, feeding him cucumber sandwiches and cakes, stroking his long blond hair and tinkling with laughter. Far from being flattered by her attentions, Jack told me afterwards, he had been acutely embarrassed, especially when she made him take her through the woods to see the folly.

'A crackle-head, if ever I met one,' he told me and I found myself unable to disagree.

–

I took a train to Stolham St Ernest. It was only ten minutes away, being the first stop on the line to Thetbury. The platform was deserted when I dismounted, apart from a jolly porter who inspected my ticket with great care, though I doubted that he had ever come across a forgery. He clipped a cardboard crescent moon out of the corner and told me merrily that there were no cabs to be had.

'No call for 'em.' He returned my ticket. 'You can walk into and out of the village in less time than it take to…' He ruminated on a useful comparison. 'Do somethin' wha' take longer.'

'But I wish to get to Stolham Hall.' I swotted a tiny black fly that was hovering between us and the porter flinched as if I had tried to slap him.

'Most foreigners like yourself send a telegram to his lordship to be met.'

But Lady Violet could not have done that, Hefty declared loyally. *She is too scatter-brained.*

'What about the ones who do not message?' I asked.

'Wellll.' He screwed his little finger into his ear. 'They have two choice.' He unscrewed his finger. 'Either they walk or either they dint.'

'But it is four miles,' I protested as he inspected the extracted digit.

'It is.' He licked the tip. 'But the further you goo the shorter it get.'

I gazed at the gathering clouds and wondered if I should go home, send a message, and return another day, but I was a Thorn, I told myself, with a proud history of…

Treachery, Ruby chipped in for it was only because Sir Giles had changed sides at the battle of Brandon Ford that he was given Thetbury Hall and its estates.

'I wonder if the vicar has a trap,' I mused aloud, for the Rectory was only a hundred yards away.

'I wonder tha' too.' The porter returned to his ear. 'For he dint have one yisdee or the day afore or…'

'I shall walk.' I set off through the station gate but I had hardly gone twenty paces when I saw a trap approaching, drawn by a chestnut horse and driven by a familiar figure.

'Hallooo,' he hailed me, waving his cap as if he had just won a race.

'Uncle Tiberius.' I waited until he had pulled up beside me. 'How did you know I was here?'

He might be coming to catch a train, Hefty pointed out quite reasonably.

'Your man, Gerrund, sent me a telegram.' He slid over on his bench. 'Climb aboard, my dear.'

I scrambled up to deposit myself beside him and kiss the small, shaved area between his bushy mutton chops and profuse moustaches.

He looked about through round gold-framed spectacles, his eyes magnified by the lenses to make him look like a furry nocturnal creature.

'You have no luggage?'

'I have only come for the day.'

'Pity,' he sighed. 'Oh, the pity, the pity of it all.' Flattering though this was I could not believe that the brevity of my visit was such a tragedy. 'I get so few visitors these days.'

'How are you, Uncle?' I asked.

'All the better for your presence.' He flicked his whip in the air, tugged on the reins to turn us around and set us on our way. 'I haven't seen you for years. My word how you've...' he hesitated.

'Not grown,' I contributed, and he chortled and patted his stomach.

'Whereas I am not sure that I have stopped.' He was a big man with a surprisingly high voice. 'The only...'

Uncle Tiberius slumped sideways to lean heavily against me. When I was a child, his narcolepsy used to alarm me, but I became used to it. My only concern now was that we were travelling at a brisk pace along a country lane. His horse seemed happy enough though and continued to trot steadily, turning left along another lane without hesitation. I took the reins just in case but there was no need for me to use them. One of the many complaints I had heard about motor vehicles was that you could not take a nap whilst driving one for they never knew where they were going.

There was little else on the road, a few farm labourers on foot and a waggon that pulled over to let us pass. It was loaded with sheep, and I lowered my eyes guiltily for they to me were what I had been to the panther.

A young girl came running from the porter's lodge as we arrived and heaved the high gates to let us through. I threw her a few coppers which she caught with a deftness that would have done credit to many a professional cricketer.

The driveway went up a small hill and it was only when the ground levelled that I could see Stolham hall. It was a large square brick building four storeys high and guarded by a white, stone-pillared portico. We did not stop there however but went around the side, past a smithy's where a fine black stallion was being reshoed, and on into the stable block.

Uncle Tiberius stretched. 'Dear me are we here already? Or did I—'

'You fell asleep,' I confirmed.

'Dear oh deary me.' He brushed a leaf off his trouser knee. 'Oh dear.'

A groom came up to take the bridle and we both dismounted, watched by four other horses over their stable doors. His carriages stood gleaming under a sloping pantile roof, maroon with his gold shield on the doors.

'Igitha used to scold me when I fell asleep,' he told me as we left the yard, relieving me from having to raise the subject.

'Have you seen her recently?' I asked as casually as I could.

'Not since you invited her to stay with you.'

I could already hear the hoots of monkeys as we skirted a horse trough.

'Actually, she just arrived,' I told him.

'Gracious, how naughty of her.' We stopped to face the lawn, so unkempt it was more a paddock now.

'I hope you do not mind me asking,' I began cautiously, 'but are you and Aunt Igitha actually married?'

No members of the family had been invited to their wedding and it was not announced in any newspaper that I had read.

'Most certainly,' he assured me. 'I have seen the certificate.'

'Why would you need to see it, Uncle Tiberius?' I asked and he rubbed the back of his neck.

'If truth be told, dear Violet, I could not remember the ceremony to save my life, but Igitha assured me that we had been through it and so, I suppose we must have.' He rubbed the back of his neck. 'My memory has never been what it used to be.'

We crossed the lawn diagonally towards a copse.

'Who was the vicar?' I enquired.

'Forget the name.' My uncle took off his hat. His hair had been Thorn thick and black once. Now it was wispy white rather like a dandelion, and I was half-tempted to blow on it. 'Went off as a missionary to Africa, I am told.'

'I should like to see that certificate,' I said.

I have, Hefty claimed, *and it is counterfeit.*

Tibby, as the family called him, tugged at his whiskers. 'But it has been lost.' For a moment he looked lost too, but he soon brightened up. 'Would you care to regard my menagerie?'

'Very much,' I said. It had been a highlight of our visits when I was young for one never saw exotic animals in Suffolk unless a circus came to town.

And the clown ran away to join the metropolitan police. Ruby was in my cherry blossom dress with its matching bonnet, her third change of costume since we had boarded the train.

Get back up that rope ladder. Hefty would never let Ruby forget how she had been a trapeze artist in *Blood on the Sawdust*, an unfinished short story.

We passed around the wooded area and through a gate in a high flint wall. The noise had been increasing as we approached but the stench hit me all at once. The first cages were filled with chimpanzees, throwing themselves around, shrieking and rattling the bars. One reached through and tried to grab my hat, but I jerked my head away just in time.

A small crocodile lay motionless in a shallow pond of green water. When I was a child I loved to poke at it and leap back as it came instantly to life, snapping at my stick. Now I showed it more respect. A python slept coiled in a glass tank, its middle bulging with its last meal – a rabbit, my uncle told me.

My favourite, though, had been an ancient lion who had always snarled excitingly when I approached but it was long dead now and replaced with a tigress who watched us sourly from her prison.

'Her mate died recently.' Tibby sucked his lower lip. 'Now she has so much space she does not know what to do.'

'You kept both of them in there?'

'Oh yes.' He tugged his beard. 'They were very cosy – quite inseparable.'

A wolf paced back and forth, its enclosure only allowing it three steps before it had to turn.

'Would they not be happier in the wild?' I asked.

'A moot point.' He clicked his tongue but made no attempt to answer it.

An orangutan was sitting sadly in a pile of dirty straw. 'Don't let its appearance fool you,' Tibby warned. 'They are the most ferocious beasts in the jungle.'

I found that difficult to believe as it ambled over, reaching a paw out towards me. My uncle raised his cane.

'It is all right,' I murmured to them both and held out my hand. Its fingers closed gently around mine.

'Well would you credit it?' Tibby gasped. 'The man assured me it was fierce, but it appears I have been defrauded.'

The orangutan's other paw passed through the bars.

'Give it your hand,' I urged.

'So that it can kill us both?'

'Please.'

Cane still raised, my Uncle offered his left hand, and the creature took that too. 'Well, I'll be blowed.' He grinned like a child.

I do not know how long we stood there enraptured before the orangutan sneezed, uncurled its fingers, and settled back into its bedding.

'Perhaps next time I could get into the cage with it,' he proposed.

'That is a lovely idea.' We moved away. Feeling a little self-conscious, I gave the animal a wave and, mournfully, it returned my gesture.

'Haven't had that much affection since my nanny was dismissed,' Tibby said, 'for allowing my father to seduce her.'

'The hussy,' I sarcasmed, for we both knew the duress to which female servants could be subject.

'Indeed.' My uncle struck the head off a red rose with his cane.

We came across an empty cage near the perimeter.

'Is this where the panther was kept?' I asked in dismay, for it was no bigger than the wolf's cage.

'In the height of luxury,' he told me. 'See that?' He pointed with his cane. 'Why they even had a water bowl.'

'They?'

'Neither her previous owner nor I were aware that she was – excuse my language – gravid when I purchased her. She gave birth to a male cub but, for some reason, she could not feed it. We took it from her to nurse it. Her cries were quite…' He chuckled at the memory. 'Piteous.'

'What happened to it?'

We sat together on a low bench.

'Why it died, of course.' He sounded incredulous that I should even need to ask. 'I sent it to be stuffed but it has yet to be returned. Hence the old saying *As slow as a taxidermist.*'

Or As stupid as an uncle, Ruby coined.

Hefty occupied himself in measuring some faint tracks in the grass at the back. *A gauge peculiar to vehicles from the Iberian Peninsula.* He strode off to follow them.

A thrush flew overhead.

Free as a bird, Ruby said sadly.

'Oh Uncle,' I sighed. 'All these animals are so unhappy.' But he was fast asleep again, leaning against me, his great head on my shoulder. Within a minute he had awoken again with a contented smile.

'Oh.' He sniffed three times and, for some reason, shot me an anxious glance.

'What is it?'

'Probably nothing.' He edged away.

'Do you know who stole your panther?' I asked and he took off his hat to fan himself though the day was mild.

'I have my suspicions.' He fiddled with the lining. 'It was definitely a woman.'

'How can you know that?'

Inspector Hefty reappeared, combing through the long grass with a miniature hand rake from his evidence bag.

'I found a ladies' handkerchief nearby,' Uncle Tiberius declared. 'Dear me, I forgot to show it to the police.' He patted and rummaged through his pockets. 'There it is. Perhaps you could give it to them.'

He handed it over, a little nervously, I thought.

I did not need to hold it to my nose. It was strongly fragranced.

Your perfume, Ruby said though I had already recognised it, *Fleurs de Bulgarie by the House of Creed.*

'Aunt Igitha,' I breathed.

'Oh really?' Uncle Tiberius said. 'For one dreadful moment, as I caught your scent, I thought it might be you.'

'Do you really think I would do such a thing?' I asked in wounded surprise.

'No,' he said. 'It was just a fleeting fancy just as I never really suspected you of strangling my giraffe.' He dropped his hat into his lap. 'If only Igitha had been a fleeting fancy too. Do you know she tried to kill me more than once?'

'How?'

'The last time there was a shotgun with the barrel stopped to make it explode in my face. I lent it to my keeper. Deuced near took half his face off. Blind for life, what there is of it.' He waved his hand. 'Other times I tried to pass them off as accidents – a loose stair rod that almost tripped me up, a banister that gave way when I leaned on it. That sort of thing.'

'Did you tell the police?'

'Didn't want the scandal, besides, it was then she told me that you had invited her to stay.'

I gaped.

'Could you not have warned me?'

'I did, or at least I thought I did but, come to think of it, the boy I sent to post the letter ran off to sea that day… or so Igitha informed me.' He ran his fingers though his hair. 'Oh dear. I seem to have been rather stupid.'

'I would not say that.' I patted his hand.

Very stupid indeed, Hefty gave voice to my thoughts while I retraced our conversation.

'Did somebody really strangle your giraffe?'

'So I was led to believe but the stupid animal made it all up. The blood never reaches their brains you know.'

At least they have one, Ruby retorted.

Uncle Tiberius got to his feet. 'I expect you would like lunch.'

I certainly would. Hefty clapped his hands with gusto.

'Cook has prepared a delicious tiger stew.'

'Thank you but I think I had better go home.' I had had more than my fill of great cats lately.

-

Agnust greeted me with relish. 'Bad news.' Few things gave her more satisfaction than the dissemination of it. 'Tha' Hettie Granger…'

'Has she taken a turn for the worse?' I asked in alarm.

'She take a turn for the better,' my maid replied grimly.

'But why is that bad news?'

I genuflected to unlace my boot.

'It mean any day now she be up.'

My neat bow had transmogrified into the Gordian Knot.

'But surely that is a good thing.' I wrenched at the knot, making it even tighter.

Agnust humphed. 'When she get up, she get about and, when she get up and about, she get into trouble and, when she get into trouble, you get into trouble.'

There was some truth in Agnust's statement. Hettie and I had been in a few scrapes together over the years, but I doubted that she would be up to many of those in the foreseeable future. That was a shame because I would have appreciated her support on my next escapade.

16: THE CREEPING HOUSE AND THE SINISTRALS

THE LIGHTHOUSE STOOD on the edge of Upper Montford. It had been built by Pertinance Quail, a much-removed cousin of my mother's, in the '60's. It might seem a futile exercise to build such a structure some fifty miles from the coast but the countryside surrounding the town was unlit. Having lost his bearings in the fenlands for an entire night and almost drowning when his trap rolled into a drainage ditch, Quail decided that the time had come to act.

He had toyed with the idea of beacons but was advised that lighting them might start an invasion panic. There was already talk of war with France over the scramble for Africa.

In the end Mr Q settled upon the idea of a lighthouse. This had the added advantage that he could scan the surrounding countryside from its height and ensure that his labourers were going about their work and that sheep rustlers were not.

The lamp, I had been told, was fuelled by whale oil. It did not burn as brightly as paraffin products, but Quail preferred a tried and tested fuel. The lighthouse had been unoccupied for years, however, since he had disappeared. He had been drowned in a shipwreck, it was put about, but I was more inclined to believe that he was trying to escape his creditors. Building inland lighthouses is a costly and unprofitable business.

'Time to accost the hag of Anglethorpe,' I announced to myself, creeping fearlessly into the hall, before Agnust could discover that I had not finished my breakfast.

Probably best to wait until tomorrow, Hefty wavered but I was already selecting my attire. It is an irrevocable rule of mine that, once one has an umbrella in ones grasp one cannot withdraw from ones expedition – not unless one wants to at any rate.

-

I would have asked Gerrund to hail me a cab. He was good at that, but he was occupied with pulling the bones out of a pike, an endless task, to judge by the spikey mound he had created. It already looked bigger than the fish from which it had come.

Now try to reassemble it, Hefty challenged, affronted that he had not been allowed to pickle a human head in the kitchen for his own display stand in the Black Museum.

Freda, the bearded lady, was sitting on the kerb. 'Spare a bottle o' gin for a poor old widda woman,' she begged piteously. Not having one on me, I gave her thruppence only to be thanked with, 'Miseryabald uddercat.'

Seraphim Square was busy. Pilgrims were gathering to commemorate the martyrdom of Aegbald, the last king of West Suffolk. He was also the patron saint of Montford and those afflicted by the terrible curse of left-handedness.

The sinistrals, Ruby hissed, forgetting that she was to be counted amongst them.

In an earlier conflict with the pagan hordes, Aegbald had had his right hand amputated, but it was miraculously restored to him so that he could wield his sword – unsuccessfully it transpired – for Jesus. The broken remains of his shrine still stood in the ruins of the monastery and people flocked there in order that they or their children could touch the memorial stone, in hope of a cure.

The crowds were usually a good sign because the cabs that brought people into town would wait in hope of picking up fares back to the railway station.

A hansom approached from Market Square, and I hailed it with my furled umbrella.

'Not gooin' tha' way,' the cabby called though he could have no idea of my intended destination.

He probably thinks you are a child and will be sick on his upholstery, Ruby taunted, for she was tall and looked like what I was too – an adult.

I think Milady is well-mannered enough to vomit on the floor, Hefty said staunchly.

There were three more hansoms parked in front of the Splendid Hotel and the crossing sweeper was helping a lady to disembark from one of them, doubtless in expectation of a tip.

I put the whistle on my charm bracelet to my lips and blew. Two cabbies glanced at me but neither of them came over. I marched to the Splendid.

'All of us booked for a trip to the shrine of Saint Aegbald,' the first driver told me.

'But that is only across the square and through the monastery gates,' I objected.

'Not when we goo the scenery way.' He winked and I wandered off.

Another hansom approached, the driver's head down and covered in a broad brimmed leather hat, the face muffled in a huge patchworked scarf, its ends dangling over a long rabbit skin coat. There was little to recognise the man by except that he wore this outfit all year round, varying it only by discarding his scarf and leather gauntlets in the height of summer. He had sported a pith helmet once, but it had caught fire when he drove past a faulty gas lamp.

The horse was equally unmistakeable – a small animal, dappled grey with a piratical black patch around her left eye and an odd slow lolloping gait.

I had no need to flag them down for Old Queeny, catching sight of me, came to a halt and turned her head expectantly. Once I had absentmindedly left my handbag open and she had nosed into it to munch on my train ticket to Sackwater and a bag of Mackintosh's Celebrated Toffees. Ever since then, Old Queeny had regarded me as a friend or a provider of treats which, in the animal world, amounts to the same thing.

I conducted a hurried search and came up with a pack of Beeman's, but I was not going to share it with a horse. I had to import my chewing gum from Cleveland in the faraway lost colonies of America.

Having found and offered Old Queeny a furry mint, which she accepted with an ungracious snuffle, I clambered aboard.

'The Lighthouse,' I called through the open hatch overhead.

'Wha' 'bout it?'

'I wish you to take me there.'

'Then you do well to get in my cab,' he reassured me. 'If you ask me to take you to Seraphim Square I have to say we are already there.' The obvious was never quite obvious enough for Friendless. He clicked his tongue and Old Queeny twisted her neck and revolved her eye in a way of which only horses and inebriates are capable. He shook his reins and she coughed. 'Goo on,' he urged, and she sneezed. 'Please.' Off we set.

'Thought of a good joke,' he chatted as we left the tar-surfaced square to rattle over the cobbles.

'And you are going to tell it to me,' I sighed.

'How you know tha'?' he marvelled.

'It was just a guess.'

'Why?'

'Why what?'

'It's the start of the good joke.'

'Please continue.' *Before I die.*

'Why do they call it a lighthouse?' Friendless sniggered and Old Queeny sighed. Perhaps her load was growing too much for her, or could it be that she had heard the joke before? I knew that I had. 'When it int a lighthouse at all. In point of a fact, it's very…' He caught his breath. 'Hu…' he managed. 'Hu… Hu… heavy.'

To this day I do not know how I managed not to collapse in mirth.

'How heavy would you say it is?' I asked, secure in the knowledge that he would spend the rest of our journey attempting to calculate the answer.

'Three thousand, six hundred, and three ton.'

'How on earth do you know that?'

'I do work it out,' he replied to my astonishment. This, after all, was a man who believed that the stars were pinholes in the sky. 'It's the tallest buildin' in town and tha's the tallest number my dear old mumby teach me.'

Friendless's *dear old* mother had let him pick up a hot coal to teach him a lesson when he was a toddler; It had *cockled*, or withered, his left hand; but that was not the only example of her cruelty towards him and yet he always spoke of her with great affection.

'It is a very good number,' I assured him, my attention caught by two dogs fighting over a bone.

The femur of a red-headed, long-sighted, presbyterian cabinet maker, Hefty deduced.

A hambone, I told him as a crow landed on Old Queeny's withers.

'Get your own horse.' Friendless flicked his whip over his new passenger. It ruffled its feathers resentfully and flew away.

It probably thought she was carrion, Ruby said grimly, though not heartlessly, for it was she who had reminded me when it was Old Queeny's birthday.

Down Old Bakery Street we went, pulling over, one wheel on the pavement to make way for a waggon laden with beets. They did not usually come up that way since the road was even narrower at the top.

'Not much room,' I commented.

'Can't make my cab more big just for you.' Friendless watched anxiously but the waggon squeezed past without touching his paintwork.

'I meant there was not much room for the waggon.'

Friendless snorted in amusement. 'No room at all for a waggon in there with you, nor even if you get out.'

'I…'

Do you really want to have that discussion?' Ruby slotted a Little Queen into the mouth of her silver snake.

'I suppose you are right.' I surrendered to his incontestable logic.

'Hear tha', Old Queeny?' Friendless crowed. 'She say I am right which mean she is wrong, so I am better than royalty.'

I thought about explaining that, far from being Royal, I was probably not much higher in line for the throne than he was, but a sharp *Don't* from Ruby silenced me.

We passed through a court surrounded by terraced houses once grand, now delipidated, for we were too close to the more unsavoury Lower Montford to make them desirable. Plans had been made to clear the area but, there being fears that the occupants would drift towards the town centre, the schemes were dropped.

Friendless broke into song though he paid scant attention to the chromatic scale. 'My love has got a red red nose,' he wailed. 'She wipe it on my sleeve. I save tha' sleeve for ever more. For she die of disease.' He inflated his chest to its maximum concavity. 'For sheeee die of dis-ee-ee-ee-ee-ease.' We bumped violently over a sack. 'Make tha' song myself,' he boasted. 'I do.'

'I am sure you did.'

'So am I.'

We swung around another corner.

'There it is,' Friendless declared from his high perch with great satisfaction. 'I know it will be.'

This was not the great surprise that he seemed to believe it was. To the best of my knowledge the building was not in the habit of wandering about the county.

A good plot for my next book, Scotland Yard's premier detective suggested hopefully. *The Mystery of the Creeping House, part one of an Inspector Havelock Hefty trilogy.*

We were too close to the buildings for me to see our destination but, as we rounded the corner it rose before us.

What rose – the corner? Ruby quibbled. She was sulking because I was wearing the hat that she had chosen for herself. *It makes you look like a squirrel,* she had told me bafflingly. It was more like a giant crimson butterfly, the outspread wings resting in my hair and its oversized body made up of a tiered bow.

We entered a large, potholed square. Behind us and to our left were the backs of the houses. Dyer Road came off the far left-hand corner along the side of a dilapidated warehouse. To our right was a low flint wall, tumbling in places, and I knew from childhood visits that this separated us from the edge of the chalk quarry. It was a good thirty-to-forty-foot sheer drop to the bottom of that.

The lighthouse stood about eighty feet high, striped in blue and white on a huge stone plinth. Red and white was more traditional but so was a coastal location. At the top was the lantern room, glass-paned and surrounded by a balcony.

'Here we are,' Friendless announced because I probably thought that we were somewhere else.

He did not pull on the reins, however, until his aged steed had already stopped and was cropping a clump of bracken growing out of a crack in the pedestal. I had a feeling that she was not supposed to eat that, and it was soon apparent that Old Queeny had the same feeling for she spit it out of her mouth almost immediately, head twisting and eye swivelling to look at me accusingly.

'I did not tell you to eat it,' I defended myself.

'She dint,' Friendless concurred, 'but she dint say daint.'

The area was deserted except for a score of skeletal cats who galloped over in the hope of food that I did not have with me. They were all mangy and many were battle-scarred, one hobbling with a missing front paw.

A waggon came clattering up from Dyer Road. This was a convenient turning place for them when Lofter's Yard was full. It swung about and back the way it had come.

'You have to walk from here,' Friendless told me though he could not have got closer without Old Queeny clambering onto the platform.

'I expect that I can manage. Will you wait?'

'For what?'

'For me.'

'You do want me to, do you?'

'Yes please.'

'Then I do believe I do.'

He pulled on his cord to unlock the flaps and I scrambled out, pretending unconvincingly, that I had not slipped on the running board. Jack had once told me that I moved with great grace and poise – for such an accident-prone woman. Not surprisingly this had led to an argument in which I told him, absurdly, that there was something unmanly about the shape of his earlobes. Was that why he had jilted me? No, it was before he had proposed, I remembered as I climbed the three steps onto the plinth.

The front door was arched, solid and painted patchily. To the right was a rusting stirrup on a chain. I took hold of it and tugged. It was so stiff that I almost had to swing on it to pull it down. I listened but heard nothing.

One should always hear something, Hefty lectured, discounting the number of criminals who had crept up on him during his investigations.

I tipped my head back but was too close to see anything other than the towering… I leafed through my mental thesaurus and came up with… *tower* in front of me and the iron base of the balcony high over my head.

It was then that I was stabbed in the back of my leg.

'Ouch!' I spun around and an enormous grey cat spun with me, clinging onto my dress.

Enormous? Ruby scoffed, for this was the woman who had hunted a man-eating tiger.

For an almost domestic cat, I justified my statement. After all, I was the woman who had been hunted by a panther.

I unpeeled my attacker's claws and shooed the beast away before I heaved on the bellpull again. There being nothing else to do, I waited.

How many three letter words can you make out of the word cat? I asked myself. *Act*, myself replied and, having exhausted that game, I yanked on the lever.

A heavy bolt slid back. Another bolt grated, followed by the rattle and clack of a lock followed by the clack and rattle of another.

The door squealed open, and I found myself facing one of the tallest men that I had ever seen. Gerrund was about six feet, but this man was at least half a bottle of Bollinger higher.

He was also one of the thinnest men I had seen outside of the Lowers. His skin was so tightly bound to his hairless head that the cheekbones looked ready to burst through it. His dark, almost black eyes sank deep beneath an overhanging brow. A great deal of his hair appeared to have migrated to create eyebrows that resembled miniature military moustaches.

I held out my card, but he did not even glance at my beautiful copperplate offering.

He was watching me as closely as a jeweller who has foolishly admitted a beggar to his shop and shown her a tray of diamond necklaces.

'Can I help you?' His tone reminded me of the policeman who had wanted to know why I was skulking in the shrubbery at the back of the vicarage.

'My name...' I began because it occurred to me that he might be unable to read.

'I know who you are.'

'How?'

'I have watched you at your window.'

A shiver – too taken unawares to run – tottered up my spine. I knew, of course, that I was on view to the square in my living room but there was quite a difference between being seen and being kept under observation.

'When?' He had eyelashes, I noticed, that Old Queeny might have envied, if she were vain about her appearance, which I did not believe she was. I tried to return his gaze, but my cervical spine was not designed to hinge ninety degrees backwards, so I made do with staring at his ash-grey waistcoat.

'Recently,' the butler – as I assumed he was from his wearing evening dress in the morning – replied.

'Why?'

He raised his hand and I thought for a moment that he intended to strike me, but he was swatting a fly.

'Mine is not to reason.' His face was so blank that I could have used it for making notes.

Well, I have enjoyed our chat, I thought but said, 'Is your mistress at home?'

'Yes.'

He stood still and erect in the doorway.

'Then I wish to see her.'

The butler puzzled over my words as if struggling to translate them. 'She has instructed me to admit you.'

'Then do so.'

Look at those hands, Ruby warned. His fingers were thick and extraordinarily long. *Just one of those could snap your neck.*

I'd like to see him try. Hefty proved that the Trafalgar spirit was not yet dead, though I might be, if the challenge were taken up.

The butler slid backwards, opening the door wide, and I stepped into a circular stone hallway surrounding an iron spiral staircase.

'Come this way.'

I had been arrested with greater deference, on the first occasion at any rate.

I glanced to where the stairs pierced the ceiling. It looked rather high. Up we went. Whilst I clung onto the banister rail, the butler's hands hung down his sides and his back remained vertical as a plumbline.

I felt slightly dizzy by the time we reached the first floor. A solid oak door came off the circumferential landing but that was of no interest to my guide. Our travels, it transpired, were not complete and we set off up another flight.

'Goodness,' I puffed as we arrived on the next floor, 'that was quite a climb.'

'Was it?' He put his foot on the next step.

I took a breath and followed.

Actually, Ruby quibbled, *you have been taking breaths ever since the midwife dropped you on your head.*

'What is your name?' I asked, if only to give my heart an opportunity to slow from *prestissimo* to *vivace*.

'Scratby,' he replied sourly as if aware that it sounded like an itchy disease, and he set off again.

I was more than slightly dizzy by the time we reached the next landing.

Thank goodness, I thought but, if goodness could, it would have smiled self-depreciatingly, knowing that it did not deserve my gratitude and that there was one more flight to go.

Hefty was already on the top floor, scraping a sample of rust from the banister into a manilla envelope.

I was gasping for oxygen and my legs almost buckled as I leaned against the stair rail, but Scratby had not even the courtesy to pretend to be winded.

Here the stairs ended on another circular landing and yet another wooden door to one side by the foot of a steep ladder with light flooding down it. Scratby put his hand to the door handle.

At least I can thank goodness that I will not have to climb that, I told myself, but goodness would have shrugged in embarrassment when my guide jerked his head sideways.

'Up you go,' he said.

It's a trap, Hefty warned. *Once you're up there he will take away the ladder and leave you to die a lingering death with your bones picked clean by the buzzards.*

I thought this unlikely, but it did give me cause to hesitate.

'After you,' I gestured.

'I am not employed to scramble up that,' Scratby demurred.

'Neither am I.'

I had lost my fleeting fondness for ladders when one, that I was on, had toppled backwards and this one did not look especially inviting. It was not even fixed but rested against the edge of the circular hole above.

'It does not look very stable.'

'It was supposed to be temporary.' Scratby stepped back as if afraid that it might collapse on him as he spoke. 'But I believe that Mr Quail had a disagreement with the iron forger over the price and so the permanent one was never made. Her ladyship has used it frequently without fear.'

I nearly told him that I had no intention of emulating her example but the superciliousness of Scratby's manner goaded me to lean my umbrella against the wall, slide my handbag up to the crook of my elbow and put my foot on the first rung.

Stay here and guard the ladder, I told my characters. I knew that they could not really do so, but I did not want them distracting me.

The ladder wobbled but I was determined that my resolve would not. Having no desire to give the butler a sight of my calves, I was just about to tell him to look away when he went off through the door.

You could at least have feigned an interest. I trod tentatively on another rung wondering, if I fell, whether I would plummet down the spiral staircase and end up twisted in the hallway or merely shatter my skull on the floor below. Eighteen rungs later I was relieved to find that neither of those fates had befallen me and I emerged into the dazzling whiteness of the lantern room.

'Goff,' I wheezed and shielded my eyes. About twenty feet in diameter, I estimated, the room was surrounded by diamond-shaped glass panes in an iron lattice. I peered under my hand – my eyes battling to perform their functions.

Aunt Igitha stood tall and angular, her mouth a pale laceration beneath her falcon nose, her wire wool hair glinting in the sun. She was dressed in what I believed the fashion magazines called *electric blue*. Whatever its exact colour, the dress gave an eerie glow to my aunt's ashen complexion.

Heels clattering on the slabbed floor, she stepped towards me, supporting herself on a silver cane. Why did she need that? She did not have a limp.

A sword stick, it occurred to me. This, after all, was the woman who I had evicted from my home, whose last words to me were veiled threats and whose last letter – if it came from her – had ripped that veil away.

'Veety,' she said in a tone that could have been stored in my parents' icehouse.

'Aunt Igitha.' I sized her up as I had seen pugilists do whilst calculating who would throw the first punch.

She held out her hand and I forced myself to take it. Her fingers were as gelid as her manner. She leaned forwards. Was she going to rip out my throat? I wondered not entirely preposterously for I had compelling reasons to suspect her of setting that panther on me.

Aunt Igitha presented me with her cheek, and I pecked it gingerly.

Fleurs de Bulgarie, I recognised, though it was fainter than usual. Was the unfortunate woman running short of my perfume?

'Why have you come?' She released my hand but kept hers raised as if about to greet me again.

'I have some questions for you.'

'And I have another for you.' She smiled acidly. 'Is there a prize for the correct answers – a copy of one of your trashy novels perchance?'

An uprising of characters was fomenting in my cerebellum.

'There is not.'

'Then I shall play, nonetheless, for the glory, the joy of crushing your…' She leant forwards until our heads nearly touched. 'Spirit.' Her breath smelled strongly of rotting meat, and I struggled not to recoil.

'Very well.' I would start with the less contentious of my accusations, I resolved. 'Did you write me a letter?'

'When?'

'Just after—'

'You threw me like so much rancid rubbish into the gutter,' she broke in. 'What if I did?'

'Why did you write it?'

'I have not said that I did.'

Confront her, I urged myself.

'Did you send a crate to my house?' I readied myself for her denial.

She released my hand. 'I might have.'

This, I supposed, was as close as I would get to an admission. 'Why?'

Aunt Igitha surveyed the room though there was not much to inspect. A peripheral iron ledge served as a window seat with lockers underneath it but without so much as a cushion on top to make it comfortable. In the centre was the oil lamp, far bigger than any I had seen before, partly shielded by a mirror – parabolic, I conjectured uncertainly. I had daydreamed during that lesson. The lamp stood on a dustily greased pole rising from dustily oiled machinery whose function must have been to rotate the whole thing, rather than just the mirror.

'Why are you wearing that hat? It makes you look like a squirrel.'

'You have not answered my question.'

'Nor you mine.'

I decided to forgo an I-asked-you-first exchange and try a different tack.

'What did you mean when you said that I would regret asking you to leave?'

'What did you mean when you said that I was distracting you from your work?'

'You always talked when I was trying to concentrate.'

'I was helping you.'

Relying on the unwritten rule that one answer deserves another, I tried again.

'Why did you send the crate?'

'Again, I have not said that I did.'

'Do you know what was in that crate?'

'Don't you?'

'This is a pointless conversation.' I gave up trying to hold her gaze.

'I did not ask for it nor have I encouraged it.' This was probably the first reasonable response she had granted me though I was still none the wiser.

You will never be that, my old governess, Miss Kidd, bobbed up briefly before sinking back through the surface of my brain.

Aunt Igitha splayed her eyes, and I wondered if the strain of these movements on her optic muscles would give her a headache. A bit of me hoped so. The rest of me was wondering if it were for this that I had clambered up what felt like hundreds of steps.

'You are an impertinent child.' She tapped the floor sharply with her cane, the sound reverberating. 'I shall not be interrogated in my own home.'

'And I shall not be imperilled at mine.'

Aunt Igitha touched her broach. It was rather a fine little cameo of a young woman, her ringlets tied in a bow. I would check my jewellery box when I got home.

'How pretty it must be,' she smiled sourly, 'to believe such a thing.'

'Are you threatening me?'

She stroked the carved profile.

'I have no need to do so.' She walked a circle around me while I stared fixedly ahead like a soldier under the scrutiny of his sergeant major. 'Come with me.' Aunt Igitha gestured to a door in the glass wall.

I hesitated. 'Why?'

'I wish to show you something.'

At least she had started to answer my questions, I reasoned. Perhaps, if I stayed, she would respond to some more.

'After you.' I stood back, not wishing to risk being shut out.

My aunt stepped onto the balcony and, warily, I followed.

The wind, hardly noticeable at ground level, buffeted me immediately. My hat fluttered its wings, but like the butterflies in Romulus's collection, it was securely pinned.

It was a good job that I had a head for heights, I told myself, because eighty feet looks more like one hundred and eighty feet when you are standing exposed to the elements at the top of it. There was only a worryingly thin, perturbingly rusty, and alarmingly low balustrade between me and proving that, of all the talents I had inherited, flying was not amongst them. I had become exceedingly adept, as a child, at falling, though. Rather like riding a bicycle, it is not a skill that one ever forgets. Landing unhurt is a very different matter.

The wind had gained in strength and speed up there and, my hat flapped wildly in its struggle to escape. Unlike the butterflies in my father's collection, I discovered, it was not securely pinned at all. I put a hand on top of it, leaving only one free to clutch the rail.

Glancing down I wished that I had not for, on this side, we looked straight into the quarry, and I did not need Hefty's tape measure to calculate that that was much further down than I would have liked it to have been. The world spun. I know it does anyway, but it speeded up alarmingly.

To my left I glimpsed Lofter's Yard crammed with waggons. The old warehouses surrounded it. They were still in use though the adjoining canal basin was largely filled in. A channel ran into the River Angle but was no longer navigable since the banks had crumbled and weeds had choked it.

'Walk with me,' Aunt Igitha suggested.

'I think I shall stand here.'

'Just a little way,' she urged, strolling as carelessly as she would were we on terra firma rather than the terrifying infirma on which I teetered. I inched a few minutes clockwise in her wake.

The lighthouse swayed or, more likely, I did.

We came to a stop about a quarter past where we had started. Far below, Friendless was stroking Old Queeny's mane while she had her face in her nosebag. The feline tribe was patrolling its territory. Ragged children hung listlessly around, probably in hope of the pennies that Friendless would not give them.

'Look.' My aunt swept her cane so suddenly that I would have jumped away, had my hand not become welded to the rail, but she was only indicating the panorama of Upper Montford. I could make out the Great Gatehouse easily and, across a bustling Seraphim Square, the observatory of the top of my home. The River Angle wound in a grey ribbon through the fields and ruins of the Monastery Gardens. Beyond them was Lower Montford, its ramshackle houses sprawling along tangled confusions of alleyways and courts. The toppers gave way to cloth caps, decorated silk bonnets to tattered straw hats, and the carriages petered out until there was not a hansom to be seen.

'It is a splendid view,' I admitted queasily.

'View?' she said scornfully for, apparently that was the last thing that I should be noticing. 'Look at all those *people*.' She uttered the last word in such revulsion that someone, who had never come across it before, might think it was some kind of untreated sewage. 'The teaming masses,' she sneered. 'Who would miss one of them or even a dozen?'

'Their families.'

'They have no proper families.' She conducted a silent celestial choir with her cane. 'Most of those so-called husbands and wives are not even married.'

I saw no point in arguing that many could not afford the licence.

'Their friends.'

'They have none of those either.' She curled her lips. 'Throw them a handful of coins and see how they fight for farthings like a pack of wild dogs over a carcass.'

'I have seen a starving woman give her last crust to her child,' I protested.

'Just as a bitch will vomit food for her pups. It is in their instinct to propagate their species.'

I had never liked my aunt and had come to dislike her but now I found her repellent.

'They may be less fortunate than us, but they are all human beings.' I made no attempt to hide my disgust.

'Insects,' she continued. 'I could crush them all.'

'Is that what you intend to do?'

'It is what I am doing already.'

A strong gust whipped up my dress to well above my knees, but I did not want to let go of my hat, and I could not let go of the rail even though it seemed to wobble.

'How?' I asked and her head dipped.

'Did you send that crate to my house?' I tried again.

'Oh Veety,' Aunt Igitha sighed as the wind dropped. 'You have never understood me.'

She propped her cane against the wall.

'And I shall never want to,' I retorted, so incensed that I let go of the rail – though not the hat. It only occurred to me afterwards that I had been readier to take a small risk with my life than a large one with my millinery.

I had intended to leave but Aunt Igitha's hand shot out and she grasped my free wrist.

'Let go of me.' I struggled uselessly.

Her nails dug in, but I would not give her the gratification of seeing that she was hurting me.

'Ungrateful wretch,' she hissed, bringing her face close to mine, 'sending the police to interrogate me as if I were a common felon. You think you can attack me in my own home with your crazed accusations? Why don't you join the stinking rabble?' She pulled me towards her and hooked her other hand around my shoulder, spinning us around so that the rail was behind me.

'Let go,' I insisted but she was pushing me, bending me backwards so hard that my feet lifted off the platform.

I kicked her on the shin, and she bared her teeth.

'Do that again and I will toss you over the edge.'

This threat was actually quite encouraging, I told myself, for it meant that she did not intend to throw me over as a matter of course.

'If you do, I shall make sure to take you with me.' I tried to twist my right arm free, but her grip was too tight.

'It is useless to struggle.' She sprayed my face with putrefying droplets.

'Sorry, hat.'

Aunt Igitha looked puzzled. Was I the only one who had conversations with inanimate objects? None of them sought to reassure me that I was not.

I pulled out a pin and let my hat go and the rapacious wind snatched it away, carrying it sailing over the deepest part of the quarry, circling and dipping like a seagull in search of sandwiches.

'Excuse me.' My aunt scowled. 'I am the one who is supposed to be mad.'

'No, dear Aunty.' I smiled sweetly. 'You are the one who is supposed to be in pain.'

'What the devil are you prattling about now?'

'This.' I raised my pin and stabbed it into the hand on my shoulder.

'Ow!' She pulled her hand away and shook it as if she were being stung by a wasp. I jabbed the hand that held my wrist.

'Ouch!' She released me to inspect her wounds. 'They will probably bleed,' she forecast in horror. 'Blink my crittels! They ARE bleeding! By Jupiter's elbows you will pay for this, girl.'

Wielding the pin like a rapier, though with not quite the panache of D'Artagnan, I thrust my not-very-rapier-like makeshift-foil towards her face to ward Aunt Igitha off. Unfortunately, she chose that moment to step forwards.

'Argh!'

I let go in shock as Aunt Igitha jerked back, the pin buried a good half of its five inches in the bridge of her aquiline nose.

'You shall suffer for this.' She tugged at the pin, but it must have penetrated the bone and was possibly bent because it did not want to be extracted.

It was a favourite pin with a carnelian gemstone in its silver framed head. Deciding, however, that I would rather save myself than my bauble, I turned on my heels and ran.

'That's right,' Aunt Igitha bawled after me, 'scurry back to your vermin.' I reached the door and wrenched it open. 'I should have known better than to expect you to understand,' she screeched, still struggling with the hatpin. 'You have never been one of us.' An odd taunt, in retrospect, since her claims to family membership were highly dubious. 'Your blood is tainted,' she ranted. 'Why you are not even a Thorn, except in my side.'

That was not a bad riposte for a woman struggling to unimpale herself, I thought, and wondered if she had prepared it in advance.

'Enjoy the view,' I yelled, not sure that she would be able to hear me for the same winds that carried her words towards me, were sweeping mine away.

I stepped back into the lantern room, slamming and bolting the door. It was not clear to me whether Aunt Igitha had realised what I had done for she was still ranting and thrashing the air with a blur of her silver cane in a much more musketeerial manner than mine.

Down the ladder I went, feeling my way carefully one rung at a time.

Scratby was standing in the corridor, eyes down to respect my decency.

'Are you afraid of ladders?' I enquired and he blinked.

'Yes, actually I am.'

'That is unfortunate,' I commiserated, 'for I have marooned your triply-perforated mistress on the outer balcony.'

'But…' His tense skin tensed. 'Why?'

'Yours is not to reason,' I reminded him and made my way back down the spiral.

17: THE RUSSET AND THE REEF OF DESPAIR

OLD QUEENY WAS still munching contentedly in her nose bag and Friendless was dozing in his high seat when I exited the lighthouse. He had slumped so far forwards it was a wonder that he had not slid off. I tapped the sole of his boot with my umbrella, and he shook himself like a dog after a swim.

'Have a clever dream,' he told me after he had worked out where he was. *Clever* meant *nice* rather than intelligent. 'Nothin' happen and then…' he grinned happily at the memory, 'nothing else happen neither.'

A bow-legged boy approached clutching a lumpy brown paper parcel tightly. His head was shaved as was the case for many of his class as a way of dealing with nits. The bulbous brow and oddly domed back of his head were typical of advanced rickets.

'Apple for your nag,' he offered. He had corduroy trousers patched at the knees and tied around the waist with a piece of torn cloth.

'Clear off.' Friendless took his whip from its sheath. 'Blimmid street slug.'

'Free on charge.' The boy unclasped the nose bag.

Old Queeny shifted uneasily as did I.

'Wint tell you 'gain.' Friendless raised the whip but I knew that he would never use it on a child.

'If I give you tuppence…' I started to negotiate. Whatever was in that package it was not a Suffolk Russet. It was too long and thin and I thought that I saw it move in his grasp. 'Stop it,' I shouted but the boy dropped his parcel into the bag, hooked the strap back in and scarpered. 'Let me out,' I bawled.

Friendless yanked the cord to release the door catch and I half rose but too late. Old Queeny screamed, shook her head wildly and reared up, lifting the forks, and tipping the cab, throwing me backwards into my seat.

She came down with an almighty clatter of iron hooves on cobblestones, still thrashing her head.

'Woah, girl.' Friendless tugged on the reigns but the discomfort of a pull on her bit must have been nothing compared to the pain she appeared to be suffering and – with six or seven hundred pounds of bone and muscle – she was much too strong for any man to hold.

Old Queeny stepped backwards, hooves high as if trying to stamp out a forest fire. She spun around so sharply that she almost capsized the cab and charged towards the low wall. If she tried to clear that, all of us would die. The hansom rocked to the left, crashing down as she set off, flinging the vehicle squealing in a sideways skid, the back of it smashing into the wall, uncemented rocks flying in every direction. I felt the wheel go over the edge of the quarry and the axle crack down onto the stones. A section of wall tumbled far down into the chasm beneath me. The cab slid and I jumped.

Lord alone knew how I managed to tumble out. My head struck a boulder and my whole body was jarred but at least I was on solid ground, scrambling over the rubble just behind Old Queeny. For some reason she had calmed a little, though she was still very jumpy. Her screams had subsided into a whimper, and she was stamping but not kicking.

The hansom had wedged with one wheel over the precipice and the other a foot or two off the ground.

Friendless, I saw, was some yards away. He must have been thrown off his seat and was picking himself groggily off the cobblestones.

Stumbling to Old Queeny's head and, not bothering with the clips, I wrenched the strap over her ears and threw the bag aside. Something slid out of it, a rat, its hind quarters crushed presumably by her frantic bites at the source of her pain. Old Queeny saw it and reared again, and I knew better than to try to hold her. Friendless had no such fears though. He staggered over and grasped her harness.

'It's all right, Darlin'.' He patted her. 'It's all right now.'

She shook her head violently, blood pouring from her muzzle, and I was aware of people gathering at a safe distance. Nobody wanted to get too close to a runaway. She was a small horse, but one kick of her hoof could kill a man. Presumably they came from the houses backing the square. They were as shabby as the properties.

Old Queeny was panting and pawing at the cobbles, but she made no attempt to break away. Friendless was speaking softly in her ear. 'We have cheese tonight, Darlin'.' He always maintained that she was partial to a hunk of cheddar. 'And I'll tell you a bedtime story.'

I ran to a drinking trough in the corner, doused my handkerchief into the water and hurried back again. Friendless was taking the bit from her mouth.

'Will she let me wash her wound?'

'Dint know.' He waited. 'Will you, Darlin'?' He tipped his head towards her as if she could talk like Bali-something and the other horse, whatever-its-name-was, in Greek mythology. 'She will,' he confirmed, 'Only...' I glanced over and saw that he was close to tears. 'Goo gentle.'

'I will.' I dabbed Old Queeny's muzzle and she shied away. 'I am sorry.' I stroked her nose on the other side and dabbed again. There was a nasty tear in her flesh.

'It will need stitching,' I said and Friendless shied too as if he were the injured party.

'Wint let a nanimal vetnerian near her and she wint neither,' he insisted.

'What about a doctor?' I dabbed the cut again, but it was still bleeding heavily.

'Not old Cronshie,' he objected.

'Dr Cronshaw is dead,' I reminded him.

''Specially not him then.'

'Dr Thorn,' I said. 'My cousin.'

Friendless nodded approvingly. 'Old Queeny like him – dint you, Darlin'?' He stroked her cheek. 'He bring her a bag of carrot he do and advise her on keeping reg'lar hour.'

I was not sure if Rommy would be available, but I felt certain that he would come if he could.

'Do you have a clean cloth?' I asked. 'To stanch her bleeding.'

Friendless patted his pockets, delved in, came out with a squashed slice of pork pie, and put it away again.

'My neckerchief.' He untied a long patchwork cotton scarf, unwound it, and handed it over. Clearly, he and I differed in our concepts of hygiene but, short of ripping a sleeve off my dress, I had nothing better to offer. I folded it and, making what I hoped were reassuring noises, pressed it gently to Old Queeny's wound. She flicked away.

'Now remember what we talk about,' her master reasoned. 'Lady Violet may act funny and have a funny way of speak but tha's not her fault.'

'I am very glad to hear it,' I breathed.

'And she int near so crabbity as they all say.'

Who? I wondered, running through a list of acquaintances that we had in common.

'But tha's only for their jealous for she's beautiful.'

I waited for the next line to crush my vanity but Friendless added, 'Int she?' and Old Queeny submitted to my pressing the scarf to her muzzle.

People were coming closer.

'Best thing's a red-hot poker,' a man with a whalebone leg said. 'Cauterise it like they do my stump.'

'Nobody touch my horse,' Friendless warned. 'I got a human doctor come special from abroad to treat her.'

He had a sketchy idea of where the county of Norfolk was even though it was adjacent to Suffolk.

'If he can come.' I did not want Friendless to set his hopes too high.

'Old nag like that be best in the knacker's yard,' a woman struggling with two buckets of manure, contributed. Had she collected them from Old Queeny?

'Old nag like you best goo there first,' Friendless retorted. 'When the time come, my Old Queeny is set for a home for horses of good character.' He raised his head proudly.

I had mentioned a charity once that took in some retired horses, but I had not made any promises.

Typical of you, Thorn, Ruby flicked her cigarette and blew smoke in the woman's face. *Build up people's hopes then dash them on the jagged reef of despair.*

She made a valid point for I had ruthlessly eliminated every man with whom she fell in love but kept her arch enemy, Count Vorolski Zugravescu, alive and skulking at the end of every adventure.

She is a cruel woman, Hefty concurred incautiously, for his fate still hung in the balance. *I shall never forget how she killed my beloved what-was-her-name?*

By the time the flow of blood slowed, I was soaked in it for the second time in days. Friendless found a length of string he had been saving for a special occasion and we tied the pack around Old Queeny's nose. She was restless again, tossing her head and stamping her front left foot.

'Did anybody see what that boy did to her?' I asked.

'I do,' Friendless said.

'Apart from you.'

'You have to ask them.'

'I was.'

'How do I know tha'?'

'I had my back to you.'

'You have your back at me all the time in my cab, chatterin' away like a hodmedod.'

A what? Ruby asked.

A hedgehog, I translated.

'Does anyone know who the boy was?' I tried to a series of shrugs.

'Int possible to pick him out anyways,' Friendless said. 'Street slugs all look the same.'

'I would recognise him,' I said, and he mulled that over.

'Would int the same as could.'

'We will need assistance.' I raised my voice. 'I shall give sixpence to any of you who help pull this hansom free.' I did a quick calculation. The square had gone from being a haven for stray cats to bustling scene of spectators drawn by the commotion. 'To the first ten of you,' I added but, clearly the inhabitants of the area were not enthusiastic about the prospect of labour and most of them either drifted away or hung back to watch the fun until I doubled my offer.

It only took eight of them five minutes to drag the cab up onto level ground though Old Queeny did most of the actual heaving with Friendless solicitously at her head. Amongst the great advantages of Joseph Hansom's design were the facts that his cabriolet was light and well-balanced, making it easier than rival carriages for a single horse to manage. I paid them all, some disgruntled that they were only given one shilling whilst others were getting two sixpences, four threepences or even a handful of coppers.

The hansom was badly damaged with the running board snapped, the glass shattered, and a lot of paintwork gouged. Luckily, the wheels and axle were intact making it driveable, though the cabin, we soon discovered, was lopsided.

'Oh dear,' I said. 'It does not look good.'

'Course it dint not look good,' Friendless said mournfully. 'It look bad.'

'Let us see if we can get it back to yours,' I suggested. 'We shall get Old Queeny treated first and then we can find a carriage maker to look at this.'

'More like a job for a carriage breaker.' Friendless gave himself a good scratch and I could not disagree with his diagnosis.

'It might not be as bad as it looks.' I found I could disagree with his diagnosis after all.

'Get it when my uncle die.' He ran a hand over a side panel. 'Never afford another – cab, not uncle,' he explained.

'Perhaps we should walk back,' I suggested, 'and give Old Queeny a modicum of rest.' But Friendless would have none of that.

'So we int good 'nough for you now?'

'I did not mean that.'

'And 'wha's a modicron?'

'A bit.'

'Said she speak funny,' he reminded his horse and jerked his thumb towards the running board. 'Hop on then and we say no more 'bout it.'

My Grandmother would have had him flogged for such insolence, which might explain why her groom put a viper in her bed. Legend recounts how it bit her and died but my family history was riddled with conjecture and myths.

Friendless made a stirrup with his hands and, with a great loss of dignity, I managed to scramble up into the seat. My dress looked worse than the cab, but I could not complain about that for, though it would make a dent in my bank balance, I knew that I could replace it.

I half-expected Friendless to walk alongside Old Queeny until I remembered that the hansom is constructed so that the driver's weight lifts much of the load from the back of the horse.

'Whenever you're ready, dear,' he said softly and Old Queeny, head down, began to haul.

'I really think…' I began to protest but she was raising her head and walking quite briskly now.

I glanced back up at the lighthouse as we set off and saw a flash of electric blue and the shape of a woman leaning over the balcony.

Your evil aunt, Igitha, Hefty felt it necessary to explain because there were dozens of other people who were likely to be up there.

Dozens, he pencilled in his notebook. *I shall need all their names and addresses.*

I watched the figure until Friendless gently eased Old Queeny's head around. Was that the figure of a woman in one of the doorways, dressed all in green? If so she melted into the shadows.

Friendless started to groan, I thought, but he was singing mournfully, 'My love is ever so pretty, as everyone confirm, but now she lie in a wooden box, eaten by the worm, eaten by – my oh my – eaten by the worm.' Just when I thought he had finished he repeated his ditty ending, 'the worm what squirm.' He cleared his throat. 'Tha' song always cheer her up, it do.' And treated us both to an unsolicited encore.

Balius and Xanthus, I recalled. *The talking horses of Achilles in the…* My mind went briefly blank. *Iliad.* I treated myself to a fresh stick of Beeman's.

18: CRUELTY AND KINDNESS AND THE MEZZANINE FLOOR

ROMULUS CAME STRAIGHT after receiving my message. Once Thetbury was a day's ride away, but the railway had reduced the journey to less than an hour.

He arrived in the late afternoon, a time that was always a limbo in Thetbury Hall. Afternoon tea would be over, there would not be time to play tennis or croquet, and it would be too early to have a sundowner or dress for dinner. In Break House it was usually time to read through what I had written that morning, unwrite most of it and despair.

Friendless kept Old Queeny in a shed at the end of End Street. It had been used as a store for rabbit skins until a virulent outbreak of snuffles almost eradicated the local population. The rabbits were back in their hordes now, but the furrier had gone bankrupt and Friendless had taken over the building, though I doubted that he had any legal claim to it.

He was waiting outside, smoking a long clay churchwarden pipe, when we arrived.

'Int my place to thank a fine nobleman for comin' 'cross the sea,' he greeted Romulus, 'but, if it is, I thank you with all my kidney.'

'I only hope I can help.' Romulus touched Friendless's arm briefly.

'Hope spring internal,' Friendless expounded and we made our way in. 'She's still a bit fizzed,' he warned, *fizzed* meaning *annoyed*.

'I do not blame her,' I said.

'She dint blame you neither,' he assured me, 'for you try to save her even if you are no use.'

The stable was cleaner than many a house in the area, the floor having been swept and washed down. The hay was neatly stacked in a corner, the tackle hanging off hooks on the wall. The wrecked hansom was parked to the left of a horse-shoulder-high wooden barrier and Old Queeny stood patiently and untethered on the other side. The scarf was still strapped to her nose.

'Hello Queeny,' Rommy greeted her.

'Old Queeny,' Friendless corrected him.

'I beg both your pardons. May I take a look?'

'Take it where?' Friendless asked but my cousin was stepping alongside the horse.

'Could you hold her head?'

'Course I could.' Friendless stood hands in pockets.

'Will you hold it please?'

Friendless did as he was bidden and Rommy put his gladstone bag on a small wooden table which, along with a spindle-backed wooden chair, was the only furniture on the ground floor. Above was a mezzanine loft.

'Tha's my bedroom,' Friendless indicated. I had not known that he slept there but I had seen large families crowded into far more cramped and less salubrious accommodation.

Rommy untied the string to lift the scarf away and Old Queeny shifted uneasily.

'Good girl,' he patted the side of her neck.

'Int a girl,' Friendless said though I had heard him call her that on many an occasion. 'She's a horse.'

Blood was still flowing from the bite and Rommy whistled.

'You're right about one thing,' he told me. 'It will need suturing.'

'I thought you goo stitch it,' Friendless objected.

'It is just another word for stitching,' I explained and he tisked.

'Steam engines, metal ships who float sometime, machines for makin' machines, talkin' frogs,' he marvelled. 'And now 'nother word for stitchin'. What-tever will they think on next?'

I was not sure about the amphibian invention but, in my experience, cabbies often know about things long before the rest of society.

Rommy draped his coat over the chair and rolled up his sleeves. 'Do you have any clean water?'

'There's Old Queeny's bucket,' Friendless offered.

Rommy glanced at it. 'Never mind.' He brought out a hipflask.

'Need to steady your hand?' Friendless asked anxiously.

'To wash them.' Rommy sighed. 'What a waste.' He poured whisky over them both and dried them on a small white towel before bringing out a large C-shaped needle already threaded with catgut.

'Now you aren't going to kick me, are you?' he asked as Old Queeny shifted uneasily.

'She dint kick,' Friendless said indignantly. 'Only sometime.'

'Let us hope this is not one of those times,' I said.

'Now then, darlin',' Friendless put his arms around her neck. 'We talk about this. It hurt, it do, but dint you kill the nice doctor.'

'Perhaps…' Rommy hesitated but he did not like to see a living thing in pain if he could do anything to help. 'Here goes,' he said grimly and put a hand on Old Queeny's nose to steady her. She shifted uneasily.

'Say tha' thing wha' make her laugh,' Friendless urged me.

'What thing?'

'The one about waitin'.'

'Will you wait for me?' I tried in puzzlement, and he grinned.

'Tha's it.' He raised his voice to a shriek that a coloratura soprano would have been hard-pressed to match. 'Dwivaaah weel yooo hwait fowr mih?' He imitated. 'Do it 'gain.'

'I do not sound like that.' Also, I never addressed him as *driver.*

'You do a bit,' Rommy said, and I was so incensed that I hardly noticed that he had passed his needle through Old Queeny's skin and was pulling it out on the other side of the wound. She must have been distracted too for she whinnied softly but made no serious attempt to pull away.

'I…' Friendless rhymed my personal pronoun with *hay*. 'Doo nort sowund like thaaat. Do the first one 'gain.'

'Will you wait for me?' I repeated in a perfectly normal voice to her master's mirth.

'Do another one,' he urged.

'What?' I asked. 'Take me home please?'

'Tha's it,' Friendless guffawed. 'Taaake mih hohhhme plis, dwivaaah.'

Romulus tied a knot but chuckled as he snipped the catgut.

'What is so amusing?' I asked and both men roared, and I was half-convinced that, when Old Queeny snorted, it was more in amusement than discomfort. Even Rommy opened his mouth, probably to offer his own imitation, but thought better of it. At least, I consoled myself as he started the next stitch, all this was distracting the poor animal.

'Take me to Stolham St Ernest,' I tried to an awkward silence.

'Can't do tha',' Friendless said indignantly. 'Dint you see she's undisposed?'

I told you she was heartless, Ruby declared though I could not imagine when she could have conversed with Friendless.

-

'Well, we did not get kicked or bitten,' I commented as Romulus and I walked back towards Seraphim Square.

He selected a Brutus cigarette thoughtfully – though all six of those in his silver case must have been identical – and put it between his lips.

His full lips, Ruby purred.

I thought you were rather taken by Anthony, I said.

I am but he isn't here.

'She's a good horse,' my cousin commented, unaware that my lady adventuress had linked her arm through his. He struck a match, cupping the flame in both hands, and dipped his head to light his Brutus. It was described as having a mild and delicate flavour though how burning leaves could have either of those qualities was beyond me. 'An excellent example of how much better they respond to their owners' kindness than cruelty.'

'He loves her,' I said, stepping around the maggoty corpse of a dead pigeon.

'And she him.' He smiled. 'That's why she trusted me.'

'Why would that boy have done such a thing?' I wondered and he shrugged.

'A cruel joke, if that's what it was, and not much of one if he couldn't hang about to watch the result of his prank.' He inhaled deeply.

'Do you think someone put him up to it?'

'It's possible.' He slowed his pace, aware that his stride was several inches longer than mine and that I was having to break into brief trots to keep up. 'Was anybody laughing?'

'Not that I noticed. There weren't many people about until they came out to see what was happening.'

We waited at the side of the road for an omnibus to pass.

'Now there's an example of what I mean.' Romulus waved his cigarette towards it. 'Even empty that vehicle is one heck of a load for two healthy animals but there must be at least twenty passengers on board, and I doubt those horses have had a decent meal in their miserable lives.'

The driver cracked his whip, lashing a piebald mare, and my cousin gripped his cane.

'What wouldn't I give to see him in harness getting a taste of that?'

He took my arm, brushing an indignant Ruby carelessly aside and we crossed the road.

'Do I really sound like that?'

Rommy laughed. 'Not remotely but it kept Friendless distracted from what was going on and, while he was amused, Old Queeny was more relaxed. Nothing like a distraught owner to alarm a horse or nervous parent to frighten a child.'

'I have not asked about Jane,' I remembered guiltily.

Not that you care. Ruby flicked a stone aside with one of my best umbrellas.

I had been too preoccupied with Old Queeny to talk about his wife when my cousin arrived.

'It is quite obvious that you do care.'

'What?' I puzzled and he managed a hint of a smile.

'Ruby does not always keep her views to herself.'

'Oh Lord,' I sighed. 'Have I been thinking out loud?'

'Again,' he confirmed.

'How is she?'

'Suffering,' he said in a muted monotone. 'In all honesty, Violet, I am surprised that she is still alive.'

I stopped in shock. He had told me many times over the last year that she was not getting better and, once before, that her life expectancy was poor, but this was almost as if he had passed the death sentence on her himself.

His face was frozen as we approached my front door.

'Oh Rommy.' I took his hand.

'I must go,' he said.

'Have you not even time for a drink?'

'God knows I could do with one.' He squeezed my hand. His voice went up the best part of an octave. 'Bat I weesh to ketch the nehxt trayn to Thaytford if I cahn.'

'I hate you,' I laughed and punched his arm.

'Goodbye Violet.' He bent to kiss my cheek, but I took told of him and held on tight.

'Don't. Please.' He pulled away. 'You're a strong woman, Violet. Be strong for Jane and me.'

And, with that, he was gone.

Am I strong? I wondered as I watched him stride through the crowd.

You could be in a travelling show, Hefty assured me, *bending iron bars over your back.*

I went inside to dip that dagger in curare.

19: THE BLOOD OF THE WASP

GERRUND HAD GONE out to confront the butcher over the amount of filler in his sausages.

'Enough sawdust to carpet the floor of Ye Olde Cock Inn,' he had complained to me. At Hettie's request he had prepared pilchards and toast for her lunch. Agnust was busy being Agnust and so I, having nothing better to do other than decide Havelock Hefty's fate, took Hettie's tray up to her.

Somewhat to my surprise, my friend was out of bed and in the process of getting dressed.

'I know you want to keep me prisoner here forever.' She glanced at her reflection in my cheval mirror, apparently satisfied with the way that her hair was almost pinned up. 'And I don't want to seem ungrateful, Violet, but I do think I ought to make an effort to go home.'

'I quite agree,' I said, and she cocked an eyebrow. 'You must get on with your life and work when you feel up to it, but not yet.'

'Yet never comes.' Hettie reached behind but gave up. 'And neither does never.' If there is one reason that every lady needs a sister, a friend, or a maid, it is because it is almost impossible to fasten one's own dress. I went behind to assist. 'Anyway,' she said as I fumbled with the first button. 'Agnust has told me all about your adventure.'

I nearly asked to which one she was referring but that would have revealed that I had been in peril more than once.

'What did she tell you?'

'How poor Old Queeny nearly crashed over the edge of the quarry.'

'She had no business worrying you whilst you are unwell.'

'She seems to think it was all your fault.'

I was still struggling. Hettie made most of her clothes herself and the buttonholes were often slightly too big or a fraction too small.

Do not pretend that you understand fractions. Miss Kidd tossed my exercise book aside.

'If Agnust caught a cold while I was fifty miles away, she would blame me.'

'Are you alright though?'

'I was a little bruised and shaken,' I managed three more buttons and the second came undone. 'But nothing was broken other than Friendless's cab. Poor Old Queeny came off the worst. Her lip was quite badly gouged.'

'By a rat, I heard.'

'A street boy dropped it into her nosebag.'

'The little horror,' she said. 'I hope it bit him in the process.'

'Sadly not.' I forced another button through. 'Romulus stitched her up. Breath in.'

'Has he asked you to check my respiration?'

'No, your dress is too tight, and I cannot get the sides to align with each other.'

'Gerrund has been overfeeding me.' Hettie inhaled and tucked her waist into a shape that might arouse the attentions of any red-blooded male wasp that she encountered.

'And me.' I got the second button back in. Only five to go.

Ruby picked up a nailfile. *Wasps do not have blood, red or otherwise.*

'How will Friendless manage?' Hettie asked.

'Old Queeny should be able to work again soon.' I finished the buttons at a rush 'But his hansom is in a bad way. However, I told him that I know a man who owes my family a favour and will repair it for free.'

'Really?'

'Yes, I really told him that.'

She looked at me severely.

'And were you telling him truth?'

'Not quite.' I wrapped a wide cream ribbon around her waist. 'It is irreparable and so I have ordered a new one.'

'But that will cost you a fortune.'

'I still have Great Aunt Herbena's bequest.' I tied the ribbon in a bow at the side and helped myself to a triangle of her buttered toast. She owed me that much and it was nice and crispy.

How lovely for you. Ruby replaced the file on my dressing table and unscrewed the lid of my pot of Hodges and Hodge, Cold Cream of Roses. *When you have made me eat quivering…*

Don't. Hefty shied away because it was certain to be something disgusting.

Quince jelly. Ruby sat at my dressing table.

'You cannot spend all that,' Hettie worried, and I retraced my steps to remind myself that she was talking about my inheritance.

'I will not starve without it, but Friendless and Old Queeny will without a hansom.' I took another bite of toast. 'You must never tell him that it is a new one.'

'But surely he will know.'

'I have commissioned the carriagemaker to fit all the old upholstery into it.'

It would take a month, he had forecast.

'Do it in a week and I will pay you double,' I had bargained.

Bargained? Hefty expostulated for I had refused to let him travel in the comfort of RMS Azalea.

'It must be costing you two fortunes,' Hettie fretted though she had not worried when she had spent a month's allowance on a Greek statue that was made in Southend. 'Are you mad?'

Ruby dipped her fingers in my face cream. *Do you really have to ask her that?*

'As you are well aware.' I waved my half-triangle of toast airily, scattering crumbs over the sheets. 'My books bring in far more revenue than I could ever hope to spend.'

'Oh Violet,' Hettie said sadly. 'You used to be such an accomplished liar.'

'And you did not even thank me when the Azalea sank with no survivors,' I scolded Hefty who had done little but complain recently.

Did I imagine it or did Hettie edge away?

'Azaleas?' she puzzled. 'Are you sure it was only me who had a head injury?'

'Yes,' I said less confidently than I might have. 'Anyway, I am glad to see you up and dressed but you must not leave until Rommy gives you permission.'

I braced myself for an outburst about her not needing permission from a mere man, but Hettie only shrugged. 'Very well.' She flopped back onto the bed, the effort proving too much for her. 'But please leave me now. I can't bear you looking at me as if I were an orphan in the snow.'

I laughed. 'I shall never think of you in those terms.' And went off to pay the carriagemaker half his fee.

There was a faint rumbling sound as I made my way home. Could it be the sound of Great Aunt Herbena rolling in her lead-lined coffin in the Strainge family vault?

20: *SQUIRE WOOLTON AND THE HOOK*

AGNUST OPENED THE door whilst I was unlocking it. Many people rang a bell to be admitted to their own houses rather than go through the considerable drudgery of inserting and turning a key. None of those people had the slightest consideration for a servant who might be on another floor at the other end of the house.

'Another on those letter come,' she declared as I stepped over the threshold.

'When?' I asked.

'After you go out and afore you come back.' She folded her arms, watching to ensure that I was wiping my feet the regulation eighteen times on the mat.

'In the post or delivered by hand?' I hung my cloak on the hook, unpinned my hat, and laid it on the table.

'Deliver by hand,' Agnust replied, 'in the post.' She looked at me critically. 'What happen to tha' dunt hat you stick on your head yisdee?' *Dunt* meant stupid though I could not see why everybody had taken against it. Mrs Grayside had assured me that it was quite the thing.

'I lost it.' I knew better than to admit that I had been fighting with Aunt Igitha. My maid would be certain to blame me.

Agnust tutted, took my cloak down and rehung it on the adjacent hook.

'Brawlin' with your aunt, I daresay,' she daresaid.

'She attacked me,' I protested.

'You should have defend yourself.'

'I did.'

'You should have stuck her with a hatpin.'

I stepped back to look into those plumbless brown eyes. Did the woman have mystical powers? If so, I wished she would use them to get rid of the spiders who were shrouding my ceilings in lace.

'I did.'

'And left her on her balc'ney, I s'pose.' Agnust returned my cloak to its original hook. 'Scratby came and go and, in the 'tween times, he say you owe him the thruppence he have to pay a street slug to goo let her in. I tell him he owe you thruppence for a new hat.'

I was not sure when, if ever, Agnust had bought any headwear that cost so little but, at that moment, there were more important concerns.

More important than ones costume? Ruby slotted her umbrella into the stand. *I hardly think so.*

'Where is the letter?' I put a stray tress behind my ear, but it dropped forwards again.

'I put it on your desk.' Agnust blinked so slowly that I was beginning to wonder if she were falling asleep. 'The one downstair.' She refused to call it an *escritoire*, being convinced that the word was indecent.

We went into my sitting room where Hefty awaited me, extra-powerful-magnifying spectacles clipped to his nose. Agnust had weighted the letter down with a book at each corner to ensure that it could not escape. The address had been written in red ink again. I slit the envelope open to find, as before, a torn-out sheet of paper.

> YOU WERE LUCKIER THAN SQUIRE WOOLTON. HE GOT THROWN OFF HIS HORSE AND BROKE HIS NECK. THE POLICE NEVER NOTICED THERE WAS A TACK UNDER THE SADDLE. HA! HA! NEVER FEAR I SHALL GET YOU NEXT TIME. MM.

Gerrund joined us.

'Are you recovered from your accident, milady?' He glanced over. 'Another One? What does it say?'

'See for yourself.' I passed it to him.

'Hell's teeth,' he breathed, running his finger under each word, though he was perfectly literate. 'MM,' he read aloud.

March Middleton, Ruby suggested. She could never forgive the goddaughter of Sidney Grice, the famous Gower Street Detective, for existing in the real world. *Anyone can do that,* Ruby scoffed, *but how long does she think she could last in your warped imagination?*

'The Montford Maniac,' Gerrund said so softly that I suspected he had not intended me to hear, before raising his voice. 'We must go to the police.'

'I must go,' I declared.

'Then I shall come with you. You cannot go out alone, milady.'

I nearly protested that I would be perfectly safe before realising that I had no grounds for such an assertion. On the other hand, I would not spend the rest of my life going out and about with an escort.

If you do not, the rest of your life might not be very long, Ruby warned.

I shall send for reinforcements, Havelock Hefty promised, and I was sure that his intentions were good. Unfortunately, I was equally sure that they could not be of any practical help.

'Lot of use you do be if he come at her with an axe.' Agnust spoke so confidently that I wondered if she were privy to the plot against me.

'I shall take my gun,' Gerrund vowed.

'Lot of use that do be if you get stuck with a sword from behind.'

'And what good would you be if you do?' he challenged.

I had envisaged an uneventful walk to the police station but, now it appeared that I was stepping into a pitched battle.

'How many times you been stabbed?' she countered.

'Once,' he admitted.

'Well,' Agnust rested her fists on her hips. 'I been stabbed two time, one in my head. So I do have more experience than you.'

All these incidents were news to me, though I had known my maid all my life, but I was more concerned with the immediate future than their squabbles and disquieting reminiscences.

'We shall all go.' I pretended to decide what had been decided for me. 'But I shall speak to Inspector Stanbury alone, if he is there.'

If only you had invested in one of those new electrical talking machines, Ruby swivelled her eyes and I followed their gaze.

'I shall telephone to make an appointment.' I was getting quite good at simulating decisiveness, I thought, but my characters were not impressed.

Real decisiveness would be better, Hefty told me as I went to call the operator.

-

As I had expected – or hoped – our progress to the police station was uneventful, the most dramatic event being when Hefty arrested a police constable for impersonating a police constable. Fortunately, I was the only one to notice.

Time to live in the real world, Thorn, I told myself.

Don't listen to yourself, Ruby urged as we arrived.

Agnust and Gerrund waited outside. It would not do to enter the station with a bodyguard.

Sergeant Webb was at the desk as usual. He was currently engaged in the construction of a matchstick model. It had doubled in size to almost six inches high since I had last seen it. He would not say what it was meant to be, and I suspected that he had not yet decided.

'The Inspector say goo straight through,' he told me, and I hoped that he would be able to open his charge book when it was next required for there was glue over the cover and down the side.

Alfred Stanbury listened to my account of the crash with only a few interruptions for clarification.

'And you are quite recovered?'

'Just bruised and shaken.'

He clicked his tongue. 'Your mother always claims that the Thorn women are indestructible, and I am beginning to believe she is right.'

'It would be nice to think so,' I said though I could name a goodly number who had done what we all must do, sooner or later, and quit this earth. 'And then I got this.' I handed him the letter. 'It arrived while I was out, but Agnust does not know when.'

'Same handwriting.' He opened the envelope. 'So presumably from the same person.'

'It seems to be,' I concurred as he read it.

'Not so easy to dismiss as the last one. I don't suppose you have that with you?'

'No but I can drop it in.'

He held the letter up to the light.

Try these. Hefty proffered his special extra-powerful-magnifying spectacles.

If you want to look like an owl. Ruby put them on herself to demonstrate how enormous it made her eyes.

Give those back. Hefty reached out but she whisked away.

'I remember Squire Woolton,' Alfred mused, oblivious to the tussle that was occurring in his office. 'I was sergeant at the time, and it was not one of my cases. Lived in one of the Hams, Stolham St Ernest, I think.' He picked up a pencil for no other reason than to put it down again. 'I'll check the files, but the chances are that the letter is right and that his death was reported as an accident. It would be almost impossible to contradict that verdict now.'

'It is a Silver Lane postmark again,' I pointed out. 'That should help a bit.'

'Not very much.' He rose to consult a large, framed map on his wall. 'There are nine post boxes in the Silver Lane area.' He prodded all the red dots with his fingertip. 'And each of those is emptied six times a day. This must have been posted between six in the evening and seven the next morning but there would be dozens, if not hundreds, of letters in the first collection. I can send a man to enquire – an address written in red ink would stand out – but it's unlikely the writer was stupid enough to go into the post office in person – and nobody would notice somebody dropping a letter in a box.' He went back behind his desk, and I sat to face him across it.

'What about my Aunt Igitha?' I asked. 'She must be a prime suspect.'

'For the letters or the attack on Old Queeny?'

'Both – and the panther.'

He picked up his ebony rule.

'Did she know you were calling on her?'

'I think she was expecting me, but she could not have known when I would arrive. Not unless…'

Alfred tapped his rule on a pile of papers as if performing a magic trick.

'What?' he leaned forwards.

'Scratby, her butler, said he had been watching me so I suppose, if he heard me announce my destination, he could have gone ahead and warned her.'

He laid the rule flat. 'You don't seem convinced.'

I picked a loose stray black hair from my sleeve. It was almost certainly one of mine but Hefty sealed it in an envelope.

'He is a striking man, very tall and skeletal. I am almost sure that I would have noticed him.'

'Almost?'

'I was busy looking for a cab.'

He exhaled heavily. 'I will go and have a word with your aunt.'

'Can I come?'

'You cannot.' He rolled the rule to and fro under his palm. 'No doubt, she will deny everything but, at least, it might give her pause for thought to know that she is under suspicion. In the meantime, I shall put a man on your front door.'

'Is that really necessary?'

'I hope not but it's a sensible precaution.'

'I would rather that you did not,' I said. 'People will think that I am under surveillance. Half of Montford probably thinks that I am a loose woman, living alone with gentlemen calling. Besides which, I have Gerrund and Agnust to protect me.'

'As you wish.' He half-shrugged and completely clicked his tongue.

'If it is not her.' I took a breath. 'You do think it possible that it could be the maniac?' Even as I spoke the words, I knew how foolish they sounded and Alfred Stanbury grimaced.

'If you want the truth...'

I was not sure that I did but found myself saying, 'I do.'

'That thought did occur to me, but I did not want to alarm you unnecessarily. As you know, the original killer was never apprehended though my predecessors hoped that he was dead. It might be an imitator but yes,' Stanbury concluded, 'it is possible that the Montford Maniac has returned.'

21: *A QUIET FUNERAL*

SAMMMY FLOWERDEW WAS given a quiet funeral. As a suicide, he could not be buried on consecrated ground. The family did not want the shame of having him lying in a grave outside the cemetery along with assorted drunks, bankrupts or wronged women driven to taking their own lives. And so, Sammy was laid to rest in the grounds of his family home in Blockborough. No announcement was made and, despite my request in a letter of condolence, I was not informed when the interment would take place.

He had been such a happy child but his decline, I believed, had started with an accident.

Jack had called at Thetbury Hall. Would I like to play with him and Sammy?

'I hardly think so,' Polly, the maid, said haughtily, for all boys were nasty and rough to her mind, but I was already lacing up my outside boots. Excepting Hettie, I much preferred the company of boys and the three of us had been friends for years by then.

Sammy had been given an air rifle and we all took turns shooting at tin cans balanced on a fence. Apart from being older than me, the boys had played at this before and were much better than I. Neither of them mocked me, though they ragged each other over their misses. The gun was more powerful than I had expected, tearing holes in the metal as if it were paper.

It was Sammy's idea to do a variation of William Tell's feat and shoot a can off my head, but I declined. Jack was less timid, or more foolhardy, and volunteered to let Sammy perform the trick on him. I begged him not to, but the game went ahead. Sammy's first shot went to one side; his second was too high; but the third sent the can flying. It was Jack's turn with the rifle next, again, I declined to take part. Again I implored them to stop but Sammy stood in front of the fence laughing at my concerns as his friend took aim.

On the first shot Sammy cried out and fell to his knees, clutching his face. When Jack rushed over and pulled his friend's hand away, Sammy's eye was a bloody pulp. Jack tried to stanch it with his handkerchief. When that failed, he ripped off his shirt and I clamped the tail to Sammy's face while Jack, being more fleet of foot than I, ran back to the house for help.

'It wasn't Jack's fault,' Sammy claimed repeatedly. 'I jumped.' It was noble of him, I thought, to be more anxious to save Jack getting into trouble than about his own injury.

Our family doctor came, and Sammy was taken into the scullery where at least there was a plentiful supply of clean water and towels. Jack waited with me in the nursery. He was so pale and shaken that one might have thought that he was injured which I supposed, in a way, he was.

'Why couldn't Sammy have shot me?' he wondered shakily. 'Then this would never have happened to him.'

'And he would be feeling just as you are now.'

'It was a dashed stupid game.' He toyed absently with the whip from my spinning top. 'I must have been mad to have played it.'

'Sammy suggested the idea.'

'I don't understand it. I've always been such a good shot.'

'I saw him move and Sammy told me himself that he jumped,' I tried to console him, but Jack's face was glistening.

'I'm not crying.' He flung the whip down.

'I know you are not, and I would never tell anyone that you were.'

Jack blew his nose. 'You're a good sport, Violet.'

Agnust came to report on Sammy's progress.

The doctor had managed to stop the bleeding, but he could not save Sammy's eye. Nor could he operate in such conditions with so little equipment and, anyway, it was probably safer to leave the pellet where it was, lodged deep in Sammy's brain.

Afterwards Sammy used to joke that it had probably drilled some sense into him, but he changed after that. He always had a serious side but now he became anxious and prone to periods of deep depression. Sometimes he would stop talking in the middle of sentences, oblivious to our voices, clicking our fingers or waving in front of his eyes. Romulus told me later that these were episodes of *petit mal* – minor epileptic attacks.

Sammy was given a glass eye but found it painful to wear and so he sported an eyepatch and learned to live with the other boys calling him *Blackbeard*.

Through all these events, the three of us remained good friends and possibly even closer, for I was never keen on hunting and Sammy, once a keen rider, was forbidden by his parents to mount a horse. Jack became very protective of him, fighting more than one village boy who had mocked the slight hesitation that developed in Sammy's speech or made piratical noises. His greatest anger though was reserved for Shillidge, the pigman, who had tossed a shovel of manure over me – accidently, he claimed – but I had had too many mishaps at his hands by then. Shillidge was a big man and built like a prize fighter, but Jack knocked him to the ground with a flurry of punches.

Having left Shillidge sprawled in the filth of the yard that the pigman was supposed to keep clean, Jack picked me up and carried me towards the house.

'I can walk,' I admitted reluctantly, for I rather liked his attention. Also, I was aware of the envious looks that a milkmaid had given me.

'I know,' said Jack with a wink, but did not put me down.

–

Hettie made her escape from the confines of Break House. I tried to dissuade her, but she was missing her studio.

It is cruel to keep her here, Hefty scolded me for my friend was yet another distraction from my deciding his fate. *Reprieving me,* he clarified.

'Your home is too comfortable,' Hettie explained. 'Artists are meant to suffer.'

'Millais lives well,' I pointed out.

'Which proves my point.' She lit one of her monstrous cigarettes largely, I suspected, to help convince me that she should go. 'When Millais was poor, he painted *Ophelia* in her beautiful death. When he became wealthy, he churned out *Bubbles.*'

We all helped her home and made sure that she was settled in. Gerrund still cooked for her and Agnust or I delivered her meals three times a day until she told us that she preferred to fend for herself. She grew stronger and my visits less frequent. Anthony often came with me or went by himself.

'She wants to paint me,' he told me one afternoon. 'But who would want my portrait?'

Actually I would, I wanted to say but muttered cruelly, 'I cannot imagine.' His face fell. 'Who would not,' I added hastily, and his wounded pride healed in an instant.

How fickle men are, Ruby commented. *Thank goodness.*

–

Lancelot Overstrand cursed and lunged forwards.

I put my Magic Pencil down, opened my little box of Beeman's, took out a stick and paced the room. If I killed Havelock Hefty, I wondered, would he disappear from my imagination? He annoyed me sometimes and his observations could be distracting. On the other hand, he was brave and loyal and at least kept an eye on Ruby.

He was no use when I was trapped in a coffin over a furnace, Ruby pointed out, though she would never have forgiven me if I had sent a man to rescue her.

‘Oh, for goodness’ sake.’ The builders were hard at work next door, and it sounded like they were trying to demolish my house. I returned to the desk and picked up my pencil.

But Scotland Yard’s premier detective was too quick for him, Hefty prompted.

There was a tapping at my window. I tried to ignore it, but it continued. The local pigeons were becoming a nuisance because of visitors to Montford feeding them. Gerrund had suggested putting spikes on the sills, but I was concerned that they might make a hasty escape difficult in the event of a fire.

The knocking grew louder. I glanced over and saw a hand rapping on the glass. Had the workmen set up a ladder in my back garden? If so, this was an intolerable intrusion. I replaced my pencil and still-wrapped chewing gum on my blotting pad.

I shall have them arrested, Hefty volunteered, *except,* he remembered, *trespass is not actually a crime.*

Men, Ruby snorted. *They are all useless.* But I noticed that she was no help either.

Sighing, I rose to my feet. There was a rope hanging down. Were they lowering a bucket onto my patio? Builders on the other side had spilt cement onto a flowerbed once. I went over just as a woman’s head appeared with long grey-brown hair straggling loosely over her face. Stupidly, I was about to remonstrate with her when I realised that something was very wrong. Her complexion was maroon, and her mouth gaped as if she were gasping for air. The head rose another foot or so and I saw that her other hand was clawing at the rope and that it was in a noose, tight around her neck.

I ran the last few steps, undid the catch, and wrenched the lower sash up. At about ten inches it jammed. I could not remember the last time that I had opened it and the wood must have warped. Reaching through, I managed to grasp one shoulder of the woman’s dress, but I could not lift her, nor could I possibly drag her through the gap.

‘I am sorry.’ I let go of the cloth and rushed to fling open the door. ‘Gerrund!’ I yelled. ‘Agnust! Come quickly. Both of you. Now! This is an emergency.' I blew my whistle. 'Agnust! Gerrund!' But there was no response.

I looked about for something else with which to make a noise but there was nothing except myself. I screamed and heard some movement downstairs.

'If tha's a hairyleg,' Agnust called up. 'You need goo catch it yoursel'.' She was the one who was afraid of spiders which might have been why she steered clear of their woven traps.

'There's a woman being hanged outside my window.'

'You writin' one on your stories?'

'A real woman,' I yelled.

'I'm coming, Milady.' Gerrund appeared at the foot of the stairs.

'Bring a knife or something. We need to cut her down.'

'Be there in a minute.' He disappeared towards the kitchen.

Agnust came pounding up the stairs.

'Through here.' I pointed though she knew, as well as I, where my study was.

She stopped. 'How do she get there?'

'She just appeared.'

The woman had her hand through the window now and was clutching the lower frame presumably trying to pull herself up. Agnust grasped the sash and heaved.

'Stuck.' She banged the side of the sash and tried again, the muscles in her neck bulging and her veins standing out. 'Proper stuck,' she declared to the sound of heavy footsteps approaching fast.

Without a word Gerrund barged her aside, put his knife on the sill, hammered each side of the sash and strained to raise it.

'Stuck,' he diagnosed and picked up his knife. With its long, heavy blade, it was what I called his ox-slaughterer. 'I'll have to cut her down.'

I knew I had suggested that, but another problem occurred to me.

'The fall will kill her,' I objected.

‘Might not,’ he reasoned, ‘but the rope surely will.’

The woman’s grip loosened, and her hand fell away. I tried to grab it but was too slow.

‘Wait on,’ Agnust said. ‘I’ll catch her.’

She made for the corridor.

‘But,’ I objected, ‘she could kill you.’

‘Wint do tha’,’ she sniffed. ‘She int in no condition to kill a fly.’

‘No I…’ But Agnust was thundering back down again before I could explain that I meant the weight of the woman falling from such a height.

More footsteps and a pause and then we heard her calling, ‘Wha’ you waiting for? A written invitation?’

‘Excuse me, milady.’ Gerrund brushed by, crouching to reach through the gap and hack at the rope. It was little more than a cord. The strands frayed and parted almost immediately. There was one thin twist of fibres left and, with a last slash, it split, and the woman fell out of view.

‘Did you get her?’ I called but there was no reply.

‘Agnust?’ Gerrund shouted but, again, she did not respond.

We pressed our faces to the pane but could not see any closer than a holly bush some ten feet from the house.

‘Do you think…’ I hesitated.

‘Soon find out.’ Gerrund rushed from the room with me in pursuit. Down the stairs we hurtled, along the corridor and through the open back door.

Agnust lay on her back, the woman prone in her arms.

‘Near kill me, you do,’ she gasped. ‘Just ’cause I say I’m ready, dint mean I am.’

Gerrund went on his haunches and lifted the woman off. Her limbs hung limp as Gerrund laid her on her back on the gravel. Grass had never grown well in my back garden and so I’d had the scant lawn dug up and replaced by gravel. I crouched. Her face was darkest purple. The cord had dug deep into the flesh of her thin neck, and I could not slide my fingers underneath it.

'Leave it to me, milady.' Gerrund unhinged a clasp knife. 'There's a knot at the side here.' Carefully he worked the blade into it, flicking upwards to cut and pull the noose apart. I watched the woman's eyes the whole time. They did not move or even flicker but stared wide at the cloudless sky. Gerrund threw the rope aside and bent over to listen for any breath. As I had proved with Hettie I was not very good at finding pulses, but I knew, even as I tried, that there would be none to discover.

Agnust was struggling to her feet, a major undertaking since she had nothing with which to pull herself up.

'Dead,' she diagnosed. Somebody had to say it.

I looked in fascinated horror. 'I do not understand.'

'It mean she int alive,' Agnust explained.

'No. I do not understand what has happened.'

'She got hung outside your study window.' My maid prodded the remnants of the noose with the square toe of her outsized boot.

'Yes, but how and why?'

Gerrund got to his feet and surveyed the scene. 'I can tell you how.' He pointed towards my roof. 'See that pole there?' I shielded my eyes. It was about fifteen feet long and attached high on the wall, just under the eaves, next door. A mechanism of metal wheels was fixed to the free end of it and the third-floor window nearest to my house was open. 'She was hung from their top floor and swung out on the pole. A child could raise and lower her with that pulley system.' Gerrund folded his clasp knife.

'The man or men working on next door's roof,' I realised, and he nodded.

I surveyed the dead woman again and judged her to be in her sixties. Her face was raw in several places, probably from it being scraped against my wall. She was dressed in black bombazine.

The heels of her shoes were polished, but the toes were scuffed, and her fingers were raw. The results – I conjectured – of her scrabbling as she tried to climb up through my window.

Rather late I remembered to pray. 'May the Lord have mercy upon your soul.'

'Amen,' Agnust and Gerrund responded.

Together we straightened the dead woman's clothes and hair as best we could and folded her arms across her chest before I closed her eyes. The lids crept open again. We would need two coins.

Something white caught my eye. A sheet of paper fluttered by and Agnust stamped at it but missed. Gerrund bent and picked it up. 'Another letter.' He handed it to me. 'Most likely came out of her pocket.' He pointed to where a black handkerchief poked out of a slit in the side of her dress.

A LITTLE PRESENT FOR YOU, I read. *DON'T WORRY THERE ARE PLENTY MORE. HA HA HA! YOUR OLD FRIEND, MM.*

I went inside to make a telephone call.

Ruby was reclining on my chaise longue browsing a copy of The English Ladies' Magazine. Her lips parted but she did not speak and, when I looked again, she had gone. Even Ruby knew when her presence was not appropriate.

–

Alfred Stanbury came with two men in uniform. I recognised the lean weather-beaten one as Constable Cooper. It was he who had attended when I saw a woman die outside my house and I had not been impressed by his performance. The other I had come across but did not know.

Alfred scrutinised the body and searched the pocket, finding only the handkerchief. He clipped open a silver broach on her breast to reveal a photograph of a bespectacled man in one half and a curl of light brown hair in the other. Presumably this was for whom she was in mourning.

'Any idea who she was?' he checked.

'It might be Mrs Hatchpenny, the widow who lived next door,' I speculated.

'It do be her,' Agnust declared.

I looked again. 'I believe you are right.'

'Right is as right do,' she pronounced sagely.

'Did she live alone?' Stanbury clipped shut the broach, a memento of two people separated by death and, one could only hope, reunited by it.

'Just her maid and a live-out cook.' Agnust closed Mrs Hatchpenny's eyes, and I was about to tell her that we needed two pennies when I saw that the lids had stayed closed.

Alfred paced around the garden. 'Well the evidence would appear to support your theory of how it was done,' he told Gerrund and crouched to pick up the rope. 'Whoever it was knew his knots.' He stood up. 'Stay here, Bunleigh,' he ordered one constable. 'I'm going to see if there's anybody in next door. And you, Cooper, get a stretcher and a blanket from the van.'

He was back a few minutes later.

'No reply.' He glanced at me. 'Is that back gate locked – apart from the bolts, I mean?'

'I'll get the key,' Gerrund volunteered.

'How well did you know her?' He asked. 'I know you didn't recognise her, but faces can change a lot in a hanging. They swell and darken dramatically.'

'I do not think I had more than three glimpses of her coming out of or going into her house since I came here and I think she was wearing a veil,' I replied. 'She was so quiet I was hardly even sure if she was there or not most of the time.'

Gerrund came back and unlocked the back gate.

'Wait here,' Alfred told us all and disappeared into the lane.

The constables lifted Mrs Hatchpenny onto a stretcher, covered her with a blanket and took her away. At their superior's insistence they used the back gate and brought a black maria along the lane. There was little point in advertising that she had died on my property.

Agnust was sitting on my garden bench. I had never seen her so subdued.

'Promise your parents I look after you,' she said.

'And you do,' I assured her. 'You cannot hold yourself responsible for what happened today.'

'I daint.' She untied and tried to retie her apron, but the bow proved too complicated for her distressed state of mind. 'And I daint entirely blame you.'

'But why would you blame me at all?'

She was still fumbling with her bow. 'Trouble follow you like a butterfly follow a cloud, it do.'

I had not heard that expression before and was not sure that it was true.

'I do not think this had anything to do with me.'

'Nothin' to do with you?' She looked at me incredulously. 'Havin' dead bodies climbin' up the side of your house?' She cleared her throat. 'Wha' kind of behavin' way is tha' for a young lady of old breedin'?'

I sat beside her. 'Would you like to go back to Thetbury?'

'And leave you to get up to your tricks?' Agnust jutted her jaw. 'I'd sooner eat jam.'

'But you like jam.'

'Tha's why I'd sooner eat it.'

Alfred returned.

'The back gate and door were unlocked,' he told us. 'I found the maid.' He rubbed his chin. 'She was dead.'

'How?' I asked.

'Throat cut,' he said, 'and by the looks of her, she had been dead a good few days.'

Anthony said he had spoken to her, I recalled but decided to wait until I had talked to him before I said anything to the police.

Alfred lit a cigar.

'I want you to go home, Violet,' he said.

'Lady Violet to you, Inspector,' Agnust corrected him.

'I *am* at home,' I told him.

'To Thetbury Hall,' he clarified. 'I do not think you are safe here.'

I rose to my feet and said, 'I cannot put my family in any danger.' But did not give him the real reason for my obstinacy. He would never let anybody drive him from his home and I was blowed if I would either.

22: *THE BLACK WIDOW*

WORD DID WHAT it often does when you do not want it to; it got out quickly. *The Chronic* produced a special evening edition and, in response to the newspaper seller's chants, Gerrund had gone out to purchase a copy on my behalf. It was a slim affair, slender on facts but bloated with sensational speculations.

THE BLACK WIDOW, the headline proclaimed, going on to state, as if it were an unequivocal fact, that Mrs Hatchpenny had murdered her servant and hanged herself in remorse. The maid was Annie Waters and was fifteen years old. She had come from Norwich two years ago. The reporter at least got some facts right, according to Agnust.

In the second paragraph I discovered that she had lived next door to *Lady Violet Thorn, the mysterious, reclusive writer of penny dreadfuls.*

Tuppeny shockers surely, Havelock Hefty seethed.

As a matter of fact I wrote books and had short stories published in fairly reputable magazines. A junior sub-editor of *The Strand* had even gone to the trouble of writing a personal – possibly too personal – rejection letter to me.

Hefty clenched his jaws on a new briar pipe so hard that I heard the mouthpiece cracking. *Blow and botheration,* he cursed. I had had both those words deleted from one of my manuscripts.

I skimmed over the rest of the article. Vivid and lifelike – i.e. deathlike – illustrations were promised for the morning edition. At least they did not know that she had died in my garden, I comforted myself.

Nobody even thought about having lunch and I did not feel hungry when Gerrund mentioned dinner. For once Agnust did not nag me to eat.

'You alway be a greedy girl,' declared the woman who bullied me daily into stuffing myself. 'Tidy wonder you int fat.' And I was about to ask her to justify that statement when she proceeded to do so. 'Push so much food in your crop it get pushed out by the next mouthful before your lights dissolve it.'

I had an idea that the lungs play no part in the digestive process and that Romulus might dispute a few other points of her argument, but it was easier to say, 'Oh' and so I did.

'I could make you a sandwich,' Gerrund suggested. 'Cheese and pickle?'

'Thank you.'

There was quite a hubbub outside and, above it all, the cries of vendors. They were working late. A coffee stall keeper had set up his stand close by. I had sampled his wares once and never had a finer mug of chicory. Somebody else was selling gingerbread figures, a harmless trade I thought, until she yelled hoarsely, *Get your Hatchpenny figure, noose round her neck. Get your Annie, throat cut open wide.* From the number of times she croaked *There you are, sir* or *madam,* she was doing vigorous business.

Agnust had closed the curtains after a few people had pressed their faces to the window. As the Romans had proved in the Colosseum, there is nothing like cruel killings to entertain the masses and there had been two gruesome deaths over which these good townsfolk could thrill.

The doorbell rang and, whilst Agnust and I debated who it could be at this hour – 'A gawking ghoul, I'll warrant,' – Gerrund went to answer it. 'I'll soon send him packing.'

'Couldn't send a postcard to himself,' Agnust jibed but he was not yet out of earshot.

'At least I could write one,' he responded though he knew that, unlike many of her class, Agnust was literate. Her father had been the first of her family to be able to sign his name, albeit in block capitals.

The voices grew louder as Gerrund opened the door. A moment later he closed it, and the babble was muted.

'It's Mrs Bottle,' he announced on his return. 'She was getting jostled, so I took the liberty of admitting her. There's quite a mob out there now.'

Let me deal with them, Hefty said valiantly but sidled off, muttering something about fetching a squadron of mounted police when I failed to demur.

'Then you had better show her in.' I checked my hair in the mirror.

Not too bad, Ruby reassured me, *if you wish to audition for the role of Medusa.* Needless to say her coiffure was perfect.

Petunia Bottle hurried in, looking rather flustered in a striking fern green-of-course costume.

'I am so sorry to disturb you.' She took both my hands in hers. 'But I read about what happened and I was terrified that it might have involved you.'

Terrified? Hefty combed through the feathers on her hat in search of an elusive clue. *She hardly knows you.*

'Why?' Agnust put her hands on her hips. 'You think milady do it? 'Cause she might of but she dint.'

'I was worried that your mistress may have been hurt.'

'Hmmm.' Agnust viewed her mistrustfully.

'That will be all, thank you, Agnust.'

'Mind she dint attack you,' my maid advised but, since she was lumbering away, it was not clear who she was warning about whom.

'Would you like a drink?' I indicated to the row of decanters, regretting my action as soon as I did so. It had been my intention to usher my caller away but now I was encouraging her to stay.

'What are you having?'

'A whisky.'

'How degenerate,' Petunia said. 'So shall I.'

I smiled, though there was little to feel happy about, and poured us both a good measure.

'There's quite a mob out there now.' She echoed Gerrund's words so exactly that I wondered if she were quoting him. 'I spoke to a constable doing his rounds, but he said they had had no reports of any trouble and the people were not doing any harm.'

'That is true.' I raised my glass to hers. 'And I am sure they will get bored soon enough. The shutters are all closed next door and there is nothing to see.'

'There was a photographer setting up his camera.'

'It will not make a very exciting picture.'

Ruby was mixing herself a cocktail – gin and some ingredients that I did not even stock.

'Did you see anything of what happened?' My visitor touched my hand again.

I chose my words carefully for I dislike telling unnecessary lies and the truth is usually more convincing and easier to remember.

'I was at work in my study at the back of the house.'

'Did you not hear the police arrive?'

'Seraphim Square is often busy.' I looked her in the eye. 'You learn to ignore the noises.' I blinked but we are all obliged to do that sometimes.

'Did you know her very well?'

I was beginning to get the same impression I had had the first time we met, almost that I was being interrogated, but I have had that feeling before with inquisitive people.

'I never spoke to Mrs Hatchpenny,' I told my visitor.

'It is often the way in towns.' She put the tumbler to just below her lips but did not consume any of its contents before she lowered it. 'But I live in the countryside now and talk to all of what I call *my neighbours,* though some live more than a mile away.'

'It is the same in Thetbury,' I told her. 'Everybody knows everybody which has its good points but, at the moment, I prefer a little more anonymity.'

'Yes of course,' she squeezed my arm. 'Since you were…' she hesitated, presumably to avoid using the word *jilted*. 'Jilted,' she said before catching my expression.

'Have you finished your drink?' I enquired though she had not even started it. 'You must excuse me for monopolising your company. I am sure that you have other calls to make.'

'I am so sorry,' she said, and I did not care whether she referred to Jack's betrayal or her presumptuousness. Both, in their different ways, were unforgiveable. I adopted a technique my mother had taught me. Whilst appearing to put a friendly arm around a caller who had overstayed their welcome, you push with one finger in the small of their back. Unless they are willing to tussle with you, they are obliged to move forwards. With a little practice one can steer them in whichever direction is required. I manoeuvred Petunia Bottle into the hall.

Somebody was performing a jig on a fiddle close by. It was a busker, no doubt, and he or she played well if inappropriately for such an occasion.

'Thank you for your concern,' I said, which sounded more sincere than it was, and opened the door.

The pavement was crowded, and every head turned to gawk at us.

'There she is, the hermit-woman.' A woman in a patched coat pointed at Mrs Bottle.

'No it's the dwarf behind her.'

I was tired of telling people that I was petite rather than something evil in a fairy story.

'Hold still, frebbit,' a photographer called from behind his tripod. 'You'll both be all blurred.'

'Excuse me.' As Petunia Bottle pushed past, a tall man in a canary felt hat was trying to elbow his way to the front and I was about to shut the door when I recognised Anthony Appleton and saw that he was fighting a losing battle.

'Let that man in the yellow hat through,' I called. 'We have a seriously ill child in the house, and he is a doctor.' Grudgingly, they made way.

'The poor wee mite.' The fiddler lowered his bow. 'I shall light a penny candle for her, if only I have penny.'

'And you had better all stand clear,' I warned as Anthony reached my threshold. 'She has the sweating sickness.'

'Holy Mary mother of God.' The fiddler crossed himself and held out his cap for donations.

'Do not distress yourself, Lady Violet.' Anthony stepped inside. 'I'll soon have her up and about.'

'He won't,' the busker insisted. 'She'll need a lot of candles lit for her.'

I shut the door.

'Sweating sickness?' Anthony puzzled.

'There was an outbreak in Suffolk about four hundred years ago,' I told him and took his cloak.

Agnust tramped up the hallway. 'Dint know we're havin' a party.' She took Anthony's hat and punched out its carefully indented crown. 'Tha's better.'

Anthony winced. 'Thank you.' He watched her with his cloak anxiously but she only hung it carefully at the end of the rack.

'Mrs Bottle has gone,' I told her and she sniffed.

'Not much of a party then. Gerrund say wha' 'bout your cheese'nd pickle?'

'Would you like some?' I asked Anthony but he demurred.

'I had a pie earlier and it is having an argument with my stomach.'

'Then I shall have mine on a tray,' I told Agnust who trudged off muttering, 'Be eatin' off the floor next.'

Not from the way you clean it. We went into my sitting room.

'A whisky might help settle your digestion.' I handed him the undrunk one and topped up my own. With my empty stomach the effects were quite marked.

'I came as soon as I heard.' He had missed a middle button on his waistcoat. 'I saw the *Chronic*.'

'I thought you must have.'

'It sounds horrible,' he said.

'More horrible than they knew.' I accidently finished my scotch in one gulp and slumped into an armchair.

Anthony sat opposite me, perched on the edge and leaning forwards.

'Are you able to tell me what happened?'

'She was hanged off a pole outside my study window.'

'Oh, my Lord!' His fingers blanched around his glass.

'We cut her down and tried…' I broke off.

He reached over and took my right hand. 'I am sure you did everything you could.'

'Oh, Anthony,' I sighed hopelessly.

'When you said she *was hanged*, did you mean it was not suicide?'

I shook my head in despair. 'She was murdered.'

'Do the police know why or by whom?'

'Not yet. Inspector Stanbury is in charge of the case.'

'He's a good man.' Anthony put his glass down on the little round tray table at his side and took my other hand. 'Though I'm not sure he would say the same about me.'

'I believe you had an audition today,' I changed the subject in an impossible effort to distract myself from the day's images. They were so vivid I could almost have sworn they were still real.

'Yes,' he said. 'It went quite well, I think, but one never knows for certain.' There was another long gap. Anthony cleared his throat. 'You appear to be under siege.'

'It feels like that.'

'That woman who left your house as I arrived. I am sure I have seen her somewhere before.'

'Mrs Petunia Bottle,' I told him, and he clicked his tongue.

'Doesn't ring any bells.'

As if by magic my front doorbell rang so suddenly and so shrilly that we both jumped. Anthony pulled his hands away and I smoothed my dress as if we had both been caught acting improperly.

There were footfalls in the hall and Gerrund poked his head through. 'I'll deal with it, milady.'

Anthony slid back in his chair.

'Are you expecting someone?'

I shook my head. 'Probably the press.'

There was a clamour at the door and Gerrund was telling somebody to *clear off* or *be given a thick ear* then somebody else to *come in*. The voice of whoever he was addressing was drowned out by a man shouting, 'How does it feel to be living next door to a slaughterhouse?' before the door closed.

Anthony clicked his fingers.

'Inspector Stanbury, milady,' Gerrund announced.

'Show him in.'

Anthony and I got to our feet as Alfred entered.

'Mr Appleton.' He took my friend's proffered hand without enthusiasm.

'Good evening, Inspector.' Anthony fiddled with the undone button on his waistcoat. 'I was just about to leave.'

'Then I shall wish you a good night, sir.'

Anthony paused. 'But before I go. Am I correct in believing that Annie Waters was only fifteen and that Mrs Hatchpenny only had one maid?'

'You are,' Alfred replied guardedly.

'That is odd.' Anthony tugged out his shirt cuffs to show half an inch of white, an affectation that Alfred regarded as foppish. 'Because I spoke to her just after the panther was delivered.' Alfred narrowed his eyes in disbelief, but Anthony continued, 'At least I thought that I did.'

'How can you not have known?' Alfred questioned him as one might a stupid child.

'She called down to me from an upstairs window,' Anthony smoothed down his pocket flaps. No doubt Alfred viewed them also as dandyish affectations. 'But, when I think about it, I am fairly certain that I never actually saw her.'

Alfred put his left thumb in his waistcoat pocket. 'You are fairly certain…'

'That I never actually saw her,' Anthony confirmed. 'There was just a vague shape standing back from the net curtains. I didn't really pay much attention.'

'I suppose you had no reason to,' Alfred conceded. 'But what was odd about it?'

Anthony nodded in appreciation of his words.

'It's just, I was surprised when I heard that she was so young.'

'Why?' I interjected and Alfred frowned. I may have had a distressing experience, but the murder of Mrs Hatchpenny was his case and I was a mere witness.

'Her voice was not that of a girl or even a young woman.' Anthony's eyes flicked sideways before returning the Inspector's gaze. 'I paid some attention to it because there is an audition coming up for the part of Widow Twankey.'

Alfred's lips twitched. 'I can imagine you…' He caught my warning glance. 'Would find that a difficult role.'

'I would,' Anthony concurred. 'But the voice I heard would be well worth imitating.' He put his hands on his hips. 'Well, that delivery is certainly not for us,' he mimicked in a falsetto.

Alfred grinned. 'She spoke like that?'

'Like a pantomime dame,' Anthony confirmed. 'And so it occurs to me, with the benefit of hindsight, that I was not speaking to a woman at all.'

'A man,' I contributed stupidly but Anthony shook his head.

'Not just any man,' he said, 'for who else would trouble to pretend to be the maid other than the murderer?'

'The Montford Maniac,' Ruby Gibson, Inspector Hefty and I spoke as one.

23: *DEATH OF A COUNTESS*

I POURED THREE good measures of Very Old Ben Nevis.

Do you really need that? Havelock Hefty asked primly though he knew that I did not.

The best time to drink is when you don't need it. Ruby toasted her theory with a coupe of Krug Private Cuvée. As often, I found her argument, if not more compelling, at least more appealing.

Hefty put a hand over my glass, but I poured through it, and felt guilty instantly. No character cares to be reminded that they are imaginary.

'You cannot jump to the conclusion that you have spoken to the maniac on the strength of a voice.' Alfred Stanbury sniffed his scotch.

Suspiciously. Hefty dried his hand on a large white handkerchief. *He thinks you are the maniac and are planning to poison him and bury him with all the other bodies in your garden.*

'Who else would be posing as the maid?' I argued and he frowned.

'Perhaps Mrs Hatchpenny did not want us to know that her servant was already dead.'

'It was not a woman's voice,' Anthony insisted.

'You thought it was at the time.' Alfred put his glass down so perhaps Hefty's theory had not been as preposterous as I had thought. 'The mind plays tricks on us all.' He picked up his glass and sniffed it again. 'Many an innocent man has confessed to a crime that he did not commit, not from being bullied into it nor to protect somebody else but because he has been presented with such convincing evidence that he believes it must be true.'

'It is part of my profession to attend to dialogue.' Anthony tipped back his head.

'Just as it is part of mine to rebut half-baked theories based on misremembrances.'

'I know what I heard.'

'Then it is a pity you did not know it at the time.'

The whisky quivered in Anthony's hand. 'Are you trying to blame me for Mrs Hatchpenny's death, Inspector?'

There was not a ripple on Alfred's drink. 'It would appear that you are blaming yourself, Mr Appleton.'

Anthony slammed his drink down, slopping it over his wrist and cuff.

'I have had enough of this.' He brought out a canary dyed handkerchief. 'I give you what might be vital information and you accuse me of being the maniac.'

'I shall need a statement from you.' Alfred rested an elbow on the mantlepiece in a relaxed pose mirroring that of his fictional colleague at the other end. Having had suspects try to kill him or themselves, he would not be perturbed by a witness getting into a huff.

'If you wish to speak to me further, Inspector Hefty, I suggest that you approach my solicitor.' And with those words, Anthony Appleton spun – quite elegantly – on his heel and marched out.

I followed.

'I do not think that he was accusing you of being the murderer.'

'Neither do I.' Anthony took his cloak off the hook. 'I think he meant that the poor woman died as a result of my stupidity.' Never too perturbed to neglect his appearance, he re-dented the crown of his felt hat. 'Which may place me on a higher moral plane but implies that I was criminally negligent.'

'Oh, Anthony, of course you were not.' I took his left hand. 'Nobody could have foreseen what was going to happen.'

'That's what I've been trying to tell myself.' He ran his right hand through his brown hair. Darkened by an application of macassar, it was almost black in the shadows of the hall. The only light came from my sitting room. 'Did I really call him *Inspector Hefty*?'

'I am afraid so.'

An easy mistake. Havelock Hefty gestured magnanimously as he strode across my frontal lobe. *Quite naturally my name is on everybody's tongue.*

'Botheration. He will think I was mocking him.' Anthony coloured, something else no doubt that Alfred would think real men did not do. 'I don't think he will want to see me again so soon. Will you apologise on my behalf?'

'Of course.' I rearranged his cravat, only succeeding in disarranging it but he managed a weak fraction of a smile in appreciation of my gesture.

'I don't even have a solicitor,' he admitted.

'You will not need one.' I went up on tiptoe, leaned forwards and pecked his cheek.

At last. Ruby applauded.

Anthony put his fingers to the spot. 'What was that for?'

'You.' I said simply. 'But you need not think that I intend to make a habit of it.'

Every advance accompanied by a retreat. Hefty plugged his briar with a ready-rubbed Glasgow mix.

'I had better go,' Anthony said quietly and leaned a little towards me but changed his mind.

For goodness sake, Appleton, Ruby poked a finger in his face. *You are as bad as her.*

'Good evening, Anthony.' We held hands too briefly to be anything other than courteous.

'Good evening, Violet.' He pulled away and opened the door. 'The child is recovering well,' he announced to the assembly, 'but, above all else, she must have peace and quiet.'

Evidently his words appealed to their better natures because the crowd fell silent. Not a voice could be heard for the best part of ten seconds.

'Midget lady novelist interviewed by dashing police chief,' the newspaper seller trumpeted. It was not possible that a new edition of *The Chronic* could have been printed in the time Alfred had been in my home, but no self-respecting vendor would let the contents of a newspaper influence their slogans.

Alfred was still standing on the hearth rug. It had a burn from when Agnust had spilled some hot cinders, but I did not want to buy a new one. I had found it in a flea market. A man with an enormous moustache had offered to carry it for a few francs but we had entrusted a rather lovely vase to a charming gentleman two days previously. He had been staying in our hotel and it would be his privilege to take it there for us. Perhaps we could meet for a drink later. Needless to say, neither he nor the vase materialised and so Jack had lugged that rug around the streets of Paris all afternoon.

I stood back a few feet so as not to crick my neck. 'You cannot really suspect Anthony.'

'I did not until he told me that I did.' He put his drink down again. 'But think about it, Violet. He claimed to have spoken to the maid until he discovered that we knew she was already dead. I would be interested to know what his alibi is for the time of the hanging.'

'You cannot be serious.'

Alfred looked at the burn thoughtfully.

'It is a line worth pursuing, if only to dismiss it.'

'You will not find anything against him.' I too fixed my eyes on the rug and could not help but remember how I had loved and trusted Jack. *HELP ME,* I had almost read.

And one must not forget… Hefty hesitated, mindful of how his life and death were in my hands. *That Appleton just happened to be around when Hettie had her alleged accident.*

He can't have dropped the spike, Ruby rallied to Anthony's defence. He was, after all, one of the objects of her affection.

Of course not. Hefty struck a match and sucked the flame into the bowl of his briar. *But who pushed Lady Violet into the path of that chestnut horse?* He shook out the match and flicked it away.

I drew in a sharp breath.

'What's the matter?'

'Nothing.' I could hardly explain that a still-glowing vesta had landed on my meninges. 'I was just remembering how Jack and I bought that rug.'

Alfred clicked his tongue. 'I assume you have heard nothing else.'

'Nothing,' I said again, struggling not to scratch my scalp as Hefty puffed his foul fumes all over the under-surface of my skull. 'Do you have news?'

He would hardly call at this hour if he had not.

'I don't really like to distress you any further.' He picked up his glass and took a drink this time.

'But,' I prompted, 'you have not come to tell me there is something that you cannot tell me.'

'We have the doctor's report from his post-mortem examinations.'

Romulus had wanted to perform the autopsies. They were rare opportunities to operate without worrying about killing the patients, he had declared. There was also the prospect of adding to his anatomical collection. Unfortunately, he was beaten to it by Mr Ball, a local surgeon.

'And?' I urged.

'Mrs Hatchpenny was strangled and Annie Waters, the maid, bled to death from a lacerated throat.'

'Just as we expected.'

'Quite so.' Alfred cocked his head to one side. 'But, when Mr Ball examined the stomach contents, he found that Mrs Hatchpenny's was empty. Also, her nails were broken, and her fingertips abraded.'

'From trying to pull herself up my wall,' I reasoned, but Alfred shook his head.

'There was a small room on the first floor, probably a linen cupboard at one time but it is empty now. We found gouges in the door and the plaster of the wall, and her toes were bruised inside her shoes from kicking.' He compressed his lips.

'Did this room adjoin my house?'

'Yes. It was towards the back so, probably your study.' He took another drink. 'The logical conclusion is that Mrs Hatchpenny was locked in that room for at least a day.'

'Three or four.' I massaged my brow in shock, aware that Alfred was watching me carefully.

'How can you possibly know that?'

'I heard her,' I breathed. 'I heard knocking and thought it was the builders. I heard scratching and thought they must have disturbed rats in the wall. You reprimanded Anthony for not making more of the maid having an odd voice but I…'

'You cannot blame yourself.' Alfred rubbed his eye.

'That is what I told Anthony, but he was not convinced.' For no reason I looked around me. 'Dear God, Alfred,' I cried. 'I listened to that poor woman trying to escape or attract my attention a few feet away for days and did absolutely nothing.'

He reached out and touched my arm.

'You were not to know.'

'I should have guessed something was wrong.'

'I shall tell you something because I know I can trust you,' Alfred finished his drink and I poured him another. 'May I?' He held out his battered crocodile case.

'By all means.' I quite liked the smell of a cigar and certainly preferred it to the acridity of cigarettes.

Alfred puffed on his for a moment.

'When I was a constable,' he began, 'on the beat a woman rushed up to me one night. She stank of gin and had to hold onto a lamppost to stay upright. Her clothes were ragged and dirty. She was a Countess, she slurred in a cockney accent, and her husband was hunting her down with a pack of hounds. She begged me to take her into custody, but I could imagine what my sergeant would have said if I had done so on the basis of that story. I told her that I was the king of China and to clear off.' Alfred exhaled. 'The next day she was found dead in an ash heap on the other side of the lowers. She had been torn apart.' He lowered his head. 'It transpired that she had been telling the truth. A central European Count had made a foolish match when he was a young man and was anxious to make a better one. Officially he was out of the country the whole time, though a black painted ship was seen anchored off Anglethorpe and locals reported hearing the howling of hounds as it set sail in the early hours of the morning.' Alfred pinched the bridge of his nose. 'I have never told anybody this, not even my wife. She was so proud of me in uniform, how could I tell her that I had left an innocent woman to her death?' He downed his drink and let me top it up. 'I tried to tell myself exactly what you told Appleton, and I told you. I didn't know.' His voice cracked a little. 'It seemed such a cock and bull story.'

Alfred closed his eyes, and I took hold of his hand. We had held hands when we were young sometimes. He was going to join the navy and be a second Nelson, but his mother was a widow and had lost all her other children. She prevailed upon him to stay at home. I half-achieved my childhood ambition to be a great authoress. The greatness was more elusive. My other hope was quashed by a letter handed to me by the vicar at the door of the family chapel.

'Everyone makes mistakes,' I whispered, 'and you have done such good things since then.'

'Have I?' Alfred looked up. 'I did nothing to prevent what happened at Haglin House and I am doing nothing to apprehend this maniac.' He placed his drink with exaggerated care on the mantlepiece. 'I must go,' he said, and I saw him to the door.

It was quiet outside now, the public having concluded that nothing was going to happen. I did not promise to keep his secret and he did not ask me to do so. There was no need. We had always been friends but there was a new closeness between us now as I bade him farewell and watched him make his way across Seraphim Square, a hunched but not – I prayed – a broken man.

24: THE BLURRED MAN

A TRENCH WAS being dug across Market Street.

'What is it for?' I asked a man who appeared to be in charge since he was doing no work whatsoever.

'Some say gas, some say water, some say 'lectricity, some say drains.' He took hold of a shovel but only to lean on it. 'But I say some trenches is for diggin' and some for fillin' in.'

I thanked him for his insight and returned through Seraphim Square, intending to visit Elkin and Lovat's Bookshop to ask if my order of *Jude the Obscure*, had arrived. They had been loath to stock what more than one reviewer had renamed, *Jude the Obscene.* Also, I wanted to check that they still had at least some of my books on display.

I took a circuitous route up Garris Avenue, a pleasant road lined with poplars and bordered by neat rows of semi-detached villas. There was little traffic here. A pretty nursemaid was coming out from the back garden of one house, pushing a pram.

We wished each other a good morning and passed in opposite directions but I had hardly gone a dozen steps when there was a scream. I spun round just in time to see a thickset man in a sack coat leaning over the pram. He was reaching into it when the nursemaid flew at him, grabbing his left arm and yelling, 'Leave her 'lone.'

The baby began to wail.

'I warn you what happen if you dint leave my sister's husband be,' he growled, shrugging her aside. 'The chit get marked.' She flailed at him, but he sent her stumbling back with a slap across her mouth. 'Right then.'

It was then that I saw a cutthroat razor in his right hand.

'No! Please,' the nursemaid begged. 'I never goo near him 'gain. I swear it on my life.'

'You swear it last time.' He ripped the cover open, and she launched herself at him again, the pram rocking and toppling over into the road. A growler was racing towards it and showing no sign of stopping or changing direction. Running over, I heaved the pram upright and dragged it onto the pavement just as the vehicle thundered by. A low wicket gate was open and I pushed the pram through it onto somebody's front path, turning to see the nursemaid being flung to the ground.

Right. I steeled myself. This was, after all, the woman who had battled with a panther. '*Non audeo capere spinam*,' I yelled the family battle cry, and the man cocked his head, doubtless struggling to remember his classical education. Umbrella lowered, sabre-like, I charged.

The man snarled but he was weak tea compared to the ravening beast with whom I had been confronted recently.

'Do not dare to grasp the Thorn,' I translated, and thrust my umbrella straight at his face as he stepped towards the howling child. This, I hoped, would hurt him enough to make him think twice about continuing his attack. He chose that moment to stoop – no doubt to pounce at me – but he also opened his mouth and my umbrella went straight in. A sword swallower would have envied that man's ability to ingest collapsible portable canopies. I was astonished and horrified at how far my carefully rolled brolly had disappeared. The man convulsed. I pulled and extracted my umbrella, my eyes still fixed upon him as he tumbled back and sideways, doubling over, choking and clutching his throat. He vomited in the gutter, gave me a looked of hatred and staggered, clutching his neck, coughing and wheezing back up the road, off down Edgerton Alley.

The nurse had retrieved the pram and was peering anxiously into it.

'Is the child alright?' I asked, dropping my weapon onto the pavement.

'She int hurt.'

'Are you sure?'

I readied myself to demure modestly at her praise and gratitude, but she only put her hand to her mouth and said, 'Oh lor', I be in such botherin' fix for this.'

I rooted in my handbag. 'Take this.' She eyed my card disdainfully. Had she been expecting a tip and, if so, why? 'If there is any trouble, show this to your mistress. I will vouch that he was just a ruffian and that you did all you could to save the baby.'

She stuffed my card into her apron pocket. 'You dint understand,' she cried and, leaving me to wallow in her praise and gratitude, hurried on her way.

Unfortunately, I pondered, I probably understood all too well.

I'm proud of you, Thorn. Ruby brushed a speck off my cerise dress, the one that she was wearing. *I could have done with you when I entered* The Corridor of Death. I had not read that one, never having written it.

Well. Hefty grasped his lapels. *We made short work of him, didn't we, milady?*

How kind of you to share the credit, I sarcasmed and he did what I had intended to do a few minutes ago, demurred modestly. *Any other big strong hero would have done the same.* He puffed out his chest.

All the better for sticking a knife into it, Ruby reminded us both.

I retrieved my umbrella. It was a horrible soggy, stinking mess so I left it propped against a lamppost. Somebody would be glad of it. Somebody was always glad of something.

-

Mr Appleton was not at home, the porter told me when I called at Marmaduke Maudsley Mansions. I visited Hettie who came to the door in a particoloured turban, doubtless to hide her wound and the tonsure that Romulus had shaved around it. She had a client – a man who might have modelled for the decrepit and corrupt portrait of Dorian Grey, she whispered, before shutting me out.

I did not feel like browsing the shops so I went home, but I could not write. When I sat in my study, I found myself jumping at the flutter of every pigeon's wings and casting fearful glances at the window. The pole was still in place. It did not appear to be anybody's responsibility to remove it especially as it was evidence in a murder enquiry.

Closing the curtains was no use. I kept wondering what was going on behind them.

Notebook in hand, I climbed the stairs onto the roof and into the observatory – a glass roofed and sided octagon built by a previous occupant. From there I had a clear view of the lighthouse. Idly I swung the telescope around and aimed it at the lantern room. A blurred man stood, the huge binoculars in his hands trained in my direction. He was bearded with long dark hair. For an instant we gazed at each other through our optical instruments, and I was still trying to focus mine when he lowered his head, spun around and walked briskly away to vanish behind the lantern. I watched but he did not emerge.

Aunt Igitha made an appearance, gliding to where the man had stood. She was all in red, my colour, I noted indignantly as she stared in my direction, though she could not have seen me with her naked eyes. Aunt Igitha waved, not the sort of cheery greeting one might expect from one with claims to be a family member, but the gesture some might use to dismiss an underling. I was in my own home, however, and determined to stand my ground. With a shrug she too disappeared.

-

It was my idea to go hacking with Jack. I did not especially care for riding but knew that he loved the pursuit and thought that it would please him. He had, after all, given up many an afternoon to play tennis and croquet with me when neither game interested him. He rode to Thetbury on an enormous black stallion, leading a modestly sized brown mare for me. She was very well-tempered, he reassured me. This was thoughtful of him but, egged on by Ruby, I took offence at the implied slight on my equestrian prowess. Did he think that, because I was a girl, I could not ride as well as a man? In truth I was never truly happy in the saddle. Horses always seemed such clumsy, unpredictable animals to me.

We set off at a gentle jog across the flat countryside and I was getting on tolerably well until we came to a ditch with a low hedge on the other side.

'I usually jump that,' Jack told me, 'but we can easily go around.'

Without a word, and ignoring Jack's warning shouts, I spurred my horse towards it. I was sure the horse could clear the obstacles. The horse, however, lacked my confidence and came to a sudden halt. Taken unawares, I flew out of the saddle, over the mare's head to land in the shallow water, temporarily stunned.

'Dearest!' Jack cried and, by the time I came fully around, he was crouching beside me. 'Are you injured?'

I got up onto my knees on the gravel bed and inspected myself. My face was bruised and my right hand and wrist were strained. The thing that hurt most, though, was my pride, or so I thought until I tried to stand. The pain shot through my right ankle, and I would have toppled, had Jack not caught me.

'Could be broken.' He picked me up and, unlike the time he had fought Shillage, I did not protest that I could walk.

Luckily that was only a sprain too but a nasty one and I was unable to walk without a stick for weeks. The wrist was more annoying. I could not write, and Ruby had just discovered, after trekking miles over burning sands, that the oasis she had seen was a mirage.

-

Neither Jack nor I went to university. In my case, not only was it not expected, but it was actively discouraged. An education would have been of no benefit to me, I was informed. It was in vain I argued that the average gentleman made no use whatsoever of the three years he spent studying ancient Greek or philosophy. My father was adamant. It was a waste of time and, more importantly, money. Jack spoke on my behalf. There was no reason why a woman should be deprived of knowledge, and I was a great deal more intelligent than some who came away with degrees. Besides all that, he promised, he would wait for me.

'Wait for me to do what?' I asked but he only gave me a wink.

In the end I let my father think that his will had prevailed. I stayed at home, but the truth was I did not want to be away from Jack for so much of the year. Was I really such a milksop, Ruby raged, but love makes weaklings of the best of us. 'Not me,' she said proudly, forgetting that she had been so besotted with Prince Rudolph that she went into a convent when he broke off their engagement.

Jack did not go away because he had unexpectedly inherited Blockborough Hall, his family seat in Norfolk. His older brother had died of typhoid and their father followed two months later. Jack, left with a widowed mother, took the running of the estate on his own shoulders. It was not what he had planned but it had become his duty. His mother died too within the year.

Sammy Flowerdew did go to Cambridge, however. He studied divinity at St John's and came back to Thetbury with a first to take up a position as a curate. This was the first rung, we assured him, on the ladder to a Bishopric. Sammy was not so sure.

'I am supposed to be officiating at a wedding next week, but I get in such a muddle,' he admitted when we paid him a visit.

'You just need to practice,' Jack reassured him. 'We are your friends. Pretend that you are marrying us.'

We went into the chapel.

'Some bride I would make,' I joked for my face was still bruised from my fall in the stream. I still used a walking stick and my wrist was bandaged.

'We need an audience to give it authenticity,' Jack suggested.

'It is called a congregation,' Sammy corrected him. 'I have a friend staying, if I can drag him away from his studies, and there must a servant that my mother can spare for half an hour.'

The friend was called Amos and I wondered why I had not been introduced to him before.

'I only arrived this morning,' Amos explained though I had not given voice to my query. Sammy had met him in Cambridge though they were studying different subjects.

Sammy's mother's maid, Lucy, had also been commandeered to attend. A young girl, she was quite pink with excitement.

'I do love a good weddin' I do.' She fiddled with her hair breathlessly.

'It is only pretend,' I explained.

'Oh.' She went even pinker at the imagined scandal. 'Well I wint split on you.'

Sammy got a key from the rectory, and we all went into a small chapel down the lane. He was clearly nervous and got quite flustered when it came time to go through the vows.

'You may now kiss the bride,' he said with great relief at the end and so Jack did to laughter and applause from Sammy's friend and sobs of joy from the maid. It was not the first time that we had kissed and was, by no means, the last. That final kiss came as an X at the end of his last letter.

'You did a fine job,' I reassured Sammy. 'But I am not available for funerals.'

'I think we have all earned a drink,' Jack said. *All* did not include the maid, of course. She returned to work. Amos hung back. He was interested in seeing the parish records as it was thought that a branch of his family had originated in the area. The remaining three of us returned to Sammy's parents' house for lemonade on the lawn.

'Remember the first time I came here?' I pointed to the oak tree. 'Eunice and I did not get to the best of starts.'

Sammy laughed. 'She is a different woman now. Hasn't been in a fistfight for weeks.'

I had met his sister again recently and dismissed our scuffle as a childish tiff, but Eunice treated me to a scowl.

'I shall never forget how you trampled on all my dolls,' she said petulantly though, as I remembered the occasion of Sammy's birthday party, it was she who had kicked them. I let her remark pass. You cannot argue with anyone who has come to believe their own lies.

–

Friendless called. I had not booked him but he was anxious to show me his *repaired*, i.e. new, hansom. On my instructions the makers had knocked and gouged the woodwork in places and fitted the old upholstery.

'Do a not-too-bad job,' he conceded, 'but tha' dent…' He pointed to a faint mark on the previously smashed footboard. 'Wint there afore.'

I inspected Old Queeny. Her lip was scarred but had healed well.

'Would you like an apple?' I asked, reaching into my bag.

'She daint like apple since tha' street slug trick her,' Friendless warned but she munched quite happily on the slightly shrivelled one that I held out for her. 'I think on a plan,' he told me, 'since you tell me of that man in London and how he get a driver to come. You can do tha'.'

This was Sidney Grice, the personal detective, who flew a green flag outside his house whenever he required a hansom.

'I do not think anyone will stop for me if I do that,' I forecast.

'I do,' Friendless insisted. 'I can see your roof from my roof so, if you fly it, I see it and come for you.'

'But how often do you go on your roof?' I checked.

'Not never if I do help it and not never if I dint help it.'

'Then you will never see it.'

Friendless protruded his lower lip. 'Only try to be helpful.'

'Thank you,' I said. 'It was a kind thought.'

'Old Queeny have another,' he said. 'We give you a free ride.'

'When?'

'Every time.'

'I cannot let you do that. It is your living.'

'Wint have no livin',' he argued, 'withou' this not-too-bad repairin' job for wha' you pay for.'

'I would prefer you to keep earning or there was no point in getting the repairs done.'

Friendless struck a statesman-like pose.

'Then I give you a ride now.'

You are supposed to be working, Hefty scolded.

'To where?'

'We find tha' when we get there.' Friendless scrambled onto his high perch with commendable agility. 'It's Old Queeny's day. Let her decide.'

'Very well,' I agreed and clambered aboard.

'Mind the 'holstery,' Friendless fretted. 'It's new.'

Off we set, Old Queeny pulling quite happily, her head held high. Unlike a lot of drivers, concerned about the risk of distractions, Friendless did not blinker his horse. 'She like to see everythin',' he would insist. 'Give us more to talk abou' of a long Thursday evenin'.' And who was I to judge somebody for holding conversations in their head? Although at least I knew that mine were imaginary. *We most certainly are not,* a chorus of characters protested.

Out of the square and up Market Street we went. The traffic was moving well, and we were soon in the suburbs with their newish detached villas and well-kept front gardens. Old Queeny, with no urging from her master, broke into a trot. The sun was shining and there was a pleasant light breeze.

Friendless opened the hatch over my head.

'She goo on for ever she do,' he forecast as we approached the crossroads leading to the countryside but his expectations were confounded for Old Queeny slowed and, taking advantage of the widening road, turned us carefully around and trotted back towards the town centre. 'Get homesick for home,' he explained.

We passed through Friar's Square to find the entrance to Angel Street blocked.

'Look like one on those motor vee-hicles break down,' Friendless informed me from his high vantage point. 'Alway doin' tha'. Tha's why they never replace the horse, do they, darlin'?'

If Old Queeny had a view on the matter, she kept it to herself.

'I can walk from here,' I told him because he would have had to make a long detour to get to Break House.

'Do tha' mean you do walk?'

'It do. I mean it does.'

He released the flaps.

I had never found a way to disembark from a hansom in a ladylike manner. The running board was too high for my short legs, and I had a choice between raising my dress or making a little jump for the pavement. I combined the two actions today and only just managed to avoid doing what I doubted I could still do, the splits.

Straightening myself out, I noticed a heavily bearded man in a long, patched coat loitering near Friar's House. There was nothing especially unusual about him. He was probably hoping to find a sympathetic cook or kitchen maid who would spare him a bite to eat. Many were glad of the male company their mistresses forbade them to keep.

Something about him caught my eye though and it seemed that he was looking back at me. Had I seen him before? I did not think so. He was not one of the usual hawkers or beggars and there was something about the way he returned my gaze, as if in recognition, but his head was down. He raised a gloved hand, touched the drooping brim of his hat, and hobbled hurriedly off as if he were trying to avoid me.

And who would blame him? Ruby challenged as I entered Break House. *Given your history with men?*

What on earth can you mean? Hefty asked and I wished that he had not for I had a good idea what she was driving at. Jack Raven had disappeared; Anthony was almost killed.

Twice, she inserted.

And Sammy committed suicide.

And you have murdered every man I have ever cared for. Ruby ground a cigarette into my hall tiles.

There was something about the beggar's clothes that was different.

And my one true love, what-was-her-name? Hefty sighed. *Not to mention your cruelly keeping me in suspense.*

I flung my hat onto the table. *Do you really want me to finish that chapter*? I demanded and Scotland Yard's premier detective paled but did not reply. 'Then I shall,' I said aloud.

I could not face working in my study, constantly looking at the window or bracing myself not to do so and so I went to my music room across the hall from my sitting room. This room also overlooked the square but had shutters which were kept closed because I never used it. The piano had come with the house and served no purpose other than to collect dust and give a holiday home to spiders. There was a stand with sheet music by Bach still open upon it. Dowager Herbena Lady Strainge used to play, and her cello case was still propped in a corner unopened.

I took the dustsheets off a small table and chair, sat at and on them, unwrapped a stick of Beeman's and set to work.

> Lancelot Overstrand cursed and lunged forwards, the blade of his dagger glinting wickedly, the tip dripping deadly poison.

But Scotland Yard's premier detective was ready for him, Hefty urged, And drew out his trusty revolver.

> Inspector Havelock Hefty reached for his trusty revolver,

I wrote. And fired at point-blank range, Hefty prompted.

But he was too late,

I wrote,

and the dagger was buried up to the hilt in his breast.

NO! Hefty screamed so loudly that I jumped and looked over my shoulder only to be confronted by *Cello Suite No. 5* which everyone except me, I expected, knew was in the key of C minor.

25: THE MAN IN THE SHADOWS AND DEATH IN THE MINE

I WAS TAKING the cork out of my absinthe when Ruby appeared dressed in black paramatta silk and masked by a heavy veil.

I am in mourning, she explained though I had calculated as much already.

But you hated him. I poured a double measure.

I pretended to. She reached for a bottle of gin.

Well, you certainly convinced me. I placed my slotted silver spoon on the glass and a sugar lump on top.

He may have been my rival. She lifted the veil back over her hat and I saw that her face was white and eyes rimmed red. *But he was my only constant companion.* My cold heart was thawing until she added, *Who else can I mock you with when you are asleep?* And the blood chilled in my veins.

What I have written, I have written, I pronounced and opened the tap of my fountain.

I see, Ruby said more icily still and swished away.

'We have not heard the last of this,' I told the green fairy but, as always, she did not reply. I have never found an answer in alcohol, but that has yet to stop me looking for one.

My reverie was broken by the strident summons of my front doorbell. I sat up in puzzlement. Anthony was one of the few people I knew who would turn up unexpectedly but even he was unlikely to arrive at – I checked my William Morris oak mantle clock. Both fingers pointed to eleven.

Gerrund had the night off and was not expected back until midnight. Agnust would be in bed and, once she was asleep, it would take the last trump to rouse her.

I went to the window and peeped around the side of the curtain. A ragged boy was running, bare-footed, away towards Market Street. Had he played a prank on me? A newt had been put through my letter box once though I never discovered by whom or why. In this instance there was only a buff envelope. Putting the chain on, I opened the front door a few inches. There was nobody there. Few people slept outside in the square since the police had adopted a policy of moving them on. I slipped the chain off again so that Gerrund would be able to get in, picked up the envelope and went back to my sitting room.

It was probably, I told myself, a begging letter, or an advertisement, but my name and address were on it in the now familiar red ink. Inside the envelope was a letter, the paper torn out, as was becoming traditional.

UNTIL NOW I HAVE BEEN TOYING WITH YOU,

I read,

BUT THE GAMES HAVE ENDED. COME TO SAINT AEGBALD'S CHURCH TOMORROW FOR THE TEN O'CLOCK SERVICE. DO AS I SAY OR THE GIRL DIES.

Which girl? The only person I knew who had been in any peril was Hettie, but she was a grown woman.

A bright light came through a gap in my curtain but, almost as quickly, disappeared. I went to the window. The Splendid Hotel was briefly illuminated then the Capricorn Brewery in the distance, St Aegbald's and the Great Gate. There was darkness then the light returned. The lighthouse lamp must have been lit and was skimming anticlockwise over the town.

The figure of a man came hurrying across Seraphim Square, tall but not bulky enough to be Gerrund. He was in the shadows but, as he neared Break House, the light swept over him and I was at the door before Alfred Stanbury had a chance to press the bell button.

Never a natty man, the inspector looked as if he had slept in his clothes. His hair was wild and his waistcoat buttoned lopsidedly.

'Are you all right?' he panted.

'Yes.' I stood back to admit him. 'Why? What has happened?'

Alfred closed the door.

'I had a letter.' He delved in his coat pocket and brought it out in a crumpled envelope.

> TELL LADY VIOLET TO BE AT SAINT AEGBALD'S CHURCH TOMORROW FOR THE TEN O'CLOCK SERVICE. DO AS I SAY OR THE GIRL DIES.

'What is this all about?' I asked. 'What girl is he talking about?'

Alfred struggled to catch his breath.

'Lisbeth.' He ran a hand back through his hair.

'Superintendent Padmore's daughter?'

Alfred nodded. 'I fear so.'

I had met Lisbeth a few times – a pale shy girl, aged about sixteen.

'Come into the sitting room.' I led the way and, without asking, poured him a very large Very Old Ben Nevis. His eye fell on my fountain. Another time he might have lectured me about my habit but, at that moment, it seemed a trivial issue. 'Is Lisbeth really in danger?'

Alfred swallowed a good mouthful of his whisky.

'We tried to keep it quiet,' he told me. 'The kidnapper threatened to send her back in pieces if we alerted the press.'

'She has been abducted? When?' I sipped the residue of my absinthe.

'When we announced there was a burglary. A canteen was stolen but, much more alarmingly, so was Lisbeth.'

'Oh, dear God. The poor girl. She must be terrified.' I had a fleeting image of Lisbeth locked in a dark cell. 'Has any ransom been demanded?'

'Not yet.' Alfred paced to and fro. 'There was a message written on Padmore's blotting pad saying that she had been taken but that was it.'

'I have never heard of anyone being kidnapped in Suffolk, at least not in modern times.'

'There was a case in June last year – an Ernest Gimlet.'

'The man found dead in an old flint mine?'

'The very same.'

'I thought that was an accident.'

Alfred rubbed the back of his neck. 'Yet again this is confidential.'

'Of course.'

'He was abducted from his home in Stolham St Ernest. They demanded a thousand pounds, but his wife did not have it. He was only an undermanager at the horsehair factory. We think they mistook him for Terrence Gimlet who owns the place, along with a string of racehorses. She called us in too late. He was already dead – strangled.'

I greeted this news with surprise. 'As I remember the coroner's court ruled that he had fallen down the shaft.'

'We kept it quiet to protect her. He was insured but only against accidental death.' He looked away. 'I have to say I was not happy with that. We were colluding in defrauding the insurance company, but it was not my decision.' He flicked his fringe back.

'Five minutes ago, a street boy put this through my door.' I passed the letter to him. 'He ran away before I got a proper look at him.'

Alfred put his tumbler down on the mantlepiece.

'My note came about twenty minutes ago. I was in bed.'

'Why would he want me to attend a service?'

'I can only think that he means to harm you.' He picked up his glass again. 'But you can't possibly go.'

'I cannot possibly not go,' I argued. 'If Lisbeth were to be…' I baulked at saying *murdered*. 'Harmed because of my cowardice, I could never forgive myself.'

'And if you were to be hurt,' he argued, 'how would I feel?'

'She is little more than a child,' I said, 'and she has no choice in the matter. I have.' I reached for the absinthe, but my hand fell away.

'I cannot allow it.'

'How will you stop me? Will you put me under arrest?'

'No, of course not.'

'The letter does not tell me to go alone.'

Alfred tugged the front ends of his waistcoat down, but it was still askew.

'That much is true.' He drained his drink.

'Whoever wrote these messages must be moderately well educated,' I commented.

'I suppose the spelling is accurate,' he conceded.

'Especially of Aegbald.' I pointed. 'Not everyone could get his name right and he has even used an apostrophe correctly.'

'He has.' Alfred scratched his cheek. 'I doubt most of my men are even aware of the sign.'

I had not heard it open, but the front door closed.

'I am back, milady.' Gerrund appeared in a long black overcoat. 'Did you…' he caught sight of my visitor. 'Good evening, Inspector.'

'Gerrund.' Alfred acknowledged him with a dip of his head.

'Might I ask what's happening?' my man looked from one to the other.

'You can rely on Gerrund's discretion and, when it comes to it, Agnust's,' I promised.

'I hope so.' Alfred reached for his pocket watch, but he did not have it with him.

'You can,' I assured him. 'I would trust them both with my life.'

'Let us hope you don't have to,' he said bleakly, and I poured another three whiskies.

26: DEATH IN THE AISLE

ALFRED ARRIVED AT about a quarter to ten, looking a great deal tidier than he had the previous night. He was accompanied by three uniformed officers.

'This is Constable Green.' He indicated to one of them with his thumb. 'He will stand outside your front door. There is another man in the lane at the back – just in case this is a trick to lure you out and leave the place unprotected.'

'There must be simpler ways to burgle my house,' I commented as I admitted him, and he shrugged.

'I'm not taking any risks.'

'Neither am I.' Gerrund tapped his coat over a slight bulge. 'Got my Enfield.'

He had tried to persuade me to take my Lady Derringer, but I did not like the idea of firing it at the best of times, still less in a church.

Agnust clunked her handbag on the hall table. 'Got mine too.' I had seen her use it once when she had blown a hole in a wall into which I could have put my fist. It did not bear thinking about what it could do to a man.

And I have mine, Hefty declared, but I shooed him away. This was no time to lose myself in fantasies.

'I have an officer at the entrance to the church,' Alfred said as we all set off. 'And four inside. That's all I can spare, with our other investigations underway.'

'You wint never find tha' cutlery now,' Agnust told him. 'Be all melted down.'

'Probably,' he agreed absently.

Seraphim Square was busy with sightseers investigating the stalls. The main trade was in garish souvenirs – models of the gatehouse or the shrine, miniature framed prints of Aegbald – all designed to catch tourists' eyes and loosen their purse strings. I wondered how many would regret purchasing ornaments which, surely, would look out of place in anybody's home.

Alfred walked to my left, his head moving side to side as he surveyed the scene. Gerrund was on my right, his hand under his coat. Agnust marched ahead, clearing the way like an icebreaker in arctic seas.

'Man finds nest of mouses in his beard,' the newspaper vendor thundered.

I hoped that tomorrow's headline would not be *Lady Novelist Murdered in Belfry* or wherever my correspondent intended to make his attempt upon my life. We walked on.

St Aegbald's was a medieval church, the statues of its patron saint and the apostles stood in niches above and either side of the studded oak door. They had all been beheaded or defaced in the puritan campaign to rid us of idolatrous images.

The constable at the door saluted his inspector and we passed inside. It being a weekday of no special significance, the church was scantily attended; a family of six was seated near the back, the children fidgeting already; two couples were about halfway down to either side. A solitary man in a shabby suit sat alone, three rows behind my pew.

The Strainge family had established a large endowment for the church in exchange for which they were given exclusive use of a private pew on the right-hand front row. It was boxed in with a door opening into the aisle. Before we even got there, I could see that an elderly lady in light mourning was occupying my place.

She looked around as we approached.

'Oh, you are Lady Violet, are you not?'

'Good morning. Yes, I am.'

She began to gather her handbag and prayerbook. 'I am so sorry, but I have never known this pew to be occupied during the week.' In truth it was rarely occupied on a Sunday either. 'I took the liberty of sitting here for warmth in the winter,' she explained because there was a grid running across the church at that point with hot water pipes underneath it. 'Also I find it easier to read near the candles.' There were two of them in front of my box, one at each end – thick white columns, their flames wavering in a draught. 'I fear I got into the habit.' She half-rose. 'I must apologise for the intrusion.'

'Do not disturb yourself,' I told her. 'It matters little to me where I sit, and you are quite welcome to take my place at any time.' As a rule, communion was something I only attended at family services in Thetbury.

The lady looked doubtful. 'Are you sure? You are too kind.'

She settled back while we occupied the row behind, Gerrund first to my right and Agnust to my left. Alfred went to speak to a constable. He had stationed one in each corner of the church. Gerrund slowly revolved three hundred and sixty degrees, scrutinising our surroundings before he settled next to me. Alfred rejoined us, sitting beside Agnust. She folded her arms and glared at the vicar as he shuffled from the vestry. She was a follower of Ethel of Ickworth who had preached that gospels of Mark the Evangelist were forged by Satan in 666 AD. Therefore, anyone who accepted his writings was a devil-worshipper.

The vicar was a wispy-haired man with a vague look in his eye. I examined the stained-glass windows, either not destroyed by the iconoclasts or reinstalled since the restoration of the monarchy. King Aegbald, in red robes and a golden cloak, wielded a sword with his miraculously restored hand.

The vicar blessed us all and began a prayer, but my mind was not on the words. It was difficult to envisage any of that congregation attempting to harm me or that, if they did, they would be able to succeed. The lady in front was leafing through her prayerbook. The man behind kept clearing his throat noisily.

Perhaps Alfred was right, I reflected, and somebody just wanted to get me out of the house. It seemed an unnecessarily drastic way of doing so.

Something clattered and I heard a grunt and we spun round. A constable had knocked a pile of hymn books over. He looked apologetically at his inspector and bent to pick them up. The vicar did not even pause.

There was a strong, sweet smell. Alfred and Gerrund must have noticed it too for they sniffed and looked about.

Chloroform, I thought at first but there was a distinctly different pungency to it. Where had I come across it before? It reminded me of when I had uncontrolled hiccups for three days as a child. The doctor had dripped a medicine down the back of my nose. But why, I wondered, could I smell it in church? The smell was getting stronger, and I felt a little light-headed.

'Is somebody trying to drug us?' I whispered to Alfred.

'Get milady out of here.' Gerrund made no attempt to whisper, and the vicar scowled.

Alfred took my arm, sliding the catch back on the door.

'Come on. Quickly,' he urged.

The candles flared. There was a bang, a whoosh and the lady in front was engulfed in flames. They shot around and high above her. For a moment she did not move and neither did I. It was so unreal that I was transfixed. She brushed her dress, as if there were just a cinder on it, then raised her arms to her head, turning towards us uncomprehendingly.

A woman screamed behind us, and men were shouting, but it was almost as if they were in a different world.

'Get out of here,' Alfred commanded me, flinging the door wide. 'Cloaks, blankets. Anything,' he shouted, ripping off his Ulster.

The lady was beating her dress now.

Agnust went towards her, but Gerrund barged her away. 'Your dress will catch too.'

The lady reeled to our right, wrenching uselessly at the closed end of the pew before turning back, whimpering in pain and fear.

Alfred reached through the fire and tried to get hold of her, but the heat drove him back. Somehow she got to the door, fumbled it open and staggered into the aisle. Swaying side to side, she lurched towards the altar. Flames still rose from the grating. The vicar stood transfixed, his hands raised and parted in the midst of his benediction. For some reason she changed course again before she reached him, a human torch, stumbling up the aisle.

'Stand clear, milady,' Gerrund shouted, pushing me roughly away.

Alfred threw his Ulster over the lady's head and she tripped to land face down. Gerrund added his coat and I passed him my cloak. The two men turned her over onto her back. The constables rushed up, using their coats too, swathing her to smother the fire.

I was surprised how little she struggled and how quickly her movements weakened. The sweet smell had faded but was replaced with the stink of charred cloth and, more horrifyingly, the stench of burnt flesh.

Alfred lifted his coat from the lady's face to reveal it transfigured, her hair singed to the scalp, her features eaten and blistered into a travesty, hardly recognisable as a person.

I knelt under the hanging cross of Jesus to touch her seared neck. Her skin was hot, hard and crisp. It did not feel human. There was no pulse. I checked very carefully but I knew, as I did so, that the woman, to whom I had spoken a few minutes ago, was no more than a scorched carcass.

Most of the congregation had fled and the constables were clearing the rest away.

The flames had died down.

'What's under here?' Alfred demanded but the vicar still stood, arms raised as if he were transformed to stone.

Gerrund was crouching. He touched the iron grating but, from the way he pulled sharply away, it was still hot.

'Leave it to me.' Agnust joined him, jammed her umbrella through a hole and levered, hinging one end up an inch or so. Gerrund put his boot under the free edge, heaved a section up about four feet long and sent the ironwork clattering onto the stone floor.

There was a gap with the heating pipes running through it but still leaving a space through which a man could crawl. A pile of cloths still smouldered under the pipes.

'Broken glass.' I pointed to the shards scattered through the tunnel.

'What's under here?' Alfred repeated.

'It goes to the crypt.' The vicar had come back to life and was kneeling beside the dead woman.

'How do we get in?' I asked.

'There is an entrance at the side of the church.' The vicar pointed. 'Through the vestry.'

'Wait here, you men,' Alfred ordered.

He, Gerrund, Agnust and I ran out and found a flight of worn steps leading down to an open door. In we rushed to hunt between the stone tombs and stacked coffins. Agnust wrenched a heavy oak door open but there was only a small storeroom filled with broken furniture and mouldering vestments. A drape of dusty cobwebs hung in front of a dead-ended room. Through it we could make out a heap of coal and, beyond that a furnace but it was obvious that nobody had been in that part for months.

'Gone,' Agnust said.

A light came through a rectangular hole in the ceiling. I went over and saw the grating and the face of a constable staring down in shock.

'Two men stay there and two of you search the graveyard for an intruder. Hurry.' Alfred shouted up. 'Are you all right?' he touched my shoulder.

'Ether,' I realised. 'There must have been a flask of it under the grating.' I remembered now, Romulus telling me what a good anaesthetic it was, but he had stopped using it because it was so flammable.

Alfred ordered me home and one of his constables to accompany us and it was only as we recrossed the square that my numb mind came to the obvious conclusion. The old lady had died in my place.

27: THE TOMB OF THE HURRENS

UNSURPRISINGLY THE POLICE found no-one suspicious near St Aegbald's. A passing maid thought she had seen a man hurrying from the crypt but could neither be sure nor give any description except that he wore dark clothing.

'Don't they always?' Alfred muttered.

The lady had been a regular parishioner at St Aegbald's. The vicar told Alfred that her name was Mrs Williams. As her attire had suggested, she was a widow. She had lived a quiet, blameless life in Nelson Road with a maid who was almost as elderly as her mistress and a live-in cook. Mrs Williams had been solicitous enough to provide for them both in her will but the legacy was not considered sufficient motive for murder. Neither woman would have been capable of accessing and crawling under the grating. Alfred Stanbury never gave serious consideration to any theory other than that the inferno had been intended for me.

A faint waxy residue had been found smeared on the sides of the tunnel, probably the remnants of a candle that had been lit beneath the flask.

Alfred Stanbury sent men to enquire at hospitals, pharmacies, vets, anywhere that might keep ether, but none reported any missing.

'I must find out when and where the funeral is taking place,' I said but Alfred cut the air with a straight hand.

'You cannot possibly go. He will be expecting you to be there, and I cannot offer you full protection.'

'He say as a boy he be a famous admiral one day,' Agnust reminded me, as if Alfred were not present. 'But he's wrong. He's even wronger when he say tint your fault you're all stunted, but…' She raised a hand as if conducting an orchestra. 'He int wrong about this. It's too full on danger. Your Ma and Pa tell me to look after you with all your head-in-the-cloud ways and tha' is wha' I do.'

I opened my mouth to object.

You cannot help being a fool, Thorn, Ruby said severely, *but you could try not to be a dead fool.*

'If you do go, milady, you would be putting our lives and those of the police at risk,' Gerrund reasoned. 'You can pray for her just as well in the safety of Break House.'

I held out my palms. 'I suppose you are right, but am I to be a prisoner in my own home?'

'You cannot venture out until we apprehend the man,' Stanbury insisted.

'But, if this is the Montford Maniac, he has been on the loose for over a decade,' I reminded Alfred and he clenched his jaw.

'It is different now.' He flicked his fringe back. 'I am on the case, and I shall catch him.'

Or her, Hefty said and I was about to proffer that option when the letter box rattled.

'S'pose I'm s'pose to get tha',' Agnust grumbled to Alfred as if it were his job really.

'I believe you are,' he primped his moustaches as if making himself presentable to receive my mail.

'Two letter.' She returned with them on a silver tray, rather than toss them on the escritoire, as was her habit when we had no visitors. 'One bill and this.' She held up the envelope for all to see the red-printed address.

'Let me see.' Alfred took it from her and clipped on his spectacles. 'Judge Street post office this time,' he observed. 'It's quite crumpled and smudged.'

'Perhaps the writer kept it in his pocket,' I suggested.

'Or got a street child to post it,' Gerrund said.

'I can get my men to inquire.' Alfred picked up my silver knife and slit the envelope open. 'But countless urchins run errands.'

'Wint trust one with my messages,' Agnust said.

'I would,' Gerrund argued. 'They are usually reliable because they hope to get other jobs from you.'

'The trouble is,' Alfred slid the letter out. 'They are not keen on talking to us and, if we offer a reward, dozens of them will claim to have done the job.'

He flattened the paper out on my desktop.

> SO YOU ESCAPED ME BY PUTTING AN OLD WOMAN IN YOUR PLACE, DID YOU? YOU ARE ALMOST AS RUTHLESS AS ME. YOU MIGHT THINK YOU LEAD A CHARMED LIFE, LADY VIOLET, BUT IT IS CURSED. COME TO THE HURREN TOMB AT TEN O'CLOCK TONIGHT. DO NOT BE LATE OR YOU WILL GET A HAND IN THE POST TOMORROW.

'Why would he threaten to murder her the first time but now only to amputate her hand?' I wondered.

'Probably worked out what a good bargaining counter she is,' Gerrund suggested. 'He can only kill her once, but he can cut bits off her countless times.'

'I know what you are thinking.' Alfred looked me straight in the eye. 'But you cannot possibly go.'

'Will you?' I asked.

'Of course.' He gripped his right lapel. 'It might be my chance.'

'Then I shall be with you,' I vowed to a cacophony of dissent. 'Do you really think I will sit here and let Lisbeth be mutilated.'

'Your motives are laudable.' Alfred released his lapel and smoothed it down. 'But equally I cannot allow you to risk your life again.'

I picked up the letter. 'He or she becomes more garrulous with every note and addresses me by name this time.'

'She?'

Igitha. I kept the thought to myself. 'The gentle sex is not always as gentle as men like to think.' I folded the letter back into its envelope.

Alfred sniffed. 'The landlord of the Stoat's Head could confirm that. He had half an ear bitten off by a woman last week.'

I came to two decisions. We would have coffee and, 'I shall go,' I said firmly.

'You most certainly shall not.' He took off his spectacles.

'There are three possible courses of action,' I propped the envelope up on my escritoire. 'Either I go with police protection, or I go with Gerrund…'

'And me,' Agnust chipped in though I had been about to name her too.

'I cannot allow you to be so reckless,' Alfred said angrily.

'Or,' I continued, 'we allow Lisbeth to be mutilated. Clearly we are at an impasse.' I returned Alfred's glare steadily. 'I wonder what her father thinks.' I went to the telephone. 'Shall I ask him now?'

Alfred exhaled heavily for he must have known full well what Superintendent Padmore would say.

'Very well.' He pinched the bridge of his nose. 'But you will go with a police escort.'

'As you wish.'

'And do exactly as you are told.'

'She wint never do tha',' Agnust warned.

'I will,' I assured him before remembering my first resolution. 'And we shall have coffee now, Agnust.'

'Not for me, thank you kindly,' she said, stroking the furry mole on her upper lip as affectionately as Friendless with Old Queeny.

-

I would have preferred to reconnoitre the site, but Alfred had made me promise to stay indoors until he came for me. He had stationed two constables to guard the house again. Gerrund went in my place.

'You are not to let anybody in,' he instructed Agnust firmly.

'Not even you?' she enquired innocently but did not try to prevent his return an hour later.

'The place is already crawling with constables,' he told me as he wiped his feet, though not the eighteen times that Agnust had tried to impose upon us. 'And they are going to be on guard all day.' He hung his coat on a hook. 'The man at the entrance wouldn't let me in.' Gerrund dropped his cane into the stand. 'But Inspector Stanbury was there and told him to admit me.'

'What did you find?' I watched him brush his navy-blue bowler hat to ensure a perfectly smooth nap.

'Inspector Stanbury showed me round. The graveyard is surrounded by iron railings about twelve feet high with just one gate that was originally padlocked but it's hanging off its hinges now with a large gap. The grass is knee high, and the paths are thick with weeds.

'Judging by the way they've been trampled, a lot of people have found their way in. The constable told me it's a favourite spot for courting couples.'

'Rather a ghoulish place to rendezvous,' I commented, and he shrugged.

'Not many private spots in the middle of town,' he said. 'The Monastery Gardens are patrolled to stop vagrants sleeping in them, but the graveyard is the private property of the Hurren family – not that they've used it for years.'

'I am not sure that there are any Hurrens left.' A fresh thought struck me. 'Perhaps he does not intend to attack me within the cemetery. What if he uses his crossbow again or has a gun?'

'Inspector Stanbury thought of that,' Gerrund replied. 'He can't screen the area off in such a short time, so he intends to have everyone carry an open umbrella and surround you from view. He's got a man on the roof of the Splendid, overlooking the square and another on the tower of St Aegbald's with a view of the graveyard itself.'

'He appears to have considered everything,' I commented.

'Good day to commit a crime,' Agnust observed. 'With all those bluebottles taken off the streets.'

That is exactly what he wants, Hefty hazarded. *He intends to rob the Fynce and Drove Bank.*

'I had an idea.' Gerrund folded his arms but unfolded them immediately. Servants are not supposed to be so casual in their employer's presence, but the pose never offended me, unless done in a defiant way. 'If nobody can see you properly, why don't I try to find someone of your build and dress her in your clothes? There's plenty of women who'd be glad of the money.'

I closed my eyes briefly.

'Is it not enough that one woman has died in my place already?'

'I had to make the suggestion.' Gerrund held up his hand. 'But I knew you would turn it down.'

His faith in me was so gratifying I did not like to admit that Ruby had made the same suggestion and I had seriously considered it until Hefty had angrily retorted that his creator may be stony-hearted and ruthless but was never a craven coward.

28: THE MARK OF THE MURDERESS

AS INSTRUCTED BY Alfred, I wore black. My habitual red would make me too easy a target, he had pointed out. As a rule, I only wore it for funerals and mourning. Once I had donned it in memory of March Middleton but, fortunately, it transpired that the reports of her death were false.

I selected an umbrella. 'Are you really that desperate to stand out?' Alfred tutted at my foolishness and Gerrund lent me one of his.

'If you unscrew the ferule, there's a spike.' He demonstrated. 'One jab in the face will fend any man off.'

I had already, at his insistence, given way and put my Lady Derringer in my handbag but rejected Agnust's offer of a lucky horseshoe. She stuffed it in her own bulky bag along with her revolver – the only maid I had ever come across who possessed a firearm. Gerrund had joked that she had bought it to capture a husband. 'Never meet a man yet worth the air he breath, let 'lone worth catchin',' she had retorted, careless of the offence she was causing.

There were a dozen policeman outside the front door and a small crowd had gathered.

'Catch up with you at last,' a man in a patched mainly brown coat crowed. 'I know you're a wrong 'un from your size. Somethin' sneaky 'bout goin' 'round so small.'

'I hear she poison both her husband,' his female companion, who was even more petite than I, declared. Clearly, she was ignorant of the fact that I had never had even one spouse of whom I could have had the pleasure of disposing.

'Move along there,' Sergeant Webb barked but nobody showed any sign of intending to do so. It felt odd to see him out from behind his desk and I wondered who was manning it in his absence.

'Throw away the key and lock her up.' A tobacco-chewing woman spat on her own shoe. 'Now look wha' she make me do.'

The constables pushed the onlookers aside to clear a path.

'They'll put a noose around your tidy nape,' a corduroy-clad clodhopper predicted, rubbing his wart-encrusted hands in eager anticipation.

A neat little girl with freckles held out a notebook. 'Make your mark.'

'Why?' I asked as she trotted backwards alongside me.

'I collect autographs.' She tried to push a pencil into my hand. 'Got three footballers and an actor who nobody has heard of, but I've never had a murderess before.'

'I am sorry to disappoint you...' I began.

'See how she dint deny it,' a woman I took to be her mother crowed and the little girl tripped on the kerb. 'And now she attack my daughter?' She swung at me with her handbag and caught a constable on the ear but made no attempt to help her howling child.

A woman in green stood to one side and I recognised her at once.

'There must be some mistake.' Petunia Bottle looked genuinely distraught. 'Would you like me to contact a solicitor?'

'Thank you but no.'

Stanbury took my arm.

'We need to go,' he muttered which was what I had been trying to do.

An egg flew past and hit the same constable, but on his other ear this time.

A young man in a grey suit stepped in front of me. 'Any comments for the *Montford Chronical*?' He too had a notebook. 'We can pay good money for a confession.'

My escorts barged past him.

'Mysterious recluse, Lady Violet Thorn was unable to deny the allegations,' he read out as he scribbled his report.

A black maria stood in the road.

'What do we…' I was going to add *need that for?* because the cemetery was an easy walk away, but Alfred shushed me and ushered me inside along with four constables and Gerrund.

'Squish up.' Agnust squeezed in alongside.

'We need to throw them off the scent,' Alfred explained in a low voice. 'Can't have a mob milling around us.'

Two more constables followed, the last of whom – the one who had been struck twice – shut the door.

'Have to sit on your knee.' He looked at me, and I was not convinced that he was joking.

'Stand and hold the rail,' Stanbury commanded, and the constable grabbed a pole that ran along the ceiling, steadying himself as we lurched off.

'String her on a giblet,' somebody yelled, and a lump of soggy vegetable flew through the grilled window in the door, splotting into the constable's face.

'A regular Aunt Sally,' I commented as, spluttering, he wiped himself with a rag.

The officer nearest the door closed the hatch, muffling the voices and casting us into darkness. We rattled around a corner. Six constables were not, I discovered, as fragrant as one might hope. I put a handkerchief to my nose.

'Hay fever,' I explained before remembering that nobody could see what I was doing.

A constable struck a match, dazzling us, and lit a cigarette to befoul the air even more.

'You know the rules, Lawson,' Alfred snapped. 'No smoking in uniform.' With a scowl, the constable shook the match and tossed it away, leaving us in darkness again but with a sulphurous fug this time.

'Crip me,' a colleague yelped. 'You burnt my hand.'

There was another rasping, and a second match was struck, Alfred dipping his head into the flare, a half-used cigar in his mouth.

'But you say…' Lawson began.

'Am I in uniform?' His superior enquired through an acrid pungency. I had told him a number of times that I did not mind his habit but, on previous occasions, we had not been crammed into the black hole of Montford. Now it caught in my throat and made my eyes water. What on earth possessed people to regard sucking in the fumes of miniature bonfires as a pleasure? I wondered, not for the first time.

Mercifully, two minutes later we came to a stop. There was a scuffling noise – presumably the driver descending from his seat. The door opened and we scrambled out into a neat court. The last man handed umbrellas to his colleagues.

'Put them up,' Alfred commanded, setting the example.

One young officer was struggling, and I opened it for him. I had never seen a policeman carrying one before.

'We can cut through Parsons Lane.' Alfred walked alongside me, Agnust and Gerrund close behind. There was only room for two abreast. We turned right down a wider road until we came to Hurren Square on the south side of St Aegbald's. The images and sounds of the terrible events we had witnessed in the church with the death of Mrs Williams swept over me again.

The main graveyard lay on the north side of the church creeping around the back.

There were gas lampposts in the corners of the square, but they were not in use. Luckily the cloudless sky allowed the full moon to illuminate the town and each policeman lit an oil lamp.

A paved path ran around a high iron fence surrounding the family cemetery. Hundreds of years of use had raised the land into a mound a good foot or two high. It was, as Gerrund had described, overgrown from years of neglect. Hogweeds sprouted through the tall grass and brambles were overgrowing most of the tumbling graves. To judge by the arced gouge through the moss, the gate had recently been forced open wider.

'My men did that,' Alfred told me. 'So you wouldn't have to scramble in.'

We must have looked an odd sight as we passed through the gate with me surrounded by umbrellas on such a clear night, lamps swaying in the men's hands.

The mausoleum stood in the middle of the private cemetery. It was a miniature chapel built of flint, supported by a bulky buttress at the back. Halfway up the walls were niches occupied by knights, heads bowed over their shields. I was not aware that the Hurrens had a military history about which they could boast. None of these statues had been defaced because they were relatively recent features. There was a heavily barred stained-glass window at the front and, below that, a solid iron door.

'Two men tried to open it,' Alfred said, 'but it's jammed solid.'

Gerrund took hold of the barley twist ring handle and twisted it anticlockwise, and we could hear a latch click up but, strain as he might, it would not move. He put a shoulder to it. 'Won't budge,' he confirmed and crouched to examine the hinges.

'They don't look rusted,' Stanbury commented.

'Take a woman to open a door.' Agnust barged Gerrund aside and grasped the handle. It clacked round and she pushed.

'Now d'you believe us?' Gerrund demanded.

'Believing is as believing does,' she declared gnomically and tried the handle again. There was a squealing of metal on metal that seemed to come from the other side. She applied her weight again and almost stumbled through the open door to the mausoleum.

29: THE FALL OF THE HOUSE OF HURREN

GERRUND CAUGHT AGNUST'S arm to stop her toppling over.

'Told you it take a woman,' she crowed, wrenched herself free of his grasp and made to enter the mausoleum.

'Stop!' Stanbury shouted and Agnust paused, her left foot mid-air. 'Stand back,' he told her and, reluctantly she lowered her foot and reversed.

Alfred furled his umbrella tightly. He took a lamp from a constable, hooked it on the umbrella handle and advanced it inside. The interior was about twenty feet by fifteen and unadorned. Stone chests ran along the length of the room to either side with no effigies. The ornamentation was all outside for the world to see. The floor was slabbed, and the pitched ceiling sagged in the middle. It was supported by a few transverse beams and three vertical ones in the middle. A frayed rope dangled from the top. The wall was propped up at the back with wooden boarding about eight feet high and six wide and a few planks had been left lying flat.

'There's nobody here,' Alfred announced. 'So how on earth did he unlock the door?'

We looked at the bolt, but it was a simple affair with no mechanisms to withdraw it automatically.

'Could he be hiding in one of the sarcophaguses?' I suggested and he stepped warily inside.

'Let me help, Inspector.' Gerrund followed and together they struggled with a stone lid, but to no effect.

'Men.' Agnust tossed her head in contempt and went in.

Never one for being left out, I joined them. The four of us heaved but the lids were all solidly fixed.

'What was that you were saying?' Alfred asked my maid and she sniffed.

'Say a lot of thing, I do and do a lot of sayin',' she pronounced as if imparting great wisdom.

'The floor is solid,' Alfred said, 'apart from that drain and, nothing much more than a rat could get through that, especially while it's half-covered in timber.' The drain hole was circular and no more than six inches diameter. 'I wonder what's behind that boarding.'

'One way to find out,' Gerrund went over.

'Be careful,' I said. 'If that supports the wall, you could bring it down.'

'Don't think so, milady,' he tapped it. 'It's too flimsy.' He rapped it with his knuckles and frowned. 'Sounds hollow.'

'Do you think there could be somebody behind it?' I gave voice to what must have gone through everybody's head.

Alfred drew out his gun while my man grasped one end.

'It doesn't even touch the wall,' he declared and pulled.

Agnust took the other end.

'The buttress must be behind that,' I said.

Gerrund and Agnust stepped back, swinging the boarding out and dragging it sideways. Alfred stood to the side, peering into the growing gap.

'There's some sort of a niche behind there,' he announced, revolver at the ready. He raised his voice. 'I am an armed police officer,' he warned. 'Stay where you are.'

'Is there somebody in there?' I asked as, with a final heave, Agnust and Gerrund pulled the boarding aside.

'Don't look, milady,' Gerrund cried and held up a hand in an attempt to block my view but I had already seen what he was trying to hide.

A man stood in the uncovered niche at the back of the mausoleum, but it was obvious at first glance, that he was dead. He was stripped naked, a rope around his chest and under his arms, tying him to a statue behind him. Most horrifying of all, his abdomen had been hacked open and his bowels spilled out, hanging in slimy coils down his legs.

I covered my mouth.

'Get her out of here,' Alfred said.

I glanced at Agnust. She gulped for air. A plank near her foot shifted and rose, hinging up then falling aside.

'Get out!' I cried. 'All of you. It is a trap.' I grabbed my maid's forearm, my fingers hardly going halfway around it. She was still staring in horror. 'Come on!' I yelled in her face and she shook herself as if from a sleep, grasped my hand and ran, dragging me with her. The base of the central beam was shifting sideways. I heard it creak and crack as we raced into the open air closely followed by Gerrund. Plaster and stones were falling from the ceiling. Something hit Alfred. It crushed his sturdy bowler hat and sent him sprawling.

'Stay there, milady.' Gerrund dashed back in, rubble smashing around him, and I made to follow but Agnust yanked me back.

'Let me go,' I ordered her.

'Blowed if I do.' Her grip tightened.

Alfred was laying prone, more rubble landing on his back and legs when Gerrund reached him, crouched, took hold of the inspector's arms, and heaved.

A larger block fell, striking Gerrund on the back of his head and he dropped to his knees, scrambled up and ran but he must have been disorientated for, instead of making for the door, he threw himself at the back wall.

'Men!' Agnust threw me aside, marched in, bent over and lifted Alfred up. A beam toppled onto her. 'Stop tha',' she scolded and tossed it aside.

A cloud of debris billowed around her as she emerged, Alfred in her arms. I could not see Gerrund now and there was no reply as I called his name. Just as I was about to go in, there was a loud creaking and a deafening crash, and the roof came down.

'Gerrund!' I cried again.

'Yes, Milady?' He appeared, scrambling over the rubble.

'I thought you had been buried.'

'Fortunately not.' Gerrund rubbed his scalp gingerly. 'Still intact,' he said.

'Skull six inch thick most likely.' Agnust inspected a tear in her dress in annoyance.

'But you went further in,' I said, baffled.

'I met a man from California…' He wiped his face with a handkerchief, but his nose was still dusted white. 'Who had been in an earthquake, and he told me the safest place when a building is falling down is beside the walls.' He blew out through his lips. 'Obviously knew what he was talking about.'

I went to where Agnust was crouching beside Alfred. He was stirring groggily and trying to sit up, but she pushed him down again.

'Now then Alfie.' She used to call him that when he was a boy, and he had not cared for it then, but he had greater concerns at that moment. 'Lay you back 'til you recover your sense – wha' there is of it.'

The constables had gathered around in concern for their superior, but they sniggered upon hearing her words.

'I need to get up,' Alfred said and Gerrund pulled him to his feet, helping him to stagger to the ruins of the mausoleum. The walls were broken to six feet at their highest point, apart from the buttress which still stood almost intact. The niche was covered, almost to the top with tumbled stones, roofbeams and chunks of ceiling, hiding the dead man from view.

'What happened?' Alfred asked me groggily. 'How…' He put his fingers to his temple. 'Did you know it was a trap.'

'I saw the board on the drain lift up,' I explained. 'There was a rope running out of the drain and along under the plank. It must have been tied to the main supporting beam. Somebody pulled at the other end.'

Alfred rubbed his brow.

'Half of you,' he instructed his men, 'go out and find where the drain emerges. This ground is higher so it's probably not far. The rest of you stay and guard Lady Violet.'

Three of the men marched towards the gate. A discarded umbrella lay across the path. Two constables turned to the right and one to the left, all following the perimeter fence, lanterns held low to inspect the ground.

Alfred addressed me. 'It seems I owe you my life.'

'You owe me a drink.' I picked some splinters out of my hair. 'But it was Gerrund and Agnust who went back in to get you out.'

'Gerrund,' Agnust snorted. 'As much use as a pickle in a jar, he is. Take a woman to...'

'Thank you all,' Alfred broke in and she scowled.

'Wint have bother if I know you talk on the top o' me like tha'.'

'I beg your pardon.' Alfred bowed his head a fraction and it was immediately obvious that he regretted the action. He staggered sideways. Gerrund took his arm and guided him to a low chest-shaped tomb.

'I can't sit on a grave,' Alfred objected, stumbling backwards, and proving that he could.

'Whoever is in there will not mind,' I reassured him.

'Might be glad of the company,' Gerrund chipped in.

Agnust peered at the inscription carved inside a raised wreath. 'Reginald Hurren,' she read. 'Funny name for a dead person.'

I did not know what propelled her to that conclusion, but it hardly seemed worth discussing.

'Are you feeling dizzy?' I asked Alfred.

'I was,' he admitted, 'but I'm all right now.'

'You should probably sit a while and keep your head down,' I suggested.

'Probably,' he agreed.

'Inspector.' A shout reached us. 'I've found it.' It was the policeman who had gone left.

Alfred jumped up, wobbled and made his way, unsteadily, out of the gate with all of us in tow. The path ran outside the fence, below the level of the mound and, as we followed it around the corner, we came across the constable standing by the opening of a stone pipe.

'This must be it,' the constable declared proudly, but spoilt his moment of triumph by tripping and having to run three steps to regain his balance.

'And there is the rope.' I pointed to where it crossed the path and ran off in front of the church towards the graveyard.

'Follow it,' Alfred barked. 'Find the other end. Leave one lantern here. Quickly.' He swayed and Agnust put a hand behind him surreptitiously so that the inspector's men could not see his weakness.

The first constable rushed off with Gerrund in hot pursuit, two more men at their heels and me, trailing as closely as my short legs and long dress would allow. The rope was slack as it meandered between the old, tilted gravestones and, about twenty yards in, we came to the end of it.

'Look,' I shouted.

There was a figure, about another thirty yards away, on the main path that led to the front door of St Aegbald's – a woman moving quickly away from the church to disappear through the Great Gate. There was something familiar about those long strides. Gerrund and the policeman chased after her, stumbling on the rough ground, their lanterns swinging wildly with each pace until they too were lost to sight.

I made my way back to Alfred and Agnust. The beam illuminated his face for a moment, and I did not like what I saw. Alfred looked pale and queasy.

'You need to see a doctor,' I advised, and he nodded weakly. 'When this is over.'

Will it ever be over? I wondered but said, 'I do not think Romulus could get here at this time of night.'

'I'll get the police surgeon to look at me in the morning. He's a reliable man.'

‘Never change,’ Agnust said. She was still supporting him. ‘Get into scrapes when you’re a boy. Get into bigger scrapes when you’re a man.’

‘Inspector Stanbury is just doing his job,’ I defended my friend.

‘Should be a vicar.’ Agnust removed her arm carefully and he remained upright. ‘Like your old pa want.’

This was news to me and, to judge from his expression, to Alfred too. His father was not an especially religious man.

For a moment we were lit then cast into shadow.

‘The lighthouse.’ I watched the beam skim over the rooftops.

‘Wha’ever that old witch get up to now?’ Agnust wondered.

‘Nothing good,’ I said.

The glass of the observatory on the roof of Break House glittered briefly as the beam swept by.

Alfred raised his hand as if in salute but really to shade his eyes. He leaned forwards touching a memorial to steady himself. ‘What the hell?’ And I too glimpsed something in the roughly scythed grass – a mass of hair and blood.

I picked up the lantern and held it forwards. Beside a tangle of rough gardening twine was a rabbit, a noose around its neck, tied to a wooden peg in the earth.

‘Disembowelled that as well,’ Alfred observed bleakly.

‘But why?’ I stared in disgust.

‘How would you get a rope along a forty-foot pipe?’ Alfred asked but followed his own question with another for me. ‘Remember when your parents brought electricity to Thetbury Hall? How did they get the cables through your mother’s garden?’

‘They used the old drainage system,’ I recalled. ‘And…’ I snapped my fingers and Agnust tutted at my unladylike behaviour. ‘They got in the rat catcher. He sent a ferret along the pipe with a string tied to its collar and used that to pull the wire through.’

‘And how did they get the ferret to go along the pipe?’

‘They lured it along using a rabbit as bait.’

‘And there it is.’ Gerrund prodded his foot in the unfortunate creature’s direction.

A length of cord lay across the path. 'He probably used that to draw back the bolt.' I conjectured.

'But how could he bolt the door and get out?' Gerrund wondered.

'Loop of string and you can slide a bolt home from the outside,' Alfred explained.

There were voices and footsteps and we looked across to see the three men return.

'Thought we had her in Seraphim Square, sir,' one constable announced. 'But witnesses say she's been there all the time.'

'Damn it,' Alfred cursed and Agnust made to show him the back of her hand for such foul language but, remembering his position now, she scratched her ear instead.

'She might just have been visiting a grave,' I suggested.

'Strange time for tha',' Agnust commented. She had sat all night for a week by her mother's place of burial for fear of body snatchers – a breed made extinct long before then by the Anatomy Act.

'It's possible,' Alfred concurred. 'In fact, probable. It must have taken a great deal of strength to shift that main post.'

'Not if it were sawn through at an angle,' I theorised. 'Then it might slide apart much more easily.'

Alfred cocked an eyebrow. 'Could do with you in the force,' he said to loud cackles from his men. 'Did any of you think of that?' He challenged and the laughter was cut off rather like conversations often were by problems with my telephone.

The constables shuffled their feet. 'Must be tha' knock on his head,' one mumbled and his companions sniggered.

'What was that?' His superior demanded, though he must have heard, and they all went back to scraping their shoes on the ground.

'I just say we must look ahead,' the mumbler explained, 'to the day women be policemen.'

I had to admire his powers of extemporisation and Alfred piffed in disbelief but let the matter drop.

'What do we do now, sir?' one of his men, having shuffled a hole in the moss, enquired.

'We get shovels and wheelbarrows, and we clear the rubble off that poor soul.'

'But where we get them from?'

'Freenes' ironmongery.' Alfred touched his hair, and his fingers came away bloodied.

'Very good, sir. First thin' in the marnin'.'

'Now.'

'But he'll be closed.'

'Then bang on his door and tell him to unclose.' Stanbury brought out a handkerchief. 'Remind him I can look more closely into where he gets his stock from.'

The constable hesitated then grinned. 'Yes sir.'

'Three of you go. You other three will accompany Lady Violet and her servants back to Break House. The rest of you stay with me.'

'Servants?' Agnust repeated indignantly, never a one to accept what people referred to as *her place*. I half believed that I was still a child in her eyes. After all, she had scolded me and protected me when I was little and continued to do so now that I was less little. Alfred ignored her.

'I might be able to help,' I argued and was glad that he did not ask what possible use I could be.

'I cannot take the risk.' He fumbled to strike a match and his hand shook as he relit his cigar. 'Whoever it was could still be here and may strike again.'

I opened my mouth to object.

'It might be best, milady,' Gerrund counselled.

'You will see a doctor?' I checked quietly.

'When I have the time,' he promised.

I took a last look at the tumbled ruins of the Hurren Family mausoleum. They must have thought, when they constructed it, that they were enshrining their name for all time and yet the family was all but extinct now and their memorial had not lasted a half century. I could not help but remember the words of Shelley about the transitory natures of power and glory.

> Look on my Works, ye Mighty, and despair!
> Nothing beside remains. Round the decay…

–

I was too shaken to even consider going to bed.

'Would you like me to sit with you?' Gerrund asked when he brought my fountain.

'If you are not too tired, I would be glad of your company for a few minutes.' I watched the sugar lump begin to crumble under the steady drip of chilled water. 'I am sure you would like a drink.'

'Thank you, milady.'

He helped himself to a neat brandy.

'Not too late in bed,' Agnust admonished us both and went to her room to shout her prayers. 'The lord dint listen to those who mumble,' she had often told me, 'and silent praying int any use. God has better things to do than poke about in your muddled head.' Her supplications often reached me from her bedroom for she always left the door slightly ajar so as not to shut out her saviour. 'Make Lady Violet see some sense,' was a frequent invocation. 'Help her grow to a respectable height.' Tonight, though, she prayed for the man we had found so brutally murdered.

'How can anybody be so cruel?' I stood in the middle of the room while Gerrund positioned himself with his back to the unmade fireplace, rather like Inspector Hefty readying himself to reveal the identity of the murderer. If only real life were so tidy.

'We can only hope he was killed quickly,' Gerrund said, 'and… those things done to him afterwards.'

'Why is somebody doing this?' I watched the green goddess tremble in my unsteady hand.

'I wish I knew, milady.' He swirled his brandy. 'I cannot think of anyone you could have offended so badly, least not since I entered your service.'

We sat to face each other in my high-backed leather chairs, the room lit only by a lamp on my escritoire.

'Feel free to smoke.' I sipped my drink.

'Never in your presence, milady.'

'What did you do before you came here?' I wondered, and he grimaced.

'Things best not put into words,' he said.

We drank on in silence until, at last, Gerrund excused himself and I was left alone with the Green Goddess and my characters for company. Havelock Hefty emerged through the fog of my grey matter wearing a checked deerstalker hat. He would certainly not be allowed to wear that in any of my stories.

That woman you saw in the graveyard, he pronounced, *was dressed entirely in green.*

'You could not possibly tell in that light,' I argued aloud.

Electric blue, Ruby insisted but it could have been either or neither.

I stared into the glass, but it held no absinthe nor any answers. It was probably not a good idea for me to have another in my state of shock and so I had two more and I must have fallen sleep in my chair for I woke briefly to find Agnust putting a blanket over me, before I fell back into a troubled sleep. It was filled with nightmares, but none so horrible as what we had witnessed that night.

30: FIGHTING WOLVES AND LAUDANUM

ALFRED STANBURY CALLED.

'You look a mess,' he told me, and a proverb came to mind – something about pots calling kettles.

He looked a bigger mess and exhausted, his face grey and drawn. His suit was crumpled and dusty and his shirt grubby. He was all right he assured me, but he did not look it.

There was no time for him to consult a doctor or for him to share my pot of coffee but, it transpired, he did have time for a very old malt. I was not sure that he should be drinking alcohol but at least it put a little colour in his cheeks.

'We have taken him to the mortuary,' he told me. 'Unfortunately, word got out. We can't screen the cemetery off. So there's quite a crowd of spectators, though there's little to see now, except the ruined mausoleum. The press have been taking photographs and asking questions, of course.' He took the whisky from me. 'Needless to say, the word *maniac* has been much bandied about.'

'Have you any idea who the victim was?'

Alfred half-drained his glass. 'One of my men recognised him. He was a Mr Amos Trandel.'

'I think I have heard that name.'

'You may well have. He had a bicycle repair shop in Shepherd's Lane.'

'Oh yes. Hettie took hers there once after she had collided with the coalman's cart.'

Alfred snorted. 'That sounds like her.'

'I never met him, but she said he was a nice man,' I recalled. 'He told her that he was an ex-don who had tired of Cambridge academic politics. He did not charge Hettie very much to straighten the wheel and demonstrated how to apply the rear brakes a fraction before the first to stop her going over the handlebars.'

Alfred laughed, the weariness lifting from his face for a moment before his despondency returned. 'Speaking of Hettie, how is she now?'

'She is slowly recovering but still getting headaches – more, I think, than she admits.'

'She has my sympathies.' He touched his temple.

'I can send Agnust out for some laudanum.'

'I need to stay awake.' He scowled.

That was rather tactless if you don't mind my saying, Hefty replaced my copy of the Police Gazette into my walnut Canterbury rack. *You must be aware that his wife is an opium fiend.*

I had heard rumours to that effect but not paid much attention to them until I saw Alfred's expression. She had started to take the medicine, it was rumoured, during the birth of their second child.

'You could try some of Agnust's toothache mixture,' I suggested, and his lips crimped.

'Her willow water? She gave me some of that when I had broken ribs. It shrivelled my tongue for a week.'

I glimpsed myself in the mirror. I had not washed, changed my dress or done anything to my bedraggled so-called coiffure. Alfred's use of the word *mess* was more than justified. It was not a pretty sight.

It never is, Ruby drifted across my cerebral cortex, cigarette in hand, and rather fetching in my flamingo pink ball gown, but one glare from me into my brain had her gliding gracefully away. She had fought off two wolves once and still been elegant enough to dance with a crown prince afterwards.

'Does anybody know why he was killed?'

Alfred inhaled deeply through his mouth and breathed out through his nose.

'Not yet.' He paced to the window and stared out. 'This was always the safe part of town before I joined the force.'

I went to stand beside him. 'You cannot blame yourself.'

'How can I not? It is my job to protect people.' His left eye ticked. Had we not been on public view I would have hugged or shaken him or both.

Three boys ran across the square towards the Great Gate carrying their sticks and hoops. I indicated in their direction. 'Children can still play in the gardens without fear.'

'For how much longer?' he asked bitterly, and I knew that it was pointless to try to reassure him.

'What will you do now?'

He stared at his drink. 'I'm off to see Superintendent Padmore. We need more officers. The men looking for Lisbeth are getting nowhere. They would be better employed searching for the killer.'

'I assume you think he or she and the kidnapper one and the same person?'

'That seems a fair assumption for now but it is less and less likely to be a woman.' He drained his whisky. 'I'll let you know if we make any progress.' We went into the hall. 'In the meantime,' he continued, 'I am doubling the guard front and back.' He slipped his arms wearily into his coat sleeves and looked me in the eye. 'I can't stop you but please don't go out.'

'I won't,' I promised.

Good, Havelock Hefty appeared, elbows on the mantlepiece in his characteristic pose. *You will be able to concentrate on saving me.*

Leave me alone, I snapped and I was absolutely sure that I had not said it out loud but Alfred shot me a curious glance as he bade me goodbye.

'Father of twenty-four shot in mistake for a rabbit,' the newspaper vendor bellowed as he passed my door.

31: BLIGHT'S BLACK AND A CONFERENCE OF CHARACTERS

GERRUND BROUGHT MY fountain.

'No ice,' he told me in much the same tone that a doctor might tell me to go straight to the undertakers and not to stop for a coffee on the way.

He could have broken that more gently, Ruby glowered for she had taken to chilling her gin cocktails lately. They looked delectable but she had never offered to mix one for me.

'But I thought we had enough for another week.'

'We did but a mouse got in and it's not fit for human consumption now.'

Hefty produced his magnifying glass. *It is obvious from the slight whitening of his fingertips that he has been secreting a supply of the aforementioned frozen water for his own personal consumption.*

It is not a catastrophe, I consoled myself as Gerrund returned to his kitchen.

It is cataclysmic, the Green Fairy hissed. *My magical powers are reduced if I am not chilled.*

I dripped water over the sugar lump.

Speaking of Petunia Bottle, Hefty said though we had not been. *I have been reviewing her case.* He sucked on his pipe for so long that I thought he had finished and was raising my torsade glass to my lips when he recommenced. *Thirty-six concerns spring immediately to mind.*

Oh Lord. Ruby flicked her cigarette. *It is going to be a longer night than when he set out to prove that all the Ripper victims committed suicide.*

He adopted his declamatory stance by the fireplace. *Do you not think it odd that there were no accounts of the alleged attack upon her person in any of the newspapers?*

Perhaps the police wanted to keep it quiet so as not to cause alarm, I suggested, *or so that the maniac would know that they were on his trail.* Even I found both of those ideas unconvincing.

Also, he continued as if I had not spoken, *she told you that she had grasped the knife and yet only her palm was scarred, not her fingers.*

Never seen a knife that was only sharp on one side? Ruby flopped onto my chaise longue. *Unlike the one Lancelot Overstrand is wielding with such…* She paused to give greater emphasis to her next word. *Deadly effect.*

Wisely he ignored her. *In my illustrious career—*

Was this before you became a policeman? Ruby enquired innocently.

Scotland Yard's premier detective went through entire novels to bask in the glory of his denouement, however, and he was not so easily distracted. *I have made something of a study of ink. And the letter you showed me contained a pigment known as Blight's Black, which was not used by Gregson and Fry until the end of '93. Tetracarbaperchlorinatium,* Hefty asserted so confidently that I almost believed him.

Even if you are correct, I reasoned. *They might have been copies that she made. The originals would be with the police.*

If she copied them at the time, she would have used the older formula of ink, he countered.

What if she made them recently from memory?

Even to the extent of ripping out the same kind of paper and scuffing it – just a little too much for natural wear and tear?

The hedge, Ruby prompted him before I could respond.

What first aroused my suspicions of Mrs Bottle – he pointed with the stem of his briar and I glanced over my shoulder, mildly bemused to find the armchair still unoccupied, – *was her account of her attacker lying in wait behind the* beech *hedge. Mr Splitbury, the farmer, only planted it in eighty-seven after he inherited the house. He wanted a windbreak for his alleged wife's purported vegetable plot. This was two years after the Maniac had made his first appearance.*

What about your fourth point? I asked and Ruby clapped a hand to her forehead.

We will deal with those another time, Hefty said airily. Clearly, he had not thought of anything else yet.

I was not sure that any of his points were valid, but I was sure that I did not feel comfortable in the presence of Mrs Petunia Bottle. Nor did I trust her.

Never trust a woman, Ruby advised sagely, *especially me.*

I sipped my absinthe. It was tepid but, whatever the fairy had averred, her powers were undiminished.

-

The subject of our conference called at Break House the next morning. If I had been propelled out of a lady's house by a finger in my back, I would not have returned, certainly not without an apology and an invitation. Even then I might have declined on a matter of principle i.e. pride. I was coming to realise, though, that Petunia Bottle quite happily took some things, such as liberties, but was unwilling to take others, such as hints.

In she sailed, all bottle green bearing a brown cardboard folder tied in a black ribbon.

'Violet.' She leant forwards to kiss me. 'Thank you for seeing me.' I sidestepped, pretending not to have noticed her intent.

There would be no ushering her to a seat this time, I determined, nor did I offer her a drink. I did, however, get straight to the point.

'What can I do for you?' I could not bring myself to *Petunia* her. Seemingly oblivious to my slights, she settled into an armchair and, not wishing to be left standing before her like a naughty schoolgirl called into her headmistress's office, I sat to face her.

Mrs Bottle raised her folder an inch or two off her lap. 'There is something I would like you to read.'

Having been waylaid by aspiring authors on a number of occasions, I greeted this news warily. Flattering though it was to have people seeking my opinion, I found they rarely welcomed it.

'I would prefer not to do so,' I told Mrs Bottle and prepared to rise in the hope that she would follow my lead.

'I really think you should.' There was a nastiness in her tone I had not witnessed before in our short acquaintance. Was I being menaced in my own home?

You are, Ruby confirmed. *Offer her a whisky. That should drown the taste of cyanide.*

'And why should I read it?' My words could have chilled my absinthe.

'Because it is in your interests to do so.' My visitor out-froze me with ease.

The last time I was told that something was in my interests was by a solicitor wanting me to put my inheritance under his control. Luckily, I took Ruby's advice that I should not trust him with my ashtray and declined. Two months later he set sail for South America to purchase an estancia with his other clients' savings.

Have a look at it, Ruby urged for she was even nosier than I.

'Very well.' I took the proffered folder. 'Before I look at this...' I untied the ribbon. 'I must ask you something.' I saw her lips tighten. 'Did you send me those anonymous notes?'

'You have had more than one?'

Well done, Thorn. Ruby applauded. *Yet again you have given her information with nothing in return.*

'Did you?'

'Certainly not.' Mrs Bottle clenched her fists and I braced myself for an assault that never came. 'The very thought of it.'

'But you wrote the ones that you showed me,' I stated.

'I might have,' she half-admitted shamelessly.

In for a penny, Ruby said.

'And you made up that story about being attacked.'

'How did you know?'

'There were too many inconstancies in your account.'

Hyperchlorocarbamtetraheliumbate, Hefty reminded me though I had a feeling that it was not what he had called it the previous night.

'I had to gain your trust somehow.'

'You never had it,' I assured her. 'But I am still puzzled as to your motives. Did you intend to recommend a private detective agency who could extort money from me in pretence of investigating the case?'

Mrs Bottle laughed. It was quite a natural, careless laugh.

'You are well suited to your profession, Lady Violet,' she told me, 'and would probably excel at mine.'

'And that is?'

Journalism, Inspector Hefty deduced. *You can tell by the Fleet Street frill on her cuff.*

'I am a journalist,' she confirmed. 'Your story interested me, but I feared that you would tell me to mind my own business if I approached you in my official capacity.'

'Which is exactly what I am telling you now,' I said coldly. 'You would appear to have wasted your time.'

She shrugged.

'On the contrary you have given me a great deal of information.' She opened her folder. 'Which is how I was able to write this, the first of a series of articles, about you.'

She held out the folder and I took it.

There were a few pages neatly typed.

LADY NOVELIST RECEIVES DEATH THREATS, I read silently.

> Lady Violet Thorn, the reclusive writer of gory shilling shockers has recently had a taste of her own medicine in a manner reminiscent of the lurid tales which she inflicts upon the unsuspecting public.

I glanced up at my visitor who sat, hands folded primly in her lap.

> Dwarfish Lady Violet, lives in Seraphim Square guarded by an immense, dull-witted maid and a mysterious man. We are not privy to the nature of his relationship with either woman. Lady Violet has been the recipient of a written death threat, the contents of which she divulged to our own reporter.

I broke off reading. 'Every other word is libellous.'

'The *Montford Chronical*'s editor does not think so.' She folded her hands in her lap complaisantly. 'In fact, they would welcome a lawsuit for the publicity that it would generate.'

'The whole article is malicious.' My words were met with indifference. 'Alfred Stanberry,' I read aloud. 'You have misspelt his name. It is b-u-r-y.'

'You see,' she said serenely. 'You have already assisted me.'

'That was not my intent.' I went back to the page. 'A married Inspector at Montford police station with whom Lady Violet confessed to having a personal relationship…' I slammed the paper down. 'It was not like that at all.'

'You told me that you know him personally.'

'I did,' I admitted. 'But I also told you that there was nothing untoward in our relationship.'

'And I have said as much.' I read a lower line. *'Lady Violet, smiling coquettishly, denied that any impropriety had taken place between them.'*

I had a powerful impulse to fling the folder in her face.

'Inspector Stanbury is a devoted family man,' I said as calmly as I could. 'He is also a dedicated officer. If you publish this, you will damage his career and injure his wife and children.'

I should have known that there was no point in appealing to her better nature for it was apparent that she did not have one.

'Are you asking me to supress the truth?'

'I am asking you not to hold a distorting mirror to it.' It was obvious that I was wasting my time. 'What do you want?' I demanded. 'Are you trying to blackmail me? I am not a wealthy woman, but I can pay you more than the *Chronical* if you will sign a promise to withdraw your article.'

Mrs Bottle leaned back. 'Thank you.'

'For what?' I asked warily.

'For giving me more material. A panic-stricken Lady Violet tried to bribe our reporter to…'

'You are a disgusting woman.' I threw the folder across the room, scattering the pages over the floor.

'When this failed, her behaviour became insulting and violent.'

'Get out.'

'And she forcibly evicted our reporter onto the street.' Petunia Bottle passed smilingly into the hall.

Agnust lumbered up.

'I tell you she's a wrong-un.' She folded her arms. Now that I thought of it, I had not heard her walk away after showing my visitor in nor approach. 'Been listenin' at the door,' she confirmed before I could even ask.

'How interesting,' Mrs Bottle, if that were her real name, said. 'You have six fingers on each hand.'

'Int got no business countin' a woman's parts,' Agnust bristled and gestured with a thumb over her shoulder rather like the landlord of the Thetbury Arms when customers got too rowdy – Hettie and I on one occasion. 'Out.'

'Good day, Lady Violet.' My visitor held out her hand, but I did not take it.

'Go,' I said, and my maid hustled her out.

'If she try get in this house again I leave her damaged on the doorstep, I do,' Agnust vowed and I had no doubt, as she tramped off to her room, that she meant it.

I told you she was a mountebank. Hefty tapped out his pipe in the fireplace.

'Silence, both of you,' I yelled aloud as Ruby appeared. 'All of you,' I added as a stray constable dithered in my limbic lobe.

I snatched at Ruby's whisky but my hand went straight through it.

Of course you couldn't grasp it. Ruby added a splash of soda. *You never grasp anything.*

Because you are merely a figment of our imagination, Havelock Hefty explained.

–

I spoke to Romulus on the telephone.

'Leave it with me,' he said. 'I know Brasker-Fulton, the editor. He's an unpleasant fellow as you might expect from one who glories in people's misery for a living but he owes me a favour. I was on hand when he was knocked unconscious by the husband of a woman he had insulted in print.' But I did not dare to relax.

Anthony called in the meantime in a very busily patterned jacket. 'Remembered where I saw that Bottle woman before,' he told me. 'She talked to my Aunt Sarah after she was robbed in the gardens. Aunt Sarah thought that she was being sympathetic but…'

'She is a reporter,' I interrupted. 'Rather a pity you did not remember sooner.'

I was about to tell him why when Rommy rang me back. 'Bad news, I'm afraid. He told me I was only doing my job when I helped him just as he is doing his now. Oleaginous swine. Next time I shall leave him in the gutter.'

I knew, as I replaced the receiver, that Rommy would do no such thing. He might hate a man, but he would never refuse him medical attention.

'Thank you for trying.'

'Not that I suppose it will do any good, but you have a few days' breathing space. He wants to finish a series about the decline of the wool industry first.'

'I suppose a delay is better than nothing. Give my love to Jane.'

'I shall flay the blighter,' Anthony vowed when I had explained. 'Do you think Friendless would lend me his whip?'

I told him that I thought it unlikely.

'I shall go to see him myself,' I announced.

'But what can you do?' he asked quite reasonably.

Grovel to him, Ruby predicted.

How dare you? Hefty fumed. *Her ladyship may be a fawning toadeater, but she NEVER grovels – well almost never and then not very much.*

'Probably nothing,' I replied to Anthony. 'But I have to try.'

'Then I shall come with you.'

'You shall not,' I assured him and went to select a hat.

Not that one, Ruby advised. *It makes you look like a…*

Lady violet looks nothing at all like a horseshoe bat, Hefty protested so loyally that I was sketching his funeral plans in my head even as I opened the front door.

–

The *Montford Chronical* was based in a tilted medieval terraced building sandwiched between the premises of a seed merchant and a furniture shop. Only by a brass plate on the Suffolk pink stucco frontage could one discern the business of the premises. The actual printing was carried out in a converted warehouse in Middle Montford.

The front door was ajar and, there being no bell or knocker, I entered. Three clerks perched at high desks cratchiting mournfully away with long quill pens which I thought had fallen out of favour along with steel-caged crinolines.

And Inspector Hefty stories, Ruby contributed unkindly.

'Good afternoon Miss. May I be of assistance?' The oldest and, therefore, probably the senior clerk lowered his head to peer over the top of his half-moon spectacles. The other two, deciding that I was not worth more than a cursory glance, returned to their tasks.

'I have an appointment to see Mr Brasker-Fulton,' I prevaricated, handing him my card.

The clerk tipped back his head to peer through his half-moon spectacles. 'Ah yes, milady.' He wheezed and passed the card to the youngest and, therefore, probably the most junior clerk. 'Give that to Mr Brasker-Fulton right away.'

The junior went to the central door behind them, knocked and went through.

'What?' I heard. 'She's got a nerve.'

I have one in my left shoulder, Hefty complained.

But none in your head, Ruby added.

The junior reappeared, announced, 'He will see you now,' and returned to his desk.

A pointy-faced man – presumably Brasker-Fulton – stood beside a huge heavy oak desk, sniffing the air suspiciously as his eyes alighted upon me. He was younger than I had expected, probably no more than thirty.

'Come to gloat, have you?' He demanded though, if I were to list my motives for attending his office, it would not have occurred to me to include that one.

'What do you mean?'

'You understand English, don't you? Or is mine not good enough for your highborn, highbred hoity-toity ears? Gloat – G-L-O-A-T. You know what the word means, I take it.'

'You think that I have come to glory in having my name and reputation besmeared in your feculent rag?' I demanded.

He twitched. 'On the contrary, I think you have come to glory in not having your name and reputation besmeared in my fec— whatever rag.'

'What on earth are you talking about?'

The editor picked up a black cardboard box file and thrust it at me.

It is full of venomous shrews, Hefty warned as I cautiously opened the lid to find the box full of venomous newspaper articles. I flicked through them – *Lady Violet Thorn and the Police Inspector* – *Dwarf Emerges from Den.*

Who was gloating at whom? I wondered.

'Take it.'

'But what…'

'Now get out.'

'But why…' I was going to enquire why he was giving me the box but he was loosing a stream of, 'Why? Did you really imagine that you would be welcome here? I could have run that story for at least a dozen editions and now I have a paper with no headlines.' He ran his fingers through his wispy goatee.

You did not mention that he had one, Ruby pointed out.

Does it matter?

It could be a vital clue, Hefty said though everything was a clue to him, and all clues were vital.

'I do not understand.'

'Then let me spell it out for you.' Was this turning into an English lesson? If so, I had better get out my slate and chalk. 'You may feel you have beaten me, Lady so-called Violet, but you had better watch every step you take from now on. There is nothing whatsoever to stop me from publishing other stories about you.'

I thought I had not understood before, but I had hardly dipped my toes in the pool of incomprehension.

'I did not come here to make an enemy of you,' I assured him.

'You did not need to come here to do that,' he tugged at his previously unmentioned flimsy moustaches. 'You had already done so.' He went to fling open the door before realising that I had not shut it. 'And don't come back.'

'I shall,' I retorted defiantly before realising there was no point in making an enemy of an enemy, 'not.'

I went back to the outer office where the two younger clerks returned hastily to their tasks. The door slammed behind me.

The senior put down his quill.

'Allow me to escort you to the door, milady.'

'That will not be necessary, thank you.'

'It would be my privilege.'

'Very well.'

'Carry on with your work Smith and Snow.' He panted as we walked to the front and out onto the street as if we had made a steep ascent. 'If I might make so bold, Milady, am I correct in assuming that you are not aware why you have been given those documents.'

'You are perfectly correct.'

A fly whisked lightly by.

'If I might explain, young Mr Brasker-Fulton who you have just met, has only just taken over the *Chronical* from his father and is determined to prove himself worthy of the role. I believe that he failed in a few other ventures including an otter farm. He wanted to publish those articles to boost flagging sales.'

'But they contain lies and perversions of the truth,' I protested, and the old clerk raised his eyebrows.

'As I suspected.' The fingers of his right hand, I noticed, were hooked and noduled by rheumatism. 'Mr Brasker-Fulton senior would never have sanctioned such scurrilous things. Young Mr Brasker-Fulton was so excited about his coup that he could not resist showing the advances to his father. The door into the inner office has a large gap under it and, whilst I should not wish to eavesdrop…'

'You could not help but overhear.'

'Quite so. From what I could glean from this and my friendship with Mr Brasker-Fulton senior's valet, the old man immediately summoned Mrs Petunia Bottle to his home and offered her £100 for these and any other stories that she might produce concerning you.'

'A princely sum. What is the going rate?'

'She would have been lucky to get five pounds for them all.'

A motor vehicle came along. There was a bull's head mascot on the front, but I did not recognise the make nor the driver with his scarf-swathed face. While the clerk clamped a voluminous ink-stained handkerchief over his mouth I clamped my hands over my ears as it rattled and banged past spewing fumes. Horses shied, drivers fighting to stop them rearing or stampeding.

'So why offer so much?' I shouted when the noise had subsided sufficiently.

'So that she would sign a contract assigning the exclusive rights to him. Whereupon he immediately ordered that the documents be handed to you and all copies destroyed and made it clear that there was no point in her writing anymore.' He coughed chestily.

'Why on earth would he do that?'

'I believe it was because of information given to Mr Brasker-Fulton by his valet about his granddaughter's nanny, Kettine.' He caught his breath. 'The valet had overheard Kettine talking about how she had been attacked. She had already boasted to the kitchen maid that she was having an… assignation and leaving her charge unattended in his front garden. You see, Lady Violet, Kettine was the nanny with the child that you saved from being disfigured by the betrayed wife's brother. Needless to say, she was dismissed without a character.' He broke into a spasmodic cough. 'This is Mr Brasker-Fulton's way of saying thank you for saving his granddaughter.'

'He could actually say it,' I sulked, but the old clerk shook his head.

'I gather he is in no fit state to do so. The effort of negotiating the agreement exhausted him.' He chewed his lower lip. 'It may have been his last significant act.'

'If you see him perhaps you could thank him from me.'

He smiled tightly. 'I am a clerk, milady. I do not get invited for afternoon tea.'

'Thank you for telling me.'

The old man shrugged lightly. 'It may be my last significant act too.' And set off breathlessly back up the corridor.

32: THE DEATH OF A DEAD MAN

AGNUST HAD GONE to the laundry to complain about a rip in one of my dresses though I was not sure that she had not created it, taking their tag off. Gerrund had set off for the butchers to purchase some lamb cutlets for dinner.

Left alone, I sat in my usual chair by the window, watching the newspaper vendor bellowing, 'Woman bitten by kipper loses finger' when I noticed a man, respectably but shabbily dressed walking unsteadily towards my house. Five yards away, he stopped, looked straight back at me then continued towards my front door. Surprisingly – for beggars are rarely that presumptuous – it seemed that he was about to ring the bell but he looked at me again, lowered his face and limped hurriedly away.

I got up and went to my escritoire to start a letter to my father. He had made me promise to send regular reports. Hardly had I got past the obligatory salutations when the doorbell sounded.

It was Alfred and he looked exhausted.

'We have found Lisbeth,' he announced the moment I had closed the door behind him.

'Alive?'

'And well.' He dropped his cane into the stand. 'Or as well as can be expected after such an ordeal.' He slipped out of his coat.

'Thank God.'

'And the Suffolk Constabulary.' He put his bowler on the table.

'How did you find her?' I wondered briefly why he was not more triumphant.

'Spot of luck really.' We went through into my front sitting room. 'And an alert officer.'

I was not aware that such a creature existed, Ruby jibed but Hefty did not rise to the bait. He had found an unexpected ally in Miss Gibson and did not wish to alienate her.

'It was Sergeant Webb. His sister lives down East Kelham way and noticed a light in an old farmhouse which she thought was deserted. Luckily for everyone he went to investigate.'

So, it was a woman who was alert really, Ruby carped, *but, of course, all credit must go to a man.*

'He peered through a crack in the shutters and saw Lisbeth sitting at a kitchen table with a man who had his back to him.' Alfred paced the room as he recounted his tale. 'Webb was out of uniform and went round to the front of the house intending to pretend to be asking for directions. The kidnapper answered the door and Webb recognised him immediately. The eyepatch helped. It was Samuel Flowerdew.'

'But Sammy…' I began.

'I know.' Alfred raised a hand. 'We all thought he was dead and buried.' He glanced towards my sideboard. 'But you have to bear in mind that the dead man's face would have been blown away.'

I raised a decanter and he raised his eyebrows and nodded. 'But he wrote a note.'

'So he did,' Alfred concurred as I poured him a Scotch, 'but only to mislead us, just as he dressed the dead man in his own clothes.' He took my outheld tumbler. 'Judging by the blood-stains, Flowerdew must have made him dress in them before he shot him.'

'But Sammy is not a murderer.'

'Unfortunately, he was.'

'Was?'

'I'll come to that.' Alfred swirled his drink. 'By Webb's account, he made no attempt to resist.'

'I doubt he could have overpowered the sergeant anyway,' I commented, for Webb was a substantial man.

'Most people would have at least tried or made a run for it,' Alfred argued, 'but he sat meekly back at the table while Webb asked Lisbeth if she was all right.'

'And was she?' I knew, of course, that he had said she was well but the way he referred to her *ordeal* gave me pause for concern.

Alfred grimaced. 'This is, as it all is, strictly confidential.'

'Of course.'

'I'm afraid poor Lisbeth was outraged.'

'Oh, dear God.' I put a hand to my mouth in shock. 'By Sammy? Surely not?'

'I fear so.' He looked down into his whisky. 'She tried to tell Webb that she had been treated well.'

'Few girls will willingly admit to being violated.' I poured myself a drink, splashing some over the silver tray. 'Which is one reason so many men escape justice.'

'Many a maid could attest to that,' Alfred agreed, 'but they are afraid to lose their positions with sullied reputations. Their attackers always say they were led on.' He rattled his fingerplates on the sideboard. 'Flowerdew openly confessed to his crime and admitted that she had resisted him with all her strength.'

As I recalled, Alfred had known Sammy quite well but was clearly unwilling to use his first name now.

'I cannot believe this. He was such an innocent.'

'Sadly, it transpires that he was not.' Alfred sighed. 'He told Webb that he had seen her at a garden party, but she had spurned his advances and told him to leave before she called her father over. He left but his desire for her grew into an obsession.'

'And so he kidnapped her?'

'At knifepoint. He took a carver from the canteen and threw the rest of the cutlery, box and all, out of the window into the moat. I think, in his muddled way, he thought he was concealing evidence.'

Alfred put his glass down and put a hand inside his jacket. 'May I?'

'By all means.'

Alfred produced his crocodile case and drew out a cigar.

'According to Webb, his account became quite muddled after that but, having had his way with Lisbeth, he was losing interest in her. By his own account, he was offended that she did not welcome his advances once she had been… taken.' He shook his head. 'Obviously she knew who he was and so he had two choices – to kill her or himself – until a third occurred to him.'

'To pretend to have committed suicide,' I concluded.

'Exactly.' Alfred struck a match. 'He found a man close enough to his size to fill his suit and of course…' He sucked at the flame and shook out the match. 'The suicide note was in his handwriting.' Alfred drew on his cigar.

'You have still not told me why you refer to him in the past tense.'

'When Flowerdew had finished his confession, Webb arrested him. He asked if he could get his coat, opened a cupboard, and took out a shotgun. Naturally Webb thought that it was to be used on him or at least to threaten him. There was a table between them and so Webb had no chance of overpowering him. He was about to bluff that several other officers were on the way when Flowerdew turned the gun upon himself and pulled the trigger.' Alfred picked up his glass again. 'As you can imagine, it blew half his head off, just as had happened to his substitute.'

'And Lisbeth witnessed all this?'

'Unfortunately, yes. Needless to say, she is in shock but at least she is safe back at home now.' He rested his cigar on the edge of the mantlepiece and I fetched him my Limoges ashtray. 'He also left a long, detailed written confession to the murders.'

'The recent ones?'

'And the old ones. He started after he was shot in the head. Thought that he should not be the only one to suffer.'

I took a drink. 'I still cannot…' I pinched the bridge of my nose. 'But why was there a gap?'

'According to his account he was nearly captured when he killed Damaris Jones. You may remember that case.'

'She was found dying,' I recalled, 'in the Capricorn Brewery yard.'

'Flowerdew was seen stabbing her. I'm sorry if…'

'I had read all the details,' I assured him.

Her face had been hacked to pieces.

'Two men gave chase and he only just managed to elude capture. It frightened him so much that he stopped for a while and then he went to Oxford.'

I was about to have another drink when a thought struck me. 'You do not think that he was the Oxford Strangler?'

'That did occur to me but those killing started before he went there and continued after he left.' Alfred shrugged. 'Besides which they were not his style.' He grimaced. 'None of them were mutilated.'

'If Sammy was so bloodthirsty, why did he not kill Lisbeth?'

'He loved her,' Alfred said simply.

'Some perversion of love perhaps.' I tucked a stray tress behind my ear. 'Would you like another drink?'

'I should get going.' Alfred hesitated and I knew that look all too well.

'There is something else.' He rubbed his temples. 'I think you should sit down, Violet.'

'Why? I—'

'Please.' He gestured and I sat on an upright chair.

'What is it?' My mind raced but came up with nothing.

He crouched in front of me and took both my hands, his face deeply troubled.

'Alfred, what is it?'

'I have something awful to tell you, Violet...'

'What?' I demanded, frightened now. Had Sammy hurt Harriet? I had not seen her for a few days. 'Tell me please.'

'It concerns...' he swallowed. 'It concerns Jack, Violet. I'm very, truly sorry to tell you...' He hesitated.

'Is he dead? Did Sammy kill him too?'

Alfred's lips moved and I thought I had gone deaf, but I could still hear the traffic outside my window. 'I'm sorry,' he managed at last. 'Flowerdew saw it as revenge for the accident.'

'So he kidnapped Jack?' My head swam. 'And made him jilt me?'

'Yes.'

I jumped up and Alfred rose too, just in time to steady me and guide me back into my chair.

'Tell me.' I stared into his troubled eyes.

'Flowerdew tortured Jack – he did not tell Webb how – to make him write that letter.'

'God forgive me!' I gasped. 'I hated Jack for what I thought he had done.'

'You were not to know. None of us knew.'

'I should have trusted him.' My voice rose. 'I should have spent every penny of my inheritance looking for him.'

'It would have been wasted. Flowerdew killed him the moment he had signed his name so he must have written his secret message before that.'

'How?' I breathed and Alfred looked puzzled. 'How did he kill Jack?'

Alfred broke his gaze. 'I do not want…'

'You are my friend, Alfred.' I clutched at a fold in my dress. 'I would rather hear it from you than at the inquest.'

Alfred took my hands again and I gripped his with some absurd idea of preventing his escape before he had answered me. He licked his dry lips.

'Flowerdew cut his throat.'

Despite his attempts to stop me, I struggled to my feet.

'Is something wrong, milady?' I had not even heard Gerrund enter.

'Very wrong,' Alfred told him, but it was my news now.

'Jack is dead,' I cried, aghast at my own words. 'Abducted and murdered.'

Gerrund reached out and took me in his arms. 'Oh, milady,' he said softly, 'if I could take your pain, I would do it gladly.' Others would also be distraught at the news but I knew then that this particular anguish could only be, and would always be, mine.

'Alone,' I whispered and buried my face in Gerrund's embrace.

Time is not, whatever the adage tells us, the great healer. It does not heal at all. It scabs over the wounds but the scars never fade. At best it teaches us that we can endure suffering because we have no choice. At first, I relied on alcohol to anaesthetise my feelings, but it only confused them. Perhaps, if I had been able to attend a funeral for Jack, or if there had been a grave to visit, I might have found a degree of comfort but his body, Alfred reluctantly told me, had been weighed down and thrown into the sea at Sackwater. Jack once joked that he wanted to be buried at sea, but in a Viking ship set ablaze to drift out into the ocean, not in the potato sack that Sammy used.

Sammy's family refused to accept his body. They gave it up for dissection. The police exhumed the man who had been buried in his name but were unable to identify the remains. Both of them would end up in unmarked paupers' graves, though not, given the delay in burying Sammy, side by side.

No inquest was held for Jack. Neither the chief commissioner nor the coroner believed that the evidence of a deranged man was sufficient cause for declaring him dead before the statutory seven years had elapsed when his death could be presumed.

Winter came and brought the desperately needed rain too late for that year's crops and in such sudden storms that the water often did more harm than good. The Angle burst its banks and low-lying areas were flooded. Much of the lowers were underwater and some who lived in cellars were drowned. So fearsome was the reputation of the inhabitants, though, that few efforts were made to help them. Gerrund, Agnust and I took food and blankets but were lucky to escape with our lives when a gang mugged us on the way there to take our supplies not to those who were most desperate but to those who had the most money.

I almost spent Christmas at home. Why ruin everybody else's festivities, I thought, until I remembered that Agnust would not get the opportunity to visit friends and family in Norfolk and

Gerrund would not get the time off that I had promised him. He had been mysterious when I asked what his plans were.

Either he is going to steal the crown jewels, Havelock Hefty forecast – I had still not finished or even named what was intended to be his last book – *or he has the offer of a better job.*

Agnust and Gerrund were both adamant that I would not be left alone for the festivities.

'Think I trust you with my duster?' Agnust challenged because it was such a sacred object that it was rarely brought out of its shrine i.e. the cupboard.

'Think I trust you in my kitchen?' Gerrund challenged with more justification. My cooking skills were overstretched by baking jacket potatoes in the ashes of a bonfire.

I saw the season through at Thetbury Hall. Rose, my sister, tried, but failed, to buck me up by persuading me to sit precariously on a horse. The poor creature became almost as melancholic as me. My mother sought to console me with readings from the bible. *My Brother Esau was a hairy man,* being a favourite. My father managed a retraction of the assertion he had made on the day that we had thought I was being jilted. Possibly the fellow was not a filthy coypu after all. Strangely, their ineptness helped a little.

I never appreciated quite how lucky I was with my staff. Agnust and Gerrund worked hard to try to distract me with other topics. Agnust taught me how to sew – though I cannot pretend that I had ever wanted her to do so – and Gerrund how to play brag properly – a much more useful, if less ladylike, skill. I even won fourpence from him in one game. I cannot remember how much I lost in others.

My friends were stalwarts. They came often and supported me in their different ways. Hettie began a fresh portrait of me and rarely had to scold me to sit still for, at times I was virtually catatonic. Rommy pressed me to stay at Suthy Hall where Jane proved excellent company. I had expected to be nursing her. But, as Count Vorolski Zugravescu, Ruby's arch enemy once said, the proverbial boot, fitted on the alternate foot. At my request, Alfred took me fishing, scolding gently when I did not notice that my float was submerged and racing upstream. Even Friendless proved that his name was not entirely justified. He called on a number of occasions to take me for rides and regale me with tales of his adventures almost all of which involved Old Queeny losing a shoe.

Anthony, however, was my greatest rock. He visited every day when I was home, amused me with unlikely accounts of his aunts and auditions; sat with my hand in his in comfortable silence for hours sometimes; held me when I sobbed and made no attempt to take advantage of my vulnerable state.

A true gentleman, Ruby observed, *but an even truer fool.*

Not for the first time my heroine was wrong. Anthony was too sensitive to my feelings and cared too much for me to press his case. Because he did not ask for my affections, they developed into something unexpressed but deeper.

For all the support I was given, I was still in pain. Although I was bereaved, I did not wear mourning. I existed in it.

33: THE MAN WITH THE WOODEN HAND

I HAD ARRANGED to meet Hettie, but she sent a note to Break House by a street urchin to inform me that she had been given an unexpected commission. It came from a lady who wanted her portrait done in time to spoil her husband's birthday and Hettie could not afford to turn her away. *Besides*, my friend wrote, *I get itchy when I am not working.* I had no grounds for complaint since my friend had devoted a great deal of time to me in recent months.

I gave the girl thruppence and she frowned.

The Straculiar *lady say you give me a tanner.*

I had thought that *straculiar* – strange and peculiar – was unique to Thetbury but it must have strayed over the border into Suffolk along with anthrax or woolsorters' disease, as it was commonly known.

Hettie, I knew, would have said no such thing, and had probably paid her already but I put another three pennies in her outstretched hand. Though she was probably no more than ten years old her fingers were already calloused from work. As a rule, she would be lucky to reach two score years and ten, two decades less than those who regarded themselves as her betters.

I nearly stayed in after receiving Hettie's message, but I had work to do – a powerful motive for going out.

The Empire Café was quiet.

They have all been abducted and are being shipped off to Tangiers, Hefty hypothesised. *But fear not, Lady Violet, I shall rescue them in your next book.*

You couldn't rescue a haddock from drowning, Ruby taunted and he gritted his teeth in an unconvincing grin. *What a wit you are, Miss Gibson.*

I was shown to a table with four chairs by the window and had hardly settled before I was asked for my order and served.

There were probably no more than thirty people in Market Square, browsing the wares, but one man caught my attention. He was respectably dressed but hatless. He had a severe limp and wore leather gloves as many did in this inclement weather. I watched him making his way between the stalls. It seemed to me that he was looking straight at me and I was sure that I had seen him before. As he came closer my suspicions were realised. This was the man who I had seen approach my house as if to ring the bell – just before Alfred had come to tell me of Lisbeth's rescue and Jack's death. Anthony had sent him away from outside my house at least once since then to my knowledge but may not have wanted to worry me if the event had been repeated.

The man came to the door.

His hair was lank and unkempt; he had a heavy stubble; and his clothes were well-made but worn rather than ragged. Either the suit had been passed on to him or, if it was his from new, he had fallen on hard times.

He shares Havelock's tailor, Ruby quipped with little justification for Scotland Yard's premier detective was a dapper man.

It fits too well to be a hand-me-down. He ignored her remark.

The waistband is too large, I objected.

If he has become poor, rather than always been poor, he will have lost weight, Hefty reasoned. I hated it when my characters were more logical than I.

The man closed the door behind him and stepped forwards but Mrs Frow-Fulford, the manageress, blocked his way. Although she was a slightly built woman, she had a commanding air which brooked no nonsense.

'Tradesmen to the back,' she said haughtily, though one could have argued – if one were feeling especially brave – that she was in trade herself.

'I would like a table,' he told her.

'There is a coffee stall in the square.'

'I prefer your establishment,' he replied, quite pleasantly for a man who was being insulted, and reached into his pocket. 'I have money.' He held out a handful of coins. 'And I shall be no trouble. You have my word on it.' His voice was soft but carried and his manner was courteous.

'Very well.' Mrs Frow-Fulford shrugged for she had not enough business that day to turn customers away.

The waitress showed him to a corner where he sat directly facing me across the unoccupied tables.

The man's gaze had settled on me. I lowered my eyes but, when I raised them again, he was still staring.

Hefty touched his left shoulder. *My wound always tingles when I am close to a murderer.*

Not in real life, I told him, and he stalked off in a fit of pique.

With some difficulty, the man rose and, as I warily watched, unsteadily approached.

'I am sorry to disturb you.' He had a well-educated voice indicating that he had, as I suspected, probably seen better days. 'But am I correct in thinking that you are Lady Violet Thorn?'

He is going to beg for money, Ruby forecast but I motioned her away.

'And who are you to ask?'

'My name is Arthur Beech,' he said softly, and I grasped my cake fork. It was not much of a weapon, but it was all I had. He raised both hands, still gloved, in surrender. 'I see that you remember the name but, please, don't be alarmed. I mean you no harm and I want nothing from you.'

'Then what *do* you want?' I asked warily.

'May I ask, first of all – and, believe me, I do not wish to pry into your personal life – but did you marry Mr Raven?'

I almost told him that he was being impertinent, but his manner was so gentle and unassuming that I found it difficult to be abrupt with him.

'I did not,' I told him, wondering why I was not feeling frightened.

'And – one more question, if I may – are you still in contact with him?'

Highly presumptuous for a man who does not wish to pry. Hefty beckoned a waitress. *A pot of China tea.* But none was forthcoming.

At one time Arthur Beech's question would have aroused anger in my breast because of my belief that I had been forsaken. More recently it would have torn open the wounds inflicted when I learnt of Jack's death and was confronted by the knowledge that it was I who had betrayed him by doubting his love. Now my emotions were no better controlled but much better hidden.

Arthur Beech waited but his wait, I resolved, would be in vain. I had no intention of explaining any of this to him, but a slight involuntary shake of my head must have given him his answer.

'Now you can answer my question.' I hoped that he was not as aware as I was of the slight tremor in my voice. I looked him in the eye, and he returned my gaze openly. 'Why did you try to kill me?' I waited for him to tell me that he had tripped up and readied myself to refute his version of events.

'I did not,' he began as I had expected. 'Why would I? You had done nothing to offend me. I did not even know who you were. If I were a murderer, would I really make an attempt on your life in full view of your companion and my friends?'

I found myself unable to refute that logic. Only an uncontrolled madman would have acted in such a way, and Arthur Beech did not strike me as a lunatic.

Not all crackpots have wild eyes and wilder hair, Hefty pointed out. *Exempli gratia, Lancelot Overstrand was suave and urbane until he tried to kill me but FAILED.* He placed so much emphasis on his last word that I was surprised it did not collapse under the weight.

Arthur Beech shifted to his right as he awaited my reply.

'So you are sticking to your claim that you stumbled into me?'

'No.' The man winced. 'I am so sorry, but I must sit down. I have been walking all day and my stump is bleeding.' He tapped his left leg and pulled out a chair, leaving it well clear of the table so as not to impose too closely on me.

'I am expecting a friend at any moment,' I told him, 'and he is a police officer.'

Arthur Beech's eyes flickered. 'I have had unpleasant experiences at the hands of his metropolitan colleagues.' He held out his open hands. 'But, just as you have nothing to fear from me, I have nothing to fear from him – if he is a fair-minded man. I will go away the moment you ask me to.'

There was nothing threatening in his manner nor any malice in those deep-set hazel eyes.

'What do you claim happened?' I asked, replacing my fork on the plate.

'I know that you will not believe me, but I can only tell you the truth.' His right cheek ticked. 'I was trying to save you.'

I snorted incredulously.

'You are right about one thing. I do not believe you.' I leaned towards him. 'And now I should like you to go.'

He sucked his lips in and put his left hand on the arm of his chair in preparation of rising.

'As I promised, I shall go but I was probably a yard away when you fell. I rushed to grab your arm, but Mr Raven fought me off.'

'Of course he did,' I asserted. 'Now leave.'

Arthur Beech struggled, grimacing, halfway up, the chair rocking sideways. He fell back into his chair with a grunt, rattling the crockery on my table. 'I'm so sorry.' He braced himself again.

Even by your standards this is heartless, Ruby rebuked me, putting her unseen hand on his arm.

It was only then that I realised why he was wearing gloves. Arthur Beech had had his right hand amputated.

Well done, Ruby clapped slowly.

'Please do not get up,' I urged since he was obviously in pain, and he relaxed his grip.

'Thank you. I shall leave as soon as I have steadied myself, but I fear I feel quite dizzy.'

Aunt Igitha had told me once that the poor suffer dizzy spells from drinking too much strum and some did but the majority were suffering from poor nutrition. Romulus had tried to organise a cooperative where people could purchase food at little more than it cost but opposition, sometimes violent, from local tradesmen had soon put a stop to his scheme.

'Then you must rest.' A thought occurred to me. It was unlikely that he would be able to afford the railway fare. 'How did you get here?'

'I cadge rides.' He rocked side to side, presumably in an attempt to make himself comfortable but it seemed obvious that he had failed. 'There is a regular flow of waggons taking food from Montford to London and bringing luxury goods back. Most of the drivers work alone and are glad of a bit of company. It helps if I make a few jokes first.'

Despite myself I smiled. 'I am sure it does.' I waved to the waitress who ignored me. She probably had no wish to serve such a disreputable-looking character, so I kept waving until she could no longer pretend not to see my signal. 'Do you prefer tea or coffee?' I asked as she arrived, and he gaped at me, his eyes wide in surprise.

'Coffee would be delightful.'

'With cream?'

He gaped as if hardly believing his ears and yet it was such a small thing for me to offer him. 'Yes please.'

'And cake?'

His hand trembled. 'Your chocolate cake looks rather good.'

'An extra-large slice,' I ordered, aware that Mrs Frow-Fulford was hovering, probably debating whether or not to evict us both. It was obvious that she did not approve of Hettie, but I was stretching her tolerance to its limits with my latest companion. There was a danger that I would find myself banned from the two best Cafes in Montford.

The waitress looked for instructions from her employer who nodded reluctantly.

'Will that be all, Madam?'

I glanced at my hand. Nobody had slipped a ring on my finger, nor would anybody ever.

'Milady,' I corrected her for there is no point in having a title if one does not flaunt it. The waitress was new, but Mrs Frow-Fulford knew full well who I was. It did no harm, though, to remind her that the gentry were frequenting her establishment.

'Milady,' the waitress bobbed in a curtsy, and I instantly regretted my high-handedness. She was little more than a girl and I had intimidated her.

'Yes, that will be all for now, thank you.' I gave her a smile, resolving to follow it with a tip, and she scurried back to the counter.

'Why are you doing this?' Arthur Beech rubbed his stubble.

'I am not sure.' I toyed with my cake knife. 'Let me be clear about what you are claiming. Are you telling me that Mr Raven misunderstood your intent when you ran up to me?'

'That is exactly it.' Arthur Beech swayed. 'But I believe that I misunderstood his intent as well.'

'Then why...' I tried to marshal my thoughts. 'But I felt you push me.'

'Not me,' he said quietly but firmly. 'Somebody pushed you and I thought, at the time, that it was your companion.'

'This is absurd.' Maybe the man was mad after all. 'He fought to save me.'

Arthur Beech puffed. 'I believe now that he did, Lady Violet. At the time I thought he was trying to kill me.'

'Why, in heaven's name?'

'I believed myself to be the only witness to his intention and the one who was foiling it.'

'This is all rubbish,' I said as the waitress returned with a tray.

'I'm sorry Milady. Have I done wrong?'

'Not in the least.' I hoped I was not frightening her off her employment. 'I am sorry I was talking to my guest.'

Relieved, she unloaded the tray and left us. Arthur Beech bit the end of his left glove to pull his hand out of it and let the glove fall onto the table.

'I said you would not believe me,' he reminded me. 'But I thought he was some kind of maniac. I did not know at the time that he was your fiancé.'

'Then why did you change your story?'

'Because I began to doubt it myself. Another man had just gone past, very close to you and I could almost swear that he laughed. Perhaps he pushed you.'

'Describe him,' I challenged.

'Tall.' He felt the pot. 'Very tall.'

'And cadaverous?' I heard myself asking.

'Do you know him?'

'Was he?'

'I am not sure. I only glimpsed him before all hell broke loose.'

Scratby, Hefty hissed as I tried to marshal my thoughts.

And failed. Ruby lolled in the chair between us to my right.

'You had better drink your coffee before it gets cold,' I said, and he lifted the pot to refill my cup first.

'What happened to you after...' I hardly liked to call it an accident.

'I was an architect and doing quite well, but I could not draw with my left hand.' He peeled the cuff of his right glove down a fraction to show me the carved wooden substitute inside. 'My mother was a widow with a small pension, and I had nobody else to turn to. I tried numerous jobs, but nothing suited me. I became quite good at writing slogans to advertise products but there was little financial reward in that, and it was not unknown for companies to take my ideas and pay me nothing.' Arthur Beech pinched his left earlobe. 'I try my hand –' He smiled ironically at his pun, probably unintentional '– at whatever comes along.'

'Why are you contacting me now?' I stirred my coffee vaguely aware that I had yet to add any milk or sugar.

He lowered his head. 'I wanted to put things straight.'

'You came to my house.'

'I did. But I lost my nerve.' He raised his head wearily. 'And, when I regained it and returned, a visitor of yours threatened me with the police.'

That would have been Anthony.

'Why did you not tell the police this at the time? Surely your friends would have supported your account.'

'They all said they had not seen what happened.' He puffed out his cheeks. 'But I suspect that none of them wanted to be embroiled in a case where, if the verdict went against me, they would be associated with an attempted murderer.'

'Some friends,' I commented, and he trembled, whether from emotion or exhaustion, I could not tell.

'I can only repeat that I was telling the truth when I said I was trying to save you.' His eyes glistened. 'Somebody pushed you.'

'This is absurd,' I said more loudly than I meant to, and Mrs Frow-Fulford looked at us sharply and came over.

'Is this man causing trouble, Lady Violet?'

I nearly told her that he was, but something restrained me.

A faint spark of human decency, Hefty suggested.

'Not in the least,' I assured her, and she looked askance but returned to her desk by the front door.

'Why on earth would a complete stranger have wanted to kill me?'

He cut a tiny piece off his cake, evidently planning to savour every mouthful.

'And yet that is exactly what you believe of me.' Arthur Beech's voice softened. 'But when I see a lady with your – forgive me for my forwardness – charms, my instincts are to cherish and protect, not to hurt her.'

On any other occasion I would have found such presumptuousness outrageous, but I felt sure that he meant no harm by it.

'Even if what you are saying is true,' I told him as calmly as I could. 'Why have you waited until now to set matters straight?'

Arthur Beech chewed and swallowed. 'That day haunts me. Obviously, my injuries prevent me from forgetting it ever but there is more to it than that. It has always plagued my mind that two people should think me a potential murderer and then I saw an interview you gave at the beginning of the year.' He cleared his throat. 'I was in a reading library trying to keep warm and dry. You spoke of the incident. It is hard enough to gain employment as it is and I was terrified that, you might in a future interview, mention my name. I wished to appeal to you not to do so.' He coughed into his napkin. 'And so, I came to Montford but, as I said, I funked it outside your house. I knew you would not believe me and that you could have me arrested for pestering you and bring about the publicity I dreaded.' He dropped his napkin into his lap. 'So I decided there and then to go back to London and not to trouble you.'

'What changed your mind?' I asked.

'On my way to the waggon yard I saw him.'

'Him?'

'Mr Raven.'

I sat forwards. 'You were mistaken.'

'No. I saw him as clearly as I see you. I was walking down Old Bakery Street and he was coming up it in a carriage. My head was down to look at the cobbles. You can't afford to miss your step with an iron leg.' He tapped his knee with his cake fork. 'A gang of waggoners was coming down the road behind me. I remember wondering how we would all get past each other. It was a substantial vehicle, nearly scraping the sides so I stepped into a doorway to let it pass. It was then that I saw him.'

'You did not,' I said firmly but he continued as if I had not spoken.

'Mr Raven's appearance was somewhat altered. He had dyed his blond hair black, but I knew at once who he was. You cannot change your eyes and, from the way his widened, it was obvious that he knew me too.

'He called out *Stop* and the carriage came to a halt immediately. It was going very slowly anyway. He said something else and made as if to open the door but the waggoners started singing, some bawdy song about a donkey and I could not be sure of his words.'

'*Old Danny's Donkey*,' I supplied as if it mattered.

'That's the one.' Arthur Beech agreed. 'Mr Raven…'

'It was not him.'

'Even as Mr Raven reached through the open window for the handle, he was jerked backwards. The singing was getting louder but I heard *Drive on. Quickly, man.* The curtain closed and the carriage set off again.'

'Curtain?'

'Yes. It was a fine carriage, maroon with a gold shield on the side.'

Your Uncle Tiberius. Hefty sat, bolt upright in the chair to my left. *I never trusted him with his wispy hair.*

The design is not unique, I said uneasily.

'You had a glimpse of a dark-haired man and yet…'

'It was him,' Arthur Beech insisted. 'And there was something else.' He glanced at Ruby's chair, unaware that it was occupied. 'He was frightened.'

'He was never afraid.'

'He most assuredly was when I saw him.' He dabbed a few crumbs with his forefinger. 'I had to turn back to warn you.' He rubbed his brow as if he had a headache. 'I fear he may have been kidnapped.'

'No,' I said flatly.

'He looked about him as if in a panic and his words, as I said, were drowned out but I am as certain as I can be that he had mouthed *Help me.*'

I chewed on his statement but there was one unanswerable reason why I could not swallow, let alone digest it.

'Jack Raven is dead.' I surprised myself at how easily I said those words.

Arthur Beech greeted the news with every appearance of genuine surprise. 'Might I ask when he died?'

'In July last year.'

He wrinkled his brow. 'Did you see his body?'

'He was buried at sea.' Spoken, it sounded a much more ceremonial affair than it would have been.

Arthur Beech bit off a chunk of cake and chewed thoughtfully, washing it down with his coffee.

'I fear you have been deceived.'

'His murderer confessed.'

'He or she was either lying or deluded.'

Why was it that everything he said sounded more reasonable than anything I could articulate? I watched him finish his cake.

'I do not know what else I can do or say to convince you, Lady Violet, but I swear by all I hold holy that Jack Raven is alive, and I am genuinely afraid for him.'

None of this makes sense, I told myself.

'Would you be willing to come with me and report this at the police station?' I asked, ignoring the fact that I had pretended that an officer was about to join us. 'I have a friend who is an inspector. He is a good man and will listen with an open mind.'

And send him packing, Hefty was tucking into a steak and kidney pudding. I had never seen that on the menu.

'I am sorry but no.' Arthur Beech put his fork back on the plate. 'You see, Lady Violet, I have two criminal convictions.'

I told you his left temple was too bulbous, Hefty claimed though he had said no such thing.

'Might I ask what your offences were?'

'The first time I sheltered in a shop doorway against the wind and rain.'

'But surely, that is not a crime?'

'It is if you have no money. I was found guilty of vagrancy and given seven days in prison. So, ironically, as punishment for the offence of seeking shelter, the government gave me food and shelter for a week.' He laughed mirthlessly. 'The second time I saw my old employer coming out of his office. I had been a good and loyal worker. He had told me as much himself and so I approached him for a small loan – just enough to buy a square meal. I was desperate and genuinely meant to repay him when I could. He summoned a constable and reported me for begging. I was given one month's hard labour.' He picked the last specks of cake off his plate. 'I have never met a policeman yet who took the word of a criminal.'

'But my friend is a reasonable man,' I assured him.

'I am sorry.' He struggled to his feet. 'But I have done what I came to do.'

'Can I write to you if I need more information?'

'Of course you can.' He smiled lopsidedly. 'Mr Arthur Beech, no fixed abode. It is bound to find me.'

'You know where I live if you have anything else to tell me.'

The table rocked under his weight. 'I have told you everything I know.'

He has spun you a cock and bull story. Ruby drew on her cigarette in a long, slim ebony holder.

I am sure that you are right, I agreed, *but I am equally certain that he believes it and came all this way to warn me.*

I unclipped my handbag and brought out my purse. 'At least let me help you.'

He held up his false hand. 'And get me arrested again?'

'Please.' I found two ten-shilling notes and emptied out my change. 'I must give you something for your trouble.'

He took the money without a word, gave me a warning look, and stumbled out. I put my purse away then remembered that I would need it to pay the bill. 'Botheration.' It was only then that I realised I had no more money on me.

Have a care you don't get arrested, Hefty warned but we both know that a smart appearance, an upper-class accent and a title give one legal immunity for almost anything.

You call that smart? Ruby fingered my new russet coat as if it were something at which the rag and bone man might turn up his nose. She was wearing one of my alizarin crimson dresses and looked much better in it than I.

'This is a little embarrassing,' I told Mrs Frow-Fulford and explained the situation.

'That's quite alright, Milady.' She smiled graciously. 'Just leave your handbag as security whilst you go home to fetch the money.'

Slink meekly away, Hefty recommended and I had no option but to follow his advice.

34: RELIGIOUS ORDERS AND THE PEARWOOD PAWN

SERGEANT GORBALS, OR *Bushy*, as he was known, for his extravagant facial hair, was on duty when I arrived at Montford police station. He was inspecting Sergeant Webb's construction.

'Wha' d'you s'pose it might be?' He asked in wonder, his voice almost as big as him.

That does not make sense. Ruby leant on the desk as if it were a saloon bar.

'A model,' I told him, and he raised a shaggy eyebrow.

'Clever.' He turned it this way and that admiringly. 'Wish I can make one. Need to take up smokin' first though, I do believe.'

I had not given that point any consideration but, when I gave it a little, it appeared that Webb must have lit his pipe a few thousand times to have amassed so many matchsticks. I doubted that he would resort to rooting through the ashtrays and bins for other men's cast-offs.

'Is Inspector Stanbury in?'

Gorbals frowned – at least I fancied that he did so behind his poorly pruned shrubbery. 'Tha's a tricky one. If I say he is, you want to see him withou' a' n'appointment and you int allowed. If I say he int, I am lyin'.'

'Thank you.' I set off down the corridor.

'Bu' I int said he is,' Gorbals protested.

'Your non-committal was very eloquent,' I called back.

'Thank you very much, milady.' I could imagine him fluffing up his facial plumage at my imagined compliment.

Alfred was at his desk, or rather, partly on it, his head down on his folded arms. I crept in. It seemed a shame to wake him, but I wanted to talk. I cleared my throat.

'Ask Mummy,' he said but did not stir.

'Alfred,' I tried.

'For goodness' sake, woman, aren't four children enough for you?'

'I want at least thirty,' I said and he sat up, hair hanging over his brow, cheeks creased by the folds in his jacket sleeve.

'Thirty what?' he asked in confusion.

'Of them.'

He shook his head which, whatever storybooks say, never clears people's thoughts.

'Is this conversation worth pursuing?'

'It most certainly is.' I pulled out a chair. 'Not.'

Alfred put a little finger in his ear and wiggled as swimmers do when trying to rid themselves of a little of the North Sea.

'Good afternoon, Violet,' he started again. 'What can I do for you?' We had a rule that, whilst he often visited me for social reasons, I never called on him at the station for anything other than work. 'And please don't tell me you are on the track of the Chessman of Chester or any other of your alliterate villains.'

'I met a man today.' I sat opposite him.

'And?'

'He had an interesting story to tell me.' *Interesting* was rather an understatement but I did not wish to sound dramatic.

Alfred combed his hair back with his fingers. 'And you wish to share it with me,' he guessed wearily but, to give him credit, listened attentively when I did so.

'I know madmen do not necessarily look mad,' I concluded, 'but he seemed so rational.'

'And he did not ask for anything?'

'Nothing. I gave him a little cash to help him home, but I had to press it on him, and we have both seen enough poor people feign reluctance to know the genuine ones.'

'And he was absolutely sure that it was Jack? I mean he only saw him once before, when they had a fight.'

'He was positive, and he was certain that Jack recognised him.'

Alfred took a half-smoked cigar from his ashtray and chewed upon it.

'I never like murder cases where there is no body,' he admitted.

'But why would Sammy Flowerdew confess to a crime he had not committed?' I unwrapped a stick of Beeman's.

He waved his cigar. 'Some people, who know they are or will be condemned, add to the tally of their murders for the notoriety.' Alfred rattled a box of matches. 'Numerous men have claimed to be the Ripper as they stand on the gallows. But…' He slid the box open and shut again. 'Padmore would think I was mad myself if I told the men to hunt for Jack Raven.'

He sucked on his unlit cigar and blew a non-smoke-ring.

'How is Lisbeth now?' I had written to her but received no reply and I did not feel that my visiting would do anything but distress her.

'She is greatly changed from the child you knew.' Alfred balanced his cigar on the rim of his glass ashtray. 'She was always shy, and she is still very quiet but now she has a strangely…' He searched for the word. 'Assertive air about her, almost a steeliness.'

'Her ordeal would certainly have destroyed her girlishness.'

'She talks of entering a religious order.'

'Becoming a nun?'

He opened and closed his matchbox again. 'I believe she said that no man would want her as his wife so she might as well be a bride of Christ.'

I closed my eyes for a moment. 'I would hope that any mother superior would reject Lisbeth if she applied on those grounds.'

Alfred gestured hopelessly. 'It is not in our hands. Anyway, despite you catching me napping, I have work to do.'

'So you will do nothing about Jack?'

'What can I do?'

'You are the policeman.'

'I am.' He let the box fall onto his desk. 'But you know better than most civilians how limited my powers are. I cannot order a search of the town and, even if I could, we have no idea if Jack is still in the area or even the country or even if he was really here at all.' He got to his feet and I, reluctantly to mine.

'I realise that,' I admitted. 'It is just that sometimes one hopes for miracles.'

Alfred half-smiled. 'Hope all you like, Violet, but don't expect too much.'

–

Two days later I received a letter.

> Dear Lady Violet,
>
> Forgive my illegible scrawl but I am still not adept at using my left hand.
>
> First, I wish to thank you for listening to me and for your kindness. You cannot know what a treat cake and coffee are to me now and the money you gave me is more than I have had in my pocket for many a year.
>
> Second, I felt I had to write to you because of my stupidity. I was tired and in pain and my nerves were overstretched. I said that I had told you everything, but I missed out one detail which struck me as odd at the time – unusual for a gentleman's carriage, that is. As it went by, there was a strong smell of fish about it.
>
> It may be of no import whatsoever, but I felt that you ought to know.
>
> I hope you will exercise great caution. If the man who is holding Mr Raven is still in Montford, I fear he may also mean you harm.
>
> Believe me I wish you nothing but the best,
>
> Arthur Beech.

I thought about going back to Alfred with this new information, but I knew that his response would be the same.

You should send him a brass plate for his desk, Ruby suggested, *NOT MUCH TO GO ON.*

Not much on which to go, Miss Kidd, my old governess chalked squeakily on the blackboard, and I had thought that correct grammar was supposed to make our language more beautiful.

To be fair to my colleague. Inspector Hefty tamped his pipe tobacco with the foot of a miniature pearwood pawn, kept as a reminder of one of his greatest triumphs. *He does not have my massive intellect.*

Also, he does not have a poisoned blade in his heart, I reminded him.

Nor have I. He waved a hand airily. *I erased those sentences whilst you were asleep.*

Was that possible? Hurriedly I found and opened my notebook.

But he was too late, I read, *and the dagger was buried up to the hilt in his breast.*

Cross it out now, Hefty commanded but his voice quavered.

At least make it his shoulder and give him a chance, Ruby bargained.

'Be quiet, both of you,' I snapped.

'You been drinkin' that peppermint cordial?' Agnust came in with my tray of coffee. ''Cause there int nobody here save you and me and I dint say nothin'.'

'There were some children making a racket in the square,' I told her, which was true, or at least it was yesterday.

A waggon loaded with bricks clattered by.

'Now tha's what I call a racket,' my maid commented.

On the contrary, Hefty slipped his tamper into a waistcoat pocket. *It is what I call a vital clue.*

It was probably an hour before I fathomed what he had meant.

35: RAGBALL AND THE POLAR BEAR

ALFRED STANBURY GREETED my theory with his now-habitual scepticism but at least he did not tell me that it was not much to go on.

'For what other reason would he be seen coming up from that area?' I reasoned. 'There is nothing else there.'

'First…' He peered over the top of his wire-framed spectacles. 'We only have one witness who thinks he glimpsed Jack and was almost certainly mistaken. Maybe he bears some grudge against you. He might be hoping for money.'

'He seemed sincere, and he was convinced that it was Jack.'

'Even if it was, there could be all sorts of reasons that he was down there. He might have something stored in one of the warehouses or be looking for a waggon to transport something for him.'

'He is supposed to be dead. He will not be running the estate at Blockborough Hall.' My hair was coming unclipped. I had arranged it in a hurry. 'And do not forget the smell of fish.'

Alfred scratched an eyebrow.

'I cannot apply for a warrant on such flimsy grounds.' He straightened a pile of papers on his desk.

'You could accompany me.'

'Your aunt's man, Scratby, sent me packing last time. Said he had instructions never to admit me.' He turned the papers over so that I could not read them. I liked to think he did so from force of habit rather than a distrust of me. 'And I have no authority to enter the property.' He took off his spectacles and laid them on the blotter.

Hefty looked through them. *You should try my extra-powerful-magnifying spectacles.*

He would need them to see any sense in half of your deductions, Ruby said.

'You could wait outside while I go in.'

'And how would that look if you were injured while I loitered nearby?' Alfred stood up. 'I have a better idea.' He waited for me to get to my feet. 'Don't go.'

'I cannot let this rest.'

He came round the desk.. 'Then take Gerrund with you though it sounds like Agnust was of more use when you got into that scrape in July.'

That scrape was something of an understatement. I had nearly been murdered.

'I cannot ask them. I know they would come, if I did, but they are not employed to act as my bodyguards.'

'Then take that fool, Appleton with you.'

I have never been sure where human hackles are but mine rose. 'He is not a fool.'

'Then take him.'

I shook my head. Anthony had been seriously injured in our last *scrape* and was lucky to walk away from the panther with no more than minor cuts and bruises. I had no right to endanger him again.

We'll make a heroine of you yet, Ruby applauded but I rather wished that my imaginary heroine could go in my place.

'Do you seriously believe it?' Alfred was asking.

'Not really,' I admitted miserably.

'Not much I can do anyway,' he said as I went into the corridor.

-

Gerrund went in search of Friendless and returned with him about half an hour later. He had been at home sponging Old Queeny down.

'I hope your boots int grubby,' Friendless greeted me. 'The reason I tell you is for I just shine my cab and I dint want him makin' dirty with mud or horse manure and filthy boots can do that, I do believe.'

'They are clean,' I promised unaware, until then, that cabs were masculine.

'Or pures,' he remembered. 'Dint want none o' them.'

Pures were dog droppings which the *pure men* would collect, often using their bare hands. A brimming bucket could fetch a tidy sum for use in the tanning industry. Doubtless to local relief, the original factory had moved out of town around the turn of the century and Tannery Lane was lined now by genteel houses.

I brought out an apple core which Old Queeny eyed with disdain, possibly offended to be offered my scraps, and sniffed at my handbag – a new one since the panther had taken such an interest in my old favourite.

'I am sorry I do not have any toffees,' I told her, and she nibbled at the core with curled lips. 'Did Gerrund tell you where I want to go?' I asked her master.

'He do.' Friendless swung up into his seat as I climbed aboard. 'And I wint goo there for none else but you, but I tell you this – if any street slug come near, I put his eye out with my whip, I do.' He pulled it out of its holder and, for the first time, I believed that he would use it.

'Goo on.' He clicked his tongue. 'Please.' And off we set.

The traffic was heavy and our progress slow but luckily I had Friendless, music hall's greatest loss, to entertain me and, sure enough, he slid the hatch open.

'Thought of a good joke.'

'Is it about lighthouses?'

'P'raps.'

'Is it about them being heavy?'

'No but they are. It's about why are they called lighthouses when they are only used in the dark?' Friendless sniggered at his own wit and Old Queeny huffed.

'Most amusing,' I sighed.

'Int finished yet,' he said crossly. 'They should be called… d-d-dark-houses.'

'But they have lights at the top,' I pointed out.

Why are you having this conversation? Ruby groaned. *You only encourage him.*

Friendless wiped his nose on his coat sleeve. 'Dark-houses with lights on top int so funny.'

'Probably not,' I agreed.

'Shall we have a song to lift our spirit, darlin'?' For a moment I thought that he was addressing me but Old Queeny nodded and he raised his voice. I had read somewhere of composers writing atonal works in the belief that they were being modern but Friendless had dispensed with musical keys years ago. 'My true love is a milkmaid,' he warbled. 'A lovely girl is she. She got cowpox in her hands and eyes and now she can't not see. And now she can't not see… me.'

'Did you write that?'

Friendless knitted his brows.

What size needles did he use? Ruby asked.

'Wish I do, write it,' he replied modestly, 'but I int tha' witty.' And treated me to an encore.

The traffic thinned as we approached Old Bakery Street and nothing wider than a handcart loaded with bulging laundry bags passed up as we went down. It was being pushed by a hunched woman who looked elderly but many of the poor aged shockingly quickly and she might have only been twenty years older than me.

We entered the square, Friendless turning his cab around, doubtless for a quicker exit, and looked about him nervously.

I wriggled about in a possibly indecent attempt to straighten my clothes. My dress had twisted anticlockwise and my petticoat in the contra-direction.

'Got fleas?' Friendless leaned over his hatch for a closer inspection of my activities.

'No, I have not.' I ceased my struggles.

'Dint give them to Old Queeny,' he pulled the cord. 'She have 'nough on her own, she do.'

'I shall not,' I assured him, and he narrowed his eyes sceptically.

Apart from the cats sneaking towards us, the square was quiet.

'Where is everyone?' I looked about.

'What day is it?' Friendless asked.

'Tuesday.'

'Ragball,' he announced. 'There's a game, Montford 'gainst all Hams, down Little Bardham way. They wint want miss tha'.'

Ragball was what it sounded, a game played with a ball made of old bits of material bound tightly and villagers all but killed each other for possession of it. In fact fatalities were not unknown. Most notoriously, I had heard that a team of nuns from Woodbridge had trampled a little girl to death as battle raged on a dustheap outside the lowers. Romulus assured me this was a local legend along with the polar bear so frequently and reliably sighted swimming in the River Angle.

The lighthouse still towered on its stone plinth.

Well I never, Ruby ridiculed. *Who would have thought it?*

You will not be so ready to mock her ladyship when The Mystery of the Creeping House is published, Hefty assured her, confident that the trilogy, in which he proposed to be the hero, would occupy my attention for a considerable period.

Take your time, he said gallantly. *Years if you need them.* He paused to examine a cloud before deciding that it could not possibly be a suspect. *Decades,* he added with reckless generosity.

I pulled the bell handle and had not even time to prepare myself to wait because the door flew open as instantly as if I had released a secret catch. Scratby was not as tall as I had remembered. He was taller and gaunter, if that were possible, but his grim expression had not changed one iota.

'Is my aunt…'

'Lady Anglethorpe is not at home,' he declared, 'nor shall she ever be at home to you, unless she sends you an invitation.'

'She has,' I asserted utterly convincingly.

'She has not,' he repeated, utterly unconvinced.

That had not been in the script I had prepared for him. I hate it when actors improvise.

This is not one of your dreadful plays, Ruby reminded me though a large portion of me knew that already.

'If I were to offer you a bribe...' I tried but he did the impossible and grew taller.

'I am incorruptible.' The last man I had heard making that claim was standing for parliament but was now languishing in Ipswich jail.

'I know you are and that is why I want you to stay here and guard my handbag,' I told him. 'I think that I have a gold sovereign in my purse, but I am not sure. I will check when I come back down. The purse may well be empty.'

Scratby wavered for even the most incorruptible are not really.

'And how would I explain my action to my mistress?' he asked. It was encouraging that he was discussing his means of getting away with the deed, rather than its ethics.

'I am sure a man of your imagination...'

'I have none.'

'A man of your intellect,' I tried and could see that he rather liked that. 'Would be able to think of something.'

'I went out to help an injured child,' he said.

'What was wrong with her?'

'She fell and broke an arm.'

'Then why did you not take her to the hospital?'

'A passing waggoner volunteered to do so and, being anxious not to leave her ladyship unattended, I returned to my post little suspecting that this odious midget had sneaked in whilst my back was turned.'

'I am not sure about the *odious midget* part,' I told him.

'A lie is always more convincing if it is presented on a plate of truth,' he postulated quite eloquently and even more offensively.

There is a serious flaw in your plan, Ruby warned but she was always trying to undermine me.

Scratby stood aside and I stepped in.

'I shall leave it here.' I put my bag on a little hall table but had only gone two steps up the spiral when he had marched over and was rifling through it.

Told you.

'You are supposed to wait until I am out of sight,' I objected but Scratby only growled, 'Never mind any of that rubbish.' He tipped out my Lady Derringer. 'What's this?' He picked it up, more like a toy than a lethal weapon in his massive paw, and clicked his tongue. 'Little girls should not play with firearms.'

'How dare you, you impudent flunky?' I tried to fume but I was more alarmed than angry. He was intent on unclipping my purse.

'It is empty.' Scratby threw it on the floor in disgust.

Not as stupid as you think, I told Ruby.

'I said it might be.' I stepped down. 'I suppose you are going to evict me now.'

'Oh no, milady,' he twisted a heavy iron key and extracted it. 'You do not get away that easily.' He turned another key, hung the ring over a hook on a belt around his waist and slid all the bolts home.

'What the devil are you playing at?'

'A less dangerous game than you, I suspect.' He slipped my gun into his jacket pocket.

I scanned our surroundings. It did not take long. The one window in the entrance hall was barred and there was nothing that I could use to defend myself now.

Any clever suggestions? I snapped but Ruby Gibson, my fearless lady adventuress appeared to have fled the scene and Havelock Hefty, muttering something about an emergency, hastened in her wake.

36: COWBOYS AND THE TRAIN TO BROADMOOR

SCRATBY MOTIONED TOWARDS the stairs.

'After you, milady.' And, having nowhere else to go, I went up.

'Are we going to the top?' I asked on the first landing.

'You are,' he replied.

Round and up we continued to the next level.

'The very top?'

'Yes.'

Off we set again until we arrived at the penultimate floor.

'Why are you frightened of ladders?' I waited for a tragic story of how he had fallen off one or a loved one had plunged to his or her death.

'Their parallel rails and divisions remind me of train tracks.' I waited for a tragic story of how he had slipped onto one or a loved one had been pushed to his or her death. 'And I was taken by a train to Broadmoor.'

'The Berkshire Criminal Lunatic Asylum?' I checked. There might be a Broadmoor village in Devon, famed for its cream teas, for all I knew.

'The very same.'

'Ah.' I said lamely, propped my umbrella in what was becoming its traditional place, and began my ascent. This time, however, Scratby loitered. 'Turn around,' I ordered him, concerned that he might catch a tantalising glimpse of my knees – or a glimpse at any rate.

'Don't flatter yourself,' he said but did as I had bidden.

In one of my wild west stories, a cowboy had been climbing out of a well when an Indian had speared him in the neck. This was too gruesome for my publishers and so he was reprieved. With his near-death in mind, I poked my head warily through the hole in the ceiling which instantly became the floor, and I was relieved to find myself unskewered.

Aunt Igitha stood almost exactly as she had before, draped in electric blue and supported on a silver cane, watching me ascend into the lantern room.

'Veety,' she greeted me. 'What a surprise.'

It might be better, I told myself, to at least begin on a civil note.

'Good morning, Aunt. How are you?'

As I had expected, there was a strong fishy smell in the air, for the lamp had been in use since my previous visit.

'None the better for seeing you.' The bridge of her nose had healed without a scar.

There were several wooden crates to the right of her. One, about the size of a tea chest, had a large open book on it, covered by a white card tied around with ribbons. It was the largest crate that concerned me most though. It was similar to the one that had held the panther but stood upright.

'How did you get those up here?' I wondered, not that it mattered, but the hatch in the floor and the door to the balcony were far too small for it to pass through.

'They were assembled in situ.'

'By whom?' I enquired since Scratby was afraid of ladders and I doubted that Aunt Igitha would have set to work with carpentry tools.

'Someone.'

'But what are they for?' There was nothing big enough to store in it in that room unless she planned to disassemble the lantern.

'Let me show you.' She walked over to it.

'Is there an animal in there?' It could not be a wild one or she would be in as much danger as me. A trained mastiff?

'You could say that.' Aunt Igitha put her hand to the side.

'Then please do not open it.'

'Too late.' She smirked and withdrew a bolt, and the side swung a few inches ajar.

I braced myself for a hurtling of fur, teeth and claws, but nothing burst through the gap. She took the free edge in one hand and swung it open.

'Dear God.'

A man was sitting in an upright chair, tied to it by rope around his waist, arms and legs. His head was down, lank black hair hanging loose. His clothes were old and patched. Could this be Arthur Beech? Had he drawn the same conclusions as I and come to investigate? But how had my aunt managed to restrain him? The man groaned.

'What on earth are you doing?' I asked my Aunt and she shrugged.

'Holding him prisoner.'

He raised his head, his stubbled face bloodied and one eye closed.

'Jack.' His name was no more than a whisper as it escaped my throat. 'What has she done to you?'

'Nothing that didn't hurt,' my aunt assured me.

His head lolled.

'Violet? Is that you?' His voice was hoarse and came through cracked lips. 'Oh God, has she caught you too?'

'I rather think,' Aunt Igitha replied for me, 'that our dear little Veety has ensnared herself. I did not lure her here.'

'I have a gun,' I bluffed absurdly since she could see that I did not even have my handbag with me. Was she supposed to believe that I had strapped it to my leg like Gerrund with his knife?

'And I have one too,' Aunt Igitha said. 'But mine, unlike yours, is not invisible.' She reached onto the roof of the crate and, when she lowered her hand, it held a snub-barrelled revolver.

'What are you going to do?'

'Shoot him,' she said, 'and you.'

'Why?'

'Because I can. Unless,' she proceeded, 'you sign this.'

She tapped a large open book on top of another crate.

'Don't do it, Violet,' Jack croaked. 'She tried to make me sign too.'

'What is it?' I asked.

'Take a look for yourself.'

I went over. A window had been cut in the card with just enough space for me to see the word *spinster* beside an empty column. 'A register of marriage… But who are you trying to marry me to? Surely not Scratby?'

'Old Scratters?' Aunt Igitha chuckled as lightly as she might at a garden party. 'Credit the man with some taste.'

'Then who?'

'Me,' Jack said. 'But I shall not be a party to it, come what may.'

'Neither shall I,' I vowed, rather ironically since I had intended to marry him freely the previous year.

'Let me make this simple,' Igitha said to me. 'If you have not signed by the time I count to five, I shall shoot your newly rediscovered beloved, dead. One.'

'You are bluffing.'

'Two.' She stepped towards Jack, the muzzle pointed straight at his head.

'This is lunacy.'

'Three.'

'Don't,' Jack gasped. 'She will kill us anyway.'

'Four.' She cocked the hammer.

'All right.' I rushed over.

There was a pen already resting on the open page.

'Best handwriting,' Igitha instructed, 'and no sneaky misspellings.'

I wrote my name, and she trained the gun back on me. 'Now that didn't hurt, did it? Release him.'

I greeted her words in confusion. Surely, I should be pointing the gun at her to be issuing such an instruction. A newcomer to the scene would think that she was rescuing Jack from my clutches.

Warily I moved towards the bound figure. He watched me, head dropping as if he were losing consciousness again, as I crouched to untie the knot at his ankles. It came apart quite easily and I unravelled the rope.

'If she wants you to sign…' I began.

'I most certainly do,' she assured me.

'Never.'

'Just sign it, Jack,' I urged. 'It is not a valid ceremony.'

'Give me a moment,' he whispered. 'I don't think I can stand.'

'How long have you been like this?'

'I rather lost track of time in there.' He shifted painfully. 'I don't know. About ten or fifteen minutes.'

'But surely…'

'Possibly twenty.' Jack stood up, stretched like a man after a good night's sleep and strolled to the register. 'Now, Igitha.' His voice was suddenly strong. 'Where do I sign?'

Together they undid the bows and put the card aside to uncover the whole register.

'Lady Anglethorpe,' Scratby's voice rose.

'What is it?'

'I have told him that he is no longer required.'

'And has he gone?'

'He has, milady.'

'Very good, Scratby. That will be all for now.'

Jack was leaning over the page, pen in hand. 'Well, Violet, you got your wish after all.'

'So it was all a trick.' I struggled to make any sense of what was happening.

'Just a little game,' he said.

'If you think that marrying me prevents me from testifying against you for some crime, I have to disabuse you,' I declared. 'The law of spousal privilege means that a wife cannot be forced to testify against her husband. It does not mean that she is proscribed from doing so.'

'Have you qualified as a barrister whilst I was away?' Jack sat on a crate. 'If so you have wasted your time. The information is irrelevant.'

Aunt Igitha had a bowl of water and wiped his face clean with a flannel. Wherever the blood had come from, it was not his.

'Congratulations my darling' Aunt Igitha beamed.

'Darling?' I repeated. 'You are her darling?' It was not just the word but the way that she had said it.

'And she mine.' Jack gazed at her. 'Aren't you, my angel?'

Aunt Igitha simpered. 'I certainly am, my sweetest boy.'

I stifled a mocking laugh before deciding that it had as much right as any other laugh to a life but it died as it rose from my throat and almost choked me for Jack was taking her in his arms.

'She is old enough to be your mother,' I said, a little prudishly perhaps, and he flared in fury. 'Leave Mummy out of this.'

Well that was tactful, Ruby said. *Especially as she is dead.*

'Ignore her,' Aunt Igitha told him. 'She has always been a stupid little girl.'

'Whereas you, my beloved, are a beautiful, intelligent woman,' he said and, drawing her close, pressed his full lips to her writhing worms.

I did not believe that he had ever kissed me with such ardour. 'How long has this been going on?'

'You are such an ingenue, VT.' She stroked his cheek. 'Do you really think we went into the woods to look at the folly at that garden party?'

'But he was little more than a boy.'

'Oh no, sweet niece,' she assured me. 'He was every inch a man.'

'Dearest Igitha.' Jack seemed a little short of breath. 'There is something I must ask you.'

Aunt Igitha quivered. 'Is it what I think it is? What I hope and dream and pray it is?'

'I believe so.'

'But not in front of her surely?'

'Who better to see us pledge our troth?' They kissed again. If this had been one of my plays, there would have been an outraged uproar. As it was, shock and nausea were fighting for supremacy in me. Jack went on one knee and took my aunt's right hand in his left. 'My darling Igitha will you make me the happiest man on earth and consent to be my wife?'

Aunt Igitha squealed in delight. 'Of course I will, my dearest.' And Jack rose to hold and kiss her again. Nausea was definitely winning the battle.

'I have a ring.' He looked adoringly into her wrinkled eyes. 'But let us do that part out of her earshot and away from her envious spiteful tongue.'

I was still formulating a spontaneous reply when, with one easy movement, Jack swept Aunt Igitha up in his arms and took her to the door. She reached out and twisted the handle. The wind swept in, and they swept out. Had the whole world gone mad or was it just my world? I wondered.

Jack put my aunt down and went on one knee again and she stroked his thick black hair affectionately. He reached into his waistcoat pocket, appeared to drop the ring, crouched even lower, put his arms around her spindly legs and stood, raising Aunt Igitha high in the air. She waved her arms in alarm and yelled 'Have a care, Jack,' but that was the last thing she was ever to say for, with a jolly laugh and final heave, he tipped her over the rail. Igitha fell, silently, headfirst, her long blue dress fluttering in the wind as she disappeared, too stunned, I supposed, to even cry out.

Jack peered over, rubbed his hands in satisfaction at a job well done and returned to the lamp room, closing the door behind him.

'What a terrible accident,' I commiserated, all too aware that I was the only witness. 'She must have fallen when we were downstairs.'

'We?' Jack frowned. 'I was never here. In fact,' he gave the boyish grin I had once found so attractive but now found rather menacing.

'My mistake,' I said and his grin broadened. I did not remember him having quite so many teeth, but he could not have grown any since we had last met.

'No, dear Violet,' he said with something approaching tenderness. 'Your mistake was in coming here. But do not worry...'

'Why not?' I asked uneasily.

'Because your troubles will soon be over.'

'You are going to release me.'

'I am,' he agreed to my surprised relief, 'from this life.'

'Oh,' I said, never at a loss for the bon mot.

'Your body shall be found with Igitha's. The police will assume you came to kill her and, in the struggle you both fell over the edge.' He made it all sound rather reasonable. 'Luckily she did not scream and alert anybody, so we have all the time in the world.'

'In that case, let me recapitulate.' I felt for a hat pin but decided that using it would only serve to enrage him. 'You said that you were not here. Scratby must know that you are.'

Jack chuckled. 'Old Scratters is my man. I gave him on loan to Igitha. He will disappear when I do.'

'My cabby knows that I am here.'

'It is not a secret that you came but Scratby sent him away, saying you were staying for dinner, so you will be dead before anybody thinks to look for you.'

'Did you really find her attractive?' I wondered and he smirked.

'It is not a woman's face or even her figure that makes her a desirable lover. It is what she is prepared to do for a man and let him do to her.'

I wish I had not asked. The nausea returned, invigorated by its short absence.

'But why kill her?'

'I was recognised the other day. It will only be a matter of time before I am discovered here, and she knew too much.'

'Arthur Beech told me that he saw you.'

'I wondered if he would go to you. He was a lucky man.'

'To lose a hand and a foot, fighting to save my life?'

'I would have killed him on old Bakery Street if those damned waggoners hadn't showed up.'

'Singing *Old Danny's Donkey*,' I put in. If nothing else it might make him suspect that I knew more than I did, though whether it would do me any good or not remained to be seen. 'He thought you said *Help me*.'

'He was right. I was trying to open the carriage door and get my gun out at the same time but the sight caught on the lining of my jacket.'

'So you were with Igitha? In one of Uncle Tiberius's carriages?'

'Igitha borrowed it when she left him, and you know what females are like. Lend them anything and you never get it back.'

'Men are just as bad,' I bridled stupidly at such a trivial point. 'You kept my bandalore.'

'Your what?'

'The double disc I had that rode up and down on a string.'

'Oh that. I swapped it for an apple pie.'

'How typical of a boy,' I fumed. 'It was a present from Uncle Postilius.'

Excuse me Thorn, I told myself. *There are more important issues at stake than a lost toy. Why, for instance did he try to push you under a train?*

I was just about to articulate that question, but Jack spoke first. 'Also I was not sure if you knew that was me in Friar's Square disguised as a tramp.'

'I did not,' I admitted. 'You were hardly visible behind that beard. Why on earth did you grow it?' I could make a good guess at the answer to my question.

'It was false so that I could alter my appearance quickly.'

'I knew that something was wrong with the way that you were dressed.'

'It was a good costume,' he said as indignantly as I might if somebody denigrated one of my new dresses. 'I stole it from the morgue.'

'But you had new socks on. Not many mendicants have any socks, let alone new ones.'

He raised his eyebrows.

'A bit of Inspector Hefty must have rubbed off on you.'

I could imagine Ruby's indignation at the suggestion that he was the ingenious character and her disgust at the idea of bits of him rubbing off.

'And he mentioned the smell of fish.'

'It seeps into everything but I still—'

'There are not many places you might be coming from on Old Bakery Street and also not many people use whale oil in such quantities that they stink of it.'

'I shall be glad to leave this place.'

'But, since you are in no hurry, did my aunt keep anything to drink up here?'

He indicated to the circular bench that lined the wall. 'There are lockers beneath it. The whisky is in five.' I had seen the ball handles but not noticed the numbers on them before. I went on my haunches and pulled the lid. 'You have to turn the handle.' I tried. 'Clockwise,' he added as I struggled.

'Of course.' The rest of the world, as far as I knew, unlocked things anticlockwise but why would anything be normal in the lighthouse?

The front hinged open and I looked inside. There was plenty of space but not much in it – two thirds of a bottle of Irish whiskey with a corkscrew, a cigar clipper and four tumblers. I took two of the last items and poured. The locker, I was interested to observe, had no sides but opened into each of the adjacent containers.

'I hope you don't think you can get me drunk.' Jack watched me fill one glass more than the other.

'I have never managed yet.'

I liked to think that I could hold my drink, but Jack could always consume twice what it took to make me inebriated and maintain every appearance of sobriety. I handed him the larger measure which, being a man, he would not refuse.

'How do I know that you have not drugged it?' He sniffed suspiciously.

'You were watching me,' I said. 'I did not have a phial in my hand and the idea of a tablet that dissolves instantly without residue or taste exists only in the histrionic jottings of Grantham Hogarth.' I said this with more venom than I intended for not only were his Hydrangea Devine stories more profitable than my works, but he had stolen, courtesy of my agent, some of my ideas.

'Your health,' he toasted me.

'My health.' I toasted it too.

Jack had aged more than he should have over the last sixteen months. The greying of his skin was emphasised by the jet-black hair. Arthur Beech had been right to say that Jack was much changed but that his eyes were the same. They were still bright green with little flecks of gold though possibly not as lustrous as they had been.

He looked me up and down with a clinical air. There was a time he had done so admiringly. 'You haven't grown much.'

'As a matter of fact,' I told him stiffly, 'I have not grown at all and there is still something unmanly about the shape of your earlobes.'

'No there is not.' He touched the right one.

'People never see themselves as others do.' I eyed him appraisingly. 'Black hair suits you. Your own was like straw.'

'You told me once I looked like a Greek god.'

'Kophoneastus,' I invented, secure in the knowledge that, unless he had spent the last year or so cramming for a classics' viva, his knowledge of Hellenic mythology was worse than my own.

'Was he…'

'Ugly,' I confirmed, sorry to defame a so-recently-created deity.

'Ugly?'

'Exceptionally.'

'Dear Violet.' He snorted. 'Always ready with the quip but never ready with the love.'

I gaped. 'I always loved you.'

'Not enough to give yourself to me.'

'You said that you respected me too much and that you wanted to wait until we were married,' I reminded him, and he rolled his eyes.

'Of course I did. The man is supposed to say that, and the woman is supposed to seduce him.'

That was news to me.

'Perhaps you were not worth seducing,' I suggested. 'You most certainly are not now. I suggest you stick to old hags in future, Jonathon.' He had always hated being called that. 'They cannot afford to be choosy.'

He tossed back his drink.

'Why are you trying to provoke me?'

In truth I was not sure.

'Why did you make me sign the register?'

'You can see now that I have uncovered it.' Jack motioned me over and I saw that the witnesses had already signed and dated their signatures two years ago. 'It was the day Sammy Flowerdew performed that mock ceremony.'

'But they both knew it was make-believe,' I objected and looked again at the names. 'Amos Trandel. That was him in the mausoleum. I only knew him by his Christian name. God in heaven, Jack! You disembowelled him.'

Jack smirked. 'Funny that. I always thought he had no guts.'

'And Lucy Hallam?' I already knew what had happened to her. It was the stuff of my nightmare.

'Sammy's mother's maid.' Jack smiled fondly at the memory. 'She left his parents' house and came to Montford to be close to her mother. I wrote her a note that the old trout had taken a sudden turn for the worse.'

'And you...'

'Hacked her apart in Freeman's Alley,' he confirmed. 'Lord that was fun. Her mother stood by the window paralysed by fear. I dragged Lucy over so the old ratbag could have a better view.

Lucy was weak by then, but she still put up a struggle and she was begging her mother for help with her last breath.'

I buried my face in my hands. If I could, I would have killed him there and then, but I could not and forced myself to concentrate.

'What about my neighbour, Mrs Hatchpenny and Annie, her maid?'

'The girl was a fool. I flattered her and she let me in. I took her there and then in the hallway.'

'And you cut her throat.'

'You have no idea how satisfying it is to do that – to see the white flesh open and…'

'Shut your filthy, repellent mouth.'

Jack tossed his head, but he no longer had his boyish fringe and the action had lost its charm. 'I kept the old woman prisoner while I chiselled away the wall. I calculated it must have adjoined your study.'

'It did.' I had heard him and thought it was a builder at work.

'After I had had my way with her too…'

'She was an old widow.' I could hardly gather my breath to speak. 'Is there no end to your depravity?'

'I have yet to find it.'

If Romulus had been allowed to perform the autopsies, I reflected, he would have discovered that they had both been outraged.

'And then you hanged her.'

'I intended to burst in whilst you were preoccupied in dealing with her so you could both watch each other die.'

'What went wrong?'

'I had not calculated on you calling your servants. I've seen them both and between them they could probably overpower me.'

'That was stupid of you.'

Jack's fist lashed out but stopped an inch from my face. 'I don't want to ruin your smug little priggish face – yet. Anyway…' Jack giggled and it was not an attractive sound. 'It was just as well I didn't kill you then. I had plenty of other surprises for you.'

Change the subject, I counselled myself. He would get no encouragement from me to glory in his disgusting crimes.

'Why all the subterfuge around the wedding?' I poured him another drink. 'You could have married me quite openly.'

'And I intended to. Originally that ceremony was just my insurance policy in case you broke off our engagement but then I was forced to go into hiding.'

'Why?'

'The Gimlet kidnapping.'

'That was you?' Whilst we were courting, dancing, playing tennis and planning our future, Jack was holding an innocent man prisoner.

'Me and Sammy.'

'Who strangled him?' Those hands had cradled my throat.

'I did.' Jack shrugged as if modestly accepting the credit for an act of great heroism. 'Sammy made a pig's ear of collecting the ransom and the net was closing around us, so I had to disappear.'

'Which is why you wrote the note. But why the message in invisible ink?' I asked and he frowned. 'Gimlet must have written that,' I realised.

'Written what?'

Not wishing to admit that I did not know beyond a probable *HELP ME,* I asked, 'How can you come back now?'

'Sammy admitted everything.'

'But why?'

'I persuaded him that we should both write a full confession of all our deeds so that, if one of us should die, the other could produce it.'

'And you had already decided who was going to die first.'

'You could hardly expect it to be me.' Jack shrugged. 'Besides which, Sammy loved me and was greatly indebted to me. I was one of the few people who stood by him when he went odd.'

'But it was you who shot him.'

'Can't deny it.' He chuckled. 'I suggested the William Tell game the night before. I told Sammy you thought he was boring but if he suggested the idea, you might change your opinion of him. Then I told him to move to make you laugh but really I wanted an excuse for hitting him. I've always been an excellent shot so I needed a convincing reason to hit him. Ironically my shooting Sammy was another reason he loved me. I saved his life.'

'Did he really outrage Lisbeth?'

'Oh yes,' Jack assured me. 'Though he did not know it at the time.'

'How could he possibly not?'

He raised a hand. 'Don't interrupt. It was always a bad habit of yours. Lisbeth loved me and thought that we were going to elope to Gretna Green, so she went willingly when Sammy arrived that night to fake the abduction. I pretended to have strained my back so that I couldn't assist. I told Sammy that Lisbeth loved him and, that when they got to the farmhouse, he should take her by force. She wanted him to do that to salve her conscience but, after that, she would willingly do anything he pleased.'

'But why kidnap her at all if you did not want her? You made no ransom demands.'

'It was a distraction. Three quarters of the Suffolk Constabulary were engaged in the search for Lisbeth whilst I went about my business.'

'So why did you want to marry me today? You cannot have your conjugal rights. It would be revealed at the autopsy.'

'Oh Violet,' Jack said despairingly. 'Do you pay no attention to your correspondence? You must have had a letter from Bailey Waters, the solicitors, telling you that you were coming into a fortune.'

'But that was a crude attempt to extort money from me. They did not even have an office address.'

'They had a fire and used a post office address whilst they found new premises.'

'But you are not poor,' I objected. 'Blockborough Hall is…'

'On the verge of bankruptcy. My father was a fool. He gambled away everything we had and more at the gaming tables and mortgaged the whole estate to the hilt.' Jack took a long draught of his Scotch, his hand trembling in anger. 'If I had known what a fix I would inherit, I should not have bothered killing him or my brother.'

'But they died of typhoid.'

'They did,' he agreed. 'I travelled half the country to Liverpool where there had been an outbreak. The pump handle had been removed by the police, but I told them that I was a government official and had come to take samples for analysis.'

'What about your mother?'

'Oh her.' He snapped his fingers in the air. 'She was no fun after they died, always wailing. She was costing me money that I did not have with her expensive tastes and her maids and she was draining the wine cellar at a prodigious rate. I might have tolerated all of that had she not got drunk and asked why God had taken my brother and not me.'

'And so you killed her too.'

He grinned. 'This would be terrific material for your next book, a pity you shall not live to write it.'

'It was you who tried to push me under that train.'

'Certainly was,' he admitted cheerfully. 'It was a spur of the moment thing.'

'But we were not married then so you would inherit nothing.'

'I had the signed certificate and I could have forged your signature. As I'm sure you will remember, you had a sprained wrist at the time.'

'From coming off that horse,' I recalled. 'But Sammy and the witnesses were all alive then. They knew it was just a rehearsal and I had not put my name to it.'

'As I said, it was a spontaneous act, speaking of which, you were knocked unconscious when you were thrown. I was mortified. I thought you were dead, and I had not had the opportunity to kill you myself. Then I saw that you were breathing, and I pushed you face down in the water. You gasped and bubbled but common sense took over. I had much more to gain by letting you live.'

'Did you never care for me?'

'Of course I did. I cared for my parents and my brothers, and I was fond of Sammy but – hang it all, Violet – fondness does not buy the things that really matter in life. In fact…'

'Some people believe that money does not either.'

'There you go again, interrupting me.' His hands closed into loose fists. 'And, while I think of it, another of your annoying habits is the way you speak. Always *do not* never *don't*. Always *cannot* never *can't*. This is very nearly the twentieth century, Violet. Nobody speaks like that anymore. I don't know if they ever did outside a novel.'

'Miss Kidd forced me to do so and, I suppose, I got into the habit. She could be quite cruel.'

'She was much kinder to me.' Jack leered. 'Nearly as kind as Igitha. Why do you think we spent so much time closeted together?'

'I thought she was giving you additional tuition.'

'She was.' Jack was smirking so revoltingly that I had an urge to slap his face, but I was all too aware that he could and, almost certainly would, hit back and with a great deal more force.

'What about the spike?'

'Another spontaneous act. I saw you and Hettie in the Cordoba. It was simplicity itself to climb the scaffolding. Believe it or not, a policeman spotted me and asked what I was up to. I told him I was retrieving somebody's cat and he went about his way. It was a bank for crick's sake. You'd have thought he'd have been more suspicious than that. Brainless bluebottle.'

'I assume it was meant for me, not Hettie.'

'Of course. But it was more difficult than I anticipated to aim from that height and then, of course, being the clumsy girl you have always been, you stumbled and pushed poor Hettie straight under it.'

'You feel sorry for Hettie?'

'No. I just pretended to care. Force of habit I suppose.'

Jack put his hands into his pockets and whistled a bar of something vaguely familiar.

'What about the panther?' I asked. 'Why was it so interested in my handbag?' Even as I was asking the question I knew the answer. 'That dirty tea towel.'

'You're good at this,' Jack granted me. 'A pity you don't direct your attentions to real murder. We would have made a great team.' There was a time I believed that but for very different reasons. 'Her cub died, and he sent it to be stuffed wrapped in a cloth. I hoped the scent would act as a lure.'

'Your hopes were not in vain,' I told him, 'but your efforts were.'

Jack sniggered. 'Not entirely. I watched from the top floor of the Pythagorean club. It was great sport. I almost choked with laughter when you tried to attack it with your umbrella. Who was that idiot with you?'

'He is not an idiot.'

'He tried to take it on with his bare hands.'

'Which makes him a hero.'

'Hero? Fool?' Jack shrugged. 'What's the difference?'

'I thought you were the former once,' I said, 'but clearly you are the latter now.'

Jack pulled a wounded expression that would have had me mortified once but gave me slight gratification now.

'I am not the one who was tricked into signing the register.'

'A silly game.' I gestured dismissively. 'You are a fool, Jack, because you had everything. You could have had me and my fortune willingly but now you will have neither and the best for which you can hope is the services of a hangman.'

'The best?'

'If Padmore gets his hands on you, you will beg for the scaffold.'

'Another of your fantasies, Violet.' Jack shook a finger at me. 'A superintendent taking the law into his own hands?'

'First and foremost, he is a father.'

'But Sammy was the one who violated her.'

'Do you really think that will save you?' I did not give him the opportunity to respond. 'Which of his men would speak out against him?'

'They would have to catch me first.'

'I still do not understand why you killed all those people.'

'Apart from necessity, for something that you never understood,' he told me. 'Thrills – as simple as that.'

'More whisky.' I went to the crate.

'You *are* trying to get me drunk.'

'I'm having one as well.' I replenished both glasses, making sure to leave the bottle on top of the low crate, and stood in front of the tall one.

Jack came up to take his drink, but I started to walk around him.

'What are you doing?'

'Does it make you nervous if I stand behind you?'

'No but I'm not stupid.' He turned to face me so that he had his back to the box now.

I had once paid an urchin to pretend to have an accident and fling a bucket of dirty water over a man who was pestering me. This was my opportunity to follow his example. I stumbled into Jack, tossing both whiskies into his face.

'Scrise!' He stumbled back, his hands to his eyes as I snatched up the bottle and cracked him on the brow.

'Damn you.' Jack staggered back another pace, still rubbing his eyes and definitely off balance now. With my hands to his chest I pushed with all my might. He stumbled backwards into the crate and I slammed the door, ramming the bolt home.

'Bitch,' he shouted. 'Think this will hold me?'

'For long enough,' I said, hastily unlacing my shoes and creeping around the lantern to open a locker door and put them beside it. The locker was empty.

I crept back to the hatch.

'You can't get out,' Jack warned. 'Scratby has the only keys.' He was banging on the door and I saw the nails pull out a fraction. They would not hold him for long.

The ladder was too heavy to be able to move from the top so I scrambled down it and pulled the base away until only the very top of it rested on the edge of the hatch. Back I climbed, even more gingerly than before, because I was not sure that the ladder would not slip down. Mercifully I got to the top, turned back, knelt down and pushed. The ladder slid down the extra inch and clattered to the ground far below.

Creeping back to the locker I crawled in, taking my shoes, and closing the door after myself. It clicked but Jack's pounding muffled the sound.

It was cramped and dark in my hideaway and I could not see what was happening now, but I heard the wood splinter and a crash.

'Out,' Jack cried in triumph and hurried to the hatch. 'Bitch,' he said for the second time before bellowing, 'Scratby. Scratby, come here.'

A fainter voice came up.

'I am on my way, sir. I heard the noise.'

'She has gone down and pulled the ladder away.'

'But how?' Scratby's voice grew louder.

'Never mind that, man. Just put it back.'

There followed a great deal of scraping and cursing as Scratby struggled to raise the ladder.

'She can't have got out, sir.'

'Where were you?'

'On the first floor, in the kitchen.'

'Then we shall search every room,' Jack's voice was getting slightly fainter.

I opened the door and crawled out of the locker, my legs already stiff with cramp. Cautiously I crawled towards the hole and peered over the edge.

'She is not on this floor.' Jack emerged from the doorway with his man close behind and I drew back hastily. 'A mouse could not have hidden in there.'

I controlled my breath and listened. Their boots clattered on the stone floor and I peeked cautiously to see them stopping on the second-floor landing before disappearing into the room.

Now or never, I told myself. It was not much of a choice, but I made it anyway. *Now.* I hurried to the door, opening it and stepping out onto the balcony. The door swung back in the wind, but I managed to catch it before it slammed and to hold it back with a hook on the wall. I had intended to keep my shoes but at least this would prove I had been out there. Leaving one on the floor and, leaning over, queasy at the height, I carefully dropped the other. To my relief it landed on the wall, bounced but landed back on it, still in view. Thirty feet or so below that was the twisted form of my aunt.

I crept back to the ladder and descended as quickly as I could to the landing. Upon opening the door and stepping through it, I found myself in a ring-shaped room wrapped around the wall of the corridor and stairs, rather like the doughnuts on a stick Agnust used to treat herself and me to when the fair came to Thetbury.

There was a single bed unmade – typical of Jack, I thought – with a side table, a chest of drawers and a campaign desk with a folding slatted chair. Other than that, the room as I circumnavigated it, was bare. There was nowhere to hide but I was hoping that I would not have to try.

The sound of more footsteps reached me and voices uttering *where-the-hell-can-she-be's* and *she-can't have-escaped's.*

'Can you feel that?' Jack was asking. 'There's a wind. She can't have got into the lantern room again.'

'I fear she must have, sir.'

They pounded on the stairs.

'Up the ladder, man.'

'I'm afraid of…'

'You will have cause to be more afraid if she is on the balcony summoning help.'

I had thought about doing that but was doubtful that anyone would be able to hear me above the near-gale conditions up there or that they would trouble to assist me if they did.

'Good man,' I heard at last. 'I'm coming too.'

I waited a while and opened the door a crack. Their voices were too distant to distinguish any words but, a few minutes later, the sound of the wind died and their voices came more clearly.

'But I could see Lady Anglethorpe's body,' Scratby said.

'The runt was much lighter. She could be tangled in the undergrowth. Stupid girl was probably trying to climb down,' Jack was saying. 'She had a lot of pluck, though, I'll give her that.'

'Indeed, sir.' A hesitation. 'I'm afraid I find the idea of descending even more alarming.'

'No choice, Scratters,' Jack said cheerfully. 'I am going down to write a note. A street slug will take it to the police for tuppence.'

Two pennies to go across town, I mused. *You skinflint.* Carefully I shut the door. *Bother,* I remembered. His writing desk was in that room and the thought had no sooner struck me than I saw the handle turn.

37: STALEMATE AND THE COIL

I DID NOT wait for the door to open but scuttled in my stocking feet around the central pillar. The door closed and I could hear Jack in the room with me, the scraping of his chair and the scratching of his pen on paper. It did not take him long which was just as well for my heart was pounding so hard it seemed impossible that he could not hear it.

The doorbell rang.

'Go away,' Jack muttered but it rang again, and somebody was rapping hard on the door. 'Go away, damn you,' he shouted though I doubted anyone other than Scratby and me could hear it.

The ringing and rapping continued.

'I'll give you a taste of my cane,' Jack vowed, pushed his chair back and marched from the room, leaving the door wide open.

I edged towards it and listened.

'Come quickly,' a voice called. It sounded familiar but it was not. 'There's a woman half dead out here.'

'What?' Jack asked incredulously.

'Round the side.'

I heard nothing for a minute and risked poking my head out.

'Got you.' Scratby pounced in triumph.

'Let go,' I demanded which was a sure-fire way of persuading any attacker to desist.

He had me from behind, one arm around my waist, lifting me off the floor and clamped another over my mouth.

'Make another squeak and I'll snap your scrawny neck.'

Scrawny? I seethed. *And I never squeak.* But I kept quiet, nonetheless.

'Get back inside and stay well away from the door.' I did know that voice after all. It was Anthony's. 'Keep those hands up,' he snapped.

'What the hell do you think you are playing at?' Jack raged.

'Where is Lady Violet?' Anthony demanded.

'I don't know who or what you are talking about.'

'I do.' Scratby lifted me, my legs kicking uselessly and held me over the side of the banister rail.

Far below I saw Anthony pointing a gun at Jack who was almost purple with fury.

Scratby took his hand away from my mouth and adjusted his grip to lower me further, holding me under the armpits, his hands over my breasts, his fingers palpating them disgustingly.

'Let her go.' Anthony was clearly rattled. 'Or I shall shoot your master.'

'If you do, I shall drop her,' Scratby replied serenely. 'What is it? Sixty feet? With any luck she'll land on you and you'll both die.'

'If you harm her, I shall shoot him and then I swear I will kill you very, very slowly.'

I had never heard such menace in Anthony's voice and resolved to write an especially evil villain part for him the moment, if ever, I was free.

'What you might call a stalemate,' Jack said with some satisfaction, 'except…' his foot rose in high kick, sending the gun flying out of Anthony's hand.

'What the…' Anthony dived after it, but Jack kicked out again, catching him in the neck, and pounced on the gun to smash the butt over his head.

'Well played, sir,' Scratby applauded – though not literally of course, because he was still gripping me.

Anthony tried to get onto all fours.

'Stay down.' Jack pointed the gun at him.

'Shall I drop her now, sir?' his man enquired as casually as he might suggest an aperitif.

'No,' Jack said. 'Put her back on the landing. We need to toss her over the balcony, and I don't want blood stains on the floor.'

Scratby hauled me back up over the rail and deposited me roughly on my feet.

'You filthy swine,' Anthony muttered.

'Get up and close the door,' Jack ordered him, and Anthony was still struggling to rise groggily when another man appeared. Even in silhouette I recognised him immediately.

'Tha's not overly polite,' Friendless complained, stepping into the hall. 'Tryin' to shut a man out, 'specially from my point of view when the man is me.'

'Who the devil are you?' Jack waved the gun at both of them.

'It's the cabby I sent away, sir,' Scratby explained as Friendless closed the door.

'Best you put that gun away,' Friendless advised, 'though I dint s'pose for two bits of minute as you will.'

'Why on earth should I?' Jack asked incredulously.

'So you dint get hurt,' Friendless said with astonishing calmness.

'You do realise that he has a gun?' I called down and Friendless scratched under the brim of his hat.

'I know what it is, all right,' Friendless assured me. 'And I int afeared of it when I do goh my whip on me.' He raised it into view, the leather thong wrapped in a coil. 'Which I do have now,' he clarified.

'Drop it,' Jack sneered but Friendless only dropped the thong to let it uncoil and raised the handle.

'I warned you.' Jack raised the gun a fraction and the sound of the shot spiralled up to the top.

'Tha' hurt.' Friendless winced. 'My clever ears.'

'Why the hell…,' Jack gawked. He had fired at near point-blank range. As he raised the gun again Friendless's whip snaked out, lashing him. 'Bloody hell!' Jack dropped the gun to clutch his face. 'You've put my eye out.'

'Dint think so.' Friendless did not even glance at him as he picked up the gun.

Anthony grabbed the banister post to haul himself up.

'Now you up there…' Friendless pointed straight at him. 'You let Lady Violet alone or I pull the trigger.'

'Why aren't you dead?' Scratby asked in astonishment.

'Welllll…' Friendless began but Anthony broke in with, 'he has an armoured plate under his shirt.'

'No I dint,' Friendless gawked. 'It's 'cause…'

I could make a good guess as to the reason and I was not going to wait for Scratby to work it out too.

I extended my finger. 'Look at this.'

'What? Why?'

I poked him in the eye and he emulated his master. 'That's why,' I said, snatched the ring of keys from his belt and ran.

Down I hurtled, round and round, until I reached the bottom.

'Darling, are you alright?' I panted.

'Of course I'm not,' Jack snarled, hand still over face.

'I int too bad,' Friendless replied. 'Just a touch of the old creaky hinge in my leg bone.'

'Never better,' Anthony said as Scratby set off down the stairs two at a time.

Jack stumbled towards me, his left eye swollen almost closed and a wide red weal across his cheek. Something glinted. He had a knife in his hand. Instinctively I swung the bunch of keys to fend him off but the effect was more dramatic than I had anticipated and he clutched his face again.

'Scrise! You got my other eye, you frebbing…'

'Mind your tongue,' Friendless cracked his whip in the air like a lion tamer.

'Time to go.' Anthony flung open the door. 'After you,' he ushered us, and out I ran.

'After you,' Friendless insisted.

'No after…'

'Both of you out.' I snapped. 'Now,' and they tumbled together onto the stone plinth.

'Frebbing...' Jack began again and Scratby hurtled down the last flight.

Anthony took up a firing stance, gun in both hands.

'It's loaded...' Scratby gasped.

'I know it's bloody loaded,' his master swore.

'No cussin' in the presence of a lady.' Friendless raised his whip again. 'Nor my horse.'

'Stay where you are,' Anthony barked but Scratby kept coming.

'With blanks,' he panted as I slammed the door.

Anthony grabbed the door handle, straining to stop them turning it as I rammed the key in and twisted it round.

'Tha's the last time he use fouled words on you,' Friendless vowed as if that had been my greatest concern.

'Thank you, Friendless,' I said. 'How can I ever thank you?'

'You just have,' he told me. 'Or have you forgot? No call for tha'.' He blushed when I kissed his cheek. 'Old Queeny get jealous.'

'I shall give her a kiss too.' I looked over to where she stood, patiently across the square, only a few yards from the broken wall where we had nearly died.

'No call for tha' neither,' he told me. 'I mean she be jealous of my gooin' on misbehavin' with another female.'

'I shall apologise to her.' I turned to Anthony. 'That is your stage pistol,' I nearly said *was it not?* too but, just this once, to hell with Miss Kidd still wielding her blackboard pointer but no longer a model of propriety. 'Wasn't it?' I asked and he nodded weakly, still a little unsteady from the blow to his head.

'It was.'

'Thank you.' I took him in my arms and stood on tiptoe to kiss him.

'Thank you,' Friendless said. 'I know you only do tha' to make Old Queeny think you kiss any old boy who come along, matter how he look.'

Anthony laughed then rubbed the crown of his head. 'Not much use in a fight, am I?'

'I wint say tha',' Friendless assured him. 'For it's true.'

'You both saved my life,' I took Anthony's arm as we walked away.

'It was mainly Friendless.'

'Tha' true,' Friendless nodded gravely. 'I usual find most thing are mainly me.'

'But how did you know I was here?' I asked Anthony, but Friendless answered for him.

'I goo home like the man tell me but Old Queeny fret – Dint you, girl? – so we goo Break house but nobody reply 'cept Agnust and women int no use so I dint tell her and I goo find him.' He jerked a thumb towards Anthony. 'I know he int much use neither but at least he's a man. He say *Oh my lor', she dint goo there, do she? That woman is crackle-headed.*'

'I was referring to your Aunt, not you,' Anthony clarified.

'Dint know 'bout tha',' Friendless said sceptically. 'But he get his gun and then he think of a way to get in.'

'Well thank you both,' I said as we reached the hansom.

'Goo on then,' Friendless gave me a prod with his whip handle. Why do men always think they can get familiar just because you have kissed them?

'I am very sorry that I kissed Friendless,' I told Old Queeny. 'It will not happen again.'

'You slobble on me anytime you like,' he confided from the corner of his mouth, 'only make certain sure she dint see next time.'

Anthony gave me his hand and I mounted the running board.

We seemed to be squashed together even more than the limited space of the cab required.

Anthony took my hand. 'You can slobble on me anytime too,' he whispered and so I did.

Friendless leaned over to peer down at us.

'Happen all my life,' he said. 'Let a mowther touch me and she goo wild.'

38: QUICKLIME AND THE SKEWER

ALFRED TOOK HIS revolver and four burly constables to arrest Jack and Scratby. They did not put up a fight.

A steeplejack was employed to scramble down the quarry and retrieve Igitha's body and Uncle Tiberius had her buried in the family plot. I did not attend.

–

I visited Jack in Bury St Edmunds prison. To this day I am not sure why. I did not expect remorse or regret. Perhaps I still hoped to understand how the carefree boy and the caring man, who I thought I knew, could turn into a psychopathic sadist. Was he always like that under the surface or were there two Jacks battling each other?

I was taken to a small sparsely furnished room where he was brought to me, shuffling in leg irons. Were they really necessary?

'Near 'scape once,' the warden informed me as Jack slumped, unshaven and wild-haired, onto a wooden chair across a narrow table from mine. 'He dint get a second chance.'

'Come to gloat?' Jack viewed me defiantly.

'How little you know me.'

'What then?'

'To see if you need anything.'

'A skeleton key might be useful.'

'I can hire a barrister for you.'

Jack snorted. 'There's not a lawyer in the country could get me acquitted.'

'You are still on remand so I can bring you food.'

'To fatten me for the hangman?' Jack sprang up and the warden put a hand to his shoulder. 'Go and do your good deeds for someone who needs them, Violet. I am a dead man.' He laughed bitterly. 'You thought your childish scribblings would bring you fame and fortune, but you shall be remembered for one thing only, as the whore of the Montford Maniac.' At that moment he sprang, grasping my throat. 'Or his last victim.' His fingers dug in.

'No... Jack,' I choked.

'Let her be.' The warden pulled a long truncheon from his belt and swung it, cracking Jack across the temple. Jack let go and turned in fury on him, but the guard brought the truncheon down and jabbed it into Jack's solar plexus. Jack doubled up, gasping for breath. 'It's back to the cell for you and manacles.' He half-dragged Jack from the room. 'Wha' you doin' here?' I heard him ask.

'Wanted a word with Mr Raven.'

'Get back to your cell.'

Massaging my bruised throat, I stepped into the corridor. A short wiry man in prison garb was confronting them.

'Wint tell you twice.' The warden raised his arm.

'It won't take long,' the other prisoner promised. 'You don't know me, Raven, but my name is Joel Trandel and I have something for you.' He reached into his left sleeve and came out with what looked like a meat skewer. 'This is for my brother Amos.'

Before the warden could stop him, he stabbed Jack in the side of the neck. I saw the skewer sink in and skin bulge momentarily on the other side before the tip poked through. Jack gasped, coughed and grasped the handle.

'Hurts, doesn't it?' Joel Trandel mocked as Jack gagged. 'Not so much as you hurt Amos when you disembowelled him, you depraved vermin.'

'Stand back.' The warden cracked him on the crown of his head.

Joel Trandel stumbled back against a wall, hands raised in surrender. 'I won't give any more trouble.'

I ran to Jack. He was trying to pull the skewer out.

Joel Trandel lurched towards us, 'And take this one.' He had a second spike in his fist and drove it in through Jack's larynx. 'You filthy…'

The warden felled Trandel with two more blows.

Jack gasped and dropped wheezing to his knees, tumbling forwards to lie face down. He coughed, spraying bright red droplets, then dark gouts on the stone floor.

I knelt beside him.

'I loved…' He managed with his last breath.

-

Since Jack had never been found guilty of any crime, his body was released and, as his putative wife, it fell upon me to arrange the disposal of his body. I donated it to medical science. After he had been dissected and any interesting specimens retained, his remains would be given a Christian funeral in a pauper's grave with none to mourn him. I supposed it was better than the quicklime that would have awaited him in prison.

There was some sympathy in the press for Scratby. He was portrayed in the *Chronic* as an unassuming man trying to serve his master. There was no sympathy in the court, however, and – after being forced to climb another ladder – he was hanged.

-

Lancelot Overstrand lunged. The Inspector made no attempt to move or to fend off the blow. The blade of his venom-coated dagger disappeared as Overstrand struck at Havelock Hefty's heart.

'But you are still alive,' Overstrand gasped in astonishment as he withdrew the knife. 'And there is no blood on the blade.'

'Did you truly believe for one moment that you could outwit me?' Inspector Hefty asked. 'I found

> your knife yesterday whilst you were bathing and swapped it for a magician's dagger. The blade slides into the handle. Also, I found your stock of poison and painted the handle of the knife with it. By my calculations you have about…' He drew out his trusty hunter and flipped open the lid, still dented by the bullet from which it had saved his life. 'One minute to live.'
>
> 'You're lying!' Lancelot Overstrand screamed in rage and fear.
>
> 'Am I?' Inspector Havelock Hefty, Scotland Yard's premier detective enquired with an enigmatic smile.

THE END, I wrote, put down my pencil and closed my notebook.

I knew I would survive, Hefty crowed.

Thank you, Thorn, Ruby sipped another cocktail. *I cannot think how I would cope without him…* Inspector Havelock Hefty gazed at Ruby Gibson benignly until she concluded, *to despise.*

Work done, I wandered into the sitting room.

Hefty did not approve of ladies consuming spirits but tonight he was prepared to be magnanimous. *I think milady has earned a small drink.*

It had not been my intention to have one but, mindful of his censorious eye, poured myself a Very Old Ben Nevis Malt.

Call that a drink? Ruby jogged my elbow and another double measure sploshed out. *That's a drink.*

'He said he loved,' I wondered.

He never loved anyone except himself. Hefty puffed on his briar.

'Himself least of all.' I went to stand by the window.

'Goodnight everybody,' I whispered to all my characters.

Goodnight Lady Violet, they replied in one voice.

Sweet dreams, Ruby said.

Seraphim Square was deserted except for the constable doing his rounds. Catching sight of me he tapped the peak of his helmet in salute.

'Goodnight,' I mouthed and raised my glass to the man who was keeping us all safe.

A cloud was sliding across the face of a full moon and the shadows were gathering beneath the walls of the Monastery Gates, but I took some satisfaction in the knowledge that not one of them was, nor would ever be again, cast by the Montford Maniac.